BLOOD OF HONOUR

Crete, May 1941, Jack Tanner finds himself embroiled in a deadly game of survival that will test his resolve more than ever before. Not only has a new subaltern, Guy Liddell, who seems determined to make life difficult, recently arrived on the island, but Tanner has offended Alopex a powerful Cretan *kapitan,* who has sworn to kill him. Then suddenly the Germans invade and British fortunes take another dive for the worse.

BLOOD OF HONOUR

BLOOD OF HONOUR

by

James Holland

Magna Large Print Books
Long Preston, North Yorkshire,
BD23 4ND, England.

British Library Cataloguing in Publication Data.

Holland, James
    Blood of honour.

    A catalogue record of this book is
    available from the British Library

    ISBN   978-0-7505-3552-6

First published in Great Britain in 2010 by Bantam Press
An imprint of Transworld Publishers

Copyright © James Holland 2010

Maps by Tom Coulson, Encompass Graphics Ltd., Hove, UK.

Cover illustration © Stephen Mulcahey by arrangement with
Arcangel Images

James Holland has asserted his right under the Copyright, Designs
and Patents Act, 1988 to be identified as the author of this work

Published in Large Print 2012 by arrangement with
Transworld Publishers

Magna Large Print is an imprint of Library Magna Books Ltd.

Printed and bound in Great Britain by
T.J. (International) Ltd., Cornwall, PL28 8RW

For Richard Braybrooke

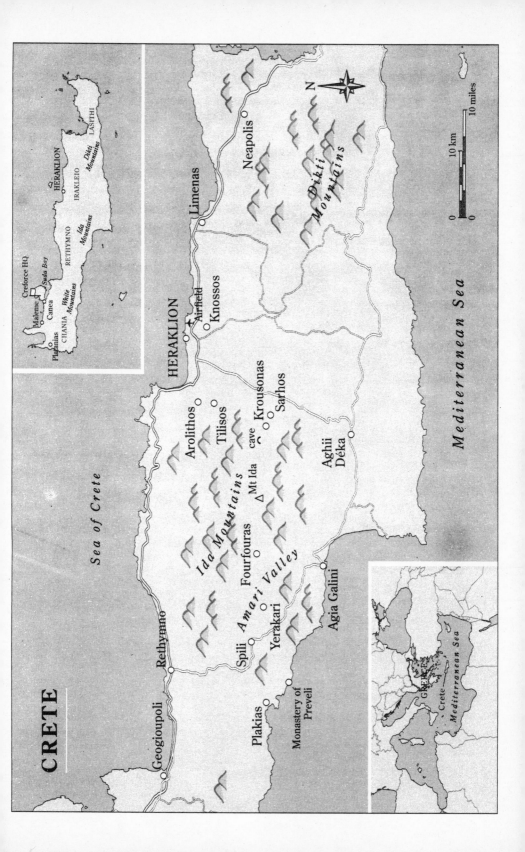

CRETE

Sea of Crete

Mediterranean Sea

GREECE

Crete

Mediterranean Sea

N

10 km
10 miles

Inset map (northwest Crete):
Creforce HQ
Maleme
Suda Bay
Canea
Platanias
CHANIA
White Mountains
RETHYMNO
Ida Mountains
HERAKLEIO
HERAKLION
IRAKLEIO
Dikti Mountains
LASITHI

Main map:
Geogioupoli
Rethymno
Plakias
Monastery of Preveli
Spili
Yerakari
Agia Galini
Amari Valley
Fourfouras
Ida Mountains
Mt Ida
Arolithos
Tilisos
cave
Krousonas
Sarhos
Aghii Déka
HERAKLION
Airfield
Knossos
Limenas
Neapolis
Dikti Mountains

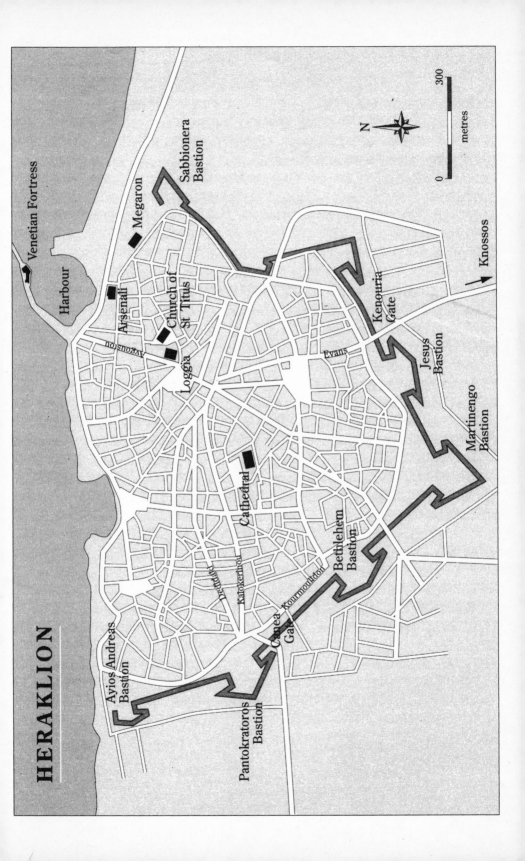

HERAKLION

Venetian Fortress

Harbour

Megaron

Sabbionera Bastion

Arsenali

Church of St Titus

Αυγουστου

Loggia

Evans

Kenouria Gate

Jesus Bastion

Knossos

Martinengo Bastion

Cathedral

Bethlehem Bastion

Dedalou

Katokenrol

Canea Gate

Kournoufton

Ayios Andreas Bastion

Pantokratoros Bastion

N

0   metres   300

1

A little before 8.25 a.m. on the morning of Monday, 28 April, 1941. A wooden fishing-boat, some eighty feet long, a painted eye on either side of its prow, was approaching the mouth of the outer harbour at Heraklion. At first glance, it was much like any other caique that had sailed the Aegean for centuries: gaff-rigged with a main and mizzen mast, light rigging either side, a prominent bowsprit, and half a dozen men manning its deck. A closer glance, however, revealed some anomalies. On its foredeck stood a single two-pounder gun, while towards the stern were a brace of mounted Oerlikon 20mm cannon. And that was not all, for fluttering from the top of the mizzen mast was a small White Ensign. His Majesty's Ship *Dolphin* was an unusual naval vessel, yet in this war there was room for all shapes and sizes in the Royal Navy – after all, needs must. A flotilla of fast motor gunboats would have been better, a godsend in fact, but Britain's war effort was already badly stretched and here in the eastern Mediterranean they had to make do with whatever was available. If that meant a wooden fishing boat, then so be it.

And the caique did have certain advantages. It was certainly a less conspicuous naval vessel, even when armed. At the faintest sound of aircraft, the ensign could be lowered in a trice, the guns covered with tarpaulins and it would look just like any other fishing-boat, plying its trade on the wine-dark sea. Similarly, if *Dolphin* was threatened, the canvas could be whipped off and they would at least have some form of defence. A versatile little boat, her skipper liked to say.

At her prow, an army officer sat, gazing towards the harbour, his arms held loosely around his knees. He was still young – in his late twenties – and wearing battledress, although his head was bare save for his mop of dark, almost black hair. A captain in 50 Middle East Commando, Alex Vaughan had been based on Crete since December – the unit had been sent to help shore up the island's defences. Somewhere along the line, his role had developed so that he was spending less time overseeing the preparation of gun emplacements around the island's airfields and ports and more helping the British vice consul, Captain John Pendlebury – so much so, in fact, that when 50 ME Commando had been posted back to Egypt, Vaughan had stayed.

A renowned archaeologist and former curator at Knossos, Pendlebury, Vaughan had discovered, had for some time been almost single-handedly preparing the islanders to resist any German and Italian invasion, should it come – an event that seemed ever more likely now that the Germans were swarming through mainland Greece. Pendlebury was an unlikely warrior, but there could be no denying either his passion or his energy. Vaughan had been impressed by the man's vision and deep knowledge of the place. More than that, he alone seemed to understand the potential for resistance of both the island and its people.

But it wasn't just ships that those on Crete were short of – it was almost everything. There were not enough vehicles, guns or other arms. It was all very well organizing the local mountain *kapitans* into some kind of resistance force, but they needed to fight with something. Despite pleas to Cairo, there had been little forthcoming: Middle East Command had more pressing concerns – the campaign in North Africa, a potential Axis-backed rebellion in Iraq, fighting in Syria, and, since April, the battle on mainland Greece. Even so, a stash of weapons and equipment had been established in the west of Crete, on Suda Island, and it was from this dump that Pendlebury was now plundering supplies to take back to Heraklion and to the local *kapitans*. So it was that the old wooden caique was carrying a cargo, not of fish, but of Bren guns, rifles, ammunition, grenades and, above all, explosives. It was something, but there was one vital piece of equipment that Vaughan was especially worried about, and that was the terrible shortage of wireless transmitters; there was not even one that could be salvaged from Suda Island. Communication between one end of the island and the other depended almost entirely on telephone, which, as Vaughan remembered all too well from his time in France, was far too unreliable once the fighting began. When communication was lost, so too was cohesion. And then the battle.

Vaughan glanced at his watch and tutted to himself. The trip from Suda Island had been uneventful, but they had set sail an hour late. The Luftwaffe had started sending bombers most

17

days – Stukas or Junkers 88s – which would thunder over to bomb the harbour and the small, ancient port. Really, this latest trip was cutting it fine. Another five minutes or so to the inner harbour, Vaughan calculated, then at least half an hour to get all the stores off and to safety. It wasn't enough, not if Jerry came over this morning at nine as usual. He shook his head. It was strange – one could set one's watch by the Germans. Why didn't they come over at different times? It seemed highly counter-productive to him to keep bombing a place at the same hour each day.

Vaughan looked down into the water. The sails had been unfurled and they were gliding into the outer harbour on *Dolphin*'s diesel engine, which chugged rhythmically, the sea slapping gently against the prow. Even entering the harbour, the water looked such a deep never-ending blue, but then they passed over a sandy stretch free of rocks and the colour turned from inky darkness to a sparkling iridescent turquoise, and suddenly the sea floor seemed not unfathomable but almost close enough to touch.

'Perhaps Jerry won't come today,' said a voice behind him.

Vaughan turned and looked up at Captain Pendlebury, standing behind him, rope in hand, squinting with his one eye against the early-morning sun's reflection on the water. Vaughan smiled and raised an eyebrow. *Perhaps.*

'After all,' added Pendlebury, 'they are rather busy at the moment.'

'Pasting our lot leaving Greece?'

Pendlebury nodded.

'Maybe,' said Vaughan at length, without much conviction. He knew Stukas were already based on the Italian-garrisoned island of Kasos, to the east. It seemed to him unlikely they would be operating against the British evacuation currently under way from the mainland. He looked ahead, up at the thick, solid walls of the fortress that guarded the entrance to the inner harbour, made with the kind of large rectangular slabs of lime-stone that he had seen in the Pyramids outside Cairo. There were no towers, no turrets, just a solid, defiant block, and he wondered how many times before the fortress had withstood an enemy attack.

Following his gaze, Pendlebury said, 'There's a sense of continuity, isn't there? The Mediter-ranean always looks so peaceful but, my God, the bloodshed it's seen. We're in good company. All the way back to Theseus and beyond, people have been arriving here from across the sea to fight.'

'Rather depressing, really.'

'Or quite exciting.' Pendlebury grinned. 'You can't tell me you don't find all this rather thrill-ing.'

Vaughan eyed him silently.

'I've spent my life digging up warriors of the past,' Pendlebury said. 'To find myself in that position – well, I'd be lying if I said I didn't find it exciting. I mean, look at us – stealing along the northern coast of Crete with a cargo of arms and explosives, desperately praying we get it into port before the enemy arrive and blow us all sky high. And the fact that it's rather important, too, Alex, adds to the sense of purpose. This is no frivolous exercise in adventurism.'

'Oh, I don't doubt it,' Vaughan replied. 'You've done a great job already, John. But I don't think I'm quite the romantic you are.'

Pendlebury patted his shoulder. 'Don't worry. It'll be all right.' Then the smile suddenly left him. 'It's got to be all right,' he muttered. 'I care about this island far too much to let the Nazis spread their vile rash across the place.'

Vaughan gazed back down at the water. Pendlebury was a fine man – an academic, maybe, but he also happened to be a natural leader of men, albeit an eccentric one. He wore an eyepatch for this trip – the glass eye had been left on his desk in his house in Heraklion – and never went anywhere without his swordstick or a rifle slung over his shoulder. But eccentrics could thrive in this war – Britain was turning out all kinds of fighting men who might otherwise never have worn a uniform. And out here, all the normal rules seemed to be going to the four winds. Good God, one only had to look at their skipper. Where had Mike Cumberlege come from? His skin was as tanned as any Greek's, his hair unkempt, a gold earring in one ear and Lord only knew how many tattoos. He was like a buccaneer of old and yet, by all accounts, he had come from a perfectly respectable background in England. Yet while there was nothing remotely military about him – Vaughan could only imagine what the bigwigs in the Admiralty would make of him – there was no doubting his knowledge or expertise. Sailing was his life. It was said that there was not a cove or bay in all the

Aegean Mike Cumberlege and his cousin Cle did not know. Well, that kind of knowledge was damned useful.

Cumberlege now shouted to them, pointing to a berth along the quayside across the far side of the harbour, between two other caiques. There were perhaps two dozen fishing-boats, dinghies and other vessels moored in the inner harbour. Vaughan saw fishermen passing nets, heard them calling to one another, seemingly oblivious to the war. Men still had to fish, to eat, he supposed. He could smell the harbour too: fish, saltwater, dust, rope and diesel. The ancient town, long ago dominated by the Venetians, rose up from the harbour's edge and climbed over the ridge behind. Beyond that, and to the west reaching out over a headland into the sea, were the mountains, still hazy but massive in the morning light. No wonder the Cretans felt bullish about resisting any invasion, he thought. *Who would want to fight them up there?*

As they neared the quayside, Vaughan glanced at the row of buildings in front of them. The whole line was the same: half a dozen classical façades with a large twelve-foot-high arched window in the centre and two smaller ones either side. Behind these seemingly deceptive frontages lay the town arsenals, with their vast curved roofs, already filling with stores – food, ammunition, weapons, even clothing, so that the soldiers could swap their thick serge battledress for cooler cotton khaki drill now that summer was fast approaching.

Dolphin slipped smoothly into the gap. Several men were waiting – some of Pendlebury's Cretans

21

and Corporal Tasker-Brown, too, another from 50 ME Commando who had been commandeered by Pendlebury.

'Here,' growled one of the Cretans, a man Vaughan recognized as Alopex, one of Satanas's local *kapitans*.

Both Vaughan and Pendlebury threw ropes to Alopex and the waiting men and, moments later, the boat nudged against the quay.

'What took you so long?' Alopex asked.

'We were late getting going,' Pendlebury replied, grabbing the first box from their stash of cargo and stepping ashore. 'Too many ships in Suda Bay.'

'So it's true? You're leaving the mainland?'

Pendlebury nodded, then looked up at the sky.

'Yes,' said Alopex, following his gaze, 'we need to be quick.' He jumped on board and picked up a box.

On the quayside, a mule and cart were waiting. Hurriedly the men now unloaded the cargo. As Vaughan swung the boxes across to ready hands on the quay, he felt the sweat running down the side of his face and tickling his back. It was hot work, but he wished they could unload and get away even more quickly. All it needed was one bomb, a chance bullet or cannon shell, and they would be obliterated. He glanced at his watch. It was two minutes to nine and they were still by the quayside.

'Come on, nearly there,' shouted Cumberlege. Vaughan grabbed another box, just as the skipper's cousin, Cle, passed a wooden crate of explosives to Tasker-Brown – but then, in his haste, let go too soon. Vaughan saw the box drop, his heart lurching as the flimsy crate split and packets of Nobel's desensitized gelignite tumbled out onto the ground. *Jesus*, he thought.

'You bloody fool!' shouted Cumberlege.

And then Vaughan heard it.

A faint whirr that made him stop his work despite the burning urgency. He glanced at Cumberlege, then at Pendlebury; they had heard it too. *Still finding it exciting?* Vaughan thought. He grabbed the last box, handed it to Alopex and jumped onto the quayside.

'Quick,' said Pendlebury. 'This way.'

Alopex yelled at the mule, sharply slapped its rump, and with a jerk the cart started moving. He cursed in Greek then said, 'The mule will only go at mule pace. These beasts will not be hurried.'

The sound of aircraft was more distinct now. Vaughan searched the skies but he could not see them at first. There was more than one, though, that was for sure.

'A curse on Teutonic timekeeping,' muttered Pendlebury.

Along the quayside. It was some two hundred yards to the end of the harbour front and the narrow alley that led to the warren of backstreets. Vaughan knew Pendlebury intended to store the stash first in a cellar somewhere in the heart of the town before distributing it to various dumps in the mountains, away from the town.

The mule was moving painfully slowly, even though they were all pushing the cart to help. *Come on, come on,* thought Vaughan. He saw

23

Pendlebury glance at him; even he looked scared now. The sound of aero engines grew louder, and this time, as Vaughan looked up into the deep blue sky, he saw six Stukas, approaching from the east. From flying in a loose vic formation, they now broke into line astern, seemed to overshoot the harbour, but then in turn peeled over and began their dives, the screaming sirens wailing as they hurtled downwards apparently aiming directly for them.

'Keep going!' shouted Pendlebury.

'Bloody hell,' muttered Vaughan. They were so nearly at the alley – thirty yards, that was all. *Thirty yards!* Damn it, couldn't this mule go any faster? He looked up again as the first Stuka released its bomb, so close he could see it perfectly, its point leaning down slightly. He couldn't help but duck but, to his surprise, the missile landed on the far side of the harbour wall, detonating with a mighty explosion of water rising high into the air. *Twenty-five yards.* The urge to cut and run was intense; self-preservation – it was a powerful instinct. The next bomb was also behind the harbour wall, but the third was inside, and so was the fourth. Vaughan clenched his teeth. *Twenty yards, fifteen, ten.* They were still in one piece despite the vast fountains of water and the terrible racket of sirens, engines and exploding bombs. Some gunners were firing their light ack-ack guns, and adding to the din, when the last of the six dive-bombers dropped its load.

The bomb exploded only fifty yards in front of them, crashing into a building by the harbour's edge, dust and shards of stone and wood hurtling

24

into the sky, but then, as the pilot pulled out of his dive, the rear-gunner opened fire, bullets raking through one of the caiques moored to the side and then spitting across the quay.

Vaughan cursed again but they were now at the entrance to the narrow alleyway. Alopex, a big man by Cretan standards, yanked the mule around the corner, while the men, grimacing with the exertion, pushed so hard that one of the cart's wheels momentarily lost contact with the ground. As they hurried clear of the quayside, a second burst of machine-gun fire hammered into the ground, the bullets ricocheting noisily off the stone just a few feet behind them.

The narrow road and high walls of the buildings now protected them from all but a direct hit, but they did not dare pause yet, the cart jolting and rattling over the stone lane. The Stukas were climbing for a second attack, the light ack-ack from the harbour and to the west of the town thumping away. It gave the men a brief respite, however, as they wound their way through the narrow network of roads, and by the time the Stukas screamed down in their second round of dives, they were passing Pendlebury's house and, opposite, the headquarters of 50 ME Commando.

Alopex finally halted the mule at the mouth of an even narrower alleyway. It was cool there, the back-street still in full shadow. He sent men to watch at either end of the street, but there was no one about. The Stukas were leaving and suddenly Heraklion was still and quiet once more, the intense racket of only a minute earlier gone as the aircraft vanished across the sea. Now the only sound was the cooing of pigeons from the roofs above. Vaughan wiped the sweat from his brow and the back of his neck, and breathed out heavily. *Thank God.*

'We'll unload here,' said Pendlebury, grabbing one of the boxes. 'Follow-me.'

He led them down the alley, under a long, shallow archway, and then up some steps. Bougainvillaea plunged over a wall bringing a sudden splash of colour, and then, beyond its fronds, there was a doorway. Pendlebury put down his box, produced a large and ageing key, and opened the door onto a small courtyard. At one end a set of steps descended to a cellar. Vaughan smiled to himself. It was typical of Pendlebury to have found such a place. A grey cat prowled along the wall above them, eyeing them suspiciously.

'He won't tell,' Pendlebury observed. 'Come on, this way.' He led them down the steps into a dark cellar, and switched on his electric torch. From the far side, further steps descended into a series of chambers deep under the town.

'This should be safe enough for the time being,' said Pendlebury. It was cold down there, the air musty. He swung his torch over the vaulted ceilings. 'Byzantine.' He grinned at Vaughan. 'Some fourteen hundred years old. Our little secret, eh?'

The Stukas had left Heraklion, but they were not the only marauding Luftwaffe aircraft that morning. A little more than a hundred miles away to the north-west a *Staffel* of nine Junkers 88 twin-engine bombers were searching for British ships

26

heading away from Greece. It had been just three weeks since the Germans had invaded the mainland and, as in Poland, Norway, the Low Countries and France, their enemies had soon been in full retreat. For many Greek soldiers there had been nowhere to run, but for the British, defeat had meant yet another evacuation, this time across the two hundred and more miles to Suda Bay in the northwest corner of Crete. The Luftwaffe had found rich pickings, repeatedly hammering the Royal Navy as it tried to get the mixed force *of* British, Australian and New Zealand troops away to safety.

'*Aussehen! Zwei britische Schiffe!*' said the *Staffel Kapitan*, Hans Brühle, over the R/T, as ahead of him, just visible, he spotted two ships, their wakes vividly white against the deep, dark blue sea. Then he added, '*Bereiten Sie anzugreifen.*' Prepare to attack.

The Junkers 88 had been designed with dive-bombing capabilities, and while unable to plummet down on its target with the kind of eighty-degree angle that the Stuka could perform, it could still dive both quickly and steeply. Brühle now brought his *Staffel* down to around three thousand metres. The two ships were still some way to the south, but he could tell now, by the wake and the speed with which they were travelling, that they must be destroyers.

The sun, already rising high in the east, dazzled across Brühle's cockpit, glinting blindingly over the perspex. He spoke into his radio once more. They were going to head east on a bearing of ninety degrees, then loop around in a wide arc,

27

so that the sun was behind them. Two *Ketten* – six machines – under Leutnant Keller would dive down and bomb the ships in quick succession, while he would lead the remaining *Kette* into a shallow dive without brakes, levelling off at two hundred metres and swooping in low for their attack. Timing was the key. It was imperative that his three low-level planes strike out of the sun just after the other six and at a time when the British destroyers were distracted. Dive-bombers were designed for accuracy, but as Brühle was well aware, hitting a small and fast-moving target like a destroyer was no easy task. Low-level passes offered the best chance of success. At only a few hundred metres above the sea, however, the risks were considerable.

'Keller,' he said, *'beginnen Sie Ihren Tauchgang, bis ich den Auftrag dazu erteilen.'* Wait until I give you the word to dive.

'Jawohl, Herr Kapitan,' Keller replied.

Brühle's mouth felt suddenly dry. He licked his lips and swallowed, then glanced at his navigator. As he pushed the control column forward, his heart was already quickening. It was always the same – nausea, but also exhilaration.

2

Colour Sergeant-Major Jack Tanner had already watched the gun captains check and recheck their ready-use ammunition and fuses on the two rear 4.7-inch guns. He had also seen the gun layer on the Quick Firing 2-Pounder, or pompom as it was known, train and elevate his weapon to its full capacity, then more than once examine its ammunition feedrails. It had been good to see. Checking and cleaning his own weapon was the first thing Tanner did whenever he had a spare moment, and since, over the past forty-eight hours, he had had very little to do other than wait in Rafina to be evacuated, his rifle had received an especially large amount of attention.

It was slung over his back now as he leaned against the stern railing. Apart from a bit of darkening and wear and tear to the butt, the rifle looked almost as good as new, glistening with a sheen of oil. As a boy, he had learned the importance of looking after weapons. It had been drummed into him by his father, and ever since he had joined the army as a sixteen-year-old boy soldier, he had carried an oiler, rags and pull-through and, wherever possible, a small flask of gin – nothing, he had discovered, could compare with gin for cleaning the firing mechanism. The spirit never congealed in cold weather, and it helped the striker hit with a clear, sharp snick.

He and the rest of the 2nd Battalion, the King's Own Yorkshire Rangers, were all aboard HMS *Halberd*. Most of the men had been bundled below decks, officers into the wardroom, ORs anywhere they could find a place to perch out of the way. Destroyers were not large vessels – in *Halberd*'s case, a little over three hundred feet long and thirty wide. Normally, she played home to just 145 officers and crew, but that had now swollen by more than seven hundred Rangers who, if not properly disciplined, could play havoc with their chances of making safe passage to Suda Bay. As the ship's captain had told the Rangers officers before they had set sail, he was expecting plenty of attention from the Luftwaffe now that more than half of the journey would take place during daylight hours. He made it clear he did not want soldiers to get in the way of the crew.

The crossing would have been considerably less tense had they left at dusk the previous evening as planned. However, both *Halberd* and HMS *Havock* had been held up on their way to Greece, first dodging enemy air attacks and then helping to rescue men from another stricken vessel. By the time they had unloaded them back in Suda Bay, the two destroyers were badly behind schedule. Not until the early hours of that Monday morning did they finally reach Rafina, and when the last of the men had been lifted, it was just before 2 a.m., with only around four hours left before first light.

Because of this delay, the crew had been almost continually at Action Stations. A small number of

30

Rangers – one section from each of the companies – had been detailed to help the crew damage-control and repair parties. Tanner could have been excused such duty, but the idea of being stuck away below decks, unable to see what was going on, did not appeal to him at all; if he had to go to sea – and he would really rather not – then he reckoned it was far better being out in the fresh air with something to look at. So Tanner, with Captain Peploe's blessing, had joined Sergeant Sykes and the rest of Corporal McAlister's section at the stern of the ship where they had taken their positions next to Y Gun, one of the ship's four 4.7-inch guns, and the one furthest aft. In any case, Sykes's platoon had lost their commander in Greece and the entire battalion of nearly a hundred men – so Tanner had been keeping an especial eye on them until their new subaltern arrived. Not that Sykes couldn't keep them in line on his own; he could, but Tanner liked Sykes, and McAllister for that matter, and furthermore, he recognized that Sykes's optimism was good for him. God knew, he needed it at the moment.

Tanner had been smoking a cigarette and watching *Havock*, *Halberd*'s sister ship. Not more than five hundred yards away and just a nose in front, she had the last remaining men from the 1st Armoured Brigade aboard, some eight hundred soldiers from the 9th Royal Rifle Corps. Then suddenly there were shouts from the men behind him, and a split second later he had heard the faint buzz of aircraft. He quickly scanned the skies, but without his binoculars he could not spot them at first. Turning round he heard the gun layer relay the orders he had received over his headset from the gunnery officer in the Director Control Tower: 'Nine high-level bombers bearing green 170.'

The gun crew were gathered around their 4.7-inch gun, dressed in navy denim overalls and wearing white cotton balaclavas beneath their helmets. Behind them were the damage-control parties, waiting expectantly, the Rangers among them. Tanner saw Sykes and McAllister scanning the skies, then looked upwards himself.

'Bearing green 160,' called the gun layer.

Tanner spotted them, then almost immediately lost them again as they disappeared in the glare of the sun. He cursed, having caught a glimpse of the sun's rays and now finding his vision affected.

'Looks like they're buggering off,' said one of the Rangers.

Tanner caught Sykes's eye and saw his friend raise a sceptical eyebrow.

'Ignorance is bliss, eh, sir?' he said, joining Tanner. He leaned out over the rail. 'And so close too – look.'

Tanner, also leaning out, now saw Crete, a dark, milky blue up ahead, lying like a sleeping maiden on the sea. He turned back, a hand shielding his eyes. The faint drone of aero engines could still be heard. 'Sneaky bastards,' he muttered.

'Can't say I blame 'em, though,' said Sykes. 'If you've got a bloody great blinding sun in the sky and not a cloud for dear money, you might as well make the most of it. And you have to admit, it's a nice day for a swim.'

'I bloody hate swimming.' Tanner glanced back at the guns. 'I hope those lads are good.'

The two stern guns, Y Gun and, behind it on the raised gun deck, X Gun, were now moving into position ready in response to orders from the DCT, clicking and ticking as they were elevated skywards. The sound of aircraft was louder now, then shouts could be heard. Tanner saw them again, high in the sky, now coming straight towards them from the east. There was something odd about them, though, and then he realized: there were now only six aircraft, not nine. Where the hell had the other three gone?

The engine pitch changed as the six Junkers dived towards the two destroyers. Tanner gripped the railings.

'All guns, rapid salvoes,' called the gun layer, which was then repeated and shouted by the gun captain. As one, the four guns opened fire, the shells hurtling into the sky with a deafening crash, while the pompom, in the centre of the iron deck, furiously pumped away, the only weapon to be able to fire independently at will. At the same time, the ship lurched suddenly as she changed course, so that Tanner nearly lost his footing. In moments, the bombers were almost upon them and dropping their loads. The whistle of the missiles could be heard amid the ear-shattering din of the guns. Then huge fountains of spume and spray erupted like sea-monsters into the sky. One bomb from the second aircraft hit the sea no more than fifty yards from the port side, spray lashing across the men on deck. Tanner ducked and cursed again, wiping the saltwater from his

33

face and hands. He glanced back at the gunners, traversing and elevating their 120mm tube in response to orders from the DCT – one man gathering the shell, the loader placing it in the breech, and the layer giving the signal that the gun was ready to fire. When all four guns were ready, the out-of-sight gunnery officer in the DCT triggered each of the guns as one. A moment later, they fired once more, the breech recoiling, then the empty casing pulled out and piled on the metal deck behind. Tanner reckoned this process took around ten seconds; six rounds per minute was not bad if firing against another vessel but against Junkers 88 bombers speeding through the air at around 280 m.p.h., it was only ever going to be a chance hit that brought one down.

The ship swerved again, and Tanner glimpsed *Havock* between the fountains of spray, her guns firing every bit as furiously and also taking hurried evasive action. Smoke and cordite hung heavy in the air, while above, black puffs of flak now dotted the sky. More bombs fell, but miraculously, none appeared to have hit either ship, and now the Junkers were climbing away, curving behind them to the north. Some of the men cheered, but barely had they opened their mouths than another roar of aircraft thundered towards them. Almost before the men realized what was happening, three Junkers had appeared low from the east, straight out of the sun at no more than four hundred feet.

Tanner ducked again as the creamy pale blue undersides of the bombers sped over the ship, a stick of dark bombs tumbling out as they did so. The 4.7-inch guns banged off another round of shells and the pompom pounded again but the elevation was wrong, their firing late on the targets, and in seconds the bombs were exploding, one landing in the centre of the ship between the port-side derrick and the pompom gun deck. Tanner turned his back and shielded his face from the blast, but even so a piece of flying shrapnel nicked his temple. Putting a finger to the wound briefly, he looked across at the other Rangers and the damage-control parties and saw most were still on the ground, only slowly raising their dazed heads.

Beneath the pompom, a large hole had been ripped out of the deck and upper side of the ship. The remains of a lifeboat, its timbers splintered and splayed, hung limply from the contorted and twisted frame of the derrick. Of the men who had been waiting there moments before there was now no sign. Nor was the pompom firing, yet between the din of the guns he could hear aircraft still circling, then spotted one banking in a wide arc in front of them.

Uncontrollable rage welled within him, and he now ran along the deck, slipped on some blood, tripped, fell, cursed and scrambled up again. Several body parts and globs of flesh lay splattered against the torpedo tube mount, the pompom mount, and across the shredded iron top deck. Through the smoke, Tanner heard the screams of dying men, pushed his way past a staggering sailor, and scrambled up the still intact metal ladder on the starboard side of the pompom deck.

Heaving himself up, he took a rapid glance at the gun position. The port side was badly damaged from the blast, while the cabouche to the front was shattered. Behind the canvas lay two dead men.

The gunner still sat in his seat at his weapon, his head lolled back and groaning. Tanner hurried to him and grabbed his shoulders, then saw that half of the man's face had been blown away, while his right arm was nothing more than a bloody mess of sinew and bone. Tanner clasped his arms around the gunner's chest and pulled him out of the seat. 'Sorry, mate,' he muttered, as the man gasped. Tanner laid him on the deck beside the gun mounting and clambered onto the seat.

Wiping blood from his face, he looked at the weapon. It seemed to be undamaged, despite some obvious shrapnel nicks; steel was tougher than flesh and bone. 'How do you fire this bloody thing?' he mouthed to himself. Either side were two large ammunition feedrails still full of two-pound cannon shells. There were hand wheels either side too. Tanner turned one to his left – *ah, elevation* – and then another on his right – *traverse* – as the barrels rose and the weapon swivelled on its mount. Beside the breech on his left there was a crank – *the firing handle?* He glanced out as the smoke cleared. Approaching from the east were two Junkers coming around for another attack, but this time they were below the level of the sun and he now saw them clearly before they crossed the blinding brightness. He was no longer aware of any sound apart from a ringing in his ears; the din of the guns, the shouts and screams of

36

wounded and dying men had gone. Traversing the gun so that it pointed directly out to sea, he turned the crank and, to his relief, a volley of shells punched from each of the four barrels. Smiling grimly to himself, he watched the two aircraft approach. One, he now saw, was heading straight for *Halberd*, the other for *Havock*.

On his own, he could not fire and change the elevation of the gun at the same time; it meant he had just one chance. *Like shooting a pheasant*, he told himself. Carefully he lined his aim on the first aircraft. The ship was still moving, but he could traverse the gun. Aim off a generous amount, he decided, open fire, and let that Jerry bastard fly straight into it. The two aircraft roared towards them – eight hundred yards, six hundred, four hundred, two hundred – *now!* Tanner turned the crank, the barrels pumped out their shells but immediately he saw his aim was wide. He swore – there was no time to traverse again – but then the ship lurched to port and the lead Junkers flew directly into his line of fire. Cannon shells tore into the cockpit and fuselage just a hundred yards from the port side of the ship. A puff of smoke, then flame.

Inside the plane, Oberleutnant Brühle had a brief moment of realization, the controls slipped from his hands and then, as the Junkers hurtled over *Halberd*, first a fuel tank and then the bomb bay exploded, the aircraft erupting into a mass of tumbling flame that scorched an arced path across the sky before plunging with a hiss of smoke and steam into the sea.

Tanner wiped the blood from his face once more. 'Got you,' he said.

HMS *Halberd* had safely docked at Suda just under two hours later, while *Havock* continued on her way to Alexandria. The remaining Junkers had turned for home after their *Staffel Kapitan* had been killed, and the ships had not been troubled again. Even so it was ironic that *Havock*, which had somehow come through the attack entirely unscathed, should be full of troops destined for Egypt, while *Halberd*, in desperate need of a lengthy stint under repair at Alexandria, should have to go to Crete first. Furthermore, at Suda, her crew learned that they would be taking their cargo of troops on to Heraklion where, it had been decided, the Yorks Rangers would be joining 14th Infantry Brigade in the defence of the port and airfield there.

Twelve sailors and two Rangers had been killed by the bomb on the iron deck. A further fourteen men had been wounded, of whom two were thought unlikely to live. Having safely unloaded their injured, the rest of the Rangers had trooped off, each company marching to an assembly area away from the quayside where they had been fed and given tea, while *Halberd*'s crew tidied their ship. In the afternoon, Suda was attacked by more bombers. This time, there were a number of anti-aircraft guns to help repel the intruders, both around the harbour and on the long ridge between the bay and the open sea. But although *Halberd* was not struck this time, a number of half-sunken wrecks in the bay showed that the Luftwaffe had had their fair share of success. As it was, some stores were hit and part of the quay was damaged, and after they had gone, a great column of smoke from the burning warehouse rose slowly into the sky, filling the air with the rich and biting stench of burning rubber.

At dusk, the men were boarded once more to begin the last leg of their journey, a trip of only a few hours. Different members of the crew were manning the guns now, and although there was still a threat from the air, the Rangers had been stood down. Even so, Tanner preferred to be out on deck and, accompanied by Sykes, returned to the stern of the ship, where they perched themselves against the hatch in front of Y Gun.

'Christ,' said Tanner, as they eased past a half-submerged wreck. He rubbed his brow; his head ached from the nick he had received earlier. A couple of stitches had closed the wound, but it throbbed. Sykes lit two cigarettes, then passed one to his friend.

He was a small man, with a lean face and carefully combed, brilliantined hair – even after long days of retreat, he had barely ever had a hair out of place. Like Tanner, he was not from Yorkshire, but while the CSM was a Wiltshireman, born and raised on the land, Sykes was from Deptford in London. As outsiders, they had recognized in each other a common bond, and as mutual trust and friendship had developed during more than a year of fighting, both men had come to appreciate that they complemented each other rather well. The time would come one day, inevitably, when they would head their separate ways. After all, the odds were that at some point one or other would be badly wounded or even killed, and if not that then the army's system of promotion and progression meant they could not remain in the same company for ever. Not that Sykes gave it much thought. He had long ago, even before the war, learned not to think too far ahead: it did not pay to brood. In any case, who knew what was round the corner? There was no point worrying about what might not happen.

For a few minutes he watched the setting sun. Only a slip of burning orange now remained on the horizon. Then he saw it drop below the ridge at the end of the bay, leaving in its wake a sky of pink that rose into a deep and ever darkening blue. He glanced at Tanner, who was still gazing out to sea. His friend was hard to read. He had always thought that Tanner was, like him, a man who took each day as it came. He had never really spoken to him about his past, but he knew that, like him, Tanner had left home in a hurry. Both men were survivors, too – another unspoken bond. Yet his friend was brooding. Ever since they had been sent to Greece, Tanner had been even more taciturn than usual.

It was Tanner's turn to pull out two cigarettes, silently, light them both and pass one to Sykes. 'Ta,' said Sykes, holding the cigarette between his finger and thumb. 'At least the air's improved,' he added, breathing in deeply. 'That burning rubber was giving me a headache.' Tanner said nothing so Sykes continued, 'And at least we should have a quieter time of things here. I mean,

I can't really see Jerry having a crack at this place. I'm sure he'll bomb us all right, but you have to admit, an island like this should be an easy enough place to defend. Mine the harbour entrances, line them and the airfields with a good load of artillery, and get the men dug in – should be able to throw any unwanted visitors back, no problem.'

Tanner turned on him. 'Haven't you learned anything this past year? Jesus, Stan, Jerry's only got to turn up with his Stukas and his Spandaus and we piss off again. What makes you think this place'll be any different?'

'It's an island. And it's got lots of sodding mountains all over it.'

Tanner was quiet.

'It's not like Greece,' Sykes continued, 'where they could come down through Yugoslavia. It's not like France either, or Norway for that matter. Where are they going to get all their ships from to bring their troops? And, anyway, we've still got the navy, haven't we? They've got to get past them, and then actually land. And you can't tell me they can possibly hope to win by dropping parachute troops. They're sitting ducks when they come down. We'll slaughter 'em.'

'Maybe. I'm just sick and bloody tired of always retreating. God knows who's leading us in this sodding war. Bunch of goojars, the lot of them. Christ, we get here and what do we see? Lots of sunken ships, and then the bloody Luftwaffe come over – *again*. I've seen too many aircraft with black crosses on in this war, and not enough with roundels.'

'Well, you got rid of one this morning.'

41

'One. One sodding Jerry plane.' He sighed. 'Where are the bloody RAF? That's what I want to know. We need planes. It's crazy, Stan, bloody crazy. Everything's so damned half-cock all the time.'

Sykes was about to reply but then turned to see Captain Peploe beside them with one of the ship's sub-lieutenants. 'Sorry, sir,' he said, scrambling to his feet.

Peploe smiled affably. 'This is Lieutenant Jewett. Lieutenant: CSM Tanner and Sergeant Sykes.'

Tanner and Sykes saluted.

'At ease, chaps,' said Peploe, then glanced back at the fading horizon. 'What a beautiful part of the world this is,' he said.

'Bleedin' lovely, innit?' said Sykes. 'It'll be nice coming out here once the war's done with.'

'I agree,' said Peploe, then patted the sides of his legs. 'Anyway.' He paused, looked at Lieutenant Jewett, then back to Tanner. 'Jack, the captain wants to see you.'

'Me?' said Tanner. 'Why, sir?'

'Either to tear you off a strip for firing his pom-pom without the required authority, or to thank you for saving his ship. Hopefully the latter.'

Lieutenant Jewett laughed. 'This way,' he said.

Tanner and Peploe followed him, past Y and X Guns, past the pompom gun deck, now fully manned once more, and to the centre part of the ship known as the waist. Up a metal stairway, onto the fo'c'sle, and then up another ladder and onto the bridge, which looked down over the bow and the two forward guns, A and B.

They found the captain outside on the bridge,

leaning against the parapet above B Gun on the fo'c'sle, a pair of large binoculars to his eyes. Tanner gazed at the array of voice tubes, high seats, wires and boxes bolted against the iron turret. It was a world with which he was totally unfamiliar. Two other officers were there, also staring through their binoculars. The position commanded a superb view out across the fo'c'sle and bow; it seemed higher up there than it really was, and the ship bigger. Away to their right, the silent mass of Crete lurked, its jagged peaks sharply defined against the fading sky. A chill was just beginning to settle, helped by a light breeze from across the inky Aegean.

'CSM Tanner, sir,' said Jewett.

The captain lowered his binoculars and turned to face his visitors. Lieutenant Commander Cross was, Tanner guessed, in his early thirties, his brow already lined, as well it might be. Immaculately dressed, despite the day's events, he had a thin, intelligent face. Tanner saluted, but Cross waved down such formality, and instead held out his hand.

'Thank you for coming up here,' he said, as he gripped Tanner's. 'We owe you our thanks. That was a fine bit of shooting.'

'It was a lucky shot, sir. If anything, it was more down to you. The ship moved at just the right moment.'

Cross smiled. 'Well, it was a brave thing to do, all the same.'

'Thank you, sir, but the braver man is the one who has to take what Jerry throws at him and isn't able to hit back.'

43

Cross turned to Peploe. 'Is he always this modest?'

'It's a trait we like to encourage in the Rangers.'

Cross chuckled, then pointed to Tanner's battledress. Next to the Indian General Service ribbon was stitched the blue, white and red of the Military Medal and the red, blue and red of the Distinguished Conduct Medal. 'I see you've been in the thick of it before, CSM.'

'A little bit, sir.'

'And been rewarded for your efforts.'

Tanner shrugged. He had always been rather ambivalent about medals. 'It's nice to be given them, I suppose,' he said, 'but I'm sure you'll agree, sir, that there are many brave men who are never given a thing, and a fair few who are given gongs they don't deserve.'

Cross nodded. He wore the ribbon of the DSO himself. 'True. And medals do mark a man, and that can be a double-edged sword. It gains you the respect of some, but resentment in others. My father, Tanner, won a VC in the last war. He always reckoned it was something of a curse.' He rubbed his chin, then added, 'In any case, medals are pointless if you lose.'

'I couldn't agree with you more, sir.'

'And, let's face it, things are not quite going to plan at the moment, are they?' He frowned then smiled once more. 'And what do you think of our ship, Tanner?'

'She's a fine one, sir.'

'Yes, she is, but destroyers were designed to counteract the threat of torpedoes from either torpedo boats or submarines. They were not

44

designed to defeat a heavy attack from the air. We have depth-charges and our own torpedoes, and our guns can make mincemeat of E-boats and U-boats, given half the chance, but against dive-bombers, the 4.7s are too slow. It doesn't help that they're centrally fired, either.'

'I can see that, sir. Can't you get more pom-poms put on?'

'I wish I could, Tanner. But what we need more than pompoms are aircraft. This war has shown us that a navy cannot operate effectively without strong aerial support. The two need to work in tandem. Unfortunately, these evacuations put a great strain on us. We've managed to get most of you chaps off this time, but I hope we won't be asked to do it again for a while.'

'You mean an evacuation of Crete, sir?' said Peploe.

Cross looked out towards the island, now no more than a dark silhouette, only just discernible. 'Crete or Malta. I'd have thought it would be hard for Jerry attacking an island rather than coming straight down through the mainland, but if Hitler does decide to have a go, you lot need to make sure you hold on to these islands. I'm not saying we can't get you away again, but it is important to be realistic – to be clear about the situation here. We've lost a lot of ships this year and particularly in the last few days. If we lose too many more, the Mediterranean Fleet is going to be good for very little.'

'And without the fleet,' said Peploe, 'Jerry can get his supplies to North Africa without much interference.'

Cross nodded. 'So you see,' he said, 'it's vital that you don't lose Crete. Absolutely vital.'

Before Tanner and Peploe had left the bridge, Cross had apologized for speaking so frankly. It had been a long few days, he explained; he and his men were tired, and it was sometimes hard to keep spirits high when their ship had a gaping hole in the deck and too many good men had been killed.

'Probably best to keep that chat to ourselves, though,' said Peploe, as they stepped back down onto the fo'c'sle.

'Of course, sir,' said Tanner. Yet Cross had been saying nothing that Tanner did not feel himself, and when Peploe told him he was heading down to the wardroom, Tanner decided to step back up to the fo'c'sle, rather than rejoin Sykes and the others from the company.

A sinking feeling had been weighing him down ever since they had heard of the German invasion of Greece through Yugoslavia more than three weeks earlier. It was something he seemed unable to shake off, and it was making him sullen and irritable, affecting his ability to do his job within the company. It was defeat that was causing this black mood. Defeat – it was like a cancer, and Britain seemed unable to stop the rot. He sighed, then lit a cigarette, breathing in deeply the sweet-smelling fumes and watching the smoke swirl away on the light breeze. Well, he had had enough of running away. Here on Crete, he told himself, if the enemy came, he would stand and fight; and if he died in so doing, then at least he would have done so with his honour intact.

46

3

Monday, 19 May, a little after eleven in the morning. In a leafy side-street a stone's throw from the imposing Holy Church of St Titus stood one of Heraklion's many *kafenios*, a café-bar that in the long summer months spread effortlessly out onto the street, the tables shaded by two evergreen plane trees, one whose branches reached out from the walled garden next door, and a smaller, younger tree growing up from the side of the street. Inside, Aratiko's was unremarkable: stone-tiled floor, rickety wooden tables and chairs, and a strong smell of cigarette smoke and coffee.

Sitting at tables both outside and in were a number of old and middle-aged men playing backgammon, their moustaches twitching, tanned faces creased with frowns of concentration or sudden laughter. The Luftwaffe might be coming over every day to attack the harbour and airfield, but that did not stop the Cretans going about their daily business – which, in the case of many of the men, meant sitting in a preferred *kafenio* for much of the day. In any case, they had soon cottoned on that the Luftwaffe could be relied upon. At around nine in the morning, and then again at dusk, thirty bombers, give or take, would fly over, aim for the harbour or airfield to the east of the town, drop their loads and head home again. The Germans

47

were despised for what they were doing but at least they were consistent.

It was Sergeant Stan Sykes who had spotted Aratiko's the day before, following the Rangers' move to join the mixed force of Greek regiments and Cretans covering the town. This realignment of 14th Infantry Brigade had been prompted by the arrival of the Leicesters, who had taken up positions to the south-east of the town between the 2/4th Australians, the 2nd King's Own Yorkshire Rangers and 2nd York and Lancashire Regiment, thus freeing up a battalion to reinforce the town. Since the Leicesters were new to the island, Brigadier Chappel considered it prudent not to place them alongside the Greeks; and because the Rangers had been closest to Heraklion, it was they who had been moved. The men were delighted – after all, a town had plenty more to offer than the countryside where there was little but olive and fruit groves.

'Here,' said Sykes, as he, Tanner and Staff Sergeant Woodman turned into the street. 'I told you it was discreet, didn't I?'

'Very good, Stan,' said Tanner. 'Now, if we can just find ourselves a little table at the back, it'll be even better.'

They wove their way past the tables on the street, through the open door and looked around. The old men glanced up, then returned to their games, but there was another group of men, younger, sitting at a table near the front, who eyed the newcomers suspiciously. Tanner caught the eye of one. Perhaps late twenties, a luxuriant black moustache and a three-day beard, wearing

48

a black waistcoat over a white shirt, loose black linen trousers and knee-length leather boots. His hair was long, swept back off his head loosely. He was a big man, Tanner noted, about his own height. Strong-looking, too.

'What about that one?' said Sykes, pointing to a table at the back of the room, close to the bar.

'Fine,' said Tanner.

They settled around the table, chairs scraping loudly on the stone floor, took off their helmets and rested their rifles against the wall, then lit cigarettes. The barman looked at them– *Yes?*

'I suppose we'd better just have coffee,' said Sykes.

'You should, at any rate,' said Woodman. 'You're the one that's got to impress his new platoon commander.' More replacements had been due in that morning, including a new subaltern for B Company. It was why Tanner and Sykes had been sent to Battalion Headquarters, newly established in an old Venetian house opposite the Jesus Bastion beside the Kenouria Gate, one of seven arrow-headed forts built along the town walls. When they had reached HQ, however, news had just arrived that the boat from Alexandria would be late. The new time of arrival was estimated to be after midday. Since it was hardly worth heading back to their new positions either side of the Knossos road they had decided to wait in town instead, slowly making their way down to the port via this bar, which Sykes had spotted earlier. But while there was nothing wrong in that, it did not pay to be seen passing the time of day in bars while others were still preparing defences and keeping watch for enemy parachutists.

Tanner held up three fingers to the barman. 'Three coffees,' he said, *'efharisto.'*

'I don't know that I want coffee,' said Woodman. 'What about a nice cool beer?'

'You go right ahead, Woody,' said Tanner.

'But you won't join me?'

'Not when the Germans might attack at any moment.'

'You're still convinced they're going to, then?'

'I'm sure of it. All this bombing – it's them softening us up. I hope they bloody well do come. Then we can shoot the bastards and kick them back to Greece.' He was talking with a confidence he did not feel. Once again, there was almost no RAF. It also worried him greatly that the Allied forces on Crete all seemed to be centred around the three main towns along the north coast: Canea, near Suda Bay in the west, Rethymno in the centre and then Heraklion. He'd been to Brigade Headquarters near the airfield and he had seen plenty of telephones and telephone wire, but little evidence of any radios. As he knew from bitter experience, once the fighting started, the phone lines were almost the first thing to go. He brushed away a fly from his trousers. The battalion had been issued with khaki drill during the past few days, and most had gladly made the change, swapping their thick serge battledress for the cooler sandy-coloured cotton. In Greece, the thick wool of their uniforms had been just about bearable during the day and they had been grateful for it at night, but now that it was May, the temperature was rising noticeably. Nobody

50

wanted to wear it in this heat.

There had been few trousers available, but both Tanner and Sykes had managed to get two pairs each, as had Captain Peploe; there were a number of perks to being CSM but one was getting first pick of anything that passed the way of the company quartermaster sergeant, in this case new uniforms. And Tanner had been mightily relieved not to have to wear the KD shorts, not because he was worried about his appearance – although he did think Bombay Bloomers looked ridiculous – but because experience in India had taught him that it was easy for bare legs to become sunburned, scratched, cut and then infected. A layer of thick cotton – and KD was sturdy stuff – provided a useful extra layer of protection. When he passed this piece of wisdom to Sykes and Peploe, they were quick to follow his lead. Tanner had also managed to get a pair of denim battledress trousers from some Australians out near the airfield, and he was particularly pleased with them. Unlike the khaki drill trousers, they still had the large patch pocket on the left leg and a smaller dressing pocket on the right, as well as the two normal hip pockets, but were every bit as light and cool as the KD pattern. It was these he was wearing now, along with his new KD collared shirt.

Tanner stubbed out his cigarette and, as he did so, noticed the barman glance at the young men near the front of the *kafenio*, and nod. He thought nothing more of it until the barman arrived with a tray that bore not only their coffees but also three full shot glasses, which he then proceeded to

51

set before them on the table.

'What's all this?' said Woody, lifting a glass and examining it closely.

'Raki,' said the barman. He inclined his head towards the men near the front.

'To our brave British allies,' said the big man, in heavily accented English. Woody raised his glass and was about to drink when the man added, 'The British who come over to Greece and then run away again, leaving our Cretan brothers stranded. Where is the Cretan Division now, Englishmen? Either dead or in the hands of Nazis. Your navy didn't think they were worth rescuing.'

Tanner stiffened, the muscles in his face taut. Pushing away the raki, he picked up his coffee instead. Sykes knew that look. 'Leave it, Jack,' he said quietly. 'He's trying to pick a fight. And he's a big bloke, an' all.'

'And now you won't drink,' continued the man. The other three were chuckling. 'We offer you raki, the hand of friendship, and you push it away.'

Woody raised his glass again, then downed the spirit in one gulp. 'Thank you,' he said. 'We're sorry about the Cretan Division but, you know, we're only soldiers, not generals or admirals.' He glanced shiftily at Sykes and Tanner. 'Come on, drink it, Jack. We don't want a bloody scene. It's not worth it.'

'He's right, Jack,' said Sykes. 'Drink it up and let's just walk out of here.' He lifted his glass, drank, then grimaced and wiped the back of his hand across his mouth.

'And what about you?' said the man, nodding towards Tanner. 'Your friends have shown some

52

manners, but not you, eh?'

Tanner sipped his coffee, but said nothing.

'Sir,' hissed Sykes. 'Please, mate. Just drink it.'

'The mighty British Empire,' said the man, scratching his cheek, 'so mighty that her army is always running away. And what are you going to do if the Germans come here, eh? Run away again. We don't want the horse that always bolts. We want Cretans to fight. Cretans who will stand their ground and fight like men for their country. For their homes.' He laughed, but without mirth. 'But, oh, no, we do not have any of our division because they were left to rot on the Albanian Front. Instead we are sent you. Cowards, men who like to run.'

At this Tanner slammed his fist into the table, pushed back his chair and picked up his shot glass.

'Don't,' said Sykes.

'Steady, Jack,' said Woodman. 'Come on, leave it.'

'No,' said Tanner, 'I've had it. I'm not listening to this crap.'

The Cretans were laughing as Tanner walked over to them. Stopping by the big man, he slammed the glass on the table. 'You can take your drink,' he said, 'and shove it up your arse.'

There was a sudden silence in the bar. The old men had stopped playing their games; the other three at the table now shot furtive glances at each other, while the smile on the big man's face vanished.

'Do you think I give a toss about this place?' snarled Tanner. 'I've lost good men fighting for

53

your country. I've lost good men in Norway and Belgium and France and North bloody Africa. Not one of them was a coward, and nor am I, and nor are my friends. Now apologize. I want to hear you take that back.' He stared at the man, his eyes unblinking.

'I'll kill you before I say anything of the sort.' He spoke to the others, turning his back on Tanner as he did so.

Grabbing his shoulder, Tanner spun him around. 'Apologize.' The man now pushed back his chair and stood up to face him. 'Outside then,' said Tanner.

Sykes was beside him now. 'It's not worth it. Walk away, sir.'

Tanner turned on his friend. 'Walk away? *Walk away?* Who do you think I am, Stan?'

'Come on, then,' said the man, clearing another chair out of his way. 'Outside.'

Out in the street, Tanner turned to face the Cretan, vaguely conscious of the watching eyes of the old men happy to observe such sport. *Where were Sykes and Woodman?* he wondered, but dared not take his eye off the Cretan, who was broad-chested, with large hands. Strength, of course, was important, but so too were agility and speed. And the willingness to fight ugly. In a boxing ring there were rules, but he knew there were none now, and although he had no intention of killing this man, he wanted to hurt and humiliate him. Tanner had fought many times, in and out of the ring, but the sport of boxing had taught him a number of useful lessons, not least the need to weigh up an opponent. This Cretan was confident

54

in his ability to take on a man of equal height, and that told Tanner he needed to be cautious until he knew the capabilities of his opponent.

For a few moments, they circled each other, the Cretan with his arms half raised, Tanner with his loose by his sides, a position he hoped would lure the man into making the first move.

'Come on, Englishman,' growled the Cretan, goading Tanner towards him with his hands.

Tanner smiled, then took two quick steps forward and swiftly dipped his left shoulder as though about to punch with his left hand, a dummy move designed to make the Cretan think he was left-handed and to encourage him to strike. The ruse worked as the Cretan swiftly flung out a heavy right punch so fast that even Tanner was surprised. Tanner moved his head but not before receiving a glancing blow across his temple, causing his footwork to falter and tipping him slightly off balance. Even so, the Cretan had overextended and Tanner was able to drive in a savage right hook – not a knock-out blow, but one hard enough to make the Cretan gasp, and in that split second, Tanner kicked his right foot hard against the man's knee, making his enemy cry out, then rammed his left boot straight into his crotch. As the Cretan grunted in agony, Tanner pushed back his right fist and, with the base of his hand, thrust a sharp jab into his opponent's neck. The four moves had taken no more than two seconds, but Tanner knew he'd not yet caused any real damage: the blow to the head had not been hard enough to break any bones, or the one to the knee. Even so, the Cretan now staggered backwards, doubled up.

Tanner stepped towards him. 'Now say you're sorry,' he said. Then something caught his eye. Looking up, he saw Woodman at the end of the road frantically waving and pointing to his left, down in the direction of the port. *Damn him*, thought Tanner.

A sudden stab of pain struck his legs and coursed through his entire body. Staggering, he saw the remains of a chair splintering at his feet, and then the Cretan was lunging at him, his bear-like arms gripping him around the waist and pushing him backwards. Tanner was already off balance, and the man's weight forced him against a table. Cracking his head first on the wood, then again as he crashed to the ground, he was momentarily dazed and, in that time, the Cretan had clasped his enormous hands around his neck and was squeezing, starving Tanner of air and pressing against his trachea. The man's nails were clawing into his neck too. The stench of alcohol, stale tobacco and sweat was overwhelming as the Cretan breathed heavily over him, grimacing with rage and effort. Tanner felt suppressed not only by the vice-like grip around his neck, but also by the hot, heavy weight of the man's body on his. Sweat was running down the Cretan's face, and a droplet fell into Tanner's eye, stinging with its saltiness.

Tanner could feel desperation welling within him, and was vaguely conscious of his legs kicking, as it occurred to him that this wild Cretan might be as good as his word and kill him, after all. With his senses now rapidly fading, he knew he had just moments in which to break free and so, despite the

56

overpowering urge to do otherwise, he allowed his eyes to flicker and his head to loll. As he had hoped, the Cretan's grip lessened fractionally. In that instant, Tanner brought both his arms inside those of the Cretan and, summoning all his remaining strength, quickly prised them apart. Then he brought his head up with a sudden sharp jerk, his forehead smashing into the man's nose. The Cretan yelled with pain and sat up, clutching his hands to his face. Still pinned to the ground, Tanner reached for a chair and swung it into the man's head, knocking him sideways. He got to his feet, and kicked again, this time into the Cretan's side, aiming for the kidney, then picked up another chair, ready to smash it down on him.

A pistol shot rang out, the report jarringly loud in the narrow confines of the street, and Tanner froze, panting, his head clammy with sweat and blood, the chair still in his hand.

'Stop!' shouted a man. 'Stop that right now!'

Tanner staggered backwards, his legs weak, and turned to see a British officer striding towards them, while a column of some forty soldiers waited at the end of the street. Hurrying behind the officer were several of his men, and, behind them, Woodman and Sykes.

Bloody hell, thought Tanner, dropping the chair and staggering towards a table, his hands groping for support. He hurt like hell – his legs, his head, his neck. Christ, he could barely speak. He tried to clear his throat.

'Get up, the pair of you,' called the officer, who, Tanner now saw, was a second lieutenant.

The Cretan roused himself, eyed Tanner with

hatred, then suddenly produced a knife with which he made a lunge. Parrying the thrust, Tanner caught the Cretan's wrist, twisted himself out of the way and rammed his elbow hard into the man's stomach, then deftly moved clear.

'That's it!' said the lieutenant, pointing his Webley at the Cretan. 'Drop that knife. Now!'

Breathing heavily, the Cretan glared at the lieutenant, then, rather than dropping it, slowly put his knife away. Tanner saw the barrel of the revolver was shaking in the lieutenant's hand. 'You!' he said, pointing to three of the new arrivals, 'put these men under arrest.' Now rifles were being pointed at both of them, bolts already drawn back. There was alarm in the eyes of the lieutenant and, Tanner saw, fear in those of one of the other men, a young lad. *New boys*, he thought. *No sudden movements.* Jesus, that was all he needed: to have survived so much only to be shot by one of his own side.

'Really, sir,' said Woodman, 'I'm not sure arrest is necessary. These two were just having a little scrap. A question of honour, you see.'

'I'll be the judge of that,' snapped the lieutenant. The Cretan's friends were now beside him, talking furiously and gesticulating wildly. He was sitting on a chair, wheezing and dabbing the blood on his face.

'Now, who are you?' he said to the Cretan. 'What is your name?'

The man spat and cleared his throat. 'My name,' he rasped, 'is Alopex. I am a *kapitan* with Antonis Grigorakis. Satanas, you know?'

The lieutenant eyed him. 'No, I don't, and I

58

don't care whether you're a *kapitan* or not. You are under arrest and you will come with us to Battalion Headquarters where I shall strongly recommend you be detained.'

Alopex glared back. 'You are making very big mistake. How long have you been on this island? Straight off the boat, eh?'

The lieutenant looked affronted. 'That is irrelevant. We can't have people brawling in the street like that. And, believe me, if you had killed this man it would have been a whole lot worse for you, no matter who you claim to be.'

'And who are you?' Alopex asked. 'Just so I know who I am dealing with.'

Again, the lieutenant seemed taken aback, and for a moment dithered as though undecided about how to reply. 'I am Lieutenant Liddell,' he said, 'of the 2nd Battalion, the King's Own Yorkshire Rangers.'

As soon as he said his name, Tanner, who had been recovering his breath quietly beside Sykes and Woodman, felt himself reel. It was as though he had been punched harder than he had by anything Alopex had thrown at him. Liddell – it was not possible. Incredulously, he stared at the lieutenant. How long had it been? Nine years now. *Nine long years.* Guy Liddell had been, what, twelve back then? Tanner closed his eyes a moment, rubbed his sweaty brow, then looked up at the lieutenant again. And now he did faintly recognize the boy in the man standing before him – those grey eyes, he remembered, because his own were much the same colour; it had been commented upon. The shape of the face too, full and round, as it had been in boyhood.

Christ, no, thought Tanner. How could this have happened?

'And you,' said Lieutenant Liddell, turning to him. Tanner followed his eyes as they noted first the leather wristband with the laurels and crown, which denoted his rank as a warrant officer second class, and then his face. Liddell's eyes narrowed – was that a flicker of recognition, Tanner wondered – and he said, 'A senior NCO like you should know better than to get involved in fights with locals. Good God, man, in case you weren't aware, we might be expected to fight a real enemy any moment.'

'He was sorely provoked, sir,' said Sykes.

'Be quiet, Sergeant,' snapped Liddell. Then, turning back to Tanner, he said, 'Name and unit?'

'CSM Tanner, sir,' Tanner mumbled. '2nd Yorks Rangers.' There were no regimental shoulder tabs on KD shirts.

'What was that? Yorks Rangers? This is just getting worse for you, Tanner. You're a disgrace to the regiment.'

'Sir,' interrupted Sykes again.

'Leave it, Sykes,' hissed Tanner.

'And you two are also Rangers?' Liddell asked, looking at Sykes and Woodman.

'Sir,' said Woodman, then told Liddell their names.

'Good. You can take us to Battalion Head-quarters. Take Tanner's rifle, Sykes, and, Wood-man, you search this man, Alopex. Then lead on.' He pointed to two of the other men. 'And you two can stay behind the prisoners. March them at gunpoint.'

'We weren't expecting you for another hour, sir,' said Woodman. 'We were in town to meet you off the ship.'

'Perhaps you were simply too busy drinking and brawling to notice the time. We arrived more than half an hour ago.'

Tanner watched Alopex whispering to his three friends and then they hurried off. He noticed that Liddell had seen this too and was clearly wondering whether he should have detained them as well. It was too late, though, so instead he straightened his cap, put his revolver back in its holster and, waving his arm, indicated to them to get moving.

'This is not over,' muttered Alopex, as they were frog-marched away from the *kafenio*. 'I will still kill you.'

'Put a bloody sock in it,' Tanner replied. He had other concerns now. *Damn it, damn it. Sod it and damn.*

Tanner and Alopex had been put in two makeshift guardrooms in the Jesus Bastion opposite Battalion Headquarters. The rooms were on either side of the tunnel leading into the bastion. Tanner's cell was dark and dank, the walls thick with cold stone, and only a small slit window providing any light. The ground was nothing more than compacted earth – clearly, these had been designed as store rooms and nothing more – but Tanner was not bothered by any discomfort. The cool air was, if anything, something of a relief. In any case, being in a darkened cell was the least of his concerns.

Being frog-marched through Heraklion would have been humiliating enough under any circumstances but was particularly so when he knew that a number of the men would soon be joining B Company. As CSM, he was supposed to be one of the figureheads of the company, a shining example. Now their first impression of him was of seeing him stripped of his weapon and placed under military arrest. Damn it all, he might even find himself court-martialled.

Sitting on the rough floor, his hands over his knees and smoking a cigarette, he sighed. His head still throbbed, and when he touched it, he could feel the slowly congealing blood of a gash that needed a stitch or two. If and when he did get out, he would have to watch his back now that a Cretan big shot was out for his blood. He knew about the kind of blood feuds these people made. Indians, Arabs, Greeks – they were all the same. If you made a vow, you had to follow it through: it was a question of honour. Tanner understood that – after all, it had been partly as a matter of honour that he had stood up to Alopex himself. The other reason had been anger. It was anger that had driven him to start firing the pompom a couple of weeks earlier and it was anger that had driven him to fight Alopex. A lot of anger. *Too much*, he thought.

And as if that wasn't bad enough, now Guy Liddell had turned up. He would lay money on Liddell being Sykes's new platoon commander. *Jesus*. Of all the people. Why the hell had he been sent here? Why wasn't he farming still in Alvesdon? What was it with these fellows? Captain

Peploe was the same – he could have been doing his bit on his family farm in north Yorkshire, away from all this. They could have avoided the fighting altogether. Tanner pushed back his hair and sighed again.

There were voices outside – English voices – and then, through the narrow window, he heard the sound of a key being turned and the squeak of hinges. Moments later Alopex was muttering in a low voice.

'You're a hot-headed old fool, Alopex,' said a voice. 'I need you fighting Huns, not our chaps.'

'He insulted me,' said Alopex. 'You think I can be humiliated like that in front of my men?'

'All right, all right,' soothed the English voice. 'Come on, let's get out of here. There's something I need you to do...'

Tanner shook his head and lit yet another cigarette. Sykes had somehow managed to purloin a stash of Player's Navy Cut from HMS *Halberd* and they had been smoking them ever since. God only knew how he had managed it; Tanner didn't like to ask. So Alopex was working for the British, he thought. He smiled ruefully to himself – a man who disliked the British, but hated the Italians and Germans more. He wondered who that English voice had belonged to. Not regular army, that was for sure, but someone who could cut through tape, pull strings. A useful friend. Tanner drew deeply on his cigarette. *Bloody hell*, he thought, *what a mess.*

He must have dropped off because when the key turned in his door, he jolted awake and felt momentarily disoriented.

'Jack, Jack,' said Captain Peploe. 'What have you been doing?'

'Bastard deserved it, sir,' muttered Tanner. 'I wasn't going to sit and listen to him bad-mouthing us and calling us cowards. It's not our fault his sodding division was left in Greece.'

'Couldn't you have just turned the other cheek?' Peploe stood over him, his round face as genial as ever. 'Sykes and Woodman managed to.'

'It's a question of honour, sir.'

'Come on, up you get.' And as Tanner got to his feet, Peploe patted his shoulder and said, 'You and your honour, Jack. Pride and a filthy temper more like. What is it with you at the moment? You've been a bear with a sore head for weeks. Even more sore now, I should think.'

'It bloody hurts like hell, sir.'

'Well? What's the matter? What's bitten you?'

'I'm sick of us running away, sir. That Cretan was right. And if I was him, I'd probably feel the same way about us too.'

'But you still felt it necessary to get into a street brawl?'

Tanner sighed. 'All right, maybe I did see red, but I'm not going to sit there listening to some Cretan wallah calling us cowards. Nor am I going to drink his drink when he's taking a lot of good men's names in vain – and men who died fighting for Greece.'

'Sykes and Woodman walked away from it.'

'Yeah, well, I think a man should stick up for himself, and his mates.' Even as he said it, he knew it sounded lame and petulant. Renewed anger and frustration swelled within him and he

64

growled and kicked the wall with his boot.

'Feeling better?' said Peploe.

Tanner said nothing for a moment. 'I'm sorry, sir,' he said at last, 'not for kicking that bastard – and, no matter what anyone says, I'd do it again – but for the trouble I've caused. I know everyone in the whole battalion will know about this, and it doesn't reflect well on me or the company.'

'More like the whole brigade.' He eyed Tanner a moment. 'Is there anything else?'

'Apart from the lack of guns, MT and almost no radios whatsoever, no, sir, I'm as happy as can be.'

'But we've no shortage of troops and we're dug in around strong defensive positions.'

'I remember what happened in Norway when we didn't have enough kit or enough aircraft. And look what happened in France. It was bloody chaos. No one knew what the hell was going on. A year on and we're still depending on telephone lines and runners. When are we going to be given some sodding radios?'

'There's a big difference, Jack. Crete is an island. They can only get here by sea or by air. They're not going to be able to bring over tanks and MT and heavy guns. We'll be more than a match for them. This is different.'

'I hope you're right, sir,' muttered Tanner. 'Anyway, let them come. I'm fed up with waiting.' He looked at Peploe. 'Will I be court-martialled?'

Peploe smiled. 'No, Jack. I can't say Vigar was overly impressed but he felt your humiliation through the town and a few hours in the glass-house were punishment enough in the circum-

65

stances. Had this been peacetime it might have been another matter.'

'And the Cretan's already been let out,' said Tanner.

'Yes – well, there was that too. Not really fair to keep you if he's been let loose.'

'An Englishman fetched him. I heard him.'

'John Pendlebury,' said Peploe. 'He's vice consul here, although he seems to be the chief of all these local Cretan *kapitans*. He's recruited them to help fight any invasion.'

Tanner nodded. *I see.*

'Actually, it's rather a thrill to meet him,' added Peploe. 'He's quite a celebrated archaeologist. In fact, he was curator at Knossos before the war. I've been hoping to cross paths with him ever since we got here.'

'You studied that, didn't you, sir? At Cambridge?'

'Archaeology and ancient history, yes. I still can't believe I haven't got out to the ruins, but there's hardly been the time. Maybe in the next few days.'

'If Jerry doesn't come.'

'Let's hope he doesn't. A bit of sightseeing first might be fun.'

Tanner chuckled.

'Hooray,' said Peploe. 'My CSM's smiling again.'

'Am I free to get back to our positions, then, sir?'

'Not quite. There's someone I need to introduce you to properly. Our new platoon commander, Mr Liddell. I think you probably owe him an apology too.' He held out his arm and ushered

Tanner into the bastion entranceway. 'Come on, he's still across the road at Battalion HQ.'

Tanner squinted in the sudden brightness. It was warm still, the sun quite strong after the cool of his cell. Birds chirped in the trees along the street and a fly buzzed by his face. Perhaps it would be all right with Liddell. After all, it had been a long time. Tanner knew he had changed a great deal from the boy he had once been; his face was more lined, more battered. There was also a slightly broken nose where before there had been no blemish, and skin that was permanently the dark brown of a deep tan, where before he had been fresh-faced, with white skin and pink cheeks. *Yes*, he told himself. *I am* a *different person now*. There was no need to worry.

'And you could do with seeing the doc before you head back up to the lines,' Peploe was saying, as they crossed the road.

In through the front door, a cool and light hallway, up some stone steps and then into a large, airy room on the first floor with windows overlooking the Jesus Bastion. Outside, a tamarisk tree waved gently in the breeze, the shadows of the leaves and branches cast across the whitewashed wall opposite. At one end, a staff clerk was tapping at a typewriter, while at the other, sitting behind a makeshift desk, was the battalion commander, Colonel Vigar. In front, also seated, was Lieutenant Liddell who, on seeing Peploe, stood up.

'Ah, Peploe, come in,' said the colonel. 'And you, CSM. Calmed down a bit?'

'Yes, sir. My sincere apologies, sir,' said Tanner, clicking to attention and saluting.

'Can't go around scrapping with the locals,' said the colonel, 'although from what I've heard it sounds as though he damn well deserved it.'

'CSM Tanner was standing up for the honour of the regiment, sir,' said Peploe. Liddell shifted his feet.

Colonel Vigar smiled. 'Well, maybe you've done us all a favour, Tanner. If we've got to fight alongside these Greek fellows, we don't want them thinking we're a pushover, eh?' He glanced at Second Lieutenant Liddell. 'Although you acted quite correctly, Liddell. Quite correctly.' He clapped his hands and rubbed them together. 'So,' he said, 'let's put this little episode behind us, shall we? We'll pretend you two haven't met yet and you can shake hands. Then we'll pack you back off to our positions. As I was saying, Mr Liddell, Tanner here is one of our most decorated soldiers. A highly experienced man, a first-class soldier and someone who I'm sure will help you settle into the company.' Vigar tapped a cigarette on the table, then popped it between his lips. 'So, Mr Liddell, this is your CSM, Mr Tanner. Mr Tanner – Mr Liddell.'

Tanner had consciously avoided looking directly at Liddell, but now, as the new subaltern turned and held out his hand, he faced him and saw his expression change.

'You!' said Liddell. 'It's you. I know this man, sir,' he said, turning to the colonel and then to Peploe. 'I can't believe I didn't notice before. Good God, you're Jack Scard – Bill Scard's son.'

4

Tuesday, 20 May. As normal, the Luftwaffe had made their morning call, albeit somewhat earlier than usual. This time, first Dorniers and then Junkers had pasted the coastal plain west of Suda Bay just after 6 a.m., others following at regular intervals until some time after seven. By half past, on the basis that the morning 'hate', as the raids were known, was over, the various men dug in along that stretch of the island were stood down, preparing themselves for another day of weapons cleaning and tanning themselves in the late-spring sun.

For Captain Monty Woodhouse, however, the all-clear had been the signal for him to report back to General Freyberg and Creforce Headquarters on the rocky outcrop of Akrotiri, above Canea and Suda Bay. A British intelligence officer, Woodhouse had been visiting the Greek regiment dug in a few miles south-west of Canea and, grabbing his motorbike, had set off through the gradually settling dust, up along lush Prison Valley, thick with olive groves, tamarisk and fruit trees, through more Greek and New Zealand positions to the south of Galatas village, and then on through Canea, normally such a thriving, bustling port, but this morning still quiet – an occasional yap of a dog, the crowing of a cockerel but curiously lacking the normal hubbub that was a feature of the island's capital.

A change of gear, and the motorbike was climbing out of the town and onto the rocky Akrotiri headland, weaving past cactus plants, more olives and rough farmsteads, until Woodhouse reached the general's villa, typically Italianate and solid. It was a stone's throw from the quarry in which Creforce was based, and no more than a few hundred yards from one of Crete's most hallowed sites: the tomb of the island's hero of recent times, Eleftherios Venizelos.

Creforce Headquarters had been chosen for the same reasons as the site of Venizelos's tomb: because the view from there was as fine as any on the island. It was around 7.45 a.m. that Woodhouse was ushered through the hallway of the villa and out to the veranda where the British commander had just begun his breakfast.

'Ah, Woodhouse,' said the general, 'will you join me? I can offer you coffee, boiled eggs and quite superb bread and honey.'

'Thank you, sir,' said Woodhouse, taking the chair shown by Freyberg's outstretched hand. The general now pushed a basket of boiled eggs towards him. 'Help yourself to coffee,' he said, dabbing at his trim moustache with a starched white napkin.

Woodhouse thanked him again and then, having poured his coffee and taken an egg, paused to look at the view before him. Below them lay Canea, the ancient harbour protecting the small array of boats like a mother cuddling a child. The pale limestone and whitewashed buildings of the town were vivid against the deep blue of the sea and the lush green coastal plain around it. Beyond, stretching west, was the long sweep of the bay. Visibility was as near to perfect as could be, and Woodhouse could clearly see the small town of Platanias some six miles away and, beyond that, the airfield of Maleme, now quiet and empty of RAF planes. To his left lay Prison Valley through which he had just travelled, and, rising majestically, the great ridge of the White Mountains.

'Hell of a viewpoint, isn't it?' said Freyberg. 'Twenty minutes ago we could see bugger-all for the smoke and dust, but it's settled down again now. So, tell me, how are our Greek friends?'

'In good heart, sir,' said Woodhouse. 'Determined not to give the enemy an inch, should he try to attack.'

Freyberg chuckled. 'Good, good. And they've got enough ammunition? Positions seem satisfactory to you?'

'Yes, sir.' Woodhouse was about to expand, but stopped as something suddenly caught his ear. Pausing, he cocked his head. Yes, there it was – out to sea, unmistakable now: the sound of aircraft approaching. He glanced at the general, who was now spreading another generous dollop of thick honey across his bread, apparently oblivious to the sound.

'I know most of them are not Cretans,' said Freyberg, 'but Crete is still part of Greece. It's still their country. Most Greek men will fight like dervishes if it's Greek soil they're defending. We're going to need men like that and, of course, they're a proud people.'

By now the sound of aero engines was a steady,

71

increasingly loud drone. Moments later, Wood-house spotted them – an air armada of Junkers three-engine transport planes and, behind, gliders. Mesmerized, he watched as a number of gliders detached themselves from their Junkers tugs and began drifting down towards the coast. Ahead, the Junkers were now shedding their loads, hundreds of white parachutes suddenly bursting into life like flower buds until the sky was awash with them, white canopies drifting down-wards.

Several gliders were heading seemingly straight towards them, and then more parachutes were dropping. Suddenly, from nearby and from the valley and coast below, firing rang out, antiaircraft guns booming, black puffs of shell dotting the sky, while amid the crashes of the guns came the steady machine-gun fire of the Bren and the individual snap of the rifle.

Woodhouse glanced at Freyberg and was aston-ished to see the Creforce commander calmly continuing to eat his bread and honey. It was inconceivable that the general had not observed what was going on, yet Woodhouse knew that to suggest Freyberg do something would be at best impolite and at worst downright insubordinate. On the other hand, Bren and rifle fire was now crackling very near at hand, from the direction of the Venizelos grave.

Clearing his throat, Woodhouse said, 'I say, there's quite a show going on, sir.'

'H'mph,' Freyberg replied, now glancing up to see the spectacle. 'I'll say one thing for 'em, they're dead on time.'

'Sir?'

'The enemy,' said Freyberg, pointing skywards with his knife, 'impressively punctual.'

Woodhouse glanced at the ribbon of the Victoria Cross and the Distinguished Service Order on the General's chest, to which had been added no fewer than two clasps, signifying he had been awarded the medal three times. Next to these was an array of other honours. Freyberg's bravery was legendary.

Soon after Freyberg had arrived to take command of Creforce, some three weeks earlier, Woodhouse had been told of how Churchill had once demanded that Freyberg strip off his shirt and vest and show him the wounds he had sustained during the Great War. According to the story, Freyberg had apparently obliged and then Churchill had carefully counted the scars – twenty-seven in all. 'Yes, but it's not as bad as it looks,' Freyberg was supposed to have told him, 'because you tend to get two wounds for every bullet or piece of shrapnel – one where it goes in and another where it goes out the other side.' Fearlessness was all very well, Woodhouse thought, but rifle and machine-gun fire were now cracking out very close to hand. Paratroopers were drifting to the ground only a few hundred yards away. Above the din, he could even hear occasional shouts, while behind him, he was conscious of activity within the villa.

'I should report in to the quarry, sir,' said Woodhouse, as Freyberg calmly poured another cup of coffee.

'Yes, yes, you cut along,' the general agreed.

Woodhouse stood up, saluted, and hurried out.

General Freyberg smiled to himself once Woodhouse had gone. The expression on the young man's face had been priceless. The truth was, however, that there was little he could do in these first throes of the German attack. He had made his dispositions, ensured his troops were as ready as possible, and had done all he could to urge the Commander-in-Chief, Middle East, to provide aircraft and guns and as many reinforcements as he could spare. Now that the Germans were actually dropping from the sky, he had to let the men get on with it. He would act only once he knew how the battle was developing.

He had known about the German plans since the beginning of the month; Wavell had let him in on some high-level intelligence. Where that had come from, Freyberg had no idea, but when Wavell assured him it was secure that was good enough for him. Yet the C-in-C had also made it quite clear that he was to guard this secret with his life and under no circumstances was he to act on what he had been told. This was damned frustrating. Any ass could see that the airfield at Maleme, just up the coast, was the key to a successful airborne invasion. Once the Huns had secured the field, they could pour in as many troops as they liked. The maddening thing was that he would have reinforced it considerably had he not known about the German plans. Now that he did, however, the risk of compromising this intelligence was considered too great. He'd rather Wavell had never told him.

This same source had also told him the Germans were planning an attack on 17 May. That had then been postponed by three days. Freyberg had woken early that morning and had settled down to breakfast on the veranda with the intention of watching events unfold from his grandstand view. And, by God, that intelligence had been bang on the money! Sure enough, almost dead on 0800 hours, down the Huns had come.

Freyberg dabbed his mouth again with his napkin. *Ah, for two or three fighter squadrons,* he thought. Three squadrons of Hurricanes or Kitty-hawks, all based at Maleme, would have made mincemeat of the German airborne invasion. As it was he could see two Junkers plunging earth-wards, long streams of black smoke following after them; one, he could see, was vividly on fire. He stood up and, for a moment, paused to lean on the balustrade. Puffs of smoke dotted the sky; more parachutes; smoke along the coast, and now a whiff of cordite on the air. Away in Prison Valley, he saw billows of silk caught in the olive groves. Guns boomed, machine-guns chattered. Behind him, in front of him, to the side of him, the battle was under way, ill-defined, confusing, messy. He put a small cigar into his mouth, clicked open his American lighter, and inhaled the sweet smoke. *It was ever thus,* he thought. Still, he felt quietly optimistic that the island would hold. He had some forty-eight thousand troops, which was way more than the Germans could ever drop in their initial assault. His inspections of the defences had also encouraged him greatly – morale was good, the men looked fit, and adequate ammunition had been dumped and stockpiled.

Freyberg glanced at his watch. Time to head down to the quarry. The German plan, he knew, was to attack in the Maleme-Canea sector first, then at Rethymno and Heraklion. And once the airborne invasion had begun, the seaborne assault would follow.

At Eleusis airfield, near Athens on the Greek mainland, it was another scorcher, but apart from a brief moment at first light, when the sky and air had been beautifully clear, the main feature of the day had been the vast amounts of dust that had been whipped up by the endless stream of transport aircraft that had been leaving since around 6 a.m. This had caused delays, slight at first but which had begun rapidly to escalate and had put the day's operation significantly behind schedule. For those men in the first wave – the battalion of paratroopers from the 3rd Fallschirmjäger Regiment – this had been frustrating enough, but for those in the 1st Regiment scheduled to be part of the second wave, this delay was causing mounting fury. The men had been in a state of fevered expectation as it was, but now the hours were ticking by and still there was no sign of any movement.

At 11 a.m., the 3rd Battalion was stood down again, and this time there was no hour-long delay but the realization that they had absolutely no chance of being airborne before two o'clock that afternoon, some four hours after they had originally been due to set off.

'I'm sorry, gentlemen,' Major Schulz told his company commanders, from the battalion headquarters tent. 'It's the same elsewhere, though. I've just spoken to Oberst Bräuer, and the entire regiment has been delayed, so it's not as though they will be starting without us.' Around the edge of the tent battalion staff were still manning radios and field telephones, while a clerk tapped away at a typewriter. Only their packs and weapons, neatly stacked beneath the trestle tables, suggested they were, in fact, ready to pack up and go the moment the signal arrived.

'I'm going to organize some food and drink for the men,' said Schulz, 'but in the meantime, go back to your companies and make sure your boys keep themselves busy.'

Oberleutnant Kurt Balthasar wandered back across the dry soil and sparse grass to his 4th Company area, a collection of patrol and bell tents among an aged olive grove. The tents had once been white, but were now a dun colour, thanks to the dust. He'd already been awake for the best part of nine hours, too nervous, too excited to sleep. Just a few snatched moments was all he had managed and then movement outside had woken him – the sound of trucks and buses, ferrying paratroopers to their gliders and transports, shouts of orders, the last-minute work of the mechanics – and from then on he had known he was awake for good. It had been the same last time, before the drop on the Belgian forts a year ago, but at least then they had been first into action. A long night that had been, but not for lack of action: they had loaded up before dawn, and had been dropping from the sky at first light. This time it was different: too much waiting.

And the airfield next to their camp was now maddeningly quiet. Across the sea, the men of the 3rd Regiment would already be fighting, yet here they were kicking their heels. The airfield was only a few hundred yards away and beyond was Athens, now shimmering in the late-morning sun. Balthasar squinted as he looked up into the bright, cloudless sky, then glanced across at the Acropolis, visible through the haze, standing, timeless, on its promontory. To the south lay the sea, where for the past couple of weeks the men had been swimming daily, keeping fit, cool and clean.

He wandered around the tents, stopping first by the men of Leutnant Neumann's platoon. Some were stretched out in their tents, others outside.

'Sorry, boys, we're delayed again,' he said. 'Stood down until two.' Groans of frustration, cards slammed on the table, a kick of the ground. 'I know, I know,' said Balthasar. 'Clean your weapons again, lose some more money on skat, write another letter. I don't want you sitting on your arses staring into space or at your wristwatches.' Mutters of 'Yes, boss,' and resigned nods. 'And Papa Schulz is trying to fix up some lunch so that you can all be sick on each other when we do get in the air.'

He continued his way around, talking to the other two platoons in turn, using the same jokes – which brought a few wry smiles. He knew the men liked him, yet he was careful not to be a friend to any of them. A bit of distance was needed. So, too, was their respect, but he had earned that with a fighting record in France and the Low Countries and, more recently, in Greece that had brought him an Iron Cross first and second class. He also made sure he set high standards. Those who followed his lead found him approachable, ready with a joke, and willing to indulge a few high jinks. Those who did not meet his expectations soon found their lives a misery, and then they either stepped up or were thrown out, or found themselves on a particularly suicidal mission.

His company now was almost at full strength – 154 men rather than the full complement of 170 – and although there were admittedly a few greenhorns, there were enough combat veterans to ensure the new boys toed the line. In any case, from what he'd seen of them so far, the replacements seemed to be shaping up well. Paratroopers were special – elite troops, as he made sure none of his men ever forgot. And elite troops were just that: the best, particularly in this battalion and especially in this company. In a year and a half of war, the Fallschirmjäger had become a force that struck fear into their enemies. This, he told them, was what they had to live up to.

Returning to his tent, he checked his equipment again. Two water bottles rather than one – who knew when they might be able to refill? – canvas gas-mask case stuffed not with a mask but three stick grenades, a gravity knife and a Gebrheller bayonet, two triple-filled MP40 ammunition pouches, a stash of rifle rounds, plus spare socks and as many dressing packs and first-aid items as he could fit into his smock and trousers. In his canvas burlap carry-sack was his parachute, while laid out on his camp bed were his firearms. It was difficult to jump out of a plane with a rifle: it could not be slung across the back because of the parachute pack, or across the front because it would get in the way. Instead, rifles were sup-posed to be placed in the aluminium canisters that were dropped with them. Over Belgium, though, Balthasar had looped his K.98 over one shoulder and it had not fallen off, and he in-tended to carry it with him this time, along with his MP40 submachine-gun, and a Sauer semi-automatic pistol. He had suggested the rest of the men do the same. The most dangerous time for the paratrooper was swinging down through the air – when they were sitting ducks – and immedi-ately upon landing when they were scrabbling around trying to shed their parachutes and offering clear targets.

On paper, the MP38 and 40 had ranges of some 200 metres, but in reality it was all but useless over more than forty. With its short barrel, it simply did not have the velocity – and Balthasar rarely opened fire with his at more than twenty-five metres. At close range it was a great weapon. At long range, it was a waste of time. On the other hand, he could drop a man at 400 metres with his rifle. When he landed, he wanted his K.98 with him, not in some canister lying tangled up in an out-of-reach cactus plant.

Balthasar sat down and looked at his watch – exactly what he had told his men not to do – then ran his hands through his hair and lit a cigarette. *Scheisser*, he thought. He considered writing to his sister, then thought better of it. What was the point? He'd barely seen her in years and he couldn't tell her very much anyway. There was no one else. Both his parents were dead – his father in the last war, his mother nearly ten years ago. Balthasar and his sister had lived with an aunt in Hamburg after that, until Balthasar had decided to leave; he'd never liked her anyway. He'd joined the Merchant Navy, sailing trampers all round the world, saved a bit of money, then tired of the sea.

Back in Germany, the National Socialists had come to power and Balthasar had seen that the new Germany held opportunities for men like him: men who were big and blond and good-looking, with a half-decent brain between their ears. Men who knew something of the world and how it worked. The Nazis didn't care if you were born in a back-street. If you had talent and could prove yourself, you could make something of your life. So Balthasar had joined the Party, then the SS and then, when Goring announced to the world that Germany had an air force, he had applied to transfer and was accepted.

Excitement had quickly turned to disappointment. Of course he had intended to become a fighter pilot – didn't everyone? – but instead of pirouetting through the sky in 450-kilometre-per-hour Messerschmitts, he was sidelined into air-sea rescue, flying biplanes with sea floats. He was an officer in the Luftwaffe but clearly his career would go nowhere if he was spending his time picking up people out of the sea. And so he decided to transfer again, applying to join the newly formed Parachute Regiment General Göring. Accepted, he knew immediately that he had chosen wisely. The training was exhilarating and he discovered he was fitter and stronger than most of his fellows. The danger thrilled him, while the knowledge of being part of a newly formed elite gave him a sense of belonging he had never known before. Three years on, he was still with the 1st Fallschirmjäger Regiment, and confident that in the ensuing battle there would be more opportunities to further his career. *If we ever get there.* He got up and stepped outside his tent. Some coffee, or something to eat. That was what he needed. No – what he really needed was a chance to get stuck into some Tommies.

Two o'clock, 20 May. The 2nd Battalion, the Yorks Rangers, were dug in beyond the town walls. The town had sprawled, however, since the Venetian days and the Rangers had wasted no time in either occupying the buildings that stood crumbling and empty, or billeting themselves among the locals. Most of the battalion's B Echelon, for example, had made their base among a number of dilapidated houses at the foot of the walls, and in the courtyard within had set up a field kitchen. So far, since landing on Crete, none of the men had gone hungry.

Even so, some three hundred yards further on, Sergeant Stan Sykes was squatting over a small fire under the shelter of a large plane tree by the side of the Knossos road. He was clutching his sword bayonet, from which hung a small Dixie can full of water. Beside him on the ground was a can of evaporated milk, a small packet of tea, a tiny tin of sugar and two white eggs. The battalion were being fed their three square meals a day, but with the lads in their positions and nothing much else going on, Sykes had bartered a couple of eggs from a Cretan girl in return for a piece of chocolate. He'd decided to boil some water, hard-boil the eggs and brew up some tea while he was about it. It was a means of passing the hours, if nothing else.

As the first wisps of steam began rising from the tin, Sykes's thoughts turned to CSM Tanner. Sykes had found him the previous evening at B Company's headquarters, a requisitioned house at the edge of town, a hundred yards behind their lines and a stone's throw from the Knossos road. Sitting beneath a sprawling tamarisk, Tanner had been drinking a brew and sharpening his bayonet. The CSM had looked up as Sykes approached. The blood had been washed from his face, but some livid purple bruises had emerged on his neck.

'You all right, sir?' Sykes had asked.

'Course I'm bloody all right,' Tanner had snapped, then added, 'Well, no, actually, I'm not. I'm bloody seething, Stan.' He had looked around, then said, 'Come on, let's get away from here for a minute.' He had led Sykes through a sparse olive grove between HQ and their forward positions, and up towards a rocky outcrop that overlooked the company's lines. He had eventually sat down on a stony seat in the rock and

83

Sykes had thought he was about to speak, but the CSM had merely pulled out a packet of cigarettes. For a while they had smoked in silence, the sun setting over the high mountains away to the west, the sky, once so blue, turning a soft purple.

'Well, what happened, then?' Sykes had asked.

'The captain came and got me,' said Tanner, then told him about Alopex's release. 'But it's your new platoon commander, Stan.'

Ah, thought Sykes. *At last.* 'What about him?'

'I know him – or rather, I should say, I *knew* him. Back home.'

'So there's another Wiltshireman in the battalion.'

Tanner drew on his cigarette, eyed Sykes carefully, scuffed at the ground, looked around him once again and then said, 'Look, his old man used to employ my dad. As a gamekeeper. But my dad died, and I left home soon after. Joined the army. Mr Liddell's old man – well, he was a good bloke. A really good man.' He cleared his throat. 'What I'm trying to say, Stan, is this: that's all anyone needs to know. When I left – there was a bit of trouble. But if you hear him saying anything, you'd be doing me a favour if you told me about it – and tried to put a lid on it too.' He looked at him, his brows pinched.

'You want me to find out what he knows?'

'Yes – but whatever he tells you, you keep to yourself, you understand? My past is no one's business. No one's.'

'No, no, of course not,' said Sykes. 'Listen, Jack, we've all got our secrets. Blimey, I was in all sorts of trouble before I joined up. That was then – this

84

is now. If you don't want to talk about it-'

'I don't. I can't, Stan.'

'And that's fine. Honestly. Say no more.' He grinned and clapped him on the shoulder, then changed the subject. 'You know, you definitely had the better of that Cretan geezer. The lads are right behind you.'

'You're just trying to make me feel better. I've suffered my share of humiliations in my life, but being force-marched at the head of a load of new recruits was more than a man should have to put up with. I fought that bastard to save our pride and ended up getting it bashed. Sticks in the gut, Stan. Really sticks in the gut.'

'I'm sure, but that was just a new officer trying to prove 'imself and nothing more. But, honestly, Jack, you can hold your head up. More than can be said for me an' Woody. What a pair of lily-livers we were, eh?'

Tanner had smiled wryly. 'We should get back.'

Sykes had left Tanner feeling little the wiser. His friend had never really talked about his past – not even his time in the army before the war. An occasional comment here and there, but that had been it. *A bit of trouble*, he'd said – something he *couldn't* talk about. What did that mean? Sykes shook his head.

The water had now begun to boil and, looking up, Sykes saw Lieutenant Liddell approaching.

'Care for a brew, sir?' Sykes asked.

Liddell paused, hands behind his back, then said, 'Yes, why not? Thank you, Sergeant.' He added, 'The men all seem to be in order.'

'Yes, I think so too, sir.'

85

'And in good heart.'

'As good as can be expected. We just need Jerry to come, sir. Don't want too much hangin' around.'

'Er, no, I suppose not.'

Sykes passed the lieutenant an enamel mug of sweet tea. 'There you go, sir.'

Liddell thanked him, took a sip and nearly choked.

'You all right, sir? I didn't poison it, did I?'

'Just a bit more sugar than I'm used to, Sykes.'

'Oh, I'll try an' remember another time, sir.'

'I'm sure I'll get used to it.' Liddell gingerly took another sip. 'Um, tell me, Sergeant, where are you from? Clearly not Yorkshire.'

'Deptford, sir. I'm a south Londoner. You're not from Yorkshire either, though, are you, sir?'

'No, no, I'm not. I'm from Wiltshire. The same village as CSM, er, Tanner, as it happens.'

'He told me once that he left there as a boy.'

'Yes. His father died – I remember there was talk that he'd been shot by some poachers. Or maybe it was an accident. I'm really not sure. I was away at the time – at my prep school.'

'His father was shot?'

'Yes, definitely shot, but how or why, I couldn't say for sure.' He frowned. 'There were rumours.'

'About what, sir? How he died?'

'Yes. It was sad. His father was a good sort. Then one of the village lads drowned. Two unfortunate deaths just like that. As I say, I was away, but I remember there being rumours – village people are like that. There's always talk. You know how it is.' He paused again. 'He was always rather wild.'

'Tanner, sir?'

'Yes. He was older than me, but it was almost as though he'd grown up out of doors. I'd run into him in the woods sometimes – suddenly he'd be there, as though he'd appeared from nowhere. Never heard him approach. I don't remember his mother at all. She must have died when he was very young.'

'So why did he leave, sir?'

Liddell shrugged. 'I suppose because there was no one to support him any more. He was too young to take over as gamekeeper – no brothers or sisters, no parents. I do know, though, that my father gave him an introduction to the regiment. He'd served with the Yorks Rangers in the last war – that's how he met my mother. He was best friends with my mother's brother, you see. I'm not sure of the ins and outs of it, but he had been in the Wiltshires and then was transferred. I don't know why – filling a hole, I suppose.'

'So that's why you joined them too?'

'Yes. I could have joined one of the Wiltshire regiments, but my father died last year and, well, I suppose I thought I'd follow in his footsteps, so to speak.'

'The CSM doesn't ever talk much about those days, sir.' Sykes caught his eye. 'Doesn't like people knowing his business – and why should he, sir? It's not up to us to pry into a man's past.'

Liddell glanced at him. 'No – no, of course it isn't.'

'But I will say this, sir. I know he thought a lot of your father. 'E did tell me that. Said he was a

87

real good man. Looked up to him.'

'Yes,' said Liddell, his brow furrowing. 'I just need to make sure he looks up to me too, don't I?'

CSM Tanner was forward of the Rangers' positions, making a further reconnoitre of the ground around them. A series of valleys fed down towards the town, valleys that were quite sparsely populated – just a few farms and clusters of houses. The land was lush, however, filled with olive groves, vineyards and small fields of still-young wheat, oats and maize. If any Germans landed, he reckoned they'd find good cover there. On the other hand, they would find it hard to advance. The British positions were pretty good: the men were well dug in, the Brens and mortars carefully positioned with excellent cover, while behind was the edge of the town, and then the huge Venetian bastions and walls of the old town. Those would take some storming.

From their positions at the edge of the town, the ground rose very gently some four hundred yards, offering as clear a line of fire as was possible in this broken landscape of vines and groves and trees. He and Peploe had considered leaving permanent pickets on the ridgeline, but then had decided there was little point: it was just too far and risked leaving the men isolated and exposed. If they were attacked in overwhelming force, it would be better to fall back to the town and the walls, somewhat crumbling after long years of decay but still a formidable obstacle.

He crested the ridge and looked down towards

Knossos. Among the plane trees he saw the Villa Ariadne, marked on his map, and a little further on, the ruins themselves. Through his binoculars he could see the walls and columns of the ancient palace, while to the east, overlooking the site, lay another long ridge, the current limit of the Rangers' front. To the west, another shallower ridge, and beyond that a further valley, narrower than the one they were currently in, and from which rose the Ida Mountains, which now, in the afternoon heat, stood clear and jagged against the cloudless sky. There was no denying it: Crete was a bloody beautiful place. He looked back towards the town, and then east, where most of the brigade were dug in. The airfield lay on flat land next to the coast. Nothing stirred; there was not a single aircraft there, and it occurred to him then that General Freyberg would have been better off destroying it, or at least disabling it.

Tanner shook his head and moved on; there was still work to be done. On his map, he carefully marked whatever buildings he came across – houses, sheds, barns and wells. When he got back to Company Headquarters, he would then make a note of the distances; he had a feeling they would be useful if it ever came to a battle.

Tanner was glad to be alone, out in the Crete countryside, away from the knowing looks and nudges. He was also grateful to be able to avoid Lieutenant Liddell. Jesus, he could have throttled him, the sodding big-mouth. He'd never liked him as a boy. Too spoiled by half. And that look on Peploe's face – what was it? Surprise – yes, but something more. *Disappointment*. Tanner winced again, just thinking about it. He'd told them he had lied about his age when he joined the army and had changed his name so that no one could trace him. Tanner had been his mother's maiden name, he told Peploe and the colonel. 'It's just a name,' he had said. Had they believed him? They'd seemed to, but now he was not the person they'd thought he was. *But I am.* He no longer thought of himself as Jack Scard; it was a name that had belonged to someone else entirely. Someone he had left behind a long time ago.

He began walking down towards the road, and as he did so, he paused to sweep the valley once more with his binoculars. They were particularly good ones, a pair of Zeiss that had once belonged to a German officer. He'd taken them in Norway, and had looked after them well ever since, even managing to bring them back safely from Dunkirk, which was more than could be said for much of their kit. Even during his time in the Western Desert he'd managed to keep the glass clean without a single sand scratch.

He now saw someone walking down the road and, focusing his binoculars on the figure, saw that it was Captain Peploe. Tanner hurried on, clambering over several walls and through a vineyard to reach the road. Peploe was up ahead, only a few hundred yards from the Knossos site entrance, when a battered pick-up truck of faded brown sped past Tanner. It was the first vehicle he'd seen in days. He watched it pull to a halt beside the captain.

Tanner ran, calling to Peploe, who now looked up, waved him on and then turned back to the

90

people in the truck.

'It's happening,' he said, as Tanner reached him. 'Germans are landing at Canea.'

'But not here.'

'Not yet.'

Tanner looked into the truck. Alopex, John Pendlebury and another British officer were sitting inside. *Bloody hell*, he thought, *that's all I need.*

'You!' growled Alopex.

'Tanner, I presume?' grinned Pendlebury. He wore a patch over his left eye. 'Captain, we could do with a couple of pairs of hands. Will you help?'

Peploe looked at his watch. 'If it's quick and you can drive us back to our positions.'

'It will be if you help, and, yes, by all means. Jump in the back.'

'Sir,' said Tanner, 'we haven't got time for this. Jerry could attack any moment.'

'It'll be quicker than us walking back.'

'We could run.'

'Stop arguing, Jack, and get in.'

Almost immediately, they turned off to the right, up the driveway of the Villa Ariadne, lined with squat palms, tall firs, clematis and bamboo. At the end of the drive, the truck pulled into a gravel circle before the house, a limestone turn-of-the-century building with a flat roof and large, shuttered windows. A flight of stone steps led up to the main entrance, but it was to a store at the back that Pendlebury now led them. Unlocking it, he pushed open the door, which squeaked, then said, 'Here. We need to get them into the back of the truck.'

Inside were boxes of rifles, several Brens,

91

ammunition and grenades.

'Where did you get all this from?' Peploe asked.

'Oh, we've been stashing it up for a while,' Pendlebury said. 'Captain Vaughan here has been helping me. How many trips have we done now from Suda Island, Alex?'

'A dozen, perhaps,' said Vaughan.

'It's been a struggle, I can tell you,' continued Pendlebury. 'I'll admit I'm not an experienced soldier, but you regulars are not very keen on helping the irregulars. London gives me the job of helping to organize and arm these local *andartes* but no one at Middle East HQ is prepared to help. We've had to rely on stealth and guile and good old-fashioned thievery. It's been fun, though, hasn't it, Alex?'

Vaughan smiled resignedly. *For some, maybe.* Suddenly a gun opened fire from the direction of the port, and then another, followed by the faint roar of aircraft and the tell-tale siren of Stukas. Bombs exploded, dull crumps to the north. The men paused.

'An overture to invasion?' said Pendlebury.

'Or maybe just the daily hate,' said Peploe.

Tanner looked at them – *let's get a bloody move on then* – and grabbed a box of ammunition.

'Yes, you're quite right, Tanner,' said Pendlebury. 'We mustn't dally.'

They began loading, taking the cache box by box to the truck. It was as Tanner was striding back to the shed that Alopex grabbed his arm and steered him to the side of the building, out of sight of the others.

'Get your hands off me,' said Tanner, shaking

his arm free.

'This isn't finished,' hissed the Cretan. 'I said I'd kill you and I will.'

Tanner felt something sharp press against his side and looked down to see Alopex had a knife in his hand. He grabbed the Cretan's wrist. 'How can you be so sure I won't kill you first?'

Alopex sneered. 'Listen to me. For now, we fight the Germans. But after...' He let the sentence hang. 'After, we have a debt to settle. So don't run away on me now.'

Tanner pressed his thumb hard into the tendons on Alopex's wrist. The Cretan grimaced with pain and the blade fell from his fingers.

'Oh dear, you seem to have dropped your knife,' said Tanner. He stared at Alopex, then turned and walked back to the shed.

In less than ten minutes they had finished loading the truck and were heading towards Heraklion, Tanner and Peploe perched on the boxes at the back. The guns and explosions were dying out, but over Heraklion and the airfield they could see a pall of grey, dusty smoke.

'Is that it for one day, do you think?' asked Peploe.

Tanner shrugged. 'They've got to come some time soon. I'm sure of it.'

Peploe was quiet for a moment, then shook his head sadly. 'Ah – so close yet so far.'

'Sir?'

'The ruins. Another hundred yards and I'd have made it. And one of life's ironies that it should be Captain Pendlebury of all people stopping me

93

getting there. Oh, well.'

'Perhaps if we kick out Jerry, sir, there'll be the opportunity after that. Did you tell him you knew of him?'

'Yes – and that I have his book on Amarna too.'

'Amarna?'

'It's in Egypt. He was excavating there half the year and here the rest of the time. I rather regretted it, actually. Made me feel a bit foolish.'

Tanner smiled. 'And what did he say?'

'Much the same as you. Said he'd take me round after we'd beaten the Germans.'

As they neared B Company's lines, the truck was waved down.

'Good luck, gentlemen,' said Pendlebury, as Tanner and Peploe jumped out.

'And you,' Peploe replied. He clapped his hand on the top of the hood, and the pick-up sped off, a cloud of dust following in its wake.

'Jack,' said Peploe, as they hurried towards Company Headquarters, 'I know this probably isn't the time, but it's going to be all right with Lieutenant Liddell, isn't it?'

'As long as he keeps his mouth shut.'

'I think he will. I talked to him about it yesterday and told him I didn't want him to tell anyone what he told us. That you are CSM Tanner and that was all there was to it.'

'Thank you, sir.'

'But, Jack, you weren't under age when you joined up, were you?'

Tanner said nothing.

'So why did you change your name?'

At this Tanner stopped, sighed, then said, 'Sir, I

94

really don't want to talk about it, but at the time I had very good reasons to do so. Can we leave it at that?'

'All right, Jack. But just assure me of one thing. It's not something I *should* know, is it? Nothing that will affect the company or the battalion?'

Tanner breathed in deeply again. 'No – no, sir, it isn't.'

And just then he heard a faint rumble, which made them both stop dead in their tracks. A moment later, the noise had grown and now both men were running up through the grove to the small rocky ridge above their positions. Away to the west, turning in over the coast, they saw aircraft, lots of aircraft.

'Here they come,' said Peploe. 'So it's happening, after all. My God, but they're low.'

And as the guns on the ground began to boom, so the first parachutes began to unfurl, their white canopies drifting down slowly through the warm early-evening sky.

5

It was not until half past three that the 3rd Battalion finally began boarding their transports at Eleusis, and not until some twenty minutes later that the Tante Jus, as the Junkers 52s were known, began to bump and rumble down the runway and finally get airborne. From being in a dense cloud of swirling dust one minute, they were suddenly emerging back into a world of clear blue, leaving the mainland of Greece behind and heading out across the sea.

Eighty minutes later, they were approaching Crete.

'Stand by!' called one of the crew. Turbulence buffeted the plane so that the men sitting on either side of the dark, corrugated fuselage knocked into one another and put out feet to steady themselves. Balthasar felt his heart beat a little faster. Clear intelligence about what would be waiting for them had not been forthcoming, but then, just as they were about to land, news had arrived that there were more than forty thousand enemy troops on the island, almost four times as many as had been thought. No one had expected the Tommies to roll over immediately, but their task was clearly going to be tougher than they had originally imagined. Men were going to die. He glanced along the men sitting opposite him, each alone with his thoughts. Some chewed at their lips, others sat with their eyes closed. Unteroffizier Schramm, sitting opposite, stared directly ahead, his jaw clenched.

The Junkers lurched again, this time the engine whining as they dropped some height.

'Get ready!' came the shout from the pilot, and Balthasar got to his feet, the others following, and hooked up his static line. It was difficult to move with so much kit: parachute at the back, rifle and MP40, and all the various bits of webbing. He turned to check that the man next to him had hooked up correctly and then the crewman was heaving off the door and the rush of wind blasted through the fuselage so that his smock and trousers clung to his body and the skin on his cheeks fluttered. Balthasar had insisted on being first to jump and now stood by the door and caught his first glimpse of Crete, blue-grey mountains rising above them as the Junkers shook and rumbled its way along the coast.

Heraklion was just up ahead, and bullets began to ping against the fuselage. Suddenly a line of them tore through the metal, leaving bright holes of daylight. One man slumped to the floor. *Dead?* Balthasar wondered. Flak now, and the plane rocked as a burst exploded disturbingly close.

The despatcher by the door received a signal from the pilot, then beckoned to Balthasar to jump. A deep breath, and he was out. *One, two, three,* and then a jolt as his parachute blossomed, the harness clamping around his chest and knocking the breath from his lungs so that he gasped. He glanced around, spotting the airfield and the town, with its immense walls and the scattering of houses beyond, stretching out into the surrounding countryside. How high was he? More than 150 metres – *too high.* Too much time in which to get hit.

Bullets and tracer arced up towards him, and just as he was trying to get his bearings, there was a loud explosion above and he looked up to see flames engulfing the Junkers. How many were out? Seven? And the rest? More tumbled from the plane, two already on fire. He watched a man – one of *his* men – plunging past, legs waving, arms and parachute ablaze. Another nearby jerked as he was hit, then hung limply from his harness.

97

This is slaughter, he thought, then felt something smack into his rifle butt – *a bullet?* More transports whirred over, the roar like a swarm of hornets. Not far now, the ground approaching, a mass of olive groves and vineyards. He could see he might land in some trees, so swung his legs. *Good*, he thought, as he seemed to accelerate down onto an old track at the edge of a vineyard.

With the parachute harness strapped to his back, he landed awkwardly, broke into a roll and winded himself. For a moment he lay still, trying to breathe calmly, but then, with his gravity knife, he cut free his parachute and unclipped his harness. Suddenly he heard movement a short way ahead among the vines. For a split second he froze, then crouched and deftly rolled onto his front, his face just centimetres from the dry, dusty soil, and peered ahead. No more than fifteen metres away he saw several enemy – their legs at any rate. Not Tommies, but Greeks, with puttees wrapped up to their knees. Carefully, he pulled back the cocking handle and took a stick grenade from his belt. Voices, excited, then another ordering them to be quiet.

Too late, thought Balthasar as he gave them a brief three-second burst. Men screamed and he saw two fall to the ground. Others fired their rifles wildly, but Balthasar was already unscrewing the metal cap on his grenade. *One, two,* he counted, then hurled it towards the enemy. He had already got to his feet and begun scampering away when the grenade exploded, the blast accompanied by more screams. Sliding below a lip in the ground, more bullets followed him, but

98

they were comfortably above his head. As he hurried through the vines, the shots and voices lessened until he emerged again, further along the track but out of sight of the enemy, now some hundred metres away.

Half crouching, he approached the same lip in the land, but further back, away from where he had spotted the Greeks. More paratroopers continued to stream down, but most, he realized, were dropping west and east of the town. Guns boomed, small arms chattered, and aircraft still roared overhead, but it was impossible to know what was going on. Clearly, the enemy were not far away – not more than fifty metres, he guessed. Ahead of him there were yet more olive groves and vineyards and a mass of trees and bushes, all bursting with leaf and flower. He took out his binoculars and peered through, then cursed as a bead of sweat smeared the glass. Wiping them, he put them back to his eyes. The walls of the town were just visible, rising over the vines and trees, he guessed around two kilometres away. Suddenly a bullet fizzed over his head, and then another, and Balthasar hastily ducked.

A whiff of smoke and cordite on the air. He looked at his watch – 1740 – and was pleased to see his hand was perfectly steady. How many had already been killed he had no idea, but it was time to get the survivors together, if possible establish a radio link to Major Schulz, gather as many supply canisters as possible, and then take the attack to the enemy. He was pleased they were up against Greek troops. They were tough fighters, but the conflict on the mainland had shown how poorly equipped they were. If the battalion could just gather themselves together, he reckoned their superior training and fighting skill would see them through.

Keeping the rise in the ground on his right, he moved through the vines and almost tripped over a prostrate paratrooper, groaning and clutching his stomach. A dark stain had seeped across the olive green of his step-in smock, while the boy's face was already waxen and drained of colour. Balthasar bent down over him and carefully moved his hands away. Underneath was a gaping wound so large he could see the soldier's guts.

'You'll be all right,' Balthasar told him, pulling his P38 from the black leather holster looped through his belt. The boy would not live; better to end it quickly now. The lad looked at him with wide, frightened eyes.

'Mother,' he called. 'Mother.'

'All right, boy,' said Balthasar, then put the pistol to the side of the boy's head and fired. The head lolled lifelessly, and Balthasar took the lad's MP38 and ammunition clips, and hurried on.

He emerged through the vines and, to his relief, saw a dozen of his men sheltering beneath the terrace of the vineyard on the track below. Among them was Obergefreiter Tellmann, the radio operator, who was squatting beside an already opened canister and pulling out an aluminium case containing the company's field transceiver.

'Does it still work?' Balthasar asked, jumping down beside him.

Tellmann nodded.

'That's something,' said Balthasar. 'Try and get

100

a link to the major right away,' he demanded. He paused and listened. Planes were still dropping men and guns were pounding, but the small-arms fire was further away now. 'The rest of you get up off your arses,' he said, 'and start looking for canisters and the others. Tell anyone you see to report back here. Go!'

While Tellmann was trying to make contact, he watched yet more paratroopers floating down from the sky, further towards the coast. More small arms chattered. Then he heard a shout nearby and a burst of machine-pistol fire. A burning Junkers plunged towards the open sea, thick smoke following in its wake. He wandered a short way down the track and spotted a Cretan man on a small cart, furiously urging on his mule. *The crazy fool*, Balthasar thought. Anyone moving around like that in the middle of a battle was asking for trouble. Unslinging his rifle, he drew it into his shoulder and aimed, then lightly squeezed the trigger. A loud crack, the butt pressed into his shoulder, and the man fell side-ways from the cart. As Balthasar had hoped, the mule soon drew to a halt; they now had transport for their supplies. Another of his men emerged into the clearing, wide-eyed and breathless.

'There are enemy just ahead, sir,' he said. 'Not Tommies – Greeks.'

'I know. I've already met them. They've all got to be killed whoever they are,' Balthasar replied, then said, 'Go and fetch that mule and cart.' He turned back to Tellmann, who nodded. *I'm getting through.*

Balthasar squatted beside him and impatiently

waved at him to pass over the headset and transmitter. Bullets were schiffing through the vines on the small ridge above them.

'Major Schulz,' he snapped, into the black transmitter.

Static hissed and crackled in his ear, and then he heard the major's muffled voice: 'Get as many men as you can, and RV at Z45D21. Have you got that, Oberleutnant?'

Balthasar pressed the red button on the transmitter. 'Yes, Herr Major.'

'Be here by nineteen hundred hours. I think I've found a way through. We've got to go in tonight. Repeat tonight.'

'Understood.'

He passed back the headphones, then took out his map. The grid reference pointed to a spot on the main coast road, west of the town. More of his men were now joining him. Two brought another of the canisters, and his second-in-command, Leutnant Eicher, emerged through the vines behind him.

'Eicher, you made it,' he said.

'Only just. We've lost a lot of men.'

'Then let's not lose any more.' Another canister had been recovered, which contained two MG34s. That would make life easier. He now had a band of just over twenty men; it was a fraction of his company, but he hoped they would pick up more as they headed towards the road. Calling the men around him, he divided them into two groups. They would move in two staggered lines, one covering the advance of the other in turn, with the machine-gun teams leading each column. Two men were also detailed to take the cart; they were to keep wide on the left flank.

'Does anyone know what lies up ahead?' he asked. 'It looked like maize at the mouth of this valley as I was coming down.'

'It is, sir,' said a man. 'But it's much flatter down there.'

Damn it, thought Balthasar. 'That can't be helped. The maize will give us some cover, and so too will the other vegetation. We will move in a wide arc. Understood?' The men nodded. 'Right. Let's get going.' And then, at that moment, a Junkers, burning fiercely, streamed across the valley from the east, banked, spluttered, then whined in a final dive. The men stopped to watch this spectacle. Moments later, the aircraft landed with a crash of tearing, grinding metal. Then a pause – brief, strange, quiet – swiftly followed by an explosion. Balthasar noticed several of the men flinch, but he was not thinking of the men who might still have been on board: he was smiling to himself. He reckoned the Junkers must have landed not far from the road, and the breeze, albeit slight, was coming from the north. Thick smoke was already billowing up from the wreck – he could see and smell it. And smoke was the perfect cover. A smokescreen, in fact.

As soon as they had seen the first parachutes dropping, Tanner had suggested to Peploe that he position himself at the top of the rocky outcrop above their forward positions and do some sniping. In his haversack, wrapped in an old soft cotton cloth, was an Aldis scope, one his father had used in the last war, and which Tanner had carried with him ever since he had become a soldier himself. He had had some pads and scope fittings attached to his Lee Enfield rifle. He did not like to advertise the fact, because he had no desire to become a full-time army sniper, but on occasion it had proved a useful tool.

With Peploe's consent, Tanner scrambled up onto the outcrop and set himself down, making the most of the rocks to find a position in which he could rest his elbows and get a steady aim. Hitting a moving target was no easy matter, but having grown up learning how to shoot game, and with plenty of subsequent practice and experience in the army, he was a fine shot, with a steady head, the ability to control his breathing and judge distance.

He could see now that most of the paratroopers were falling either around the airfield or to the south-west and west of the town. Away to his left, the Australians and Black Watch boys were having a field day. The firing was furious – planes were coming down in flames, and it seemed as though the invaders were being decimated before they had even touched the ground. It served them bloody well right: it was about time they got a pasting. To the west, the guns were now pounding the sky. Tanner rated their brigadier: he had noticed that there were many more guns around the town than had been firing during the daily enemy raids. Brigadier Chappel had evidently ordered them to keep their presence hidden. Now, however, they were all opening up and the German transports, flying low at not much

104

more than five hundred feet, were suffering a pummelling. For the first time since he had set foot on Crete, Tanner began to think they might have a decent chance after all. Damn it, they had the chance to kill every single one of them if they held their nerve.

His scope was zeroed at four hundred yards, and he reckoned the closest to him were falling a little further away than that. It wasn't a problem – it just meant allowing a little for the extra distance. Bringing the rifle to his shoulder, he closed his right eye and peered through the scope with the left, singling out falling paratroopers. They were a curious sight; he'd not seen parachutists falling from the sky before, but the straps seemed to emerge from their backs, so that each man hung there, like a puppy held by the scruff of its neck.

A plane-load was now dropping just to the south-west so, quickly taking his bead, he aimed a body length below his target, breathed in, held his breath, and fired. The first shot missed – *too high?* Aiming off a bit more, he picked out a second man and this time saw the body jerk. So, a body and a half was the aim-off length at five hundred yards. The key, he discovered, was to pick an aircraft of falling paratroopers, use the first few to judge the distance, then take aim the moment the 'chute opened.

In front of him the men were also firing, most wildly. Each time a plane caught fire, a cheer went up. The air was now heavy with smoke, so that he could no longer smell the sweet scent of May flowers and grass; the stench of battle had fallen on Heraklion. As Tanner put another two five-round clips in his magazine, he watched one enemy transport plunging out towards the sea, a body and parachute caught on the tail-plane. *Jesus*, he thought, *poor bastard*. More aircraft were dropping men further west, at the foot of the mountains near the coast, while others were landing in the maize fields and groves to the west of the town. They were too far away, so he lowered his rifle and peered through his binoculars.

He spotted some Cretan men and Greek soldiers scampering between the olives. A German had just landed in the branches and Tanner watched as he desperately tried to free himself. But now three Cretan men were upon him, dragging him out of the branches and beating him to death with their rifles. Another paratrooper, only just free of his 'chute, was attacked by several Greek soldiers charging at him with bayonets. Three men each lunged at him. For a moment the man stood, held up by the steel, then as they withdrew, he slumped to the ground. *Vicious fighting*, he thought. Everyone's blood was up. He swept to the south-west, and noted movement below a shallow ridge more than half a mile away. Taking careful aim, he fired and saw a figure duck. A miss, but it might keep their heads down.

He waited a few more minutes, then looked at his watch. *Ten to six*. It seemed clear that the two main drop zones were the airfield and west of the town; the ground in front of them to the south was quiet. Leaving his position, he hurried back down the ridge and up to the company's positions, where he had seen Peploe a few minutes before.

'Good shooting, CSM?' Peploe enquired, as Tanner reached him.

'Piece of cake, sir,' Tanner replied. 'Those poor sods are sitting ducks once you get a bead on them.'

'Rather them than me.'

'Too right, sir.'

'Well, so far so good, wouldn't you say?' Peploe peered through his own binoculars.

'Early days yet, sir.' Tanner looked around him, at the staggered slit trenches, the weapons and ammunition pits, each section carefully positioned for interlocking fire, and making the most of the trees, rocks and vegetation. These were not so much deeply dug as well positioned. It would, he knew, be hard for lightly armed German paratroopers to break through.

'I got a good view from up there,' he said, jerking a thumb at the outcrop behind them. 'All the action's over to the west. Why don't we send out a fighting patrol?'

'Where?' asked Peploe.

'I was thinking we could push out to the southwest. See what Jerry's up to. It seems to me they're going to be pretty disorganized at the moment. We could take advantage of that.'

Peploe nodded. 'All right,' he said. 'Who will you take?'

Tanner had already thought of that. 'Sykes, and McAllister's section, sir?'

'All right, but take Mr Liddell and his Platoon HQ men as well.'

107

Tanner's face fell. 'Really, sir? Mr Liddell's only just arrived.'

'Then it'll be good experience for him, won't it? I need you two to work together, Jack. Prove to me that you can.'

Tanner swallowed. 'Yes, of course, sir.'

The patrol was quickly assembled. Having sent runners to the neighbouring Greek regiment on their right and to A Company on their left, Peploe spoke with Liddell and Tanner while the men readied themselves, getting rid of any unnecessary kit. 'CSM Tanner will lead the patrol,' Peploe told them, 'but, Mr Liddell, you are the officer, and are therefore ultimately in charge. But learn from him, Lieutenant. He has a lot of experience at this sort of thing.'

'Anything else, sir?' Liddell asked.

'No, I don't think so. Just have a look around.'

'And if we come across any enemy?'

'Engage if appropriate, but don't get yourself into a compromising situation. You'll have to use your judgement, Lieutenant.' His expression relaxed. 'But you're in good hands with Tanner and Sykes.'

Tanner turned towards the men. Some wore jerseys or their battle blouses over their KD shirts, and he realized there was now the first nip of cooler evening air. The sun was lowering; soon it would be behind the great mountain range to the west. Leaning down to his pack, he pulled out his own khaki wool jersey. 'Right,' he said. 'Everyone ready?' He took out his map, showing them where the buildings and wells were that he had marked earlier. 'Any stragglers are likely to make for these,' he told them, 'so we need to be particularly careful there. I spotted Jerries here.' He pointed first to the map then to the fold in the land to the southwest. 'That's where we'll head – south first, using the olive groves for cover, then we cut across.' He turned to Liddell. 'All right, sir?'

'Yes, I think so, CSM,' said Liddell. 'And we'll use a formation for open country with the enemy in close contact.'

Tanner glanced at Sykes – *what the hell is that?* The sergeant winked. 'Something like that, sir. I'll take Chambers, Bonner and Sherston out front, Sykes can scout on the right with Bell, and you, sir, with McAllister, the Bren and the rest of the section, follow fifty yards or so behind.'

Liddell nodded. 'Diamond formation?'

'Absolutely, sir.'

'And what if we lose sight of you?'

'Try not to, sir. I said fifty yards, but what I meant was, stay behind at a distance where you can always see me.' Tanner pulled his rifle from his shoulder, one hand around the barrel, the other on the neck of the stock, his finger and thumb touching the bolt. 'Let's go.'

Tanner led them through the olive groves, jogging so that they covered ground quickly. Two hundred yards or so on, he paused, glanced behind and then across at Sykes, saw everyone was still with him, and pressed on. After another couple of hundred yards, he turned westward until he was approaching the top of a shallow ridge. A grassy track marked the boundary between the olive groves and, beyond the ridge, a north-west-facing vineyard. It was here, just on the lip, that he had seen a paratrooper show his head a quarter of an hour earlier. Glancing back at the others, he raised his arm above his head to halt them, then looked across at Sykes and Bell and urged them on.

'Stay here a moment,' he told Chambers, Bonner and Sherston, then he too crept towards the brow of the ridge.

On his belly, Tanner lifted his head, scanned the ground quickly, then rolled over. In front of him there was a vineyard, the vines full of newly bursting fresh leaves. It was not big – perhaps sixty yards across – and another track was followed by more olive groves. To his right, the land rose again, gently, so that the ground before him was enclosed in a shallow hollow. Among the olives, several parachutes fluttered; a limp body hung from the branches, but he could see no enemy troops – not live ones, at any rate. Glancing across at Sykes and Bell, he saw the sergeant signal thumbs-up, then turned back to the others. 'Hey, Punter,' he called softly, to Chambers.

'Yes, sir?'

'Signal to the others to come up, will you?'

'Sir,' Chambers replied.

Tanner scurried forward through the vines, noticing bootmarks in the dusty soil. He found Sykes and Bell standing over the body of a dead paratrooper.

'Look at this, sir,' said Bell. 'Stomach wound, but he's been shot in the head too.'

'And at close range,' said Tanner, looking down. 'Someone put this boy out of his misery.'

'There's a load of dead Greeks up there,' said Sykes, waving towards the crest of the ridge. He turned back to the dead paratrooper. 'Look at those boots, though. I'm tempted to 'alf-inch 'em.'

'Too big for you, Stan,' grinned Tanner. 'You need to pick on someone your own size.'

'All right, all right,' said Sykes. 'But I'd rather be on the short side than a big lad like you, sir.'

'Why's that, Stan?'

'Less of a target.'

'Talking of which,' said Tanner, 'let's push on. Tinker,' he said to Bell, 'you go ahead a bit with Punter. See what's round that bend. There are plenty of tracks here – see if you can follow the Jerries. My guess is they've headed north to the west of the town where most of them were dropping.'

'What about me, sir?' asked Sykes.

'I need to speak to you. Tinker, take Bonner and Sherston with you as well. If it's clear up ahead, leave two men to keep watch, then come back. All right? Now, iggery, boys.'

The four men hurried off, and Sykes said, 'I did speak to him, you know.'

'Tell me in a moment,' said Tanner, pushing on down through the vines. At the edge of the vineyard they now saw there was a short four-foot terrace alongside the track. Jumping down, they looked around. Back along the track, they could see a figure lying on the ground, ran over and found a dead, grey-haired Cretan lying face down in the grass. There was a neat hole in his back, but rolling him over they saw an exit wound the size of a fist. Thick blood had stained the front of his shirt and waistcoat and the surrounding grass.

'Shot in the back,' said Sykes.

'For his cart,' added Tanner, pointing to the tracks.

The rest of the patrol was now clambering out of the vines.

'You talked to him, then?' Tanner said, in a low voice.

'You don't need to worry, Jack,' said Sykes, using Tanner's Christian name out of earshot of the others. 'He thinks you left because your father died and because you were too young to take over from him.'

'Who's saying that wasn't the case?' Tanner snapped.

'No one, Jack. No one's saying anything. That's the point.'

Tanner sighed. 'I'm sorry, Stan. Didn't mean to take it out on you. One of these days I'll tell you all about it.'

'His old man died,' said Sykes.

'Died?' Tanner wiped his brow. 'I'm sorry – as I said before, he was a good man.'

'I told Mr Liddell you thought that. That's why he joined the Rangers and not any of the Wiltshire lot. Thought he'd follow his father.'

Tanner nodded. 'That explains it.'

Liddell was now walking towards them. 'What's going on, Tanner?' he said, as he neared them. 'Why have we stopped?'

'I've sent men on to scout up ahead, sir. We're where the Jerries started dropping. Earlier I saw some canisters coming down around here, so I thought we could have a quick look around for them while we wait for Bell and Chambers to report back.'

''Ere, sir,' said Sykes now, pointing towards an olive grove a short distance from the track. 'There's a couple of dead Jerries over there.'

'So there are. Come on, then.' Tanner and Sykes hurried across a narrow strip of rough grass, then reached the olives. Pushing their way between the young trees, they reached the first of the dead men, some twenty yards from the other, lying in the grass.

'Good,' said Tanner. 'This one's still got his weapon. Have a look at the other one, Stan.' Tanner picked up the dead man's submachine-gun, and admired it. It was light, with a comfortable grip, and beautifully engineered. He looked at the safety catch, the cocking handle and the magazine, which he removed and replaced easily and smoothly. Slinging the weapon over his shoulder, he squatted down to strip the man of his spare magazines.

'What do you think you're doing?' said Liddell, beside him.

'Taking his weapon, sir. Say what you like about Jerry, they make beautiful kit.'

'Put it back, CSM.'

'What?' said Tanner. He stared at Liddell incredulously.

'Put it back. We're on a patrol, CSM, not a booty hunt.'

'Sir, this is a good weapon. We don't have anything as good as this.'

'Nor are you trained to use it.'

'Trained? I don't need training in how to use

113

this.' He picked it up and pulled back the cock. 'Aim, fire. Sir.'

'Put it down, Tanner. That's an order.'

Tanner glared at him. 'For God's sake,' he said, flinging the weapon onto the ground.

'Right,' said Liddell. 'Now let's get back to the patrol.'

'Look at this beauty,' grinned Sykes, as he re-joined them, clutching an MP38 of his own.

'Put it down, Sergeant,' said Liddell.

'Down, sir? Why?' Sykes glanced at Tanner.

'Mr Liddell doesn't want us booty hunting,' said Tanner. 'He's worried we're not trained to use them either.'

Sykes laughed.

The subaltern had turned red. 'I'll not have any more insolence from either of you,' he snapped. 'Put the gun down, Sergeant, and let's get on with what we're supposed to be doing.'

'Give me strength,' muttered Tanner, then turned back in the direction of the track.

Chambers arrived soon after. There were more olive groves and vineyards, he reported, then a series of maize fields that led all the way to the Rethymno road. They had found tracks easily. There was also a downed aircraft up ahead, about five hundred yards away. Smoke was still billowing up from it.

'That settles it, then,' said Tanner. 'Back in patrol formation, and let's see if we can't surprise a few Jerries. Bet they reckon they're safe behind that smokescreen.' He grinned. 'Sergeant Sykes and I will head back with Lance Corporal Chambers, the rest follow as before. And keep your bloody eyes out and on me.'

Liddell now cleared his throat. 'Hold on a minute, CSM,' he said. 'What exactly have you got in mind?'

Tanner took a deep breath. 'Whatever Jerries landed round here have clearly moved on, sir, to the north. My guess is they're mustering somewhere up ahead.'

'A guess?'

'Yes, sir. I'm not a Jerry, so I can't say for certain, but they're not here any more, are they? If we follow their tracks we might be able to find out a bit more. We're reconnoitring, sir.'

Liddell bit his bottom lip. 'Very well,' he said at length. 'But we're now quite a long way from our lines and I don't want any shooting, all right? Observation only.'

Without answering, Tanner turned and strode on ahead. 'Jesus,' he muttered, as Sykes and Chambers hurried beside him.

They found Bell, with Bonner and Sherston, lying at the edge of the vineyard. Tanner got down beside them. Directly ahead was the aircraft, still smoking furiously, the plumes swirling towards the coast. The low ridge continued, gently flattening out to the west of Heraklion. From where they lay, the walls of the town could not be seen, but beyond were more olive groves, which gave way to a series of maize fields. The crop was still young, but tall enough for a man to crawl through.

'Have you spotted any movement, Tinker?' Tanner asked Bell.

'I'm not sure. I might have done. Maybe movement through the maize, but I couldn't swear to it.'

'Should have lent you these,' said Tanner, pulling out his binoculars. He peered through them. The maize and the bushes and trees at the end of each field were too dense for him to see anything; perspective seemed to condense through the lenses. But beyond, perhaps as much as three-quarters of a mile away, he could now see men moving through the groves and around a small cluster of buildings. Then, suddenly, movement caught his eye, movement that was closer, somewhere before the buildings. Quickly he adjusted the focus. Yes, there they were, now in his line of vision, quite clear: a column of men crossing a track between the fields – not crouching, but openly walking, no more than three hundred yards ahead, the smoke of the aircraft their shield.

Tanner smiled. 'Will you have a dekko at that! Can you see what I see, boys?'

'Jerry, sir,' said Bell.

'Where are those tracks through the maize, Tinker?'

'A bit further down, sir. We found two lots.'

Tanner saw a second line of Germans come into view, further across the field and behind the lead column. 'Sergeant, give me a head count, will you?' he said, as he put the binoculars to his eyes once more. He noticed one man at the front of the two columns had an MG34 slung over his shoulder, but that the others seemed to have only sub-machine-guns.

'Nine in the first, eight in the second, sir,' said Sykes.

'Good. Sergeant, you and Tinker follow the right. The rest, follow me. Let's get a move on.'

Scampering down through the vines, they found the tracks through the maize and, half crouching, hurried on. Reaching the end of the first field, Tanner led them as they crawled on their stomachs across a track a path, Tanner realized, that led back up onto the shallow ridgeline. Some smoke had drifted across there too, not thickly but it was something. Sykes and Bell were crossing the track and he signalled to them, Lieutenant Liddell and the others following to halt, because he had just remembered the cart. A plan had seeded in his mind. Where the hell was the cart? He had seen several trees a short way down the track to his left, and told Chambers, Bonner and Sherston to wait, then ran over to the trees and, carefully raising himself, peered around.

'Got you,' he mouthed. Less than two hundred yards away, working its way through the groves beyond the maize fields, was the cart. Tanner counted three men. Hurrying back to Chambers and the other two, he signalled to Sykes to join him.

'What's up, sir?' whispered Sykes.

'That cart,' he said, gesturing in its direction. 'There are three men with it. My guess is their supplies are on it. I want you and Tinker to head up this track to the right. It rises slightly, so you should be able to get a good view down towards those two Jerry columns. There's a bit of smoke, so that'll give you cover. I want you to take out the two leading men. They've got MGs, so make sure you hit them. Fire off a couple more rounds, then get back. Most of them only have sub-machine-guns, so they won't be able to hit you from that range.'

'And in the confusion, you take out the cart.' Sykes grinned.

'Me and the boys here, yes.'

'What about Mr Liddell?'

He glanced back. The lieutenant and the rest were still waiting. Tanner again held up his hand – *stay where you are*. But he could see Liddell moving forward, coming towards him.

'Quick,' he said, with a glance at his watch. 'I make it eighteen twenty-two. In three minutes – no, make that four – open fire. Do the job, then peg it. Now, iggery.' He slapped Chambers and Sherston on the back. 'Come on, let's hurry.'

They were off before Liddell could reach them, half crouching, half running down the track, and in moments were out of sight of the lieutenant. They easily found the route the cart had taken. At the far end of the maize field there was another long, narrow olive grove: the trees, combined with the smoke between them and the town, provided all the cover they needed. The cart was a couple of hundred yards ahead and, looking at his watch again, Tanner realized he had cut the timing a bit fine. Making sure they ran with a line of olives masking their approach, he delved into his haversack and felt for his scope, then thought better of it. *You don't need it*, he told himself. *Six twenty-five*. Just one minute to go. They were making ground on the cart, which was trundling through the rough grass at a slow pace.

'Rifles ready, boys,' whispered Tanner. 'I'll take

the lead. Punter, you go for the one on the left, Bonner and Sherston, the third fellow, on the right.' They continued to run forward, now moving from tree to tree. Still none of the men by the cart had looked round. *Any moment now*, thought Tanner, and he prayed Sykes and Bell would hit the men with the MGs.

A rifle crack from the ridge and then another, and now the men by the cart flinched and looked around – not behind them but to their right, the flank they must have known was their most vulnerable. On cue, Tanner leaned against an olive tree, his rifle to his shoulder. A little under a hundred yards, he reckoned. Aiming low in case his target suddenly crouched, he breathed out, held his breath and squeezed the trigger. The German was hit in the stomach and cried out as the other three fired almost simultaneously. Tanner saw that Chambers had hit his man, who had collapsed on the ground, but the other two had missed. Maintaining his aim, Tanner pulled back the bolt and fired again, this time at the third man, who had been looking wildly in their direction and trying to bring his sub-machine-gun up when the bullet slammed into his chest. Tanner pulled back the bolt again, fired a second time at his first target, then ran forward, sprinting through the long, lush May grass.

Short bursts of sub-machine-gun fire rang out, but not the lethal *brurp* of the MG. *Good*, thought Tanner, as they reached the cart. The mule was calmly eating grass as though nothing untoward had happened, but Chambers's German was gurgling softly. Tanner saw now that the man had been hit in the neck, bubbles of blood foaming at his mouth, his eyes wide. *Damn it, damn it,* thought Tanner, taking out his Webley from its canvas holster. Christ, but he hated to do this. Pointing the pistol at the man's head, he closed his eyes briefly and fired.

He turned and saw Chambers staring at him.

'He couldn't have lived,' Tanner snarled. 'Aim a bit better next time, Punter.'

Chambers nodded mutely, but Tanner was now looking at the cart. There were a number of canisters, but also a stash of rifles. He wondered what was in them, but then a rifle shot cracked and a bullet fizzed nearby. *No time*, he thought.

'Quick,' he said to them, 'move back. Run!' More shots rang out, a bullet struck the side of the cart and another hissed over Tanner's head. His heart pumping, he felt in his haversack for his grenades and took out two. He had intended to set the mule free but there was no time for that now. 'Sorry, mate,' he said to the mule, pulled out the pins of the grenades, lobbed them into the cart, then sprinted. Bursts of sub-machine-gun fire – too far, but getting closer. Another rifle bullet whistled by, and then the grenades exploded in quick succession and Tanner could not help but look back. The mule and cart had disappeared among a ball of flame and smoke, and then there was a second explosion as ammunition in the canisters detonated. Rounds were pinging as they caught fire, but then he heard the tell-tale burst of MG fire raking the olive grove, and cursed Sykes and Bell.

Reaching the track, he saw Chambers urging

Bonner and Sherston to head straight into the maize field. More MG fire, this time only just behind him, and now Tanner was among the maize too, crouch-running as quickly as he could. He knew they had nothing to fear except the enemy machine-gun but so long as the men lay flat on the ground, they would be all right. Were they doing so? He knew he should have told the lieutenant what he was planning, but there hadn't been time. No, that wasn't it: he'd said nothing because he'd feared Liddell would put a halt to it. He cursed as another burst of MG fire peppered the ground around him and he dived down into the maize, his face pressed into the sweet-smelling soil as bullets snipped through the stalks above his head.

Silence, a few muffled shouts behind him, and then he got up again, pushing on through the maize, his heavy breathing amplified among the dense stalks, until he reached the path along which they had come. Glancing back, he saw a German near the edge of the track, scanning the field. Crouching still, Tanner brought his rifle to his shoulder but he must have caused movement in the maize because the German was now raising his weapon to his shoulder. A moment later, two bullets sliced perilously close, thumping into the soil nearby. Tanner fell flat on his face as a third whined a hair's breadth from his head. Turning his face slightly he could just see the German reaching for his ammunition pouch and Tanner smiled. Quickly lifting himself onto his haunches, he brought his own rifle to his shoulder and slowly rose until he was standing there, no more than fifty yards away. The German now saw him, too late, but instead of diving for cover or fumbling at his breech, he just stood there, staring at Tanner.

Pressing the butt into his shoulder, Tanner felt his index finger squeeze against the trigger, but then something made him stop. He had long since come to the conclusion that the only useful German was a dead one, but to kill the man in cold blood like that, even in the middle of a war, felt like an execution rather than a combat killing. Why it was different from shooting a man in the back as he sat on a cart, he could not say, but he knew he could not kill the man. Instead, he began to walk backwards, keeping his aim, and stepping carefully through the maize, until at last the German turned and ran back towards his men.

Tanner turned too, running through the field until ahead he saw several Rangers crawling on their hands and knees. Recognizing Chambers, he hurried on, hoping Sykes and Bell had got away safely, and then it occurred to him that the enemy machine-gun must have run out of ammunition. *And thank God for that.* Now that he thought about it, he'd seen the cylindrical magazines on the weapons, not belts. Smiling to himself, he soon caught up with the others. Mr Liddell could go to hell. They had just destroyed eight Jerry supply canisters and, with them, a stash of arms and ammunition – weapons and bullets that those Jerry paratroopers could no longer use. And, as he knew from bitter experience, a soldier without weapons was no good to anyone.

6

Oberleutnant Balthasar was furious. Four men dead and one more seriously wounded was bad enough, but to lose the supplies like that was an added blow. More than that, it was a humiliation. And then to be caught out by that Tommy. He wondered why the soldier had not fired when he had had the chance. He knew he would have done, but it had confirmed what he had long ago come to believe: that somehow he was invincible, destined to survive this war. It had given him a chance to study the *Englander* and he promised himself that, should he ever see him again, he would kill him.

He stopped and angrily kicked the ground. The men were tough, motivated and well trained, but he knew their confidence had taken a beating so far that day. Damn it all, so had his. All that waiting around, the anticipation and nerves gnawing away at them, and when they had finally made their jumps, they had been shot to pieces. Now this. Tommies, not Greeks. He'd fleetingly seen a helmeted figure by the cart, then flashing through the olive groves, but there was no tell-tale sign of blood or, better still, a body. Those Tommies had crept up behind them – stalked them! – blown up their supplies, then disappeared again.

Balthasar had seen the shock and disappointment on the faces of the men; after what had come

123

earlier that day, it had been hard to hide. Most had lost friends in the jump. Casualties were expected, but that did not mean men were unaffected when they saw their comrades on fire, screaming, as they plunged to the ground, or trussed up in the branches of a tree with half their guts hanging out. It was at times like this that strong, decisive leadership was needed. His men trusted him, looked up to him, yet he'd allowed himself to be outfoxed – too busy watching his flank to protect his arse. Briefly, he took off his helmet, rubbed his eyes, wiped his brow, then placed it back on his head. He turned and went to rejoin the others. Time was marching on; they needed to find Major Schulz and what remained of the battalion.

A quarter of an hour later, having followed the river that flowed through the mouth of the valley, they finally caught up with most of the survivors from the battalion's jump, a couple of kilometres to the west of Heraklion town. The land before the Rethymno road rose briefly, so that the river had cut a shallow gully. To either side of the river there were olives and plentiful orange and lemon groves; among them and along the gully, paratroopers now took cover. Above, another flight of Tante Jus thundered over, parachutes blooming and drifting down. The Tommy flak guns continued to boom, so that the ground trembled, the reports of the guns resounding across the mouth of the valley. Small-arms fire crackled, sharp and tinny beside the guns, and mostly from the defenders, firing at the unfortunates still drifting towards the ground.

To his relief Balthasar spotted several more of

his men, and after ordering the remnants of his company to find cover together, clear of any direct enemy fire, he hurried off to find Major Schulz.

The battalion commander was not in the house he had initially indicated, which lay among tall palms and plane trees just before the river, but beneath a small two-metre cliff on a bend in the river.

'Ah, Balthasar, at last,' he said, as the *oberleutnant* reached him and saluted. 'Not quite what we were expecting, eh?'

'The Tommies seem to have plenty more guns than I'd thought, Herr Major,' Balthasar replied. 'Men too, for that matter. Where are the other company commanders?' It was cool now, and around them mosquitoes and other insects swarmed beside the river.

'Von der Schulenburg made it but the other two have been killed,' Schulz replied, brushing a bug away from his face. 'Thank God I jumped first from my plane, because it was hit immediately after. Everyone else was killed.'

'How many men have we lost?'

Schulz lit a cigarette. 'It's hard to say. We have a few more than two hundred at the moment. Major Schirmer dropped several kilometres west of here with his men. I've made radio contact with him but he's blocking the road and fighting off local bandits. I shouldn't say this, but General-major Student wants his arse kicking.'

'The Cretans not welcoming us with open arms?'

Schulz snorted. 'Not a bit of it. The locals have

been butchering our men. I had a paratrooper here a few moments ago who saw his best friend beaten to death by *franc-tireurs*. He only just managed to get away himself.'

'And what about Colonel Bräuer and the rest of the regiment?'

Schulz shook his head. 'We've been trying them on the radio, but we can't get through. I assume it must be broken or destroyed.'

'Maybe we should get ours to him. We've less need for it now we're here. Under darkness it might be possible.'

'Maybe. Anyway, give me some good news – how many of your men have you brought?'

'Seventeen, Herr Major. Although another forty or so are already here.'

'Seventeen? God give me strength.' Schulz drew on his cigarette and shook his head.

Balthasar had thought to spin a story about the loss of the supply cart, or simply not mention it, but he knew one of the men would say something and that the story would eventually reach the major. Far better to tell the CO straight, and now – bad news hidden beneath worse. 'Actually, we were attacked on the way,' he told the major, lighting a cigarette himself. 'I'm afraid they got some of our supplies and five more of our men. Four dead.'

Schulz said nothing. For a moment he rubbed his brow, paced up and down a few steps, then said, 'We can't stay here and do nothing.'

'I don't think we should, sir.' *Not if I have anything to do with it.* He wanted a chance to fight back, to kill these Cretan bandits and Tommies.

By God, he had an urge to make them pay for what they had done that afternoon. 'We should make an attack at dusk.' He looked at his watch. *1855.* 'In an hour's time. What do we know of the defences?'

'We've been watching them since we landed,' said Schulz. 'There are Greek troops and *franc-tireurs* manning the western part of the town. We've spotted men on the battlements but they're also on the ground below. They seem to be quite lightly armed – rifles mostly and a few machine-guns. The guns are mainly flak.'

'The British must be further round to the south,' said Balthasar. 'I'd like to have another look, Herr Major. If we can get into the town, we can make the most of our machine-pistols.' He patted his MP40. 'These will make mincemeat of the rabble inside, as will our grenades. Out here, without all our MGs and rifles, and without guns, we're virtually defenceless.'

'I agree, Balthasar,' said Schulz. 'We just need to get a toehold inside, then the town will fall and the harbour will be ours. Those Tommy guns can't get us there.' He patted a fist into his palm. 'Let's get von der Schulenberg and work out a plan of attack.'

They found Hauptmann Count von der Schulenberg, then scrambled up the bank behind the house. Yet more transports were flying over, most heading east of the town. The guns continued to thunder, so that as they entered the house, the walls shook. On the first floor they peered out of the windows across the broken land, with its groves, trees and occasional houses. The land, Balthasar noticed, was only superficially flat. All the way to the edge of the town, the ground was broken by small rocky gullies and outcrops, and plenty of vegetation. At dusk, with the light constantly changing, it would be easy to advance, flitting between the trees and groves, nothing more than shadows in the fading gloom. Their small numbers would work to their advantage. Balthasar scanned the land again. There were also too many parachutes, patches of creamy silk draped across trees or streamed out over the ground. Bodies littered the earth, and the urge to avenge those men stirred strongly within him.

He trained his binoculars on the town walls. Smoke from the crashed Junkers had thinned so that he now had a clear view. Behind him, the sun was setting beneath the mountains, its last rays casting a beam of bright orange light through the back of the house and giving the limestone walls of the town ahead an ethereal glow. Outside, Balthasar was conscious of birds singing and it struck him that the gentleness and beauty of the light was at odds with the violence of the battle. He peered now at the town walls. They had seen better days. Although some ten metres high, they had crumbled in parts and he could see trees and bushes sprouting between the slabs of stone. Beneath, buildings stretched away from the walls where the town had begun to sprawl.

He had read up on the island, and knew that it was some centuries since the Venetians had built those bastions and that, in the end, they had not been able to keep out the Turks. The town had been besieged for more than twenty years – twenty years in which the walls had taken a battering. Those invaders had finally gone more than forty years ago, at the end of the nineteenth century, but little money had come Crete's way since. It was a poor place, he knew, and now, as he studied the tired town, he realized the Cretans must have plundered the walls for stone for the houses beyond. Those battlements had looked so formidable as he drifted down, but now he realized they were not so impregnable after all.

Ahead, he could see what looked like a main bastion and gateway into the town, but to the right the walls were crumbling. There were trees aplenty there, reaching out like claws from the stonework, and houses below too. He swept with his binoculars again. There was another bastion by the sea, but between it and the water's edge there was a gap.

'Well?' said Schulz. 'Your thoughts, gentlemen.'

'We should split into two forces,' said Balthasar. 'One force should attack the gap in the wall by the edge of the sea, the other towards the main gate ahead of us. In each case, a diversion is needed while the storm troops attack the weak point. There,' he said, pointing to the crumbled bastions to the right of the main bastion. 'We don't need medieval scaling ladders to break through there. We just need enough men to make it seem as though they're making a head-on attack to draw away the enemy forces. The same by the sea.'

'Yes,' said Schulz, 'I think you're right. Hauptmann?'

'I agree,' said von der Schulenberg. 'Of course, we could do with more ammunition, but we need to be bold.' He turned to Balthasar. 'A number of canisters came down west of here and they have been mostly successfully collected. We're short of medical supplies and food, but we do have some ammunition.'

'There will be food in the town,' said Balthasar, his mood rapidly improving.

Schulz eyed him for a moment, then chuckled. 'You know what, Oberleutnant? Just the thought of it makes me feel better. Hauptmann, you will lead the attack by the sea. Take what's left of your company and those from 3 Company, and Balthasar and I will carry out the attack here.' He looked at his watch. 'Nineteen zero five. We move out in forty minutes.'

'*Jawohl*, Herr Major,' said Balthasar.

Schulz frowned, his face set. 'We'll storm those sons of whores,' he growled, 'and then they'll wish they'd shown our comrades a little more respect.'

Second Lieutenant Guy Liddell had said very little as they had woven their way back towards their lines, but inside he was fuming. Clearly, Tanner's little ruse had paid off spectacularly, yet he sensed it might well not have done. It had been a foolhardy plan, conceived and acted upon without much pause for consideration. Furthermore, the CSM had not consulted him, even though he was the officer in charge. Worse, the man had directly disobeyed his order not to open fire. He had the distinct impression Tanner had concocted the whole thing to spite him as much as anything – revenge, he supposed, for the events of the previous afternoon.

When they finally reached their positions south of the Jesus Bastion, the euphoria of the men was plain to see. Excited chatter, claps on the back, wide-eyed relief at having escaped the German return fire unscathed.

'Bloody hell, sir,' McAllister said to Tanner, 'it was some explosion. We could see it from where we were!'

Liddell had gritted his teeth and smiled along with them, but as soon as he could, he went over to Tanner and tapped him on the shoulder. 'Tanner, a word,' he had said, steering the CSM away a short distance.

'A good patrol, sir,' said Tanner.

'Tanner, I ordered you not to open fire.'

'I know, sir,' Tanner said quietly, 'but the opportunity was suddenly before us. There wasn't time to consult you.'

'You completely disobeyed me,' Liddell hissed. 'You could have got my men killed.'

Tanner smiled. 'But I didn't, sir. There's no one with so much as a scratch. The only dead ones are Jerries, plus we've got a lot of their kit.'

'I don't like having my authority undermined, Tanner. Regardless of your little success, I shall be reporting you to the captain.'

Tanner stared at him, those pale blue eyes boring into him. 'What are you trying to prove, sir?'

Liddell felt himself bristle. 'I'm not trying to prove anything. I just want you to respect the authority of an officer.'

Tanner smiled. 'Respect, eh?' And then, as he

131

had already done once before that evening, he turned away and walked back towards the men.

Liddell watched him, unsure what to say or how to respond. He felt belittled, foolish, as though somehow he was in the wrong, not the CSM. It was, he knew, unfortunate that he should have met Tanner again after all these years in such disagreeable circumstances, but it had not been his fault; he had not been the one street-brawling with the locals. He could see that Tanner had been humiliated but he should have thought of that before fighting that Cretan thug. Nor was he to know that Jack Scard had joined the Yorkshire Rangers back then. Now they were stuck with each other, but that did not mean the past could simply be ignored. His father had once been Tanner's father's employer. They were of different classes. Bill Scard had shown his father respect, so now Tanner would damn well show him some.

Looking up, he saw Captain Peploe approaching him. He was wearing a wool sweater over his shirt, his hands plunged deep into his pockets.

'Good to see you, Mr Liddell,' said Peploe. 'A successful patrol?'

'Yes, I think so, sir,' said Liddell.

'Get on all right with Tanner?'

'Apart from the blatant disobeying of orders, yes.'

Peploe smiled and said, 'Let's just move away a bit.' He led him away from the men, and down the Knossos road a short distance. The skies were at last clear and an uneasy quiet had descended; no more aircraft droned overhead, the guns were no longer booming. Only small-arms fire disturbed the evening stillness.

'You'd better explain,' said Peploe.

Liddell did so, then said, 'In my judgement, it was a reckless decision. I admit it was successful, but it could have very easily backfired. We had no idea how many there were of them or how strongly they were armed, and I had already specifically told him not to open fire.'

Peploe rubbed his chin thoughtfully. 'When you say, "we", are you sure Tanner had not made any kind of recce first?'

'I don't see how he could have done, sir. One minute we were moving through a maize field, the next he and the others were off. He knew I wanted to talk to him and deliberately rushed on ahead before I could reach him.'

Liddell saw Peploe struggling to suppress a smile and felt his cheeks redden.

'All right, Lieutenant.' Peploe looked up towards the mountains, then back at Liddell. 'It's partly my fault. I should have been a bit clearer beforehand. Tanner was leading, and I would always trust him to use his judgement. After all, he has seen more action than any of us. My reason for sending you at all was because they were men from your platoon and I thought the experience would be good for you. You also have to remember that we're fighting a war, and people do get wounded and killed. If we tried to avoid risk, we'd never get anywhere. Finally, it's good sense to take whatever weapons you can find. First, the enemy can't use them, and second, we can.'

'Sir, I–'

Peploe cut him off. 'Look, don't take this the

wrong way. Tanner should not have disobeyed your orders, but you have to understand that having pips on your shoulders doesn't mean you're expected to know everything. What did you do before the war, Guy? Do you mind if I call you "Guy"?'

'No, sir, of course not. I was a farmer, sir.'

'Funny – so was I. So you didn't have to join up?'

'No.'

'We're still civilians, really. That's what you need to understand. I'm sure you're a bright enough chap, but it's very different applying one's brains in the army. University?'

'Cambridge.'

Peploe laughed. 'Me too – that's two things we have in common. Don't tell me you studied archaeology and ancient history?'

'Mathematics.'

'Ah, proper brains, then. The point is, Guy, I'm sure your mathematical mind will be useful, but what really counts is experience. That's what makes all the difference. A year ago I was like you. New to the army and quite clueless. I learned on the job, and I had Tanner as my guide. He taught me bloody well, too. Look, what I'm trying to say is this: you can demonstrate authority in a number of ways, but I'm not sure barking orders at the best soldier in the whole battalion is the right way.'

Liddell said nothing. Shame and embarrassment coursed through him. He had hoped Peploe would back him up, but instead he'd been given a dressing down – in the nicest way, but patronizing all the same.

'Ah, the witching hour,' said Peploe. 'The light's going. We need to keep alert, Guy, in case those para boys try to catch us out.' He looked around him. 'By God, it's a beautiful place. I should be crawling over ancient ruins, not waiting to fend off Germans.' He patted Liddell on the back. 'Try to work with Tanner, Guy. Earn his respect and you'll find him a tremendous ally.'

Respect, respect, thought Liddell. *That word.* It seemed that everyone deserved it apart from him, yet he was the one who had been slighted, who had been treated disrespectfully, no matter what Peploe had said. Twice in two days he'd been made to feel he had been at fault when all he'd been doing was acting in the manner he believed both right and appropriate in an officer. He lit a cigarette and wandered back towards his men.

A leaden weight seemed to be pressing down on him, from which there was no escape. He felt trapped, because he knew, as in the back of his mind he had always known, he was not cut out to be a soldier. The patrol had confirmed that. When the shooting had begun, nausea had filled his stomach, his heart had pounded and his mind had scrambled. A feeling of panic. Only with the greatest of difficulty had he managed to stop himself standing up and running. Right now, he wanted to rant and rave and kick. He should never have left the farm. Pique: that was what it had been. Jealousy of a sister who was more capable than himself. Christ, he regretted it now. He drew on his cigarette and closed his eyes.

What the hell am I doing here? Caught up in a bloody stupid war on a dry and dusty island – and trapped with Jack Scard, of all people. He had never liked him, even as a boy. That quiet, brooding intensity, and the fact that he was so obviously good at everything. He remembered now a time when he and his father had gone to flush out a fox that had been attacking the chickens. It had been summer, so there was no hunt to call upon. Bill Scard had showed them the den and both Bill and his son had accompanied them one evening. Sure enough, the vixen had appeared, and his father had turned to him and said, 'Go on, Guy, you have the shot.'

He'd missed, but then Jack had brought a rifle to his shoulder and, before the vixen could disappear into her den, killed her dead. 'Good shot, boy,' Liddell's father had said. 'A fine shot.' And it transpired that it had been Jack who had found the den in the first place.

Liddell could remember it as though it were yesterday, the sense of disappointment and the injured pride, the tears he had tried so hard to hold back and how, as he had touched the corner of his eye, he had seen Jack looking at him. Even now, ten years on, it made him wince. It was ridiculous, because he knew now, as he had known even then, that somehow Jack Scard was better than him, and yet he couldn't be because Scard was nothing more than a barely educated wild man, while he had been brought up with all the advantages of his class: a large home, education – a degree in mathematics, for God's sake. All that had to count for something, and yet, here, on Crete, as he took command of his platoon in his father's old regiment, it seemed that it counted for nothing at all.

Liddell cursed. He'd not thought of Jack Scard in years. He'd been sorry when Bill Scard had died, but when Jack had gone, he'd felt only relief. He could walk through the woods or on the downs without fear of seeing him; in no time, he'd put him out of mind entirely. But now here he was, and the thought of this decorated war hero sneering down his nose at him was unbearable. He had tried to impose himself but had been shown nothing but contempt. Liddell cursed again. No, there had to be another way of getting Tanner on side.

Drawing deeply on his cigarette, he thought hard, and then, as he watched the blue-grey smoke waft into the cool evening air, his thoughts turned back to the death of Bill Scard. What had happened? *Think*, he told himself. What was it Sykes had said? Something about Tanner never speaking about his past. *Why not?* Some people were reticent, it was true, but the way Sykes had said it was as though it had been a threat. Liddell smiled. *Of course!* It *had* been a threat. And why was Tanner making sure of that? Because he *did* have something to hide. Christ, why hadn't it occurred to him before? His mind began to whirr and now he remembered what he'd told Sykes, that not only had Bill Scard died but so, too, had one of the lads in the village. Was there a link? He didn't know, but Tanner *did*, he was sure of that now. *Yes*, he thought. Jack knew something and was worried he might also know and spill the beans. Liddell smiled. The more he thought about it, the surer he became.

He flicked away his cigarette. Of course, he could hazard a guess at what might have happened, but that was not the point. All he had to do was pretend he knew and make that clear to Tanner; perhaps Tanner might inadvertently tell him. If he was right, then that would very quickly wipe the knowing smile from the CSM's face. He felt his spirits lift.

He was still thinking about when and how he might try out his theory when small-arms fire interrupted his reverie. It was coming from the west of the town, a burst of machine-gun fire, the crack of rifles and the dull explosions of grenades. There was shouting too, faint yet distinct on the evening breeze.

Once more nausea filled his guts, his blood pulsed and his legs weakened. *Oh, God,* he thought, *don't let them attack here.*

7

Dusk and dawn – the best times to attack. When the light is changing rapidly and the shadows are long. For the defender, it is hard to adjust to this constantly altering light, but for the attacker there is still enough light to see. Desultory small-arms fire had continued to crack out all evening, but so far they had advanced to within two hundred metres of the town without being noticed.

Balthasar paused briefly as his men crept forward, flitting between trees and through the groves. Bringing his binoculars to his eyes, he looked up again at the walls. There were men up there. *Another hundred metres*, he thought, *and then we can have a go.*

Von der Schulenberg's party had left ahead of them, circling to the north. There were just over a hundred men in each group, and in one respect this was an advantage: one did not want a large force at this stage. Infiltration and surprise were more easily achieved with fewer men. The enemy would have little idea how many there were of them, so all they had to do was hold their nerve, get that crucial breakthrough into the town, and he felt sure they had a good chance of success.

Balthasar moved forward again. There was still smoke on the air, but also a more fragrant smell, clear and sharp. Cicadas were calling noisily, almost deafeningly. Well, that would only help them. He was satisfied that the plan was the right one. A hundred metres from the edge of the town, they were all to open fire with their rifles, aiming for as many men on the walls as they could see. Then, Leutnant Mettig, from 2 Company, would lead the diversion: two hastily put together platoons, only thirty men. They were to work their way through the houses at the foot of the walls, kill anyone in their path, then make a big noise attacking the main gate. Meanwhile, the rest of them would go round to the right and storm the walls.

He was 150 metres away now, once more ahead of his men. Suddenly he heard a noise up ahead,

139

then low voices, clear enough over the sound of the night insects. Urgently, he signalled to the men either side of him, some ten metres away, to wait. Pressing himself into the trunk of a tree, he listened. Two or maybe three men were coming; he heard the click of weapons and footsteps through the grass. Getting nearer, and then voices again – Greeks. They were just a few metres away now, and Balthasar breathed in. His heart hammered in his chest. Still the approaching men had not seen or heard anything untoward; the noise of cicadas was evidently proving a good distraction.

Three men. Cretans, not soldiers, but carrying rifles, creeping forward, and past him, but then something made one turn. Balthasar knew that feeling – a sixth sense that something else was there. It was, however, the last movement the man made because, in that moment, Balthasar plunged forward with his rifle, the twenty-three-centimetre blade of his Gebrheller bayonet glinting in the gloom, and thrust it into the man's chest. A gasp, and the Cretan fell backwards, but already Balthasar had pulled out the blade and swung the rifle into the side of the next man's head, knocking him sideways. The third tried to run, but he was startled and scared and within a few steps Balthasar had caught up and had stuck the blade through his back. He fell forward with a cry, and Balthasar punched down with the bayonet again. The second man was groaning on the ground, and Balthasar kicked him hard in the side, rolled him over and then, placing the tip of the bayonet over the man's heart, pressed downwards. Quickly, he wiped his blade on his victim's side, then signalled to his men to continue forward. *Surprise.* It was such a good weapon, and now there were three less enemy to worry about.

He moved forward again, through another olive grove, this time so dense the branches were touching one another so that he had to crouch to get through. At its edge he paused again and glanced to either side of him. Yes, there were his men, ready. In front of him was a small, rough field, a donkey standing in one corner. Dogs began barking to his left. Up ahead, the first houses, mostly white with flat roofs, although some were pitched, with terracotta tiles. They stretched away towards the walls alongside rough dirt roads. Balthasar looked at his watch: *1948. Two minutes.*

He moved to his right, hurrying deftly between the trees, past men clutching rifles, until he reached Schulz.

'Ready, Oberleutnant?' said Schulz. Above, stars were beginning to twinkle.

'Yes, Herr Major,' said Balthasar. He could now see the walls clearly and a few men on top. Bringing his rifle into his shoulder, he aimed carefully, training his sights on one particular man, a Greek soldier, his helmeted head silhouetted against the fading sky.

Schulz looked at his watch. 'All right, Balthasar,' he said. 'Let us begin.'

Balthasar felt strangely calm. His heart rate had lowered, his breathing was steady. This was what he was trained to do; in truth, it was what he enjoyed doing – the thrill of the fight, the euphoria of action. His target was, he guessed, ninety metres away, moving slowly. Balthasar steadied

141

himself, waited for the man to stop moving, then squeezed the trigger.

The crack of the shot rang in his ears, but his aim had been good. Atop the walls the man crumpled, and now there was more rifle fire, a deafening fusillade. In moments, the night had come alive, and men were running forward, towards the houses, bursts of sub-machine-guns and return rifle fire filling the air. Balthasar was now beside Schulz, hurrying through the olive grove away from the main gate.

Balthasar had been half expecting enemy troops to be dug in around the edge of the town, but there appeared to be no one. The only return shots were coming from the walls and the houses in front. *Good.* As he was now up ahead he could see the crumbling walls and their point of attack. He took a couple of deep breaths, nodded to Schulz, then sprinted across a short stretch of open ground. Bullets spat around him, but he reached the wall around the first house unscathed. Others followed. He saw one man fall, but the rest were making the crossing safely. Moving off again, he hurried forward, using the darkening shadows for cover. There would be enemy in the houses, he knew, but he had told his men to ignore them as much as possible – to keep within the shadows, and to move swiftly to the walls. Shots rang out nearby and he heard the ricochet of a bullet. Forward he went, and then he was at the walls.

Slinging his rifle across his back, he swung his MP40 to his front, and pulled back the cocking handle ready. A large part of the wall had col-lapsed – the stone had evidently been taken away, reused, he supposed, so that now there was no more than a three-metre climb. Opposite, on the other side of the road, a building extended from the walls and it occurred to him that it might be possible to work their way through that and into the town. Other men had now joined him. He signalled to several to start climbing the walls, then saw Obergefreiter Möhne hurrying from the shadows.

'Möhne!' he hissed. 'With me!' He scurried across the street as several shots rang out from the windows above. Pressing himself against the wall between the window and the doorway, he took out a grenade, unscrewed the cap, dropped it beside the doorway and moved away. A blast, and then he stepped out in front of it, kicked open the shattered wood and, opening fire, ran inside. Without pause he raced through the smoke. Ahead, a set of wide stone stairs. He sped up, vaguely conscious of men following and further gunfire. Reaching the first floor, he stretched out his arms and fired another burst, then scrambled onto the landing and pounded up a second flight of stone stairs.

Men behind him, and now men ahead – Greek soldiers – coming down the stairs. Another burst, and two enemy tumbled down towards him. Were there others? Jumping over the dead men, Balthasar continued up. Then, at the top, he took out another grenade, unscrewed the cap, counted to three, and lobbed it onto the next landing. A second later the grenade exploded, the sound deafening in the confines of the stone walls so that Balthasar's ears rang. Springing onto the landing he fired again into the swirling cloud of dust and smoke, kicked open a door and fired. A pistol shot rang out but the bullet whizzed harmlessly past his head, and now one of his men was spraying the room with bullets. A cry and another man collapsed to the ground. Balthasar saw that the room was otherwise empty. *An officer*, he thought as he hurried past the dead man and over to one of the two large windows.

Quickly he pulled out his magazine and replaced it, then cautiously peered through one of the windows. Below was the street and the gap in the walls. Men were clambering up but he saw two hit and tumble backwards. *Where was the firing coming from?* A muzzle flash from a building within the walls. Unslinging his rifle, he aimed at a dark window and fired.

'Quick!' he called. 'Get some covering fire up here!'

Unteroffizier Rohde was now beside him. 'The building is secure, Herr Oberleutnant,' he said.

'Good,' said Balthasar. 'Now order some men up here. Where's the MG? Get Möhne.'

One of the other men called to Möhne, who appeared a moment later with a private, Schütze Meier, in tow, clasping an ammunition box.

'Get to the window, quick!' ordered Rohde.

Balthasar turned to him. 'We need to find a way into the walls.'

'I think maybe on the floor below,' said Rohde. 'There is a door cut into a deep recess.'

Balthasar nodded as Möhne opened fire, the room quickly filling with the sharp stench of cordite. More men came into the room. 'Show me,' he mouthed above the din. Rohde led him downstairs and into a similar-sized room below. At the far end was the recess, a good metre deep, at the end of which was a wooden door.

'This has to lead into the town,' he said. He called more men to him, and they stood back as another grenade blasted open the thick oak door. The smoke and the shock of the explosion were an advantage when storming through a building such as this. Rohde fired blindly past the splintered wood, then hurried through, Balthasar following, holding his breath. They were in a narrow stone corridor, but Balthasar now saw a rectangular opening at the far end. Only an iron gate barred their way, but Rohde tried the handle and discovered it was not locked. Beyond, a flight of stone steps descended at a right angle to the street. Rohde glanced at Balthasar, his face taut.

'Out of the way,' said Balthasar. 'I'll go first. Cover me.'

Pressing himself against the wall, he peered through the gate. Outside, he could hear fighting but the street opposite looked quiet. His heart had quickened again, but he pushed open the gate, then stepped out and ran down the steps, his body tense, waiting for a bullet to smack into him. But it did not come, and he was able to cross the street undetected, then signal to the others to follow.

As a dozen men, one by one, hurried down the steps, Balthasar looked around. The light was fading rapidly, and the sky twinkled with stars...A road ran beside the wall, but immediately opposite there was a long row of buildings. As he crouched in the shadows of one, he could see that the enemy occupied the buildings opposite the broken wall and that, even with the help of the MG firing, his men were struggling to get across. They needed to storm the building, and preferably from more than one side.

Rohde was now beside him with Gefreiter Reinert.

'Reinert, I want you to go back,' he told the corporal. 'Tell Möhne that we're about to assault these buildings, and get the men the other side of the wall ready. Try to find Schulz. Rohde, you attack from the front, and I'll take five men to the back.'

Reinert nodded, and hurried across the road. Balthasar watched him disappear safely, then divided his men and told Rohde to wait one minute before attacking. He led his group back along the road, keeping close into the shadows until they reached a narrow paved street. Turning into it, he was relieved to find a small alleyway off it that evidently ran along the back of the row of houses. Hurrying along, they rounded a bend and saw men moving from the alley into the rear of the building. Balthasar immediately opened fire, Greek soldiers screaming as they were cut down. He ran on, urging his men to follow. Pausing by the doorway at the rear of the building, he signalled to two of his men to take out grenades.

They unscrewed the caps and, at Balthasar's gesture, threw them through the open door. As they exploded, the men turned and entered. Almost at the same moment, there were explosions from the front of the building too. Balthasar allowed himself a grim smile of satisfaction, then grabbed two of his paratroopers and said, 'Stay here and guard this back door. Shoot anything that moves.'

Having given one an encouraging slap on the back, he stepped into the house.

Inside there was pandemonium. Dazed and coughing, Greek troops floundered through the smoke only to meet a burst of Schmeisser fire. Above, Balthasar heard a machine-gun clattering, so he hurried up the staircase. The stench was overpowering, but as he glanced up he saw a Greek soldier half aim a rifle at him. Before he could respond, the man had fired, the bullet grazing Balthasar's upper arm. Cursing, he opened fire himself, the soldier tumbling down the stairs. Balthasar pushed him out of the way and continued upwards, two steps at a time. The MG was still pounding, so he took out his last grenade, lobbed it inside the room and, when it had exploded, emptied the rest of his magazine. The machine-gun stopped firing.

Cautiously, Balthasar stepped inside. Sulphurous smoke filled the room, rasping at the back of his throat. One man lay slumped over the machine-gun, his arm and side shredded. Another lay flat on his back, his face hideously disfigured by the grenade blast and his chest torn open. Two more lay under the window. One was groaning, so Balthasar took his Sauer pistol and punched a single bullet into the man's chest. Blood was spreading across the stone floor, a darkening slick that was now seeping around his boot. He looked down at the MG. It was wrecked – annoying, but that could not be helped. From the back of the building came another burst of a sub-machine-gun but the rest of the house was now quiet.

'We have it,' said Rohde, from the doorway.

'Well done,' said Balthasar. 'Now let's get the rest of them across.' Cautiously he moved to the window. Across the road, men were already clambering over the walls. 'Quick!' he shouted, then looked back along the road and saw more men streaming down the stone steps from the wall house.

'Come on,' he said to Rohde, then hurried out of the room and back downstairs over a number of Greek dead to the street below. There he paused and touched his arm. It stung and there was blood on his fingertips, but he was lucky the wound was no worse. He wiped his brow, suddenly aware that he was perspiring heavily. Fighting was hot work.

My God, we're in, he thought. They had achieved the hardest part. Even so, as Balthasar was well aware, there was still much to be done before the town was theirs.

Captain Alex Vaughan had been with Pendlebury in a *kafenio* next to the Canea Gate when the shooting had begun. Already it had been a long afternoon, organizing Cretan raiding parties, helping Greek snipers pinpoint targets and distributing the booty taken from dead paratroopers. And this on top of several days of feverish activity in which he had had little sleep. He felt exhausted.

Vaughan was one of the very few people who knew that Pendlebury was not only vice consul but head of the Special Operations Executive on the island, the wing of British intelligence set up specifically to carry out clandestine sabotage against the enemy. Although Vaughan had a natural gift for languages and could hold his own in Greek, Pendlebury was almost a native. He spoke both ancient and modern Greek fluently, the latter with the Cretan patois, and having spent so many years at Knossos and excavating other ancient sites on the island, he knew the place intimately; indeed, he had walked and traversed the island more than most Cretans.

Pendlebury had established a network of informers that stretched all the way to the mainland, and three days earlier had received word from one – via a trip across the sea – that the German invasion had just been postponed but was still imminent. Over the past months Pendlebury, along with Vaughan and his fellow SOE officers, Jack Hanford and Terence Bruce-Mitford, had devoted much energy to organizing the local *kapitans* into guerrilla forces should the invasion come. Vaughan, if he was honest, had always questioned the value of Crete to the Germans, but Pendlebury had insisted the enemy would invade, and for that, he argued, they needed to be prepared. He had been proved right that afternoon and, thanks to him, they now had arms stashes all over the island, but especially in the mountains, from where Pendlebury hoped the fight could be continued should the worst happen and the British be defeated.

The previous day, Hanford had left Heraklion to organize the guerrillas in the mountains, but

Vaughan had remained behind with Pendlebury to help defend the town. 'I'm sure the Greek regiments will fight,' Pendlebury had said, 'and so will the British. But the ones who will fight hardest are the Cretans. It is their island, after all.' Therefore he had armed as many as he could, and while many of the guerrillas – or *andartes*, as they were known – had remained in their mountain villages, some had joined him in Heraklion, men like Alopex, the village patriarch of Sarhos, a village on the lower slopes of the Ida range, and the head of an influential family olive-pressing business.

Alopex had known Pendlebury for years, helping with his digs before the war and with organizing the planned resistance since the latter's arrival back on the island the previous year. It was from Pendlebury that Alopex had learned English. Vaughan had recognized that this had been a smart move: Pendlebury was universally admired by the Cretan patriarchs, and Alopex's close ties to this eccentric but beloved Englishman had only enhanced his own standing.

Alopex had also been at Pendlebury's when the paratroopers attacked, and so too had Satanas, the most influential *kapitan* of them all. Satanas was from Krousonas, a large mountain village higher in the Ida Mountains than Alopex's home. As Vaughan had discovered when he had first visited Krousonas, Satanas was the unquestioned village patriarch and a legend on Crete as a man who had fanatically fought the Turks more than forty years before. It was said that he had survived so many Turkish bullets that he must be

150

the devil himself; that, Vaughan had been told in awed tones more times than he could remember, was why everyone knew him as Satanas.

Vaughan could only guess at Satanas's age, but tall and broad, with a mass of thick white hair, a luxuriant moustache, and dark unblinking eyes, he was an imposing figure. Pendlebury had done well to win his affection; in Satanas he had one of his most trusted collaborators. And with Satanas and Alopex beside him, Pendlebury's efforts to unite the townsmen of Heraklion against the invader had been made that much easier. Satanas was also respected by the Greek commanders in Heraklion. There were three under-strength Greek battalions holding the town, around fifteen hundred men in all, and thanks to Pendlebury's urging, with Alopex's and especially Satanas's influence, the Greek commanders had agreed to line the walls with snipers. It was funny, Vaughan had reflected, that although there were Greek colonels and majors in Heraklion, it was Pendlebury and Satanas, both barely trained in soldiering, who were most assuredly in command. Some people, he supposed, were natural leaders of men.

Their leadership skills would be tested again now that the Germans were launching an attack. In the bar, Pendlebury had smiled and pushed back his chair. 'We mustn't dally here.'

Vaughan had rubbed his face and eyes, finished his coffee and raki, and followed him outside.

That had been twenty minutes ago, and although they had held off the attackers successfully at the Canea Gate, they had then heard increasingly heavy fighting just over a hundred yards to the south. Vaughan had hurried off to see for himself what was going on. At the Alpha Company, the 3rd Greek Battalion, headquarters there was heavy fighting and as he hurried along the street he heard machine-gun fire from outside the walls and from within the 3rd Battalion building. There were already a number of dead, and then he saw a squad of paratroopers, half hidden by the shadows, crouching along the edge of the street and about to storm the building.

He wondered where the hell the rest of the battalion was. Clearly, reinforcements were urgently needed, but most of the 3rd Greek Battalion was already strung out manning the walls as far as the sea. Battalion HQ was in the Bethlehem Bastion, another two hundred yards further along the west wall of the town, but there was no sign of any attempt being made to help Alpha Company fend off the breach in the defences. He wondered whether he could work his way round the back and reach Bethlehem Bastion by avoiding Plastira altogether. There was, he knew, a narrow alleyway that ran behind the houses along Plastira. Perhaps if he was quick, he could cut through that way.

Turning down Stratigou Vassou, a narrow street running away from the walls, he stepped into the alley only to be met by a burst of sub-machine-gun fire. He flung himself to the ground, bullets slapping into the stonework above his head, then glanced up to see the darkened shapes of a number of dead Greek soldiers. *Damn it*. Now the Germans had the building and could pour through the breach at will. Sliding on his front,

152

he inched out of the alley and ran back towards the Canea Gate.

Fighting could now be heard to the north of the town, towards the sea, and Vaughan realized they had been duped. The attack on the Canea Gate had been nothing more than a feint, drawing their fire and attention, while the enemy attacked two of the weak points. And yet he had reckoned that Alpha Company's defences had been good. Goddamn it, he had visited them that very afternoon. Those Greek soldiers had held the buildings beyond the gate and those directly opposite the gap in the wall. Even highly trained German paratroopers should not have been able to breach them. They might live in modern times, yet he had recognized that the walls held the key to the town's defence. Without any heavy firepower, no paratrooper, armed with rifle or machine-gun, should ever have been able to break through, even in the places where the walls had started to crumble.

But it had happened and now they needed to work out a way of forcing the enemy back. He found Pendlebury with Alopex, Satanas and a distraught Greek captain desperately trying to gather men together at the foot of the walls. Around them were a cluster of Cretans and Greek troops.

'Well?' said Pendlebury, as Vaughan reached them.

'It's bad,' he said breathlessly. 'Jerry's through between here and Bethlehem. They've got Alpha Company Headquarters. I tried to get through to Battalion at Bethlehem Bastion but failed, I'm afraid.'

'That's a bore,' said Pendlebury, 'although I guessed as much. It's why we're organizing our guerrillas here.'

It was now almost dark, but a bright moon and a canopy of stars shone a milky light across the town so that it was still possible to see clearly out of the shadows.

'We need reinforcements,' said Vaughan. 'I can't understand why the rest of 3rd Battalion haven't mounted a counter-attack.'

'Because most of their men are already along these walls down to the sea,' said Alopex.

'It's the 7th Battalion that needs to launch the counter-attack from the south,' said Pendlebury. 'Perhaps they're worried about an attack from the south.'

'Why don't I head to Jesus Bastion and see if I can get some help from the Yorks Rangers?' said Vaughan. 'I can get across town if I'm quick.'

Pendlebury nodded. 'Yes, all right. Satanas and I will stay here with Kapitan Milos and try to hold the gate. Alopex, you take some of your men and see what's going on down by the sea. Get the Garrison Battalion at the harbour if necessary.'

Vaughan glanced at the motley band of men now with Pendlebury: Greek soldiers with rifles and old uniforms, puttees wrapped all the way to their knees, and Cretan guerrillas, waistcoated, high-booted, with bandoliers around their waists and across their chests. He knew that Pendlebury was right to suppose the Cretans at least would fight with passion, but was that enough against highly trained German paratroopers? Looking at them, he doubted it. 'I'll be back as soon as I can,' he said now, then turned and began to run.

Captain Peploe and CSM Tanner had hurried to Battalion HQ as soon as they heard the fighting going on to the west of the town. It was perfectly obvious to Tanner that they should send reinforcements and Peploe was of the same opinion.

'What about holding the line here?' Colonel Vigar had asked.

'Sir, we know most of the enemy in our sector landed to the west of the town,' said Peploe. 'CSM Tanner led a patrol earlier and he was able to confirm that those troops that landed further south have been making their way west to join the rest of their forces there.'

'And now they're attacking.' Vigar scratched his chin with his thumb. 'Hmm. And we've not had any requests for help. For all we know they might be holding on easily.'

'Sir, I'm not sure how many Jerries came down this evening,' said Tanner, 'but they won't have enough to attack the west of the town and here in the south.'

'All right, Tanner,' said the colonel, a touch of irritation in his voice. 'Don't get above yourself. I do understand what you're saying, you know.' He now drummed his fingers on the table. 'I suppose we do have quite a lot of men around the airfield, but what worries me is if Jerry launches an attack from the south using those men that have dropped around the airfield. Those wallahs that landed to the west make their attack, drawing what we've got over there, and then the eastern lot attack us from the south. Jerry always has lots

155

of radios, you know.'

'That's surely unlikely, sir,' said Peploe.

'But we still need to hold the line here,' said Vigar. 'How are you proposing we manage that?'

'By leaving one or two platoons from each company. We have machine-guns here, sir, and rifles, and flares. Two platoons can hold this line even if the enemy does attack from the south.'

Colonel Vigar eyed each of them, then glanced across at Major Ryan, his second-in-command. 'What d'you think, Tom?'

'I'm with Peploe and Tanner, sir,' he replied. 'But if you're unsure, why don't I put a call through to Brigade?'

Vigar nodded. 'Yes, all right.'

Major Ryan picked up the phone and rang through to Brigade HQ to the west of the airfield. 'Yes, the enemy is attacking the west of the town... Yes... We are proposing to send reinforcements... All right.' He paused a moment and glanced back at the others. 'Yes, sir,' he said at last. 'Oh, I see. I'll tell Colonel Vigar that, sir. Yes, very good, sir.' Major Ryan put down the phone. 'They think it very unlikely that Jerry will manage an attack tonight from the south. We're to send reinforcements.'

Colonel Vigar clapped his hands together, as was his way. 'Good, good,' he said. 'All right, then. Two platoons from each company it is. Peploe, get your men ready right away.' He turned to Major Ryan. 'Tom, you're in charge. Get word up to the other companies, but I suggest Peploe and his mob get going as soon as they can. We'll send runners on ahead now – find out where we can best deploy.'

Peploe and Tanner saluted, then hurried from the Jesus Bastion back out to company lines, where orders were quickly issued. Peploe had decided that 3 and 4 Platoons should remain behind holding the lines, with Lieutenant Ivo McDonald in charge. He would lead 1 and 2 Platoons. Tanner stuffed a flare gun into his belt, grabbed extra rounds for his Enfield revolver and helped himself to more grenades, which he packed into his haversack. He then told Sykes and Sergeant White to make sure their men had also got enough grenades. 'Make sure they have as much ammo as they can carry,' he told them. 'I reckon ammo's one thing Jerry's going to be short of, so we need to make sure we've got more than him.'

In just over ten minutes they were ready and moving out, down along the Knossos road and through the town walls in double-quick time. It was there, as they passed Battalion Headquarters, that they met Captain Vaughan, fresh from seeing Colonel Vigar.

'Thank God for someone with a bit of foresight,' he said, as he joined Peploe and Tanner at the front of their column. 'We need you desperately, I'm afraid.'

'Have they broken into the town, then?' asked Peploe.

Vaughan nodded. 'I only hope it's not too late already.'

8

A little before 9 p.m., 20 May. As the Rangers hurried across the Platia Ekaterinis, the cathedral looming darkly beside them, the sound of fighting became suddenly closer, so much so that Tanner could hear the shouts and cries of men above the reports of small arms. At the end of Agio Mina, they faced Kalokerinou, the long straight road that led to the Canea Gate. Halting the men, Tanner moved cautiously forward with Captain Vaughan, and looked down towards the town walls. Muzzle flashes punctured the dark, shapes moved in and out of the shadows and bursts of machine-gun fire and rifle shots resounded sharply between the buildings lining either side of the street.

They stepped back again.

'Let me go forward and try to find out what's going on,' said Vaughan.

'I'll come with you,' said Peploe.

'No, you'd better stay here with the men. Let me take Tanner.'

'All right – but if you're not back in five minutes I'm moving the men on.'

Vaughan and Tanner slipped back into Kalokerinou, carefully inching their way down the street. The fighting seemed to be concentrated around the confluence of streets before the Canea Gate, but suddenly there was shouting and men were running back. Tanner saw German paratroopers race across the mouth of the road, spectral shadows briefly lit by the light of the moon. Then, a moment later, they opened up with several short bursts of automatic fire. Several men cried out, as Tanner brought his rifle to his shoulder. His aim was blocked, however, by the retreating rabble. Feet clattered across the stone as a group of men hurried down the street. Several yards ahead three stopped, fired back down the road, and then, breathing heavily, pulled into the shadows beside them.

'This is bloody chaos,' said Vaughan.

'Alex, you're back,' said a voice Tanner recognized instantly as Pendlebury's. 'Have you brought reinforcements?'

'Yes,' replied Vaughan, as Tanner crept past him.

'Alopex!' Pendlebury called, then said to Vaughan, 'Where are they?'

'Agio Mina.'

'Alopex,' said Pendlebury again. 'Call the men to you in the Agio Mina.'

A grunt of acknowledgement and Tanner heard him summon them. A few more now scampered back down the street, as Tanner fired a white flare into the air, then quickly thrust the Very pistol back into his belt and took out his rifle. The flare whooshed into the sky, burst with a crack, and hissed as it descended, casting a white glow over the far end of the street, illuminating the walls and the Canea Gate with a flood of magnesium and, at the same time, revealing in clear light a number of paratroopers now moving along the sides of the street. They immediately ran back but not before Tanner had aimed his rifle and fired five shots in rapid succession. He hit two men, but the aim had been to push them back for a minute or two and even to sow doubt in them.

'We need to be quick, sir,' he said, walking backwards down the edge of the street. 'That won't hold them off long.'

'Come on, John,' said Vaughan. 'There are seventy Rangers waiting round the corner.'

'Seventy? Well done, Alex, well done indeed!' All three men now took to their heels as shots rang out down the street once more. Turning the corner, they found Peploe waiting. More shots followed, and there was also gunfire to the north towards the sea.

'The Huns are all over the place, I'm afraid,' said Pendlebury. Tanner was now conscious of Alopex standing beside Pendlebury with around twenty Cretan *andartes* behind him. 'They're through the Canea Gate, perhaps have the Bethlehem Bastion, and are working their way east through the streets.'

'And what's happening on the seafront?'

'They're through there as well. The remnants of the 3rd Greek and Garrison Battalions are fighting them. But we need to knock back this lot first. Do that, and the northern prong might run out of steam.'

Jesus, thought Tanner. They needed to get a bloody move on. 'Sir,' he said to Peploe, 'what about getting some men watching on that street corner? One of the Brens, sir.'

Peploe nodded. 'Sykes!' he called in a low

160

voice. 'Get a Bren on that corner.'

'Sir!'

'I suggest we move up to the next street that crosses Kalokerinou,' said Vaughan, his voice urgent, 'and place the two Brens either side, keeping the enemy at the Canea Gate pinned down. From there we can send sections down along the streets that run to the walls.'

'All right,' said Peploe.

'We need guides, sir,' said Tanner. 'Men who know this town like the back of their hands.'

'Yes, you're right, Tanner,' agreed Peploe. 'Captain Pendlebury?'

Pendlebury spoke quickly to the Cretans. Tanner glanced at Alopex and caught his eye. The Cretan drew a finger across his neck. *Like a sodding bad penny*, thought Tanner, raising his middle finger towards him.

Peploe hurriedly issued his orders, dividing the platoons so that one was sent across the far side of Kalokerinou, and others kept to the south. As they set off, Tanner passed Lieutenant Liddell, fumbling with his revolver. 'All right, sir?' he said.

'Yes, thank you, Tanner.' A forced smile.

They moved forward, initially three platoons together, down a short, narrow road and across a wider street, until they reached a small triangle. Pausing, Tanner saw a number of palms and planes rising from the centre. Heavy firing continued to the north, but in their part of the town, there was desultory shooting only. He wondered what the enemy were planning, what they were thinking. Were they expecting a counter-attack or would they be assuming the Greek forces there

161

had fled? He gripped his rifle. Time would soon tell.

Their force now split. Pendlebury, with Peploe and 2 Platoon, headed for the far right corner of the triangle, while Tanner, with Vaughan, Alopex, half a dozen of his men and all of 1 Platoon moved towards the left.

'Boys,' whispered Tanner, 'keep well into the shadows at all times. Rifles unslung, grenades to hand.' They crept forward. Tanner's heart was hammering, and his mouth was dry. He wanted a glug of water, but he daren't reach for his bottle in case the enemy suddenly opened up.

'Sir,' whispered Corporal Hepworth behind him.

'What is it, Hep?'

'I'm not sure how much I like this creeping about in the dark. Last time I was home I saw a dead scary film at the pictures and it was just like this, all night-time and shadows. I hope a werewolf don't jump out on me.'

'Put a sock in it, Hep, will you?'

As they reached the corner of the triangle Alopex stopped, and Tanner signalled to the men to get down on their haunches. *Christ, they're noisy*, he thought – rifles knocking against webbing, soles of boots sliding on the ground. Quietly, he slid forward, then heard the sound too. Voices up ahead. German voices.

'Kourmoulidon,' whispered Alopex.

'A street that runs from here towards Bethlehem Bastion,' mouthed Vaughan.

'Tanner,' whispered Alopex, 'follow me. Captain, you wait with the men, but when the firing starts, move them forward quickly.'

Tanner swallowed and moved forward until he was beside the Cretan. 'Just up ahead, maybe twenty metres, there is a narrow turning to the left.'

Tanner nodded and then, as Alopex silently moved forward, followed. Tanner had to admit that the Cretan was as stealthy as a cat. The man wore bandoliers criss-crossed over his chest and carried a rifle, yet Tanner could barely hear him move. The moon was high above them but the old Venetian houses on their left were tall enough to cast ink-dark shadows over them. The voices were nearer and Tanner could faintly see that Alopex was quickening his step. Suddenly the Cretan sidestepped into the narrow street entrance, nimbly crossed the road and pressed himself against the stone wall on the other side. Tanner followed, trying to keep his breathing calm and measured.

'They're moving slowly down the street,' whispered Alopex. 'As soon as two men have reached the mouth of the road, we grab them, OK? You have a knife?'

Tanner pulled out his seventeen-inch sword bayonet.

'Kill them silently, then we grab their fancy guns.'

Tanner could not help smiling to himself. The enemy would be tense, as nervous as they were prowling through that triangle. Their reaction would be startled – that was human nature. For a crucial moment, they would not know what was going on. Tanner felt for two grenades. 'Here,' he

163

said, passing one to Alopex. 'Pull the ring pin, then throw.' Alopex took it.

A chink – a weapon touching some webbing – and then footsteps, quiet, but unmistakable. *How far now?* Tanner wondered. *A few yards.* He moved beside Alopex, his bayonet in his right hand, and held his breath.

Suddenly there they were, hard to see but strangely distinct, two men, one after the other, just one step away. With deft swiftness, Alopex lunged towards the second man, wrapping his left arm around his throat and, with the right, twisting the head with an emphatic jerk. Then, for good measure, he plunged his knife into his victim's heart. It took no more than a couple of seconds, but as the first man made a sudden alarmed turn, Tanner was upon him, arm tight around the German's throat and his bayonet plunging into the paratrooper's side. As Tanner knew well enough, a knife thrust through the kidney killed a man instantly, the pain so intense that the whole body ceased to function. Neither man had uttered so much as a gurgle, yet grabbing and dragging them clear of the road had made enough noise to alert their comrades.

'Müller! Kreschmann!' someone whispered loudly, not far behind, but by then Tanner had his man's Schmeisser off his shoulder and had stepped out, fired a quick burst in the direction of the voice, heard a cry, then retreated and, with his bayonet still in his hand, took the grenade from his trouser pocket, pulled the pin and lobbed it a short distance down the road. By this time, the Germans were firing wildly, the noise

164

deafening. Bullets richocheted off the walls, and then came the explosion of the grenade, and Tanner heard more shooting, this time rifle fire from away to his right. Leaning against the corner of the wall, he took out his Very pistol and fired another round, which fizzed as it rose into the sky, then burst and crackled as it descended. White light bathed the street ahead, and both he and Alopex fired two more bursts from their captured Schmeissers.

'Keep firing!' yelled Tanner, as paratroopers up ahead hurtled across the street and took cover in buildings. Several men cried out and Tanner saw at least three lurch and slump to the ground.

'Good work, you two,' said Vaughan, now beside him with Sykes and McAllister's section.

'Where's Mr Liddell?' said Tanner.

'The other side of the road,' said Vaughan. 'I left him on the corner with the rest of the platoon.'

'Sir, would you mind going back to him?' said Tanner. 'He's new and will need a bit of guidance. Alopex and I can manage here.' Vaughan smiled. 'Yes, all right. Once that flare of yours has died down.'

Tanner felt a heavy clasp on his shoulder and turned to see Alopex.

'We should go down this road,' said the Cretan. 'Maybe there are more Germans but also it cuts back to Kourmoulidon. We will take these men with us, OK?'

Tanner nodded, then turned to Vaughan. 'Sir, we're going to cut back onto this road further up, but we don't want to end up shooting at each other.'

'We'll move up the road on the far side, Tanner, and try to flush out any enemy on that side of the road.'

'Yes, sir, and we'll keep to this side.'

'Good luck, Tanner.'

'And you, sir.'

The flare had fizzled out and Vaughan left them, disappearing once more into the shadows.

Tanner now split the men into groups of four, staggered at either side of the road. As the street turned to the right, the centre was once more bathed in moon and starlight. Shots were ringing out, but there was no sign of the enemy so, at the next junction, Alopex turned right, leading them back towards Kourmoulidon.

They paused beneath a tall palm on the corner of the two roads, now some seventy yards further along. Tanner was certain he had seen enemy troops take cover in buildings further to the right and, if so, they were now behind them. For a moment, he was unsure how to flush them out. He didn't know how many or where they were; they could easily have moved on.

The street was dark again, out of the line of the moonlight, although down the middle of Kourmoulidon and almost up to the far side, milky light shone down. He wondered where Vaughan and the others were and cursed, annoyed with himself for not having paused to work out a more defined plan. *Too late now.* He moved beside Alopex. 'We need to draw their fire,' he whispered. 'See where the bastards are.'

He dashed across the road to where Sykes was waiting. 'Stan,' he said, 'I need you lot to step out and fire across at the houses opposite, but a little way down so that if they fire back you can duck behind this wall. And aim a bit high so you don't hit any of the others coming down the road.'

'And what are you going to do?'

'The same.' He ran back, unslung his rifle, took a step out into the road and fired across at one of the houses opposite. It was the signal for the rest of the men to follow, rifle shots cracking out, zipping off stonework, snapping through branches and shattering glass. Almost immediately, from directly opposite, several bursts of sub-machine-gun fire opened up, bullets flying towards them.

The men dived onto the ground but not before Tanner heard at least two cry out. *Damn it, damn it.* Another couple of bursts, bullets hissing over their heads this time, but they could stay where they were. Tanner knew there was only one way to silence them and that was to hurl a couple of grenades, then race over the road and pray that Vaughan and the others recognized him as he crossed the moonlit part and didn't cut him down. Rifle fire sounded, and another Ranger screamed. Fumbling in his haversack, Tanner felt for two grenades, took a deep breath, got up and ran around the corner to his left. He pulled the pins and hurled the bombs in turn towards the enemy fire. Muffled German shouts of alarm – then the grenades exploded one after the other, and Tanner was running across the road, rifle shots cracking out from the house, and feeling for another grenade. Sliding himself low against the wall, he pulled the pin, counted three seconds, then threw it in through the lower window.

Another burst of fire from the first floor, and Tanner glanced back to see Sykes and several of the others making a dash for it too. Where was Vaughan?

'Move! Move!' he shouted across the street, and heard running feet approaching from Kourmoulidon, more bursts of fire from above, then Vaughan and Liddell were beside him, the latter gasping. So too was Alopex, his unhelmeted head distinctive. 'We need to storm this house,' said Tanner. 'Stan? Got any grenades?'

'I've one in my hand now, sir.'

'Hepworth?' Tanner called. 'Where's Hep?'

'Here, sir.' Tanner saw a dark shape shuffle towards him.

'OK,' said Tanner. 'On three, pull the pins, count to three, then lob them through the windows. I'll put one by the door, and when they've blown, Alopex and I will go in with our new toys, and you follow, all right? Now get back from the door a moment.' He gripped the heavy metal lump, pushed his index finger through the loop and said, 'One, two, three, pull.' With a strong tug, the pin came free. 'One, two, three, now!' He heard the dull thud of the grenade landing, then bits of wood, metal and stone were blasted clear of the doorway and through the windows. Tanner crouched, his helmet forward, head ducked towards his chest. And then he was up, Alopex beside him. With their Schmeissers at their hips they opened fire and burst into the house.

It was almost pitch-dark, but there was a glow of moonlight shining down a long corridor that led to the back of the house and open French

168

windows. Tanner saw a figure jump down from above and disappear into the shadows beyond. He ran forward, through the doors, nearly lost his footing over the short step down into the garden beyond, and pressed the trigger on his Schmeisser only for it to click innocuously. Cursing, he felt for his revolver, then heard movement above him and saw, too late, a German jumping down on top of him.

Tanner collapsed face first on the hard earth, the wind knocked from his lungs. The faceless enemy was on his back and now brought a fist into the side of his head. Tanner gasped with pain but, with all his strength, pushed his knees into the ground and forced his body upwards, twisting as he did so. His assailant now had his hands around his neck, but Tanner managed to drive his elbow into his side once, then twice, and roll him over, so that he was now lying on top of his attacker. Tanner gasped again as the grip around his neck tightened, but he grabbed both hands and, grimacing, managed to prise them off him and roll free.

No sooner had he done so than the German was up, half crouching, a knife now in his hand. Tanner could see him quite clearly, moonlight on them both. A Schmeisser was slung across his back, his holster at his side. On his head was the helmet the paratroopers wore, more rounded, without the protective lip around the ears and neck. He was a big man, too, about his own size. Tanner crouched, waiting for the man to pounce. His rifle was still on his back, his pistol still in its holster, the captured Schmeisser at his side, his bayonet on his hip, but he had no time to reach for any of them because now the German lunged. Tanner parried the first blow, but the man delivered another to his head with the other hand, knocking him off balance. Then he lunged again and Tanner only just managed to grab his hand before the blade was plunged into his chest. The two men were now inches apart, straining and grimacing – and Tanner saw his expression suddenly change.

'*Sie sind es!*' said the man, and in that moment of his own incomprehension, Tanner felt the tip of the knife prick against his chest. The German pressed with both hands, but Tanner strained and pushed against him with all his strength and at last felt the blade move away. He dug into his attacker's wrist with his thumbs and his enemy gasped and dropped the knife but, at the same moment, drove his knee hard into Tanner's stomach. He gasped and staggered backwards. In the next instant, the German swung with his fist again, catching Tanner on the side of his left eye. Tanner cried out, swung uselessly back, but the German had gone, moving across the garden and out through a door to the side.

Tanner reached out to the wall of the house. Resting one arm against the cold, rough stone, he hung his head, breathing deeply. For the past minute in which he'd fought that man he had been aware of nothing but saving his life. His mind had been closed to all other sound, all other movement. It was as though the world had stopped while he grappled with the German. What was it the man had said? '*It's you!*' And then he remembered the German in the field, the one he had been unable to shoot. Bloody hell, had that really been only a few hours earlier? It seemed like a lifetime ago. *Well, I'm damned,* he thought.

He felt blood run down the side of his face, and became conscious once more of fighting nearby. From the front of the house, shots cracked out, but nearby, beyond the end of the garden, there was further firing and he realized that their counterattack must be succeeding.

He dabbed at his eye and winced. His throat was sore too – the second time in two days that a man's hands had been trying to throttle him, and yet now, for the moment, his enemy Alopex had become his ally. *Bloody hell, what kind of war is this?* And he wondered why the German had not used his pistol. Had he been returning the show of mercy? No, that Jerry had definitely meant to kill him. It was the same as before: the man had run out of ammunition. That was the fatal flaw in using lightly armed shock troops such as these paratroopers. Victory needed to come swiftly and decisively or they would lose. A soldier without ammunition could not win the fight.

Tanner began to chuckle but it hurt his throat so he stopped. Perhaps, he thought, they really would hold onto Crete after all. *We bloody well will if I've got anything to do with it.*

Oberleutnant Balthasar ran down the street, turned left, then left again, spotted two German bodies in the middle of the road and, to his relief, managed to salvage three magazines and a spare

171

clip for his Sauer. He was just moving off again when two rifle shots snapped at the far end of the road, the bullets coming worryingly close. Scurrying into the shadows he was relieved to hear return fire, a two-second burst of a machine-pistol, from the junction of another narrow street. Crouch-running towards the sound, he clamped a new magazine into his MP40, fired a short burst and joined the others.

'Good to see you, Herr Oberleutnant,' said Rohde. 'I thought they'd got you.'

'They will never get me, Unteroffizier,' Balthasar replied. 'I am indestructible, didn't you know? Now, let's move.' He hoped he still sounded calm, that he was hiding the rage and disappointment he felt. The attack had failed, he knew that now. All that effort, all those good men lost – two in that house and many more in the attack. All that ammunition spent too, and for nothing! Good God, he regretted not killing that Tommy. How had he let him get away? It was the same man, he was sure of it. Balthasar cursed. He had believed they could do it, and they nearly had, but with the Tommies counter-attacking they had never had a chance – they had had neither the men nor the ammunition.

Safely reaching the town walls, they found they were not alone. Other paratroopers had been pushed back. Furious firing was still going on around the main gate, and Balthasar led his men there, pausing by every dead body, German or Greek, to hunt for spare ammunition. They might be falling back, but Balthasar intended to take as many of the enemy with him as he could.

10.05 p.m. Still dazed, Tanner had been about to step back into the house when he heard Sykes call him. 'I'm here, Stan,' he rasped.

'Bloody 'ell, sir, are you all right?'

Tanner rubbed his neck. 'A bit of fisticuffs with an irate Jerry, but I'll live.'

'Where is he now?'

'Scarpered.' Something caught Tanner's eye, glinting in the moonlight, and he bent to pick up the German's knife.

'What's that? A memento?' asked Sykes.

'Yes. That bastard just tried to shove it into my chest. Could come in handy, though, eh?' He patted Sykes on the back. 'Come on, Stan, we'd be better get a bloody move on.'

Back in the street, Tanner found Lieutenant Liddell with Vaughan and Alopex.

'There you are, Tanner,' said Vaughan. 'House secure and nothing more up this street. I've sent a few on ahead.'

'Those Jerries are running out of ammunition, sir,' said Tanner, huskily. 'Time to press home the advantage.'

'Come on, then,' said Alopex.

They moved forward, the platoon split into sections once more, staggered at either side of the road. A short way on, Alopex led them off to the right. They could hear fighting to the west. 'They're at the Canea Gate,' he muttered, quickening his step. A few minutes later, and having passed a burning house and a number of dead, they reached Plastira, the road that ran along the walls. Thirty yards to their right, men were firing towards the gate. From back down the street, muzzle flashes shone like fireflies, the sound of small arms echoing sharply within the narrow confines. The platoon hurried forward and Tanner saw a British soldier and a Cretan *andarte* step out into the moonlight and fire.

Sykes led a section of men across the road, firing as they went, and when Tanner had reached the next junction he was firing too. Bullets ricocheted nearby, and he stepped into the shadows.

'Who's this just arrived?' said a voice Tanner recognized as Pendlebury's.

'It's us, John,' said Vaughan. 'We've got them running, then?'

'It would seem so,' said Pendlebury. 'One last push is all it needs. Some kind of charge, perhaps.'

Peploe was now beside Tanner. 'You made it, Jack,' he said. 'Much fighting?'

'A bit, sir. We lost three men – Webster, Jones and Mallerby. And you?'

'Half a dozen, I'm afraid, and three wounded.'

'Peploe?' said Pendlebury. 'I think we should storm the gate. What d'you say?'

'All right,' said Peploe. 'Straight down this road?'

'What about one group down the road,' suggested Tanner, 'and another on the walls? Can we get up there?'

'Yes,' said Pendlebury, 'just a short distance back the wall's crumbled so it's easy enough to climb up. And what about flares? Have you got any more, Tanner?'

'Yes, sir.'

'As have I,' said Peploe.

'Excellent. Captain, why don't you and some of

174

your men head onto the wall, then? When you're up there, give us a signal and we'll make our move.'

Peploe took 1 Platoon. Bullets followed them as they crossed the road, each man flitting briefly through the moonlight, but they all made it and hurried down the road, hugging the wall. The stench of blood and sulphur was still strong where vicious fighting had taken place earlier. Tanner nearly tripped over a corpse, but they found the gap and carefully climbed up onto the battlements and cautiously moved forward until they were level with Pendlebury, his guerrillas and the rest of 2 Platoon on the ground.

Tanner gave a low whistle, then took out his flare pistol and fired a shot into the air. The flare exploded almost directly over the gate. It was the signal the men below needed, and Tanner watched as Pendlebury's mixed force ran down the street, the captain himself emerging into the moonlight, waving a sword above his head.

'Is that what I think it is, sir?' he asked Peploe.

'His swordstick,' said Peploe. 'He says it's excellent for killing parachutists.'

'Jesus,' said Tanner.

It was now their turn to move forward, crouch-running below the level of the battlements. Up ahead, the Canea Gate was bathed in magnesium light. Tanner saw Germans on the walls firing down towards this new attack. *Not yet,* he told himself, his hands gripping the Schmeisser, *not until I'm close enough for this to cause havoc.* He stood up now, and ran on, ahead of Peploe and the others. The Germans had still not seen him, and now, at just under thirty yards, he opened fire, two short bursts, and saw men fall away, while others scampered clear of the walls and onto the roof of the great bastion beside the gate.

He did not follow them. Instead, he crouched and fired down on the enemy below. Men screamed and fell, and now Pendlebury's charge was upon the paratroopers. Tanner saw Pendlebury skewer one German and then others were fighting hand-to-hand with rifles as clubs, bayonets and knives. Peploe sent another flare into the sky and ordered his men on the wall to cease fire. Tanner briefly glimpsed his assailant in the garden, firing into the mass with his pistol, but before he could aim a shot, the German had disappeared under the gate.

Tanner now fired his last flare, out over the gate. Several bullets fizzed by, and one of the men further along the wall cried out and collapsed. Retreating paratroopers had already begun to fall back, away from the town, melting into the shadows, but as the flare burst, it was possible to see some of them hurrying away. Tanner pushed the Schmeisser onto his back, unslung his rifle and fired. He saw one man fall, but even with the flare they were hard to discern among the mass of buildings, trees and vegetation beyond the walls. Fighting could still be heard to the north near the sea, but by the Canea Gate the din of battle soon receded, until there was nothing more than the occasional, desultory crack of a rifle.

9

As the defenders of Heraklion were preparing their final charge on the Canea Gate, eighty-five miles away Major General Freyberg was signalling to General Headquarters, Middle East, in Cairo his assessment of the day's fighting. The old quarry high on the Akrotiri outcrop had been transformed over the past three weeks into the working headquarters and command post of Creforce. Trestle tables lined the hollow cavern cut into the rock, electric lamps had been rigged up from the rough stone roof, radio sets and telephones had been connected, with a mass of wire running out from the entrance and down the hill. Camouflage nets had been draped over the entrance to mask it from the air. Inside, staff officers tapped at typewriters, while on a map table, progress, as far as it was known, was carefully plotted.

It was ironic that Freyberg was able to send a coded message more than seven hundred miles across the sea to Cairo and yet have very little communication with his forces stretched out on the coastal plain just a few miles in front of him. Freyberg had seen more action than most, and he knew that battles were always messy, chaotic affairs. A lot of smoke, a lot of noise and always conflicting messages. From their vantage point he and his staff had seen plenty of German transport planes plunging into the sea and onto the rocky Cretan ground; they had heard the sounds of fighting all day. Other than that, they had seen very little.

Instead, they had been reliant on deciphering what messages had come through: increasingly jittery ones from Colonel Andrew, commander of the New Zealanders of 22nd Battalion at Maleme, who was clearly out of radio contact with his two companies on the far side of the airfield. Freyberg appreciated that this was always a difficult judgement for a commander. Were one's men overrun and defeated? Or was it simply that the rather flimsy telephone lines that linked battalion to company had been cut? Freyberg suspected the latter. He knew that Brigadier Hargest had initially promised reinforcements from 23rd Battalion for Colonel Andrew, but that would have meant moving them away from the coastal sector they were defending. Yet Freyberg knew what Hargest and Andrew did not: that the same intelligence that had warned him paratroop drops would be made at around 8 a.m. that morning had also advised that a further ten thousand enemy troops were to be transported to Crete by sea. True, there had been some inconsistencies in the intelligence signals over the past few weeks, but Freyberg had decided to trust the latest. Warnings of a seaborne invasion force had last been passed on exactly a week before, and since subsequent intelligence signals had proved uncannily accurate, Freyberg saw no reason to doubt that the Germans were indeed about to arrive from the sea too.

It was with this in mind that he had urged

caution to Hargest. It would be wrong, he felt, to reinforce Maleme when logic suggested that infantry armed with Brens and rifles should never be overrun by Germans armed with little more than sub-machine-guns. Elsewhere, around Galatas and in Prison Valley, it seemed the enemy had taken a drubbing, yet fighting had been heard all day and, as at Maleme, communications between units had been extremely problematic. It didn't matter how many telephone wires wound their way out of the Creforce quarry – if they were cut somewhere along the line, they were completely useless. Indeed, most information that day had come from runners rather than by phone, messengers arriving at the quarry's entrance, red-faced, sweat-drenched and exhausted.

As darkness had fallen and the fighting had at last died down, Freyberg hoped his commanders in the field were making the most of the opportunity to repair lines, get runners through to dispersed companies and prepare themselves for robust counter-attacks at first light with the troops they had. Sending massed reinforcements to panicked battalion commanders was not the answer because that would upset his carefully prepared dispositions – dispositions that had been made with the promised subsequent seaborne landings in mind.

That afternoon German operation orders had been discovered on a dead German officer in Prison Valley and had revealed that objectives for the first day had been all three airfields: Maleme, Heraklion and Rethymno. News from Heraklion and Rethymno had been sketchy to say the least, but the last communications both suggested huge German casualties and gave no sense that the airfields – or harbours for that matter – were in immediate danger.

With a tumbler of Scotch beside him, Freyberg sat at one of the trestle tables, pencil in hand, paper in front of him, ready to draft a signal to GHQ in Cairo. 'Today has been a hard one,' he wrote – and indeed it had. He took a mouthful of whisky, the strong aroma masking the dank mustiness of the cavern. 'We have been hard-pressed,' he added. 'So far, I believe, we hold aerodromes at Rethymno, Heraklion and Maleme, and the two harbours.' He paused, thinking. It was true the enemy had not taken their objectives but he was worrying about what was to come the following day: more airborne troops and ten thousand men by sea. That being so, the situation looked less secure. 'Margin by which we hold them is a bare one,' he scribbled, 'and it would be wrong of me to paint an optimistic picture.' He paused again, drank another glug of whisky. Was that too pessimistic? No, because he had always made it quite clear he felt the island was inadequately defended, and it was best to prepare his masters for the worst, should it come. However, he could always end on a brighter note. 'Fighting has been heavy,' he continued, 'and we have killed large numbers of Germans. Communications are most difficult.' He sat back, read it through again, then added one last afterthought: 'A German operation order with most ambitious objectives, all of which failed, has just been captured.'

He stood up, passed the scrawled note to a

clerk, then wandered out through the camouflage netting to the mouth of the quarry. The night was warm, although there was a light breeze. A faint whiff of smoke blended with the ever-present scent of herbs and grass. Under the light of the moon and the stars, the dark outline of the coast could clearly be seen and beyond, away to the south, the imposing mass of the White Mountains. Occasional desultory small-arms fire rang out; a dog barked in the town of Canea below. Freyberg finished his whisky, wondering whether he would be able to stand in the same place at the same time tomorrow night, or whether by then his forces would have been overrun.

Tanner stood on the battlements, looking out over the town. To the south, fighting was still going on but it was lessening now. He felt certain the Germans there would soon fall back once they knew their other thrust had failed. In any case, as he could now see, it looked as though the two platoons from A Company had just arrived – he could see Captain Bull and several others approaching Peploe from the direction of Kalokerinou; for all he knew, those from C and D Companies had already been sent to join the fight by the sea. He wondered what was happening over by the airfield. Turning his head, he listened for any sound of battle, but there was none – the airfield was surely still theirs.

Laughter from below made him look down thirty feet to the open area around the mouth of the Canea Gate. The mood among the town's defenders there was euphoric. Clear of the shadows, soldiers and Cretan *andartes* alike were exchanging excited accounts of their part in the action. Tanner knew these feelings. There was relief at still being alive and the strange elation that could happen after a fight. It was the adrenalin that still coursed through the body. Only when that had worn off would the exhaustion set in and even dark thoughts – memories of terror or even of horror: the blood, the broken limbs and smashed faces. One got used to seeing mutilated corpses, men with limbs missing, heads blown off, guts spilling out, and the mind hardened to such things, but thinking about them was never pleasant. There were corpses aplenty down there now, and large patches of blood spreading across the dusty road, clear enough even in the milky moonlight, but no one else seemed to have noticed. He watched one large, silver-haired Cretan *kapitan* embrace Alopex and then Pendlebury, who laughed, then gesticulated wildly. The man still had his swordstick in his hand and waved it in circles above his head, no doubt reliving the charge he had led earlier.

'Crazy bugger,' said Sykes, now standing beside him. 'Not your normal run-of-the-mill soldier, is he?'

Tanner chuckled. 'No, but he's a bloody good leader. He's got those Cretans where he wants them. Look at 'em. They bloody love him, don't they?'

'More than I can say for Mr Liddell. Look at him.'

Liddell was away from the rest of the men, walking aimlessly among the fallen.

182

'Poor bastard,' said Tanner.

'Why d'you think that?'

'As you said, Stan, he's not cut out for this lark, is he? I saw him earlier, before we set off to flush out those Jerries. He was bloody scared stiff. Should have stayed on the farm.'

'He'd probably be more use there. We still need scoff, and so does everyone back home, but I'm not sure we need his sort trying to tell us what to do.'

'I just wish to hell they'd never sent him here. Of all sodding people.' He lit two cigarettes and passed one to Sykes. 'Anyway, we need to go on a scavenge.' He stood up. 'Here, Hep,' he said, 'keep an eye on the lads, all right? Make sure they keep a good lookout.'

'Yes, sir,' Hepworth replied.

'Good,' said Tanner. 'Right, Stan, let's see what we can find.'

On the top of the wall and above the bastion, the moonlight shone brightly. Now fully accustomed to the light, Tanner found he could see quite well. Certainly, they had no difficulty in picking out the German dead, although he had found only a few spare magazines for his newly acquired sub-machine-gun. He did take a pistol, though. All the paratroopers, he noticed, seemed to carry these side arms, a small, nicely balanced semi-automatic, with an eight-round clip. Tanner much preferred it to the heavy, bulky Enfield revolver he had been issued on becoming a warrant officer. What was more, the Enfield could only be reloaded by placing each bullet into the six chambers, a fiddly task at the best of times, but especially so in the heat of battle when nerves and adrenalin made hands shaky. With the Sauer pistol he'd taken, he discovered he could grip the weapon and press the release button with the same hand. Out it fell, and all he had to do was shove another in place. He decided that so long as he could get his hands on enough ammunition – and the bullets were quite a bit smaller than those for his Enfield – his own revolver would be consigned to the bottom of his pack.

There was much about the German kit that he and Sykes found to admire. The cotton smock looked comfortable and had the kind of large pockets they wished they had more of on their own uniforms. Both men helped themselves to the long canvas gas-mask bags they carried. Having ditched the masks, they slung the bags over their shoulders and used them to store as many magazines as they could find. What took their attention more than any other piece of kit, however, were the paratroopers' boots. Tanner had long wished they might be issued with rubber, rather than studded leather-soled boots. The German boots were not only rubber-soled but side-laced and high enough to reach well over the ankles.

'These look about right.' Sykes whipped off one of his own and measured it against those of a paratrooper. 'Bloody beautiful,' he added, as he pulled them from the dead man. 'Will you look at that!' With the laces undone, the top of the boot opened to reveal not a separate tongue but one large piece of soft leather that folded back on itself once the laces were tied.

'Very nice, Stan,' said Tanner. 'What's the leather like?'

'Lovely an' supple. You're not going to have problems of stones in your boots with these on. Just need to get you a pair now, sir.'

Tanner walked among the dead and eventually found a man of similar height. Like Sykes, he measured his own boot against that of the dead German and was pleased to see the sizes compared.

He sprang up and down on his new boots, patted some of his new kit, then said, 'Good work that, Stan. I'll say one thing for Jerry – he does make bloody good clobber.'

He looked up and saw Captain Peploe approaching them from the bastion.

'Well done, you two,' he said, extending his hand to shake theirs in turn. 'The Cretans are over the moon, and so are Pendlebury and Vaughan. Hopefully, so too will be Brigade. We lost a few men but not as many as the Germans by the look of things. I see you've found yourselves a bit of extra kit.'

'It's damn good, their stuff,' said Tanner.

'You want to get yourself a pair of these boots, sir,' said Sykes. 'You can walk silent in these, I swear it.'

Peploe smiled. 'A good tip. I will.'

'So what happens now, sir?' asked Tanner. 'Have reinforcements been sent down to the sea?'

'Yes – A Company is going to stay here with us but the others have been directed there and it seems the Leicesters and Yorks and Lancs have sent a company each.'

'That's good, sir. A swift, strong counter-attack is the way to deal with these jokers. I tell you what, sir, today's given me heart. We can't possibly lose this island now.'

'What if there's a seaborne invasion as well?'

'With what? I thought Jerry only had U-boats.'

Peploe shrugged. 'Captured Greek ships?'

'What? Those wooden fishing-boats? You're joking, aren't you, sir? Against the Mediterranean Fleet? Those navy guns might not be much bloody good against Jerry bombers but they'd be perfect against any slow little transports. I know we lost a few ships coming back from Greece, but it wasn't that many, all things considered. If Jerry's stupid enough to try it, let him.'

'You're probably right, Jack,' said Peploe. 'I hadn't really thought of it like that.'

'So long as we keep these airfields, those para boys are done for. You can only carry so much into battle when you're thrown from an aeroplane. I bet they're already starving hungry.'

'I 'ope they are,' said Sykes. 'Serve 'em bloody right.'

'So, what now?' Tanner asked again. 'We're to stay here, are we?'

'For now, yes, we're to man the ramparts here. We're holding them between here and Bethlehem. A Company is going to hold the bastion. I'm not quite sure about the Greeks yet or what happens in the morning, which is why I'm going to head back to Battalion in a moment and see Old Man Vigar. But we need to be vigilant – just in case they try anything at first light.'

'Shouldn't we be attacking them at first light,

sir? We've got them on the run. We should be making the most of that. God knows, we might be able to wipe them out entirely.'

'Well, maybe. I'll suggest it to Vigar, but we don't know what's going on elsewhere and it's not only Jerry who's running low on ammo. We don't have that much ourselves.' He rubbed his eyes. 'I don't know about you two, but I feel dog-tired.' He gave Tanner an affectionate pat on the arm. 'Look, do me a favour. Organize watches, then try and get your heads down. Who knows what will happen tomorrow? But we're going to need our wits about us. We might have beaten them back tonight, but this battle isn't over yet.'

When he had gone, Tanner took out another cigarette. It was cooler now, and he was glad he had put on his battle blouse, which he now buttoned up. The firing had almost completely stopped – just a few shots to the south, and an occasional crack of small arms from away to the east; both sides had paused, it seemed, to lick their wounds. Men still moved around on the street below, but the town was quiet again.

But then he heard voices and both he and Sykes got up and looked down. There, clear in the moonlight, was the silver-haired *kapitan* with Alopex and half a dozen of their *andartes*. They watched them, standing there, checking weapons, until they disappeared under the archway of the gate.

'Where they off to in such a hurry?' said Sykes.

'To kill some Germans,' said Tanner. 'Which is exactly what we should be doing.'

187

Dawn had broken a short time after five. First a faint pink and grey strip in the east and then, slowly, an arc of deep orange had risen, just a sliver at first. Oberleutnant Balthasar had awoken, cacophonous birdsong sounding through the many trees and groves around them. Raising himself from his grassy bed on the edge of the river, he took out a water bottle, drank greedily, then went down to the river's edge and refilled it. The river was barely a trickle and no doubt the water had been filtered with all manner of dead animals and other bad things, but it was better to struggle with a stomach upset than to die of thirst.

He moved forward to check on the pickets. He found two of the men watching diligently from the safety of an olive grove, trees and the tall May grass providing good cover. Lying beside them, he drew out his binoculars. Up ahead were the houses and the walls – the walls that'd been briefly theirs. He and the men around him at the Canea Gate had been among the first back to the battalion command post. He had known Major Schulz had gone to try to link up with von der Schulenberg after their breakthrough; his own task had been to secure the west of the town. It'd been plaguing him that he had been the one to sound the retreat, but what else could he have done?

Schulz and von der Schulenberg had eventually reappeared with the remains of their storm troops some time after midnight. Balthasar had never seen Schulz so angry. It seemed that, with von der Schulenberg's men, they had reached the edge of the port. There, he had even taken the surrender of the town from a Greek major and the town's mayor and had raised the swastika from a flagpole at the western end of the harbour, but as they had been corralling the prisoners, they had come under attack again. The Tommies were refusing to honour the surrender. 'It is completely against the practices of war,' Schulz had fumed. He had been cheated of victory and, in the process of falling back out of the town, had lost far more men than they had when they stormed the walls. Anger was fuelled by bitter disappointment; that night, they had suffered their first defeat of the war.

He looked at the town. It seemed quiet enough.

'Have you had contact with the other pickets?' he asked.

'No, Herr Oberleutnant.'

'All right,' he said, moving into a crouching position. 'I'll send some men to relieve you shortly.' He moved along through the grove, pushed his way underneath two thick olive trees, and then recoiled. Before him, in a slight hollow in the ground, lying in the grass, were two of the pickets, side by side, their heads severed and placed on their chests. Pinned to the jump smock of one was a note, written in German: 'Ravening a blood drinker though you may be, yet will I glut your taste for blood.' Balthasar snatched the note, the paper stained with blood, then looked back towards the town. A fury he had not experienced before coursed through him, as he made his way to the command post. Quickly sending forward replacement pickets, he then found Unteroffizier Rohde and ordered him to organize a burial party. 'Wrap them in parachute silk,' he

189

snapped. 'The fewer men who see them the better.'

Schulz was up, squatting beside a radio, anxiously watching the operator as he tuned the receiver.

'Herr Major,' said Balthasar, 'two pickets were killed in the night.'

'*Scheisser*,' cursed Schulz. 'How? I did not hear any shooting.'

'They had their heads cut off.' He pulled out a cigarette, lit it, and inhaled deeply.

'My God,' said Schulz, his voice quiet.

'Here,' said Balthasar, passing him the bloodied note.

Schulz snatched it, his eyes scanning the words. 'What does it mean?'

'Revenge, Herr Major. I imagine it is a quotation of some kind.'

'Revenge?' snarled Schulz. 'Revenge? I will give those sons of bitches revenge!'

But there was little they could do that morning. A head count showed they had now lost more than seventy per cent of their force since the air landings had begun. Ammunition was low; so, too, was food. The survivors were exhausted – Balthasar could see it in the men's drawn faces. Morale, usually so high, had taken a beating. Every man among them had lost good friends, and that was hard to take. And there was the shock of defeat, too. Those who had fought in France or in Greece were used to lightning victories with minimal losses; those new to action had joined their ranks expecting those successes too. Now there was the grotesque murder of the two pickets. Schulz had tried to put a lid on it but, of course, word had quickly got round.

It was their inability to make contact with any of the other units that Balthasar found so frustrating. They knew that more men were due to be dropped that day around the airfield, and, they hoped, more supplies, but it was infuriating not to know what was happening, whether the men dropped around the airfield were making headway, whether the other drops at Rethymno and Canea had succeeded or failed. Despite repeated efforts on the radio set, no contact had been made with Oberst Bräuer and the rest of the men in Orion Sector, the designated codename for the Heraklion Drop Zone, nor had the runner sent the previous night reappeared. God only knew what had happened to him. A link had been established with Major Schirmer and his men from the 2nd Fallschirmjäger Regiment, who had now secured the Canea road, but Schirmer would only spare one company. The 3rd Battalion now had just 204 men left and nothing like enough ammunition to launch any kind of attack. They would have to stay where they were, digging in and watching out for any enemy counter-attack.

Just after seven, with the sun now risen, a radio signal from VIII Fliegerkorps was intercepted. From this they learned that the Luftwaffe would be carrying out a supply drop and bombing Heraklion some time after 8 a.m.

'Let's hope they come soon and find us,' said Balthasar, squinting up at the cloudless sky. 'It's going to be hot today.'

191

'Get a flag pinned out,' said Schulz, 'and have the green flares ready. We can't afford for those fly boys to miss us. Some supplies will give the men a much-needed lift.'

Balthasar took another glug from his water bottle. 'I know what will really lift morale,' he said. 'The chance to make those bastards pay.'

The daily hate arrived just after 9 a.m., Stukas first, circling and bombing the harbour area, and then around a dozen Junkers 88s. From their positions on the walls, Tanner watched through his binoculars. Some of the bombs landed in the sea, others on the town. The noise – the scream of the sirens, the whistle of the falling bombs, the explosions, the crash of stone and timber collapsing, and the pounding of the anti-aircraft guns – was deafeningly loud. Huge clouds of dust and smoke enveloped the harbour and then several houses were hit nearby, the ground thudding at the explosion. The dust and smoke that rolled up into the air soon drifted across to the walls, making the men there cough and choke.

And then they were gone, the smoke soon thinned and dispersed, and above them droned another wave of aircraft, this time transports.

'Here, look at this, sir,' said Tanner, passing his binoculars to Lieutenant Timmins.

'What am I looking at, CSM?' asked Timmins, a thin-faced twenty-three-year-old from Knaresborough, commander of 2 Platoon.

'The flare, sir, that Jerry's just fired.'

'What of it? I'm afraid I don't really catch your drift, Tanner.'

Tanner tried not to let his impatience show in his voice. 'Well, sir, first of all it's pinpointing exactly where those para boys are, and second, it's clearly a signal to the transports coming over to drop them supplies and maybe even reinforcements.'

'Yes, yes, I see what you mean.'

'So next time they come, if our lot to the south of the town start firing green flares, then maybe Jerry will drop us some supplies too.'

Timmins grinned. 'That would certainly get up Jerry's nose.'

'It would, sir.'

Most of the transports seemed to be to the east of the town and, once again, the chatter of small arms could be heard between the thunder of the ack-ack guns. Parachutes were blossoming behind him, but now several opened out ahead. Tanner took back his binoculars and peered through them again. *Canisters.* He counted half a dozen descending slowly to the ground, then disappearing from view behind the shallow ridge away to the west.

He had been studying the ground since first light, and already it felt familiar to him. The edge of the town spread only a short distance from the walls, then beyond were the seemingly endless olive and fruit groves and vineyards, interspersed with small grass meadows. Stretching away from the town was the main road to Rethymno and Canea, an unmetalled and dusty track that cut a creamy path through the endless green vegetation and rose up over the ridge, beyond which, he guessed, was the river he had seen the previous afternoon. Then maize fields, yet more olives and

193

finally the mountains. Just the far side of the ridge, but clearly visible above it, was a house, a farmstead of some kind, he supposed. It was from around there, just the other side of the ridge, that the flare had been fired. How far? Half a mile, maybe as much as a thousand yards. Just out of rifle range. And there would be the Germans' forward positions, with pickets sent to keep watch, just as he was watching them.

Tanner had been hoping for movement, but had seen little sign of life, apart from a brief moment when the sun had caught some glass and a blinding glint had twinkled from an olive grove. A paratrooper looking back at him, he guessed. At least now he had some definite markers. He knew the Cretans had been out scalp-hunting in the night, but his thoughts now were of patrolling at dusk, assuming the enemy did not try anything in the meantime. Certainly, there were few indicators to suggest they would: the morning hate had been no worse than normal, and the Aegean looked calm and untroubled, no sign of any German armada steaming over the horizon towards them.

Down below, burial parties were clearing away the dead from the previous evening, a grim task that was now the responsibility of B Company since they had been detailed to cover the Canea Gate and the bastion. It was a measure designed to ease the load on the Greek battalions, now back in position at either side of them. 'To buck them up a bit,' was apparently what Colonel Vigar had told Peploe. The rest of the battalion had returned to their positions astride the Knossos road. A cart of bodies was now rumbling through the gate itself and out to a pit that had been dug at the edge of town, a task overseen by Lieutenant Liddell. It was funny, Tanner reflected, how different things were now. When he was a child, the Liddells had been treated like royalty in their village. David Liddell had been a respected man, squire of the parish. Tanner had been taught not to speak to any of the Liddells unless spoken to; he'd not liked that even then, but it had been the way of things. It had existed for centuries, the huge chasm between land-owner and the families who worked for him.

The war was changing that. Second Lieutenant Liddell might be an officer and therefore still his superior, but the men knew that the CSM ran the company with the company commander. That was also the way of things. The men respected and looked up to him, he knew, something he had earned. The war was turning civilians into soldiers – men like Liddell and even Captain Peploe, who in peacetime would never have worn a uniform. And they were seeing that those from the lower classes were not necessarily another man's inferior. War was levelling the social divide. As Tanner was aware, his own natural authority and his proven abilities in battle had shown that a man like Guy Liddell was not his better any more.

Early afternoon, in a quiet street near the harbour. They were in a small Venetian townhouse, two storeys high, in a room on the first floor with white walls, crammed bookcases, a few old prints, a desk and a couple of tatty armchairs. To the side of the desk, French windows led out onto a small balcony, from which the twinkling blue of the old harbour could be glimpsed. By the door stood a hat-stand, over which was slung a Sam Browne belt, and an officer's peaked cap, and beneath it, what at first glance appeared to be an ivory-handled cane but was, in fact, a swordstick.

Behind the desk sat John Pendlebury, leaning back in his swivel chair, smoking a cigarette, while the two armchairs were occupied by Satanas and Alopex, the former also smoking, but a long cheroot rather than a cigarette. Alex Vaughan was leaning against the French windows' frame. A knock on the door, and in came Corporal Tasker-Brown, bearing a tray of small glasses and a bottle of raki. Pendlebury leaned forward to clear a space for the tray, rolling his glass eye in the process but neatly catching it as it tipped off the edge of the desk.

'Damn eye,' he said.

'The patch is better,' said Alopex. 'It makes you look more fierce.' He chuckled.

'I wonder whether the Huns have worked out their little message yet,' said Pendlebury, as he poured the raki.

'What's this?' said Vaughan.

Pendlebury glanced across at Satanas and Alopex, with a smirk. 'I wrote our friends a line from Herodotus,' he said. '"Ravening a blood drinker though you may be, yet will I glut your taste for blood."' He raised his glass. 'Your good health, gentlemen.'

'And then we caught two of their sentries,' grinned Alopex, 'killed them, cut off their heads

196

and left that note pinned to one of them.'

Satanas and Alopex chuckled.

'For God's sake,' snapped Vaughan. 'You're as bad as them. Behaving like savages.'

'They were already dead,' said Pendlebury. 'We're trying to sow a sense of discord, of fear, among them.'

'And the point of the Herodotus?'

'It was said by Queen Tamaris when she cut off the head of King Cyrus. Cyrus and the Persians invaded her kingdom of the Massagetae. She captured him, executed him and returned his head in a sack.'

'Invade our country and pay the price.'

'Exactly. I think it sent a very clear message.' Pendlebury pushed back his chair and ran his hands through his hair. 'The maddening thing, though, is that we should be annihilating that mob out there. Tonight we should be finishing them off. Damn it all, we've got way more men than they have. We could storm their positions and be done with 'em. I'm no soldier, but I know my history, and that tells me one should always exploit success. "Don't leave today what might cause rivers of blood tomorrow."'

'Our *andartes* are ready and waiting in the mountains,' said Satanas. 'We give them the word and they'll attack.'

Alopex stroked his moustache. 'Then we would attack them from behind. The British could stay here, sitting on their arses. It would be our victory. A Cretan victory. Word would quickly spread. It would unite our people against the Nazi invader.'

Pendlebury leaned forward, thinking, his fingers

drumming on the desk. Then he stood up. 'Damn it – you know what? We should break out of here now. Go and tell the *andartes* to attack. If we'd been given radio sets like I asked then we could signal Hanford and Bruce-Mitford, but since we haven't then I see no other way.'

'Don't be mad, John,' said Vaughan. 'If you must go, wait until dark.'

'No. It'll be too late then. We need to get them moving now, this afternoon, so that they can attack at dusk. Satanas and Alopex can head back to Sarhos and Krousonas, and I'll break through to Gazi.'

'But the Germans are to the west of the town,' said Vaughan. 'You'll never get through.'

'I don't see why not,' said Pendlebury, lighting another cigarette. 'We drove to see Brigadier Chappel this morning and there are supposedly German paratroopers swarming around between here and there too. We never saw a single one and we were making no effort to hide.'

'They probably moved in the night.'

'Listen, Alex, I've been trying to work out how many paratroopers we have to the west of here, and I reckon at the absolute most – and it's probably even a lot less than this – there cannot be more than three hundred. Three hundred, spread out along the reverse slopes of that ridge, is not very many. Are you really going to tell me I can't sneak through with all that lovely natural cover? Course I can.'

'If they see you, they'll kill you. After what you did last night, I don't suppose they'll be in a very forgiving mood towards any of us,' said Vaughan.

'They won't. I know these folds like the back of my hand. I can get through them, I know I can.'

'This is madness, utter madness. It's not a game. And you are no soldier. You're a brilliant inspiration and a wonderful organizer, but you've barely done any fighting in your life. Let the army boys do their job, John.'

'But they're not, are they? You heard Brigadier Chappel this morning. A fine fellow, I have no doubt, but he wouldn't even consider ordering a counter-attack. He just wants to sit and wait. Well, that's no good. We need to strike now. I know I'm right.' He looked at Satanas and Alopex for approval. Satanas tilted his head. *I think you are right.* 'We'll leave through the Canea Gate, head straight down the road and then split up. You two can go south, and I'll break through to the west.'

'John, don't. It's a needless risk.'

'Battles aren't won without taking risks, Alex.'

'Battles aren't won taking needless, stupid risks.'

Pendlebury walked over to Vaughan and clasped him by the arms. 'Alex. We need to do this. My mind is made up.'

10

It was a hot day. So hot, in fact, that the men manning the walls had begun taking off their tin helmets; the steel had become too hot to touch, let alone wear. Better to risk an exposed head than fry one's brain. A sickly stench had also begun to waft across the walls. Second Lieutenant Guy Liddell knew the smell – it reminded him of one summer when a rotting deer had reeked for days from its death-bed in the woods, a cloying, nauseous stench that seemed to get into one's hair and clothes. Except, of course, that the smell was no deer, but men who just a day earlier had been living and breathing but who were now dead and, it seemed, abandoned, missed by the burial parties, their bloating corpses left to bake and rot in the May sun.

It could have been me, thought Liddell, as he looked out from the walls towards the endless lush groves, fields and trees, bursting with life and framed by the mountains beyond. A vision of beauty, but to Liddell this place was hell. Home-sickness welled within him, his sense of entrapment overwhelming. He was hungry and thirsty, yet that smell made him feel sick, so that the last thing he wanted was food. Images from the fighting the previous night kept filling his mind: limbless men, the sound of bullets whistling over his head, the fear he had felt. Christ, he had even pissed himself – the only consolation had been that, at night, no one had noticed. He had poured water over his crotch and by dawn his shorts had dried, but the thought that he was still walking around in clothes soiled by dried urine disgusted him.

Liddell swallowed hard.

'Are you all right, sir?' Sykes asked.

'Yes, yes, fine, thank you, Sergeant.' *I need some shade.* 'But I'm just going to go down to the, um, street. To get some ... water. You carry on, Sergeant.'

Sykes smiled and nodded, and Liddell hurried away, across the gate and into the bastion, its dark coolness instantly refreshing. Back out on the street, he stepped around the corner from the bastion entrance and out under the great arch of the gate. Protected by its shade, he paused, drank from his water bottle, then quickly filled and lit his pipe, the sweet aroma of the tobacco going some way to hide the stench of death. He thought about Tanner who, like Sykes, was now swaggering about in German boots, with a German Schmeisser slung across his back, as though he were some kind of ancient warrior parading his battle prizes. He realized now that he had been wrong to stop him plundering those men the previous afternoon, but it was humiliating to see the pair flaunting their new-found possessions, as though they were deliberately trying to rub his nose in it.

Liddell closed his eyes, leaned back against the stonework, and breathed in the delicious smell of tobacco. He still planned to confront Tanner, but so far there had not been the opportunity, not with the battle the previous night, and this morning he had only ever seen him from afar. On the two occasions he had made towards him, Tanner had somehow disappeared by the time he had got there.

But now there Tanner was, walking towards him from beyond the gate. Liddell's heart quickened. It was strange: he had been thinking about it and now the perfect opportunity had presented itself.

Tanner saluted lazily as he reached the edge of the archway.

'I was just getting a moment's shade,' said Liddell, then hastily added, 'And where have you been?'

'Just to get a look at the lie of the land, sir.' Tanner, too, had taken off his helmet. Beads of sweat pricked his brow, and dark patches stained his shirt. He began to walk on past, but Liddell stopped him.

'There's something I want to say to you.'

Tanner faced him, but at that moment, there was the sound of a vehicle approaching from the town, something so rare on the island that they both immediately turned before Liddell could say any more. They heard the grinding of gears, a burst on the throttle and Pendlebury's pick-up turned the corner. Tanner stepped to one side, but the truck halted beside him.

'Afternoon, Tanner,' said Pendlebury.

'Off somewhere nice, sir?' Tanner glanced across at Satanas and Alopex in the front beside him. Sitting in the back were four *andartes*. Pendlebury was wearing Cretan dress. 'I hope you're not intending to drive too far in this, sir. Lots of Jerries up ahead.'

'We're heading to the mountains,' said Pendlebury. 'I'm afraid I can't persuade the good brigadier to counter-attack from here.'

'So, you're planning to do it yourself?'

'In a nutshell, yes.'

'One fight last night was enough for you boys, eh?' chuckled Alopex.

'No, no,' said Tanner, his voice calm. 'I'm with

202

you. A counter-attack is what we should be doing. Dusk or dawn is the best time, though, I reckon.'

Liddell moved beside him. 'Can we help you, sir?' he said.

'Just what are you proposing to do, sir?' cut in Tanner.

'Trying to get away before I'm arrested again,' said Alopex. He began to laugh.

Pendlebury turned off the ignition. 'Satanas and Alopex are going to take the car, head south and up to Krousonas, and I'm going to jump out shortly and cut through to the west.'

'But the Germans are all up ahead, sir. With respect, it's madness to try and cross their positions.'

'Tanner,' snapped Liddell, 'remember who you're talking to.'

Pendlebury raised a hand. 'It's all right, Lieutenant.' He turned to Tanner. 'I'll be quite all right. I know how to slip through. It's a question of time, Tanner, and we haven't got much of it.'

Tanner looked at Alopex and Satanas, who stared back at him, dark eyes unblinking. 'Sir,' said Tanner. 'This is madness. Please, if you must go, do so with Satanas and Alopex. There are few Jerries to the south. You'll have a chance that way.'

'No time,' smiled Pendlebury. 'We need to attack tonight, while the Huns are still off balance.'

A thought now occurred to Liddell – one that could win him respect and show his authority. 'Maybe you could take some men and escort him, CSM,' he suggested.

'Maybe you could,' agreed Alopex.

'And then we all get killed instead of just Captain Pendlebury?'

'Of course, if you're scared...' said Alopex.

Tanner glared at him, but Pendlebury cut in, 'I don't need an escort. I'll be able to slip through on my own. Don't forget, I know this place a lot better than they do.'

'Excuse me a moment, sir,' said Liddell. 'Let me have a quick word with Tanner.'

'We need to get going, Lieutenant.'

'Just a brief moment, sir.' Moving away from the car, he now spoke to Tanner in a low voice: 'You were all for going out on a patrol yesterday.'

'The situation was completely different,' said Tanner, exasperation in his voice. 'They'd just landed then, and we could easily work in around the back of them. Patrolling forward when they have outposts trained on us is a completely different matter. And look at him – he's a bloody archaeologist, not a soldier. Christ, he's only got one eye, and he's expecting to hoodwink all those para boys, some of the best-trained troops in the whole Jerry army.'

Liddell thought a moment, then said, 'Look, I think you should know something. I've deliberately kept quiet about your past, but I do know what happened.' He eyed Tanner and immediately saw the flicker of alarm in the CSM's eyes.

'What's that got to do with this?' Tanner snapped.

'I've suggested we escort Captain Pendlebury. I don't want you showing me up.'

Tanner stared at him.

'Is that clear?'

Tanner glared at him a moment longer, then turned back to the car. 'Sir, give me five minutes, and I'll get some men together. We'll come with you. Lieutenant Liddell is right. We can create a diversion.'

Pendlebury glanced at Satanas and Alopex.

'It is a good idea,' said Alopex. 'You should accept the offer.'

Pendlebury stepped out of the car. 'Very well,' he said. 'And thank you.'

As they hurried back from the arch, Tanner clenched his fists, an intense anger welling within him. Rarely had he so wanted to knock a man cold as he did Mr Liddell right now. Perhaps the man was bluffing, but that was hardly the point. He was being blackmailed, and that was unforgivable. And it was crazy to be heading out like this, however much he sympathized with Pendlebury's reasons. *Bloody hell.* And who was he going to take? It felt like a suicide mission, yet he knew there was something in Liddell's suggestion. He reckoned Captain Pendlebury had virtually no chance of getting through on his own, but by creating a diversion, those odds might lengthen a fraction. Would it be worth it? Christ only knew.

'Sergeant!' Tanner called, once they were through the arch. 'Sergeant Sykes!'

Sykes appeared. 'Yes, sir?'

'Organize five volunteers and get them down here, iggery!'

'Volunteers? I don't like the sound of that.'

'Just do it, Sergeant,' barked Tanner.

At the noise, Captain Peploe emerged from the

bastion. 'What's going on?' he said, striding briskly towards Tanner and Liddell.

Liddell cleared his throat. 'Captain Pendlebury is attempting to break through enemy lines, sir, so I suggested Tanner take a patrol with him to try and cause a diversion.'

'You did what?' said Peploe, incredulous. 'But it's broad daylight. What the hell is he thinking of? What were *you* thinking of, Mr Liddell?'

'His mind is made up, sir. It's the only way he has any chance at all of getting through.'

'Where is he?' said Peploe. 'He's not taking my men.'

'Sir,' said Tanner. 'Mr Liddell is right. We won't dissuade him. I know it's foolhardy but he hasn't a chance without us. Perhaps if we get close to the Jerry lines and create a diversion, it might distract the enemy while Captain Pendlebury slips through.'

'Well, I damn well hope you're intending to go too, Lieutenant,' snapped Peploe.

Liddell looked taken aback. 'The CSM has volunteered to lead it, sir.'

'But it was your idea.' Tanner could see that Peploe was livid. 'You lead by example, Lieutenant. You can't send good men out on a patrol like this and not go too.'

Liddell's eyes darted from the captain to Tanner. Then he took a deep breath. 'Yes, sir,' he said. 'Of course, sir.'

Sykes now appeared from the bastion with McAllister, Bell, Atkins and Hill, all men from 1 Section. 'Your volunteers, sir,' he said.

'Well, you can bugger off, Sergeant,' said Tanner.

206

'I only need four men now.'

'But I'd like to come, if it's all the same to you.'

He glanced at Peploe, who nodded.

'Jesus,' muttered Tanner. He sent Hill back onto the walls, then briefly explained their mission. 'Now, I had a bit of a recce earlier,' he added, 'and I think there may be a way through, a little further to the south. There's a house on the main road that I'm pretty sure is their CP, but we've got to get past their pickets first and then get Captain Pendlebury over the river, where I'm pretty sure most of them are lying up. Getting over the river's going to be the tricky bit, but there's a lot of those maize fields and, as we now know, the crop's tall enough to crawl through. Before that there are groves and vineyards and broken ground. If we use it well, with a bit of luck we'll be all right.' He paused, patted his webbing, then said, 'You all got enough ammo?' They nodded. 'Good. Leave helmets behind, and anything that might chink or make a noise.'

While the men were sorting out their gear, Peploe took Tanner aside. 'I'm sorry, Jack. This is a bloody awful mission.'

'It'll be all right, sir.'

Peploe glanced at Liddell, shook his head, then led Tanner back to the truck waiting in the shade of the arch of the Canea Gate.

'Do you really need to do this, Pendlebury?' he asked.

'Yes, I'm rather afraid I do,' Pendlebury replied. 'It would have been better if Brigade made a big push tonight, but unfortunately the brigadier was having none of it.' He smiled. 'But when it's all over, I'll stand by my promise, Peploe. I'll show you round as many of the sites as you care to see. And they're stunning. You won't be disappointed.'

'Thank you.'

'It's worth fighting for, this island – for its people, for its beauty and for its antiquity. The thought of the Nazis crawling all over Knossos or Karfi is repellent. We can't let them get their grubby little hands on them.' He adjusted his eye-patch. 'All those years I spent digging up the past, studying and learning about the lives of those ancient warriors and now I've become a warrior myself.' He chuckled. 'I never thought I had it in me. To be honest, it's all been rather instructive. I think I understand them better now.'

Pendlebury agreed to leave Satanas and Alopex at the gate, and let them continue on their own. Tanner watched the two Cretan *kapitans* embrace their English friend with an affection that was clearly heartfelt.

'And you,' said Alopex, pointing a finger at Tanner's chest. 'Don't get yourself killed. That is my honour, OK?'

Tanner had a mind to knock him down there and then; he was not in a good mood. Instead, he snarled, 'One more jibe out of you, and I'll not wait for this to be over. I'll take this bunduck here and shove it up your bastard Cretan arse.'

Alopex made to take a swing, but it was Satanas who pulled him back. They spoke quickly and angrily, then got into the pick-up and drove off.

'And you like these people, sir?' Tanner said to Pendlebury, as they watched the car head away, a cloud of dust following in its wake.

'I do, yes.' He laughed. 'They're kind, fun-loving people, fiercely loyal, but proud. You have to understand, Tanner, that there is a strict hierarchy system in Crete. It's quite feudal, really. Each village or town has its one family with the chief, the *kapitan*. Other families must accept that heredity. Satanas is the *kapitan* of Krousonas, Alopex of Sarhos. Krousonas is a larger, more important place than Sarhos and that is reflected in Satanas's status. These men expect respect and loyalty – it is a code they have grown up with since birth. If they are insulted they have an obligation to see that slight avenged. You insulted Alopex, so he *has* to avenge it. What would his men think of him if he did not? His honour would be slighted again. And I'm afraid that means a blood feud.'

'But he insulted me first. I wasn't looking to pick a fight.'

'That's irrelevant to him. This is his country and he is a *kapitan*. He feels he can say anything to you. Clearly, he chose the wrong man to insult, because now you both find yourselves in a situation where neither of you can back down. Don't get me wrong, I understand it from your point of view. In some ways you're like a *kapitan* in your company – you don't want to lose any face in front of your men.'

'A man's pride can get him into trouble, sir, but respect is important. Respect and honour. These are things I've also been taught to value. I'll fight him if I have to, but I'm not backing down. I'm damned if I'll ever apologize to him.'

'Then maybe you two are more alike than you know. But I suspect he already does respect you.'

'He did fight well last night, I'll give him that.'

'And it sounds as though you have a grudging respect for him too.'

Tanner grinned. 'We should concentrate on the job in hand now, sir, don't you think?'

'Quite so, CSM, quite so.'

They had been weaving through the narrow alleys of the town beyond the walls but were now approaching the town's edge. The stench from the bodies lying in what had become no man's land was now even stronger. The heat had seen to that. Somewhere to the south, shots rang out.

'They've been spotted,' said Pendlebury. He looked worried for a moment, then said, 'Oh, I'm sure they'll get through.' There were a few more shots, but a small cloud of dust could be seen rising just above the greenery and it appeared to be still moving southwards. Tanner, too, felt sure they had got through and, not for the first time, wished Pendlebury had gone with them. It was amazing how obtuse really clever people could be.

They paused by a low, flat-roofed building, where open country spread away from them on the far side. The sun was still high. Sweat covered their faces, and flies buzzed in front of them. On the wall above a scrawny grey cat looked down and mewed.

As they crouched in a group, Liddell said, 'I think we should all move out there together.'

'No, sir,' said Tanner, 'Captain Pendlebury should move alone on our left, away from where most of the Jerries are.' He turned to Pendlebury. 'If that's all right with you, sir? About fifty or sixty yards. Close enough so we can see you.'

'Yes, I think you're right,' said Pendlebury.

'And we don't cause a diversion unless we have to.' Tanner took out his sword bayonet and drew a rough map in the dirt. 'Here's their CP,' he said, making an X beside a line that was the main road. 'And here's the river. Three hundred yards or so to the south-west, it meanders back on itself. We'll cover his flank here, where the bend in the river juts out, so that he can cross it further back. There's a little cliff in the river on the bend and maize fields the other side, so as long as there aren't lots of Jerry there, you should be all right, sir.'

'Bravo, Tanner,' said Pendlebury. 'Sounds like a good plan to me.'

'And we get to the river by heading south a little way now, keeping the wreck of that Jerry transport between us and the enemy. There's plenty of vegetation and folds in the ground, so we should be able to stay out of sight.'

'Formation, sir?' asked Sykes.

'We'll move in pairs. Two up front, two out to the right, and two to the left, who will keep in visual touch with Captain Pendlebury. The idea is that we avoid opening fire until the captain is well across the river. Sir,' said Tanner, turning to Pendlebury, 'you should move in line with us. If we halt, you should too.'

'All right,' said Pendlebury. 'But once I get across the river I'm on my own.'

'Yes, sir. Once you're across we'll cause our diversion, if need be, and draw attention away from you.' Tanner glanced at Liddell and realized the lieutenant had nothing more than a pistol. 'I don't think you'll get very far with that, sir, if the shooting does start,' he said, then unslung his rifle and gave it to him. 'Here, you'd better take this.'

Liddell accepted it. 'And if we run into their pickets?'

'Let's hope they're taking a siesta.'

Tanner wiped his brow. By God, it was hot. He had kept his haversack on his hip along with his bayonet, water bottle, pistol and magazine pouches, and now worried he had kept too much. It creaked as he stood up. The others moved noisily too, rifle straps clicking, army boots loud on the ground. But they needed this clobber – he couldn't expect men to head out to within spitting distance of the enemy without the means to defend themselves. He looked around. Birds still chirped, a dog barked and somewhere not far away a cock was crowing too. Background noise that would help mask their approach.

'Come on,' he said, 'let's go.'

They passed the wrecked Junkers and moved around a small craggy outcrop and down into a sloping grove of dense olives. At the bottom there was a grassy track and a field, but immediately in front lay another small rise in the ground that hid their approach. Working around it they reached a vineyard and, crouching among the leaves, were able to move forward with comparative ease so that Tanner began to feel more confident about

212

their chances of reaching the river undetected. The main difficulty was navigating the correct route without raising his head to orient himself, although he could still see the mountains and had already marked a bead along which he hoped he would keep the right course. And he had his compass. The headland overlooking the river had been at about 240 degrees and, pausing now, he took a bearing. The pointers flickered, then settled. *Good.* Glancing around him, he saw Sykes and Atkins on his right, McAllister and Bell a short way back. Sykes raised his thumb, then wiped the back of his hand theatrically across his forehead. But no sight of Pendlebury. He was too far off, but it was reassuring that at fifty yards he could not be seen – or heard, for that matter. Then he turned to Liddell.

'Come on, keep going,' whispered the lieutenant, from behind him.

Another olive grove, and now Tanner saw Pendlebury to his left. The sweet smell of soil and herbs had been replaced by a familiar sickly odour. Tanner paused, sniffing to determine where it was coming from, but it was hard to pinpoint. He moved on cautiously through the long grass, but then a group of crows fluttered noisily in front of him, making him start.

'Oh, my God!' exclaimed Liddell.

'Ssh!' Tanner signalled to Sykes and McAllister to halt. *Damn.* It was precisely what he had hoped to avoid. Any picket would know those birds had been disturbed and very probably by men. Sure enough, a moment later, several shots zipped nearby. Tanner pressed his head into the ground, breathing in the soil, a pleasant relief from the stench of death. Another bullet. *How far away?* No more than a hundred yards, he reckoned, maybe less. So they were there, all right. Dust had stuck to his face and hands, but he now inched forward again and saw at last the source of the smell. A few yards away lay a dead paratrooper, his chest bright where the crows had been feeding. Tanner saw that his eyes had been plucked clear, his cheeks pecked. He had seen human beings torn and shredded many times before, but his stomach tightened and filled with nauseous bile.

'Oh, Christ,' said Liddell, behind him, and retched.

Be quiet, damn you! thought Tanner. 'Close your eyes and keep moving,' he whispered.

It was German voices that alerted him some ten minutes later. Through the grove he could see the river now, away to his left, and the planned crossing point for Pendlebury, but some thirty yards ahead and slightly to their right were what he supposed must be the German pickets. Behind him, he could hear Liddell breathing erratically, and he now cursed Captain Peploe for insisting the lieutenant should come with them.

Halting the others, he glanced across to Sykes, who pointed up ahead, then held up three fingers. Tanner nodded, then turned to Liddell. 'Stay here,' he mouthed, then began inching forward. The land rose gently in front of him, the olives thick, their branches of silvery and dark green leaves almost touching the ground. Carefully, slowly, he moved through the long grass beneath

214

the olives, cringing inwardly each time a part of his webbing or kit made a noise. He could hear their voices clearly, a short way to his right, so he moved forward again.

'*Was war das für ein Geräusch?*' he now heard one say. He froze. The man's tone had been alert, and he had caught '*was war*' – *what was*.

Silence for a few moments, while the men listened. Tanner felt his chest pound and his breathing seemed hopelessly loud and heavy as he lay there. A blade of grass was tickling his nose and he suddenly had an urge to sneeze. Carefully bringing his hand to his face, he pressed a finger hard against his top lip just in time.

'*Nichts,*' said another, in a reassuring, more relaxed voice. '*Ich habe nichts gehört.*'

Tanner breathed out with relief then inched forward again until he had moved beyond and behind the pickets. Creeping to his left, he parted the grass and saw the Germans just ten yards away, their backs to him, lying beneath the olives, looking down the shallow slope. Theirs was a good position, he now saw, for the olives thinned to the side of them and then beyond, stretching back towards the town to the south, the groves were noticeably younger, sparser, and offering a much clearer field of fire. *Thank God*, thought Tanner. It was only to their right that the endless groves and vines were so much thicker. He had chosen their approach route well.

Where were the other pickets? The ground rose again slightly to their left – not much, but enough. He guessed they were positioned for interlocking fire, but that did not mean they needed to be in

215

visual contact. Tanner thought for a moment. The men were equipped with rifles. To kill him they would have to swing those round and fire. If he could travel half the distance without them noticing, he reckoned he would have them. They were, he saw, lying together, side by side. As ever, surprise would be everything.

Slowly, he felt in his pockets for his clasp knife and German knife, desperately trying not to make a noise, then withdrew into the grass and began carefully lifting himself into a crouch. Suddenly he heard a match strike and knew that the moment had come. Leaping forward, he bounded through grass, olive branches snapping back at him as he moved. One of the men started – a grunt of alarm – but they had barely moved by the time Tanner leaped onto their backs, and with one hand plunged his German knife down through the right-hand man's shoulder into his subclavian artery, and flailed wildly with his clasp knife at the left-hand man, who gasped, dropped his rifle and clutched his wounded arm. A split second later, Tanner plunged the German knife again, this time down into the middle man's shoulder, before making a third plunge into the left-hand man's heart. Three seconds, three men. All dead.

But it had not been an entirely silent killing, and he could hear voices now, calling out. *'Was ist los?'* said someone, Tanner guessed perhaps thirty yards away.

'Nichts,' he called back. *'Alles ist gut.'* Then, breathing heavily, he moved back out of sight, the branches and long grass closing around him.

A shot rang out, not from the enemy but from

one of his own men. 'Damn it!' he cursed. In moments, a volley of rifle fire replied, and now there were shouts from beyond, from the direction of the river. More shots, both rifle and sub-machine-gun fire.

'Jesus!' muttered Tanner, now crouch-running through the olives. Through a gap in the trees he saw the river, then Pendlebury dashing through the water and running into a vineyard beyond. *No, no, no!*

'Fall back! Fall back!' he now heard Liddell call out. A new and violent rage overtook Tanner. Bullets were snipping through the olives as he slid down beside the lieutenant.

'What the bloody hell do you think you're playing at?' he spat at Liddell.

'We've got to fall back,' stammered Liddell. 'We can't hold on here!'

'Don't fall back!' Tanner called. 'Let 'em have it!'

'Fall back!' Liddell shouted again. 'That's an order!'

More bullets were scything through the branches. Tanner glanced at Liddell. Then, clenching his fist, he drove it into the lieutenant's temple. Liddell looked at him wide-eyed, then collapsed unconscious on the ground.

'Liddell down!' called Tanner, and took back his rifle. 'Is everyone OK? Keep firing! Just keep bloody firing!

'Damn it!' he cursed again. Then he took out two grenades, pulled the pin on one, hurled it in the direction of the second lot of pickets, and crouch-ran towards the edge of the bend in the river. From the cover of the grove, Bell and McAllister were firing furiously at the men moving forward from the south along the river. Tanner pulled the pin of his other grenade, briefly stood and hurled the bomb across the river. Someone cried out as it exploded, but then Bell said, 'Look, sir! There's the captain!'

Tanner saw him in the same instant. He was running through a vineyard, but paratroopers were moving in from his right, firing their Schmeissers and rifles. They watched him fall, and Tanner brought his rifle to his shoulder and fired. Frantically pulling back the bolt, he fired again, and then again, and again, ten rounds in rapid succession. He saw several men fall while, near him, McAllister and Bell were also firing. As he fumbled in his pack for more clips, he saw Pendlebury get to his feet again, his revolver in his hand. The captain fired, loosing off his entire chamber. Three men fell but as Pendlebury tried to fire, his chamber now empty, a bullet struck him in the chest. He staggered and fell backwards.

Tanner pressed the catch on his magazine, pulled it out and reloaded with two more clips. Men hurried towards Pendlebury and Tanner fired again. He saw another man fall. The paratroopers around Pendlebury dived to the ground, and Tanner angrily drove his fist into the earth.

But now Sykes was calling, 'Atkins is down!' Enemy fire was coming from the south, towards them.

'How bad?' Tanner called back.

'He's dead, sir.'

'Leave him and fall back!'

He hurried back to Liddell. 'Bugger it!' he muttered. For a moment he considered leaving the lieutenant where he was – Christ, he'd be doing everyone a favour – but then he thought of Liddell's father and the good deed that man had done him. 'Damn and blast you, Liddell,' he said, then slapped him hard around the face.

'Sir, sir!' he hissed. 'We've got to move.' Bullets continued to ping through the branches around them as the lieutenant stirred. 'What happened?' mumbled Liddell.

'Sir, get up!' Tanner hoisted him by the shoulders and slapped him again.

'Argh, my head!' groaned Liddell.

'Sir, it'll be more than your head if you don't get a move on. Now, on your feet!' A bullet zinged just inches from them, and Tanner felt for his last grenade, pulled the pin, and threw the bomb hard in the direction of the enemy fire. Liddell was now on his feet once more, crouching unsteadily.

'*Sir!*' said Tanner. 'Let's go!'

Liddell looked at him with glazed eyes but at last seemed to comprehend, and they hurried through the grove, the lieutenant veering wildly at first but quickly regaining his balance. Bullets continued to fly and Tanner cried out as a searing heat scorched his side. Grimacing with pain, he continued to run, aware that as they fled, they had the folds in the ground, the dense vegetation and their own speed to help them. If they were hit, Tanner convinced himself, it would be a lucky shot on the part of the Germans.

But, by God, he hurt. His side, his lungs – his

mouth was dry as chalk. His heart pounded. Branches had whiplashed his face and arms, and he could feel the salt of his sweat stinging the scratches across his body. A machine-gun now opened up, its rapid fire cutting a swathe behind them. *Christ* – in moments it would have its range. Up ahead was the wrecked transport, and around it charred, blackened olive trees. Men were moving through the unscathed trees, the branches shaking as another drill of MG fire rang out. Had anyone other than Atkins been hit? Tanner could not tell.

He caught up with Liddell, grabbed him by the collar and yanked him hard away from the direction of the plane. 'This way,' he growled. Another burst of fire, this time to the left. Bullets tore across the corrugated-metal fuselage with a loud clatter. On they ran, moving in a wider arc. Tanner winced again, shoved Liddell forward, then vigorously shook the nearest tree and ran. Another burst of MG fire, bullets tearing into the wood and branches around them, but now they were behind the aircraft. Reaching safety at last, Tanner doubled up, hands on his knees, gasping and grimacing.

'Sir, you've been hit,' said McAllister.

Tanner looked up, his bloodied face glistening with sweat, and glared at Liddell. 'Yes, but I'm alive, and Captain Pendlebury is not.'

Tanner was wrong. Pendlebury was alive. Oberleutnant Balthasar, whose men held the southern part of the ridge to the west of the town, had been incensed that enemy troops had infiltrated

220

so far, but then, when a one-eyed English captain wearing Cretan dress had been brought before him, his mood had changed.

Balthasar had ordered that the man be taken to a farmhouse at the edge of the maize fields and there had told the elderly owners to give him a bed. He had detailed Gefteiter Reibert, one of only two medics to survive the jump, to treat the wound.

Half an hour later, Balthasar stood in the doorway of the bedroom watching Reibert tend him. The Englishman's head lolled and he groaned. Reibert had ripped open his shirt, which lay crumpled by his side. A bullet had gone through his lower left lung and had exited his back. The man was pale, waxen, his brow feverish.

'Well?' said Balthasar, walking over and standing beside his prisoner. He saw the identity tags around his neck and pulled them off. A number and a name: *Pendlebury, J.*

'He has lost a lot of blood, Herr Oberleutnant,' Reibert replied, 'and I am no surgeon.'

'You're a medic, though, Reibert. Make sure he lives. Is there anything you need?'

'No – no, I have everything.' He took out a syringe and a phial of morphine, tapped the end of the needle, then injected the wounded man. Balthasar looked around him. It was a simple, one-storey cottage, whitewashed stone walls, stone floor and rustic furniture.

'Actually, Herr Oberleutnant, perhaps some warm water...'

Balthasar turned to the Cretan couple, watching anxiously from the kitchen. 'Neró,' he demanded. *'Neró zestó!'*

The old man muttered something to his wife, then put a few more twigs on the fire. As he did so, the woman filled a blackened earthenware pot from a ewer of water and hung it above the fire. Balthasar nodded his thanks. *These people.* They were peasants, stuck in a different age.

When the water had warmed, Reibert carried it through, took off the already bloodied bandages, bathed the wound, cleaned it, stitched the bullet hole on both sides, then applied more bandages.

'If you don't mind me asking, Herr Oberleutnant,' said Reibert, 'why is it so important to keep this man alive?'

Balthasar smiled. 'Because, Reibert, he was breaking out of Heraklion. We know he's British – he was muttering in English and, of course, he looks no more Greek than you or I. In any case, I recognize him. He was fighting in Heraklion last night, waving a swordstick, leading a mixed group of Greek, British and Cretan bandits. And, as you can see, he is wearing Cretan costume. Why? Because he was on his way to meet the Cretan bandits in the mountains behind us.'

'Is he an enemy agent, then?' asked Reibert.

'Of some sort, yes. With lots of important intelligence for us, which he is going to tell us when he is conscious again. When will that be?'

Reibert shrugged. 'The morphine will wear off in an hour or so, but he is weak. And it is dependent on him not getting an infection.'

Balthasar thought a moment. The problem was time. They still had no real idea how many enemy troops were in and around Heraklion, or what

supplies they had. Were he the British commander, he would attack that night – but he knew the
Tommies tended to be cautious. On the other
hand, there had been nothing cautious about this
man's break-out. It suggested there was some
urgency, that perhaps they were planning a combined attack that night.

He needed to confer with Schulz – he had not
seen the major since the Englishman's capture.
Perhaps Schulz had news too, from Oberst Bräuer
and the men dropped around the airfield. It had
been quiet from over there since the morning drop
– occasional small-arms fire, but that had been
about it. Clearly, there had been neither an attack
nor a counter-attack. Balthasar banged a fist
against the doorway. They were largely cut off, isolated and almost entirely starved of information.
That was why it was so important to get this man
to talk.

11

No one had said a word as the remaining five
Rangers made their way back to the town. Only
when they had passed through the Canea Gate
and on beneath the walls to the bastion did Tanner turn to the others. 'Get a drink and some
tiffin, and clean your weapons,' he snapped.

'Shouldn't you get your wound seen to, sir?'
suggested Sykes.

'No, I bloody shouldn't. Now get going – all of

you.' He leaned against the wall and took a long draught from his water bottle. He gasped and then grimaced with pain.

'I'm going to have you court-martialled, Tanner,' hissed Liddell.

'Oh, really?'

'You directly disobeyed my orders and then – I still cannot believe you did this – you had the nerve to knock me unconscious. Striking an officer, Tanner, that's very bad. Very bad indeed.'

'What are you talking about?' said Tanner. 'I saved your life. I could have left you there. Left you for Jerry. If you hadn't stopped yapping you'd have got us all killed, rather than just Atkins and Captain Pendlebury.'

Liddell's face reddened. Tanner saw the jaw muscles clench with anger. 'You're forgetting yourself, Tanner. And forgetting what I told you earlier.'

'I'm not forgetting anything,' snarled Tanner.

'Do you want me to tell the men the truth about you?'

'And what's that? What is the truth, Mr Liddell? Why don't you tell me what you know?'

Liddell glared at him. 'You killed that lad. The one who died. Cutler – George Cutler.'

'Oh, did I really?' Tanner made to wipe his brow and saw Liddell flinch. 'You don't know. You don't know anything. You can tell the men whatever you bloody well like.' He shook his head in disgust. 'How could such a fine man as David Liddell have been your father?'

'How dare you speak to me like that?'

'Look, you stupid bastard, go and report me to

224

Captain Peploe. Go on, run off and bleat. And then I'll tell him how you wrecked the whole mission. I'm beginning to think Captain Pendlebury would have got through on his own if we hadn't made such a bloody racket. And he still would have most likely got through if you hadn't gone and lost your nerve and fired that rifle. *My rifle.* No shooting, I said. What the hell did you let off that shot for?'

Liddell said nothing.

'Well?' said Tanner again. 'Why did you?'

'I didn't mean to!' spluttered Liddell. 'I had the bolt cocked and my finger ready on the trigger. It just went off.'

'Oh, Jesus,' said Tanner, clutching his hair, 'give me strength. Get away from me. Say what you want to Captain Peploe, but bloody well keep away from me.'

He staggered across the street to the house they had taken over from the Greeks as Company Headquarters, Liddell following him.

'Wait,' said Liddell.

'I've told you – keep away,' growled Tanner. Captain Peploe was not there, so he pushed past Liddell and went back to the bastion. He felt hot and weak and his side hurt, but as he went through the arched wooden doorway of the left-hand tunnel, he stepped instantly into a world that was refreshingly dark, cool and musty. The Pantokratoros Bastion was bisected by two dark tunnels that ran through its length, although only the left-hand one was being used now. At the entrance between the tunnels was an old guard-room, with one solitary oval window looking

225

back down Dedikaki. B Company had made this their mess room, a place to escape the smell and the heat.

Sykes was in the guardroom, chatting with Staff Sergeant Woodman.

'All right, sir?' asked Sykes.

'Look, I'm sorry I snapped at you, Stan,' he said.

''S all right, sir.'

'Have you seen Captain Peploe?'

'He's with the colonel,' said Woodman.

Tanner nodded and left them, heading back out into the bright sunshine. He took another glug of water, then set off down Plastira, the road that ran all the way round beneath the walls to Jesus Bastion.

The bodies from the fighting the previous night had now all been removed, but patches of dried blood could still be seen on the ground. He passed a blackened building, the site of bitter fighting. *Jesus, was it really only yesterday?* It felt a lifetime ago. The distance to Battalion HQ was not far – less than a mile – but even though he had kept in the shade of the walls, he felt light-headed by the time he reached the bastion. Captain Peploe was upstairs with Colonel Vigar, he was told, and by the time he reached the top of the stairs, he had to hold out an arm and lean against the wall in an effort to regain his composure. He paused a moment, then stumbled to the colonel's office and knocked at the open door.

'Good God, Tanner!' exclaimed the colonel, as Tanner weakly saluted.

'Jack, are you all right?' Peploe stood up and got him a chair. 'Here, sit down.'

Tanner gratefully did as he was bidden. Peploe offered him his silver hip flask. 'Thank you, sir,' he said. *Brandy*. The fluid scorched his mouth and throat but the kick from the alcohol revived him. And now the colonel was offering him a cigarette. Tanner smiled. 'Why, thank you, sir. I need to go on patrols like this more often.'

'So what happened?' asked Peploe, as Tanner exhaled a large swirling cloud of cigarette smoke. He told them – no details, but the bare facts.

'I can't believe it,' said Peploe, when he had finished. 'And Atkins, too. I'm sorry, I always knew it was a bad mission.'

'Yes,' muttered Colonel Vigar. 'Damned bad show.'

'He would have made it – Captain Pendlebury,' Tanner said. 'I could see him. He was clear of the river, but then a rifle went off and it was bloody mayhem.'

'Who fired the shot?' asked Peploe.

'God knows,' Tanner lied. 'I'd been seeing to some pickets when it went off. I'm sorry, though, sir. Two good men. I know Captain Pendlebury was an important man here. And I'm also sorry you won't now get your guided tour.'

Peploe grimaced. 'Fate has rather conspired against it, hasn't it? I've got his books, but it's not quite the same. He was a great man, though. It's sad, very sad.'

'But at least the rest of you got back,' said the colonel. 'That's something.'

'Yes,' agreed Peploe. 'I was half convinced you'd

all come croppers out there.' He now looked at the bloody mess of Tanner's side. 'Is it bad?'

'No, sir, just a graze. Bloody hurts, though.'

'Take him to the MO, Peploe, and then you'd better go and see Captain Vaughan.'

'Sir?' said Tanner, as he stood up once more. 'Tonight? Are we counter-attacking?'

'I've had no orders to that effect.'

Tanner's wound was not serious. An unpleasant gash, but when it had been properly cleaned, treated and bandaged, the MO assured Tanner it should heal quickly. His light-headedness had been compounded by too much sun, extreme fatigue and not enough water. The doctor urged him to drink more and gave him a couple of benzedrine pills. 'One of those will perk you up in no time,' he said cheerfully.

Tanner swallowed one with a large draught of water and by the time he and Captain Peploe were back outside in the street he felt decidedly better.

'Do you want me to come with you to see Captain Vaughan?' he asked.

'Perhaps it might not be a bad idea. I'm sure they can spare us both another half-hour.' Peploe squinted up at the deep blue cloudless sky, then whisked away a fly. 'Bloody hell, it's hot.'

A loud boom of guns made both men flinch, and then they heard the tell-tale hum of aero-engines. A high-pitched whine – and Stukas were high above the town, ten of them, peeling off one after the other and diving, sirens screaming. The guns around the harbour and edge of the town thundered, the ground shook, and bombs were crashing down once more.

'Come on, Jack!' yelled Peploe. 'Captain Vaughan can wait. We should hurry back to the gate.'

In the ten minutes it took to reach the company at the wall, the Stukas had gone and were now pasting the area to the east of the town around the airfield. Much of Heraklion lay smothered in a cloud of slowly rolling dust and smoke. Bombs had landed just to the west of the town and several buildings had been destroyed, but as Tanner and Peploe climbed up onto the wall once more, they heard more aircraft, transports this time, and the sky was filling with parachutes.

'Sir, with your permission, I'm going to try a little experiment,' said Tanner.

'What is it?'

'Green flares, sir. To attract the transports.'

Peploe grinned. 'All right.'

Tanner grabbed Woodman and Hepworth, hurried across the road to retrieve a Very pistol and green flares from his pack, then ran back out through the Canea Gate and to the house where they had earlier paused. A wave of Junkers was now thundering over so, aiming his Very pistol into the air, Tanner fired. The flare crackled with a green light. He fired another and, sure enough, moments later, four canisters were floating down towards them.

'Neat trick, that, sir,' grinned Hepworth.

'Thank you, Hep. Now we just have to watch where they land and retrieve them.'

Two were beyond daylight reach, but Tanner

carefully noted where they had come to rest; they could be collected at dusk. However, the other two landed close by – one in a grove less than fifty yards away, the other drifting down among the houses behind them.

'Would you bloody believe it?' laughed Woodman. 'That's going to really piss off Jerry, that is.'

'And we like pissing off Jerry, don't we?' said Tanner.

They collected the container from the olive grove, cutting away the silk parachute, folding it up, then dragging the long, rectangular aluminium box back to the safety of the house. It was heavy – too heavy to be easily dragged as far as the wall. 'Hep,' said Tanner, 'run back and get a few of the lads from your section to help pull this in.'

While Hepworth hurried off, Tanner and Woodman retrieved the second canister, which they found lying in an alleyway. Several Cretan boys and old men were already standing around it, but they moved away as Tanner and Woodman approached. This one was lighter and they moved it easily, dragging it down the dusty road to where they had left the other.

'It's like Christmas, Jack,' said Woodman, rubbing his hands. 'What d'you reckon we've got here?'

'Hmm,' said Tanner. 'Rations in the lighter one. Ammo in the other? Let's have a look.' There were indeed rations in the first, but also medical supplies.

'*Verbandkasten*,' said Tanner, pulling out one of the green-grey metal boxes. 'We can always do with medical kit.' He opened it up. On the underside of the lid was an inventory of its contents, and the box included a number of field dressings, ointments, syringes and phials. The canister contained six such boxes in all.

'How's your wound, Jack?' said Woodman. 'You can try some Jerry medicine on it and see if it's any better.'

Tanner grinned. 'Hold on, Woody,' he said, pulling out a cardboard box. 'See what that says?'

'*Zigaretten*,' said Woodman. 'Lovely job.'

Tanner ripped open the box. 'Tennis Meister! Never heard of that one before. More of a cricket man myself, but I'll give 'em a go.' He pocketed four packets and gave the remaining four to Woodman.

'Finders keepers, eh, Jack?'

Tanner lit one and inhaled. 'It's all right,' he said, breathed out the smoke, then delved back into the canister. There were more cardboard boxes, and Tanner lobbed one with *'Eiserne Portion'* stamped on the side. 'Have a dekko at what's in there,' he said, taking out another box for himself. 'This one says, *"Nahkampfpackung"*,' he said. 'God knows what that means.'

'Oh, no,' said Woodman, opening his. 'Hardtack biscuits and tinned fish. Just what I wanted.' He rolled his eyes.

'Bad luck,' chuckled Tanner. 'I've got more beadies in this one, and some chocolate. Bloody hell, there's even sweets and a couple of cigars. Bloody brilliant rations, these.'

Hepworth arrived back with two other men and Tanner lobbed him a bar of chocolate. 'Here you go, Hep. This one's on me.'

'Cheers, sir,' said Hepworth. 'What's in the other container?'

'Haven't got that far. Hold on.' Tanner opened it, then his face creased into a smile. 'Beautiful,' he said. 'Will you look at that?' Inside was an MG34 light machine-gun, spare barrels, oilers and two aluminium tins of ammunition.

'We've had one of those before, haven't we, sir?' said Hepworth.

Tanner nodded. 'The barrels get bloody hot, but they can chuck out the bullets, all right.' He closed the lid again. 'Anyway, enough of the chat. Time to get them back.' He stood up and looked at the sky. The Germans had gone, and the guns were quiet once more. It had been a good ruse, firing those green flares, but there was no doubting that many more canisters had fallen further to the west, among the enemy. Presumably more would come the following day. He felt a fly settle on his neck and slapped it, but it buzzed away.

If only they received orders to counter-attack that night. Time was everything, and he felt certain they should attack right away, while they had the chance. He wondered what was holding Brigadier Chappel back. Did he know something, some piece of intelligence, or was it just caution? Tanner shook his head. 'Iggery, lads,' he said. 'Back to the walls.'

Around the same time, Major General Freyberg was holding a conference with his commanders in the Canea sector at the Creforce Headquarters quarry, although Brigadier Vasey had also driven over from Georgioupolis near Rethymno, to report on the situation there. Overnight, the enemy paratroopers at Maleme had occupied the perimeter of the airfield and taken command there. Yet this did not unduly worry Brigadier Hargest, commander of 5th Brigade around Maleme, since he still had two battalions, plus two companies from the 22nd Battalion within shouting distance. Having talked to his divisional commander, Brigadier Puttick, that morning, he had agreed that there was no need to launch a counter-attack on the airfield until dusk. With his guns and infantry all around the south and east of Maleme, there seemed to be little the Germans could do. He would let the Huns fry in the sun all day and finish them off that night.

This mood of quiet confidence had not changed as they had settled down around a rough wooden trestle table to discuss the current situation and to plan for the counter-attack that night at Maleme. Drinks had been poured, cigarettes handed around; their faces were serious but hardly grave.

No sooner had they each given their brief reports than Freyberg was interrupted by Captain Sandford, head of the signals group above the quarry.

'Excuse me a moment, gentlemen.'

Freyberg stepped away from the table and, taking the thin, folded piece of paper from Sandford, went outside to read it in private. Clear of any possible prying eyes, he unfolded it and read: 'On continuation of attack Colorado, reliably reported that among operations planned for twenty-first May is air landing two mountain battalions and attack Canea. Landing from echelon

233

of small ships depending on situation at sea.'

Freyberg read it through again, his heart sinking, then held it out and, with his cigarette lighter, burned it, the paper curling and blackening and turning to ash. For a moment he stood there thinking. Colorado was the codename for Crete, but an attack on Canea had been spelled out in the clear. The air landing of two battalions was less of a concern because he did not see how the Germans could land at Maleme when the south and east of the airfield were still surrounded by 5th New Zealand Brigade, but a seaborne invasion was a different matter. It was what he had feared most all along, and now it was about to happen.

He walked stiffly back to the table and sat down, then gulped his Scotch. For a moment he said nothing, his brow furrowed, his mind whirring. He wished he could have shown the signal to the others, to discuss it in detail, but he had been sworn not to show such messages to any soul under any circumstances. Besides Captain Sandford, also sworn to secrecy, these signals were for his eyes only. And only he could shoulder the responsibility of acting on this intelligence.

'Are you all right, General?' asked Puttick.

Freyberg, who had been rubbing his brow between his fingers and thumb, looked up. 'Er, yes – sorry. Where were we? Yes, the counter-attack on Maleme tonight.'

Hargest cleared his throat. 'Ideally, I'd like another couple of battalions,' he said. He was a round-faced and round-girthed New Zealander, with a short, trim moustache, a farmer and politician in New Zealand between the wars. 'I've got the 21st and 23rd Battalions primed and ready to go, and the Maoris still at Platanias, but I'd far rather have an overwhelming force and make sure we do the job properly.'

'I can release you two of my battalions,' said Brigadier Inglis, commander of the 4th Brigade, based further along the coast between Canea and the village of Galatas.

'Out of the question,' retorted Freyberg. 'We need the troops here in case there's a seaborne invasion.'

'Surely one battalion could be spared, sir?' said Hargest.

'Only if Vasey agrees to release one of his Australian battalions from Rethymno to replace it.' He turned to Vasey. 'You seem to have Rethymno in hand, Vasey. Can you spare one of yours? What about the 2/7th?'

'I was rather hoping to use them to clear the road to Rethymno, sir.'

'And it'll take some hours to get them here, sir, at the very least,' said Hargest.

'Hargest is right, sir. It's forty miles and we've barely enough M/T. Then there's also the problem of moving in daylight with enemy fighters about.'

Freyberg held up a hand. 'Do your best, Vasey. Put the order through now. I'm sorry, but I'm not budging on what I said. You can't have another battalion until Vasey's Australians arrive. We've got more pressing concerns here at Canea and Suda than those few paratroopers at Maleme. What you've got should be more than enough as

it is. Damn it, man, you've got three whole battalions you can use. Those para boys must be
hopelessly low on ammunition by now. You
should be able to slaughter 'em.'

Hargest nodded. 'Very well, General.' He
glanced at his watch. 'It's nearly fifteen hundred
hours now. If Vasey's lot can get here by, say,
twenty hundred, then I'd still like to have 20th
Battalion or whichever one you can spare, Inglis.
But as you say, sir, I'm sure I'm being overly cautious.'

'Of course you are, James,' said Puttick. 'Colonel
Andrew panicked a bit last night, that's all. I don't
entirely blame him – it's difficult to know what to
do for the best when communications are down,
but we're aware of the situation now and you've
got more than enough troops as it is to deal with
it. The general's right, it'll be a slaughter. But what
we must be careful about is moving the fielder
every time the ball goes through the gap. If the
Huns try a seaborne invasion or an attempt to
break out of Prison Valley, we're going to need
troops here. Balance, James. It's all about maintaining balance.'

They left soon after, just as the latest enemy air
raids were developing. Stukas and Junkers 88s
bombed British positions along the coast from
Maleme to Suda Bay, the coast disappearing
once more amid a haze of smoke and dust. The
bombing did not appear to have been particularly accurate, but this time the planes had been
accompanied by fighters, Messerschmitt 109s,
which strafed positions in the wake of the
Junkers. As the dust settled and the smoke began

to drift away, the transports appeared, turning and flying parallel to the coast in their already familiar vics of three. From the sand-bagged sangar at the mouth of the quarry, Freyberg, tin hat on his head, peered through powerful binoculars at the spectacle. A large number of parachutes were blossoming directly over Platanias, some six miles away. They were met by furious return fire, cackling like fireworks all along the coast to the rocky outcrop of Akrotiri where Freyberg now stood. He smiled to himself. Of all the people he would least like to meet were he to be descending in a parachute, it was the Maori. Vicious little brutes.

Fierce fighting continued for at least an hour and a half. There seemed to be something going on at Maleme as well, but Freyberg soon found himself gazing out to sea, more than along the coast. The signal had been quite explicit: a seaborne invasion was expected that day, 21 May. Freyberg found himself pacing impatiently: into the quarry, back out to the sangar. Then he left the quarry entirely, and climbed up through the sagebrush over dusty red soil to the rocky ground above. Sweat ran down the sides of his face, but whether it was from the heat or anxiety, he was not entirely sure.

At half past four, unable to sit waiting at Creforce Headquarters any longer, he ordered his car and sped down the hill to Suda Bay to see the naval officer-in-charge, Captain Morse. Half-sunken ships littered the narrow bay, while along the docks, the signs of repeated air attacks were all too apparent. Part of the quayside had completely collapsed, a crane lay on its side, twisted and broken, while a number of buildings were nothing more than piles of jagged rubble. There was an air of menace and desolation about the place.

Morse's command post was in a building a short way from the harbour's edge, with a commanding view back down the length of the bay. As his car drew to a halt, Freyberg looked back at the harbour and the men clearing the rubble; it was a big task. Morse seemed slightly surprised when, a minute later, Freyberg was brought into his office – another room of smooth, whitewashed stone, a picture of the King on the wall behind the desk and a shipping chart opposite. An ashtray over-flowed with cigarette ends. Morse stubbed out yet another, saluted, then nodded towards the window. 'I'm afraid we can't keep up, sir. It doesn't matter how much we clear away, there's always more.'

'What about Suda Island?' said Freyberg. 'Have the stores there been cleared out yet?'

'Yes, sir. We finished yesterday.'

'Good.' He stroked his moustache. 'Look here, Morse,' he said. 'About a German seaborne invasion...

'As I said to you before, sir, I really don't think that need be too much of a concern.'

'Yes, you keep saying that, but we've under-estimated the Hun before in this war and with dire consequences.'

Morse could not help his sigh of exasperation. He looked tired, his eyes hollow. 'There are logis-tical issues here,' he said. 'The only way Hitler can get his men across the Aegean is by requisitioning large numbers of caiques. These are the only vessels in the sort of quantities he would need to transport any kind of invasion force.'

'What about Greek merchant ships and the Italian navy?'

'Perhaps one or two trampers as well, but nothing that would transport a serious invasion force. As for the Italians, well – the Italian fleet is not in the Aegean. One destroyer is known to be at Piraeus but nothing more.'

'But from these, Morse, they *could* assemble an invasion fleet.'

Morse chuckled. 'Well, yes, I suppose they *could*, but as I said to you before, the Mediterranean Fleet could deal with anything they put out. As you know, Admiral Cunningham now has four task forces in the Aegean. Believe me, sir, our destroyers would make light work of any German invasion fleet, let alone our cruisers and battle-ships. Surface vessels are not a problem. It's attacks from the air that you need to worry about.'

Freyberg left him soon after, still unconvinced by Morse's reassurances. The intelligence from Cairo had been uncannily accurate so far and now he had it on the same authority that a sea-borne invasion would be coming today. The sea was a big place – what if it was not picked up by Cunningham's forces?

By the time he arrived back at Creforce Head-quarters, it was some time after five. Brigadier Stewart, his chief of staff, was there to meet him, concern etched across his face.

'You'd better come and have a look, General,' he said, leading him to the observation-post sangar.

Freyberg took the proffered binoculars in silence and trained them out to sea. He could see nothing – just the same deep, empty blue. 'What am I supposed to be looking at, Keith? Can't see anything.'

'No, sir, not out to sea – at Maleme.'

Freyberg peered through the lenses. There was a lot of smoke around Maleme – it looked as though a fuel dump had been hit because at one end a huge column of black smoke rose into the air – but he could now see a German transport coming in to land. Men began leaping out, and then the aircraft moved off again, wobbling as it took to the air and disappearing into the smoke. Moments later, it re-emerged, rising safely out of the fray. Other transports, he could see, had not been so fortunate – one was still burning fiercely; another lay wrecked.

'We seem to be making mincemeat of this little effort,' he said, passing the binoculars back to Stewart. 'I'd have thought that was a gunner's dream.'

'But if they keep coming and gain a foothold, General–'

Freyberg raised a hand. 'Look to the sea, Keith, look to the sea. That's where we need to worry'

Once again, the intelligence reports had been right. An invasion fleet was on its way. Decrypts of German radio traffic reported that it was steaming for Crete. To protect this most secret of sources, Admiral Cunningham despatched a lone Maryland reconnaissance plane, which duly found the fleet, as if by accident. By dusk, three of the Mediterranean Fleet's forces were back in the Aegean, and as darkness fell Force D, of three giant cruisers and four destroyers, all bristling with a combination of heavy guns, pompoms, cannons and torpedoes, was closing in for the kill.

All this immense fire power against one Italian destroyer, two small, rusting steamers and nineteen caiques.

It was around 11.25 p.m. when a runner from Captain Sandford's signals team arrived at the Creforce quarry with important news. They had been monitoring radio traffic out at sea and had just picked up the news that Force D was about to engage. Freyberg immediately hurried outside, Stewart and other staff officers following, and clambered up to the rocky outcrop above.

Suddenly the horizon was lit by a series of flashes, followed, some moments later, by the dull crump of guns. Relief coursed through the general. More flashes, orange and red, momentarily lit the sky, then came the steady peal of the guns' thunder.

'Ha, ha!' chuckled Freyberg, jumping from foot to foot. From the signals group regular updates were brought down. An Italian destroyer, the *Lupo*, was reported sunk, then two steamers. Two caiques had gone down, then five, then ten. Eventually it was reported that eighteen out of nineteen had surrendered or been destroyed. The invasion force was dead in the water.

Freyberg looked up at the stars twinkling down on them and breathed in deeply. A hint of smoke, but mostly he could smell the sage and grass, and the dusty red clay. Gunfire could still be heard out at sea, but the invasion force was no more.

'It's over,' said Brigadier Stewart. 'Well done, sir. Perhaps we will save Crete after all.'

'Thank you, Keith,' said Freyberg. 'It's been a great responsibility. A great responsibility.' He looked at his watch. The counter-attack at Maleme was due to start in half an hour, at around 1 a.m., later than originally planned, but with 20th Battalion, released after the late arrival of the 2/7th Australians. 'Time for Bedfordshire, I think,' he said. 'Can't do much to help the boys at Maleme by staying up all night.'

Freyberg walked back to his villa, cicadas ringing in his ears, the rough ground crunching underfoot. His worst fears had not come to pass. Damn it, he should have listened to Morse.

The Creforce commander was already fast asleep by the time the counter-attack was due to begin, so he was blissfully unaware that already it had begun to unravel. Delays and more delays as troops struggled through the night meant that it was not until 3.30 a.m. that the Maori and 20th Battalion finally began advancing along the coast towards Maleme, and not until well after dawn that they would be in any position to join the counter-attack on the airfield. And all the time more and more fresh, well-equipped German mountain troops had been landing.

The invasion force at sea might have been defeated, but Freyberg had made a catastrophic miscalculation, for while he slept, Maleme was about to be lost for good.

And, with it, British chances of saving the island.

12

A little after 3 p.m., Thursday, 22 May. Another hot day. Along the walls of Heraklion and out beyond, the men kept guard, watching for any enemy movement, but the heavy, languid atmosphere meant no one was going to fight willingly. In B Company Headquarters, a house opposite the Canea Gate, Captain Peploe and Tanner had made the most of the quiet to catch some much-needed sleep, Peploe on a divan on the third floor, Tanner on an old armchair in Peploe's office – once the living room, no doubt, of a prosperous family, but which had been transformed since being requisitioned by the Greek Army. All that was left were a couple of rickety tables, wooden chairs, one sideboard and a lone empty bookshelf.

It was cooler in there than out, the thick stone walls an effective barrier against the heat, although shafts of sunlight poured through the open windows. In his half-sleep, Tanner batted away a fly, but it was a persistent creature: every time he was on the verge of dropping off, he felt it crawling over his arm or face. He opened an eye and watched a small lizard scurry up the wall next to him, then rolled down the sleeves of his shirt and took out a handkerchief, which he placed over his face. He closed his eyes once more.

It had been another busy night. Tanner had persuaded Peploe that if there was to be no counter-attack they should at least be sending out fighting patrols at dusk. In any case, they had had two further canisters to retrieve. These they had successfully found and they had proved even more bountiful. One had been filled with a dozen Schmeissers, or MP40s, as they appeared to be called from the stamp at the end of the breech, and plentiful cardboard boxes of ammunition and magazines, while the other contained one 80mm mortar and two dozen boxes of six mortar shells. These had been taken back with glee while Tanner and Peploe had led separate patrols in an effort – to pinpoint the German pickets. Having prompted return fire and noted the position of muzzle flashes, they had retreated to the edge of the town and spent the night harassing enemy positions with their newly found mortar.

It had also been encouraging to hear gunfire from further to the west throughout the night. It might not have been the co-ordinated counter-attack Pendlebury had had in mind, but the screams piercing the darkness from the ridge to the west suggested the Cretan guerrillas were causing murderous havoc among the enemy. And at regular intervals, the Rangers had kept firing the mortar, the rather hollow sound of its discharge followed some seconds later by a dull explosion. If they couldn't attack, then Tanner was determined they should make those paratroopers' lives as difficult as possible.

The morning hate had arrived shortly after eight o'clock, bombing positions around the airfield, but since then it had been quiet, and became quieter still the further the sun rose in the sky. Tanner shifted in his chair, a stab of pain from his side waking him once more. *Bollocks*. Somewhere beyond the town, several rifle shots rang out. Sparrows were chirping just outside the window, footsteps on the street below. The enemy were half a mile to the west, and yet among all this mayhem, life continued.

Tanner pulled a Tennis Meister from his top pocket and had just lit it when a runner from Battalion hurried up the stairs and knocked lightly on the open door.

'Is Captain Peploe around?' he asked.

'Not at the moment. Is it important?' Tanner replied.

'Lieutenant McDonald, then?'

'On duty on the walls – or maybe at the town's edge.'

'Oh – well, in that case, sir, can you tell them the CO will be here in half an hour?'

Tanner nodded, then settled back in his chair. He wondered what the colonel wanted. Perhaps he had news of a counter-attack after all. He finished his cigarette, put a billycan of water on the Primus in the kitchen below, then went to wake Peploe.

'Sir,' said Tanner, tapping on the door. 'Wakey-wakey.'

Peploe stirred, then stretched.

'Sorry to wake you, sir,' said Tanner, 'but the CO's coming round shortly.'

Peploe stood up and opened the shutters, squinting as the sunlight poured in. His strawberry-blond mop of hair looked more tousled and unkempt than usual. Peploe might have grown up on a farm, never destined to be a soldier, but he had turned out to be a damn good one in Tanner's opinion, a man who led by example but who was never too proud to take another's advice. And he listened. How many officers had he known who shared that trait? Not many. Yet he also admired Peploe for his refusal to be something he was not. Peploe made his decisions on the basis of what he believed the situation demanded and by using common sense; he cared little for decorum or ceremony. Tanner approved of that. Parade-ground etiquette was all very well, but in battle there were other ways of ensuring discipline. Peploe never had any discipline problems because he had the trust and respect of his men.

'Actually, you did me a favour. I was having a terrible dream. I'd been court-martialled and Mr Liddell was the judge.' He grinned. 'Can you imagine?'

'I'd rather not.'

'I didn't tell you, Jack, but he did come to see me yesterday afternoon. He said you knocked him out.'

'What did you say, sir?'

'I asked him why. He told me he had been ordering a withdrawal and that you had counter-manded that. He had insisted you pull back and then you knocked him out.'

Tanner said nothing.

'So, anyway, I then asked him who he thought had fired that first shot and, after shifting his feet a moment, he confessed that it had been him. "That's interesting," I said, "because Tanner's already given me a report and didn't mention that it was you who had fired it." He was quite surprised to hear that. "So Tanner saved you from any loss of face with me, and now you've spoiled it rather," I said. He went on about how it was an offence to strike an officer, so I told him bluntly that, strictly speaking, it was true, but considering the outcome of the mission, it might be better if he kept quiet and forgot all about it.'

'It is true, I'm afraid,' said Tanner. 'But I had to shut him up somehow. Short of killing him...' He let the sentence trail. 'Look, he was endangering us all, sir. We had to divert attention from Captain Pendlebury to give him any chance of getting through, but we also had to give Jerry some return fire before there was any remote chance of us pulling out safely.'

Peploe shrugged. 'He wasn't happy. He wanted to know how he was to get the respect of the men when you and I were always undermining him.'

'He's undermining himself,' muttered Tanner.

'That's what I said. But he threatened to take it to Colonel Vigar. I'm just warning you, that's all. It might be what the CO's coming to talk to us about.'

But when the colonel arrived soon after, he greeted them affably and happily accepted the tea Tanner offered hm. As Tanner had learned in India, hot char, as they had called it, was as refreshing as cold water when the heat became too much. He had made it the way he had been taught on first arriving in India as a boy soldier: a generous amount of tea leaves, several spoons of sugar and half a can of condensed milk, all poured into the boiling water together and stirred.

'Good man, Tanner,' said Colonel Vigar, as Tanner passed him a chipped enamel mug.

'And have a piece of this, sir,' added Peploe, passing the colonel a small block wrapped in brown paper.

'*Schokolade*, eh?' said Vigar. 'Not been pilfering from the enemy, have you?'

Peploe grinned. 'Tanner here thought of rather a good wheeze, actually, sir. He noticed Jerry was firing green flares at the transports coming over and that canisters were then being dropped. So we did the same yesterday at the edge of town. Worked a treat.'

'Care for a beadie, sir?' said Tanner, pulling out his packet of *'Für Die Wehrmacht'* -issue Tennis Meister cigarettes.

Vigar raised an eyebrow and took one. 'Now you're just showing off.'

'We're less taken with the *Knäckebrot*, sir,' said Peploe.

'Did you just get chocolate and cigarettes or anything useful, Peploe?'

'We mortared them with their mortar most of last night, sir,' said Peploe, 'and we're now the proud owners of one Spandau and twelve more Schmeissers.'

'What we really need is a flag, though, sir. Or something with which we can make a large swastika on the ground. Perhaps then we can get some more.'

Vigar nodded. 'Could always use a sheet.' He chuckled. 'Good work, you two. I'll tell the rest of the chaps to give it a go.' He sat down in the armchair, had a gulp of tea, then said, 'Anyway, I

248

came over to see how you're faring and to put you in the picture. Apart from the unfortunate loss of Captain Pendlebury, you seem to be all right, as far as I can see – keeping Jerry on his toes by the sound of it.'

'We're fine, sir. But feeling a bit frustrated, if I'm honest,' said Peploe. 'We might have got our hands on a few canisters but Jerry's got most of them. Every day that passes, more men and supplies are flown in. We should be counter-attacking, sir. We're never going to beat them staying put.'

'All right, Peploe. I've been over to Brigade this morning and talked with the brigadier and the staff there. The brig's being cautious because his orders were to protect the port and the airfield and he's determined to do that. His dilemma is that he's not sure how many paratroopers are out there, and yet our own ammunition is getting low. Furthermore, he's had only intermittent contact with Creforce.'

'What's the news from there, sir?' asked Tanner.

'Mixed. The Mediterranean Fleet have seen off a seaborne invasion attempt – apparently only one caique managed to reach the island – but it sounds as though they've lost Maleme.'

'Lost Maleme?' said Peploe. 'Then the Germans can fly in whatever they want! That's a disaster, isn't it?'

Vigar shrugged. 'Not if they can get it back again. Rethymno is stable, though.'

Tanner shook his head and walked over to the window.

'You're not happy, CSM?' said Vigar.

'No, I'm bloody not, sir. We bloody well

murdered them the first day. How come they're still out there? How can we have lost Maleme? I just don't understand it. Men armed with Brens and rifles can't possibly be beaten by men with short-range sub-machine-guns. It's not possible.'

Vigar sighed. 'I don't know, Tanner. And if it's any consolation, I agree with you – we should be taking the attack to the enemy. Anyway, you're moving from here, back to the south of the town. The brigadier is less worried about the west side now there are signs that the enemy is massing around the airfield. A group that landed further east has moved up and more parachuted into the area yesterday. He thinks the Greeks can handle this side of the town on their own again.'

'Back to our old positions?'

'Yes. Tonight at twenty-two hundred hours, if you would. The brig thinks the western lot might move across to join the rest around the airfield. The Argyll and Sutherland Highlanders landed in Tymbaki a few days ago and are going to move up from the south to join us, so we've got some reinforcements coming too.' He finished his tea, then pushed himself up out of the armchair. 'Well, thanks for the refreshments. I'll see myself out.'

At the door, however, he paused. 'By the way,' he said, turning back towards them, 'your new subaltern, Mr Liddell. What's your take on him, Peploe?'

Peploe glanced at Tanner, then back at the brigadier. 'Early days, sir.'

'Hmm. Came to see me this morning. Gave him pretty short shrift, I'm afraid. It's your company, John. If you want to give him the chop when this is over, you do that. A chap like that can always be shuffled off to become some staff wallah. I'll leave that one with you. But, Tanner, I don't ever want to hear of such a complaint again. Clear?'

'Yes, sir.'

'Good.' Vigar winked, then left them.

Of course they had needed the supplies of ammunition that had been dropped, and the rations too, but Oberleutnant Kurt Balthasar was particularly relieved to have been sent some water-purification tablets. Truly, these were manna from heaven. He was not the only one suffering from diarrhoea – most of the men were. Water was always the most important ingredient of life, but even more so when the men were spending much of the day out under a hot sun sweating so much body fluid. They had had no choice but to drink the river water, but they were paying the price. Now there was not only the stench of decomposing paratroopers.

The men were ordered to dig holes in the ground as much as possible, but since they had not landed with any entrenching tools, this had been difficult: bayonets and knives had been used to loosen the earth, and helmets to scoop away the soil, but these efforts offered only limited sanitation. The crap and decaying flesh attracted the flies as well. Millions of them seemed to have descended on the remnants of the 3rd Battalion. The men were struggling, but every other living thing seemed to be thriving on their discomfort:

251

carrion crows, flies, mosquitoes, ants – even the rock lizards that darted about. Balthasar found himself whisking his hand about his face almost continuously. It did nothing to improve his mood.

Neither did the lack of news. The only radio contact was with Athens, picking up brief snatches of radio traffic here and there. Runners had been sent out at night to try to link up with Oberst Bräuer and the men to the east of the airfield, but they had not been seen since. Most probably they had been intercepted by Cretan bandits. The attacks the previous night had cost the lives of a dozen more men – a comparatively light return, all things considered, but he for one had not slept even a minute and, from the men's faces, he was not the only one.

The decapitation of the pickets the previous night had unnerved them all, but while his own thirst for revenge had been exacerbated by this monstrous act, the reality of their situation meant that at present there was little opportunity for exacting any retribution. Rather, their position continued to be extremely precarious, as Balthasar was keenly aware. The men were on edge, suffering from various degrees of dysentery, chronically short of sleep, and with insufficient arms to properly defend themselves.

And to make matters worse, the English captain, Pendlebury, was not talking. It was Eicher who had begun questioning him that morning; the Leutnant could speak near fluent English.

Pendlebury was weak but conscious. He knew very little, he told Eicher. He was no soldier;

Heraklion had become too oppressive; he had had to get away from the smell, the death. He claimed to have lost his nerve. When Eicher had pointed out that he had tried to cross their lines with an escort of British soldiers, Pendlebury had denied it. Rather, he claimed, he had seen the patrol leaving and had crept out behind them. They had not even known he was there. It was the truth: he was an academic, not a soldier, who had been on the island before the war. His position, he said, was as vice consul – a minor diplomatic post, nothing more. His task had been to ease relations between the Greeks and the British on the island – always uneasy, and especially so since the loss of the Cretan Division on the mainland. He had never had any military training at all in his life – it had probably been obvious enough to them.

Eicher had pointed out that Pendlebury had killed three of their men. Pendlebury apologized. It had been nothing more than self-defence – they had been firing at him. He was surprised to learn that he'd killed anyone – with one eye, it was hard to aim properly. He'd had no real thought of where he might go, but he had supposed into the mountains. That was all. It was the truth.

'He's lying,' Balthasar had told Eicher. 'I saw him two nights ago in the fighting around the Canea Gate. He was leading their counter-attack. See what he says to that.'

Everyone had been fighting that night, Pendlebury told him. Civilians, Greek soldiers, British. He had joined in because, like the Cretans in the town, he felt compelled to try to force back the invader.

'He was leading the attack,' said Balthasar. 'Using a swordstick.'

No, Pendlebury insisted. He had merely joined in. Perhaps it had looked that way, but it was not the case – he had been just one of many. It was true he had used a swordstick – but that, he hoped, only went to prove how little soldiering he had ever done.

'I don't believe a word of it,' said Balthasar. 'He thinks we were born yesterday. He's a British agent, and he was trying to get through to the bandits in the mountains.'

Pendlebury denied it, and continued to deny it. Soon after they stopped the questioning: the wounded man was flagging, but so too was Balthasar, gripped with an acute pain in his stomach. 'Get some rest,' Balthasar told him. 'Build up your strength. But you will tell me all you know, Hauptmann Pendlebury.'

Since then, Balthasar had spoken with Major Schulz and Hauptmann von der Schulenberg.

'Take the note we found,' suggested von der Schulenberg, as they sat in the shade of a large chestnut behind the house next to the river. Flies darted and buzzed around them, but at least the leaves, dark and fecund, offered some shade from the sun. 'If he is an agent with the Cretan bandits, he'll know about that note.'

'Yes – yes, I will,' said Balthasar.

'And what was he doing here before the war? An academic, you say? What kind? An archaeologist?'

'I'll interrogate him more fully this afternoon,' he had told them. 'Reibert does not think his

254

wound is life-threatening, but the more time he has to rest the better.' The same applied to himself, as he well knew. He could sense his own strength sapping, and had begun to feel a little light-headed. He had eaten a biscuit, a hard, dry tooth-breaker, but it had hardly made him feel better. When he and Eicher eventually returned to the cottage where Pendlebury was being held, Reibert suggested he take a Pervitin tablet: for all their shortages, they had plenty of those energy pills. It had made a notable difference – within ten minutes, Balthasar felt the fatigue seep away.

And Pendlebury was awake when he and Eicher entered the dark, shuttered room in which he still lay.

'Tell him, Eicher,' said Balthasar, 'that we know he speaks German.'

Pendlebury smiled. 'Yes, it's true,' he said.

A correct guess. *A good start.* 'Then why did you not say so this morning?'

'You never asked.'

'I am interested to know what you were doing here before the war.'

'I am an archaeologist. I was curator at Knossos for some years.'

'For how long?'

'I took over from Arthur Evans in 1929. We carried out other digs. Many digs.' He lolled his head. 'Good days – peaceful days, they were.'

'Work that took you all over the island.'

'Oh, yes. It's a beautiful place.'

'You must know a great deal about the ancient world,' said Balthasar.

'And it was littered with despots just like your Hitler.'

Balthasar ignored the comment. He smoothed his hair, then wiped his brow. 'And tell me, Hauptmann Pendlebury, I am curious – how much do you learn from your excavations and how much from texts written at the time?'

'It entirely depends on what one is excavating. What age it is.'

'But the ancient Greeks wrote books, did they not?'

'Oh, yes,' Pendlebury replied. 'Some of the finest ever produced. Homer, Aeschylus, Herodotus. You should try them. They tell us so much about life, about history. That human nature never really changes.'

Balthasar produced the bloodied note left pinned to his headless men. 'Perhaps, Herr Pendlebury, you recognize this quote. "Ravening a blood drinker though you may be, yet will I glut your taste for blood." He eyed Pendlebury closely. His eyes were closed again, but his mouth creased into a smile. 'You recognize it? We've been wondering what it means.'

'Herodotus,' muttered Pendlebury. 'The master story-teller. Let me tell you about this. You see, long ago, there was a king – King Cyrus of Persia, the Great One. He was a cruel, ruthless emperor. Half the known world bowed down before him, but then he tried to tame the Massagetae, a wild and independent people, fiercely proud and determined not to become the slaves of Persia, as so many others had. And the unthinkable happened – Cyrus was defeated and killed and his

256

body brought before Tomyris, the queen of the Massagetae. And those were the words she spoke before she cut off his head. She kept it in a wineskin filled with blood. Rather apposite, don't you think?'

'And written by you, no doubt?'

'You will find that there are many men on Crete fully acquainted with the writings of Herodotus. He is as well beloved and read as Shakespeare or Goethe.'

'You wrote this,' said Balthasar, renewed anger coursing through him. 'You are an agent of the British and you were leaving Heraklion to organize the bandits in the mountains.'

'I understand that you might wish that to be the case, but it is not. I know very little, as I told you.'

'Perhaps you can tell us about the defences in the town,' said Eicher.

'What do you want to know?' Pendlebury replied. 'There are large Venetian walls around the town. A fort at the harbour.'

Eicher sighed. 'Men. What men are in the town?'

'I couldn't say for sure. A lot, though. There are a number of Greek and British regiments.'

'Eicher,' snapped Balthasar, 'we know about their forces. If there were as many as Herr Pendlebury says they would have counterattacked by now.'

'I told you I know very little. You probably know more than me. My role was more diplomatic than military.'

Balthasar felt his anger rising. This man was making fools of them, treating them like idiots.

'What about supplies?' asked Eicher. 'What reserves are there?'

'I wouldn't know,' replied Pendlebury. 'It's not something I've ever asked about. Everyone seemed to have enough the other night.' He grimaced, then turned over. 'I'm very tired. My chest – it's a strain talking like this.'

'Maybe we should let him rest some more, Herr Oberleutnant,' suggested Reibert.

Balthasar slammed his hand against the door. 'No!' he shouted, then stood over Pendlebury and pulled him over so that the Englishman cried out in pain. 'Listen to me,' he said. 'I know you are an agent and I know you are working with the bandits. Tell me everything.'

'I have,' mumbled Pendlebury.

'This is your last chance. Tell me, or I will have you killed. And after what you and your Cretan comrades did to my men, believe me, it will be a pleasure.'

'But I've told you what I know.' There was a look of fear in his eyes now.

Balthasar smiled. 'I don't think you have. I don't think you have told us anything.' He glanced at Eicher. 'We're wasting time.' He suddenly felt light-headed again and, stepping from the room and out into the glaringly bright afternoon sun, shielded his eyes. 'You,' he said, to the men standing guard outside, 'get the prisoner out here.'

John Pendlebury had hoped that he might yet survive. When he had been hit the day before, he had thought he was moments from death, but then he had been taken back and tended, his wound cleaned and dressed. When the questioning began, he knew he could tell them nothing, but although they were not getting the information they wanted from him, a part of him clung to the belief that perhaps he would be saved after all. His *andartes* might rescue him, or the British overrun the German positions. Maybe the Germans would keep questioning him further.

But the German officer was becoming impatient – and angry. He could see that. Not that he blamed him. It must have been a demoralizing few days for them. The man did not look well either: the sweaty brow, the grimaces of discomfort. It had been the note that had sealed his fate. The German Oberleutnant knew he had written it, no matter how much he might deny it. He cursed himself – he had walked into that trap; vanity had got the better of him.

And now two paratroopers were hoisting him up off the bed, the pain shooting through him, like a bolt, so that he could not help but cry out. Roughly, they helped him across the room, into the kitchen and out into the blazing heat. Wearing his cotton trousers, his chest bare except for his bandages, he was taken around the side of the house until they reached a windowless stone wall.

So this is it. Thirty-six years of life, of love, of learning, about to end. He was glad he was on Crete, the place he loved above any other in the world, but he was desperately sad that he could not see or speak to his wife or to his children. Daniel and Jenny – he wouldn't watch them grow up, flower into adulthood. He had not seen any of them for nearly a year, and although he had missed them, he had been too busy, too pre-occupied, to let their absence from his life trouble him unduly. And yet, in his last moments, he yearned for them. A heavy weight consumed him, one he recognized as grief.

'Your last chance,' said the German officer. 'Tell me all you know.'

'I know nothing,' mumbled Pendlebury. His mind turned to Vaughan. His friend had been right – it had been a game of sorts. A wonderful, exciting, exhilarating adventure. He'd never felt closer to those kings and warriors who had ruled and fought on this island thousands of years before, and yet like many of them, his end would be as bloody, as brutal. Perhaps it was fitting.

'Very well,' said the German. He nodded to the two men.

The cock of their Schmeissers, metal being drawn against a tight spring. Pendlebury felt his body tense: he was shaking, every muscle in his body quivering. Fear? Yes – but more than that, a deep, uncontrollable sadness and loneliness.

A sharp rattle and instantly he felt as though a huge fist had smashed him into the wall behind, and then he was no longer standing, but lying on the ground, the sun high above, the sky a deep eternal blue. There was no pain, just the sensation that he was slipping, falling, the earth closing around him.

As John Pendlebury was breathing his last amid a widening pool of blood and dirt, Major General Freyberg was considering the terrible responsibility of high command. He had the best part of fifty thousand men under him – fifty thousand for whom he was responsible.

It was a little after five in the afternoon, and although it was cool enough in their quarry head-quarters and still oppressively hot outside, he felt compelled to step out of the cavern hewn from the side of the hill. There were simply too many staff officers in there – men with drawn, taut faces, waiting anxiously for the arrival of runners with news, but who clearly already feared the worst. The whiff of failure hung heavy in the air, more pungent than body odour. Never had he felt the eyes of his staff so keenly upon him. There was no discernible sign that they blamed him; rather, he sensed they were looking to him, their brave, decorated leader, to somehow pull something magical out of the bag and resolve the situation.

The truth was, however, that he wished there was someone *he* could turn to. When he had been younger, command had come so easily. All he had had to do was make sure his men were in good spirits, then fight with reckless bravery and they all followed. Being personally fearless had somehow been enough. And he could honestly say that he had never felt scared before – rather, he had been overcome by an overwhelming wave of exhilaration, his body and mind whirring with adrenalin and vitality.

But he was not fighting any more, not per-sonally. He was in the grandstand, moving the kind of soldiers he had once been among on the battlefield, and for the first time in his life he did feel scared – not for himself, but over what to do.

261

Climbing across the rocky ground, he felt the sweat from his brow running down the side of his face. Everyone was sweating a great deal – the quarry reeked of it, great dark patches staining their cotton uniforms – but they were used to it. They were getting used to defeat as well. *Perhaps that's it.* They had developed a losing habit; perhaps it was affecting their judgement, which was being eaten away by a lack of confidence, an expectation of failure that shadowed all they did. Pausing by a smooth-surfaced rock, he saw a lizard dart away and sat down, breathed heavily in and out a few times, then took out a cigarette from an old, darkening silver case, and lit it.

It had only dawned on him that afternoon what a catastrophic mistake he had made. All morning, he had misread the situation. The counter-attack had gone in late, but Hargest had told Puttick that although there had been a steady flow of enemy planes coming into Maleme they were taking troops *off* the island, not bringing them in. Initially, he had believed this too, but then suddenly, as he had been watching and listening to the continued fighting from the OP, the penny had dropped. Moments later, news had arrived of the heavy fighting by the Maori and 20th Battalions as they had continued to claw their way up the coast. They had still not even reached the airfield, let alone won it back. He had believed the reports because he had wanted to believe them – but, of course, the Huns weren't evacuating. Why on earth would they be, when the airfield was still theirs? No, they had been bringing in more and more troops, ammunition and supplies all day.

Freyberg took off his tin helmet and rubbed his hands across his face. He had been a fool – a damned, bloody-minded fool. He had been so focused on the threat of a seaborne invasion – and, yes, he had lacked sufficient confidence in the navy and his own defences that an invasion could be repulsed – that he had failed to recognize the real danger even though it had been unfolding right under his nose. If only he had released 20th Battalion when he had had the chance! Then both they and the Maori could have attacked at dusk, with the rest of 5th Brigade, and sent the Germans packing.

Perhaps it was still not too late, but to mass his forces now in one big counter-attack was fraught with danger. If it failed, it would be the end of the New Zealand Division. He was the country's most senior commander, and the division New Zealand's biggest contribution to the land war. If it was wiped out, the repercussions would be far-reaching. Freyberg had seen enough blood in the Great War to last him a lifetime and more; he knew how much the country mourned the loss of so many of her young men. He did not want to go down in history as a butcher. *I am not confident enough of success*, he told himself. There, he had admitted it. Yet lack of confidence had never plagued him as a younger man.

He pushed himself back up onto his feet, and continued up the hill to the signals station, a small bunker lined with sandbags, whose radio mast stuck up high into the air.

'Evening, sir,' said Captain Sandford, as Freyberg appeared at the steps.

'Sandford, I need some good news. Have you any for me?'

Already, from Sandford's grim expression, he knew he could expect little.

'I'm sorry, sir,' said Sandford. 'Another caique and an enemy steamer, but a second enemy invasion force was not intercepted due to shortage of ammunition. And I'm afraid the Mediterranean Fleet has taken a pounding today. Too many ships are within range of enemy aircraft.'

'Oh, God,' muttered Freyberg.

'Two cruisers sunk, sir.'

'No! Which ones?'

'*Fiji* and *Gloucester*, sir. A destroyer, *Warspite* and *Valiant* damaged, along with a number of other destroyers. It's been a bad day. I'm sorry, sir.'

Freyberg sighed. 'No – thank you, Sandford. One must face up to these things.' He turned and left. *So that's it, then.* His decision had been made. It meant the island would most likely now be lost, but lives would, he hoped, be saved.

Reaching the quarry once more, he found Brigadier Stewart. 'Keith, I've made a decision,' he said.

'Sir?'

'We're going to abandon Maleme. I want you to issue orders for a general withdrawal to Galatas.'

His chief of staff looked at him keenly, then placed both hands on the trestle table in front of him. 'If we withdraw, General, Jerry will be able to bring in supplies almost at will. His build-up of forces will become so great we'll be unable to hold him. We'll lose the island.'

'Do you think I don't know that?' Freyberg snapped. 'Christ, man, do you think I haven't thought of it?' Then, in a quieter voice, he added, 'Keith, I don't like it any more than you. But at least most of the men might live to fight another day.'

By morning, German paratroopers from Prison Valley had linked up with mountain troops from Maleme. Little did those at Heraklion know it, but in just three days, Crete's fate had been sealed.

13

Saturday, 24 May, a little after 9 p.m. Captain Alex Vaughan walked back through the quiet streets of Heraklion after a fruitless visit to Brigade Headquarters. Here and there he saw signs of bomb damage, particularly the closer he got to the harbour – one shattered house had spewed rubble and blocks of stone almost right across the street. At last he reached the entrance to the house he had shared with Pendlebury since 50 Middle East Commando had returned to Egypt: a short flight of steps leading to a wooden doorway in a wall, and through into a small courtyard, across which stood the house. He was tired, frustrated, and not a little disturbed by what he had encountered at HQ.

News from Canea was not good, but instead of instilling some fight into 14th Brigade, it seemed that the rapidly unravelling situation in the north-west of the island was making Brigadier Chappel even more determined to sit tight rather than take the attack to the enemy. A stalemate had developed, but Vaughan feared this would not last long. Several hundred more Jerry paratroopers had landed to the south earlier that day. Perhaps more would arrive tomorrow, along with more supplies, more arms, more ammunition. On the other hand their own supplies were slowly being drained away. Jesus, it didn't take a genius to work out which way the balance was shifting.

Crossing the courtyard, he was surprised to see a light on in Pendlebury's office and that the front door was ajar. Taking out his revolver, he went to it and carefully pushed it open. Slipping soundlessly into the hallway, he stood by the door to the office, his pistol cocked, listening. He waited a moment, then kicked back the door and stepped into the room, his revolver at the ready.

'I surrender,' chuckled Alopex, holding up his arms. He was sitting in one of the armchairs, just as he had three days earlier before leaving the town.

'Alopex!' exclaimed Vaughan. 'How did you get here?'

'It's easy enough at dusk when you know the way.' He raised a small glass. 'I hope you don't mind but I helped myself to a little raki.'

Vaughan put down his revolver, went to the small sideboard and poured himself a shot. Then, sitting at Pendlebury's desk, he raised his glass. 'It's very good to see you alive and well.'

'We're all mourning Pendlebury,' said Alopex.

'So you heard?'

'Executed by the Nazis.'

'Not executed exactly – he was killed in a fire-fight trying to cross the lines. I told the bloody fool not to do it.'

'No, that's not what happened,' said Alopex.

'What do you mean?'

'He was shot then, but not killed. They took him away – he would have lived. They interrogated him, but when he told them nothing, they shot him.'

Vaughan stared at Alopex. 'But how on earth do you know this?'

'They took him to the house of an old couple down in the valley. After Pendlebury was murdered the Germans left the house and the man and woman fled to the mountains. They heard it all and saw the Germans bury him. Tossed him into a shallow pit as though he were a dog.' He spat the words.

Vaughan put his head in his hands. 'Poor John,' he said.

Alopex lit a small cheroot. 'So, what can I say? We have been attacking the enemy every night, but still the British stay put.'

'Believe me, if I was commanding here, that would not be the case.' Vaughan stood up and went to the sideboard, took the bottle of raki and poured them both another shot. 'So why are you here?'

'Satanas asked me to come. He is seeing Hanford tonight. There are rumours about the fighting in the west of the island – that the British are falling back. Satanas thinks that if you are defeated in the west, you will have to leave Heraklion and Rethymno too. He thinks you will abandon us, just as you did on the mainland. And in France and Norway.' He smiled without humour. 'I know you and Pendlebury have tried to get us as many arms as possible, but it is not enough. We will fight on – of course we will – but if you leave, we want your weapons.'

'What can I do, though? I am not the commander here. A captain doesn't count for much, you know.'

'You can talk to the brigadier.'

Vaughan nodded. 'I'll do what I can. But I can't do that unless we get the order to evacuate.'

'You can start sowing the seed.'

'Yes. Yes, that's true.' He leaned forward, hands together, thinking. The room was bathed in a dim orange light. Sitting across from him, Alopex's features were in shadow, but there was no denying the menacing impression he gave: the thick moustache and two-day growth of beard, the knitted heavy eyebrows and dark eyes that stared hard at him. Around his waist were two bandoliers, while a rifle rested across his lap.

'And there's another thing,' said Alopex. 'The stores here in Heraklion that we brought from Suda Island. They are still safe?'

'Yes.'

'We need to plan for them. We must get them out.'

'How?'

'We are going to organize a boat. It will arrive tomorrow night. You must arrange for men to help carry everything down to the harbour.'

'And you plan to sail back to safety before daylight?'

'What else can we do? The town is now almost surrounded. A man can creep through, but not a truck or a cart. We have no choice. Better that it should end up at the bottom of the sea than in the hands of those scum.'

'Yes, I can see that.'

'You must warn the port that the boat is coming. There must be no trouble. It will reach you when the German fliers have gone home, and the stores must be ready.'

'What if it's late? I don't want to have to wait on the quayside with a large stash of arms and explosives. You remember the trouble we had getting it in the first place. If Brigade gets a whiff of it they'll take it all back in a trice. Look, I'll have men and a cart ready, but the boat has to be here before I move it from its safe place.'

Alopex stroked his moustache a moment. 'All right. So long as you are ready and waiting.' He finished his raki, then stood up. 'You are a good fellow, Alex. I know I can count on you. And you will talk to your brigadier?'

'Yes. I'll do all I can.'

Alopex embraced Vaughan, picked up his rifle and stepped out into the dark of the night.

The men of the 2nd Battalion, the King's Own Yorkshire Rangers, had also seen the paratroop drop to the south that afternoon. Tanner had wasted no time in hurrying to his rocky perch above their positions and, with his rifle and scope, taking shots as they descended, while the rest of the company had also fired furiously as this latest batch of invaders drifted down. Most had fallen a good four or five hundred yards away and more. How many had been killed or wounded was anyone's guess, but there was no doubting this had been the heaviest drop since that first day. Tanner was not alone in thinking the stranglehold they had had over the enemy was slipping away.

'I don't bloody believe it,' he had heard McAllister grumble. 'We could have finished this lot off for good the other day but we let 'em get away with it. And now look.'

Tanner had watched the other men in the section gaze up at the sky to the south, filled with falling parachutes. 'Defeatist talk, Mac?' Tanner had asked.

'No, sir. Just pissed-off talk, that's all.'

'Well, perhaps tonight we can go after them,' Tanner had said. 'Jerry doesn't much like the dark. Stir up a bit of trouble for all those disoriented paratroopers. Mac, we could get you a lovely pair of boots like mine.' The men had laughed at that, but when Tanner had gone to talk to Captain Peploe about sending out several fighting patrols, he had been told that orders had just arrived from the colonel, who in turn was passing on instructions from Brigade, that it was essential ammunition be preserved as far as possible and that any counter-attacks or active patrol work was to be forbidden. For what possible reason were they to preserve ammunition? That was what Tanner wanted to know. It seemed crazy, completely illogical. What was the brigadier thinking? That it was

270

better to let the enemy slowly but surely build up his strength while they sat back and watched?

Incensed, Tanner had gone to find Sykes, a man to whom he knew he could always gripe and groan about the brass.

'We could send out a few forward pickets, Jack,' Sykes suggested, as they sat beneath a large plane tree brewing char.

'Quite a long way forward.' Tanner grinned.

'And if they happened to bump into the enemy – well, a man's got to defend himself, hasn't he?'

'He has, really,' chuckled Tanner.

So, Tanner had later suggested this to Peploe. 'I know we're not allowed to actively engage the enemy, sir,' he said, as he stood in the doorway of Company Headquarters, 'but I'd like to set up some forward pickets.'

'Just how far forward were you thinking?' Peploe asked.

'Four hundred yards or so. There are a few wells and old buildings I marked up before the invasion. I was going to take the men there. Good cover.'

'And precisely the place disoriented paratroopers would head for.'

Tanner smiled. 'Well, yes, there is that, sir.'

Peploe agreed, so Tanner took Hepworth's section and Sykes. 'But, sir,' complained Hepworth, 'we're not on duty tonight. We're supposed to be getting our heads down.'

'What do you think this is, Hep?' Tanner retorted. 'A summer camp? A whole load of Jerries dropped down over there in case you hadn't noticed. Now shift your arse and stop complaining.'

271

'Yes, sir,' said Hepworth.

Tanner had known him for more than a year now and they had served together almost continually, apart from the couple of months after Hepworth had been wounded at Dunkirk. A lean-faced lad from Bradford, with a slightly hunched look about him, Hepworth had been a Territorial before the war, as a means of eking out a few extra pennies every week. But the Territorial 5th Battalion had been destroyed in Norway. Hepworth, along with Sykes, McAllister, Chambers and Bell, had followed Tanner into the 1st Battalion and had been sent to France, and then, when France had been lost, overseas to join the 2nd Battalion the unit of the Yorks Rangers Tanner had first joined as a boy soldier all those years before in India. Tanner trusted these men although, in truth, most were barely out of their teens – hardly men at all, and even though, Hepworth especially, they grumbled and complained whenever there was the opportunity. It was why, given the choice, he preferred to have them beside him whenever there was a fight rather than others in the company whom he knew less well.

As they reached their forward positions, Tanner was met by Lieutenant Liddell. The two had been largely successful in avoiding each other the past two days, but now Tanner looked up at him, a challenging expression on his face.

'Where do you think you're all going?'

'Forward pickets,' growled Tanner.

'But these men are off watch.'

'That's what I told him, sir,' said Hepworth.

'Shut it, Hep,' snapped Tanner. 'Captain

Peploe's orders, sir.'

Liddell looked at the men and then at Tanner. 'Very well, then.'

'Password is "yorker",' said Tanner. 'Perhaps you'd tell the rest of the men, sir.'

Liddell nodded, and Tanner slung his rifle onto his shoulder, his MP40 clutched in his hand. 'Iggery, then, lads. Follow me.'

He led them forward, walking freely at first and then, as they moved further, crouching through the fields and groves. The light was fading fast. Occasional shots rang out, a dog barked, while from the trees came the ever-present sound of cicadas and crickets. Reaching an old goat shed, Tanner gathered the men around him. 'Hep, you and two others stay here.' He pointed to a well, around seventy yards to their right. 'Three more over there by that well, and the rest, I want you to make your way to that stone wall over there.' He pointed to a crumbled barn and a drystone wall around a hundred yards further to the west. 'Get behind that and keep a watch out to the south. There's still some moon and it's another clear night so there'll be light from the stars. As it gets dark, your eyes should adjust. But use your ears too. My guess is some Jerries might just come looking for shelter and water. If they do, give it to 'em.'

'I thought we're supposed to be preserving ammunition, sir,' said Hepworth.

'You've got to defend yourselves, Hep.' He looked at the Schmeisser Hepworth carried – one of the twelve to have been given out. 'In any case, that's not our ammo you're using – it's Jerry's.'

273

He grinned at Hepworth and gave him a pat on his shoulder, then glanced around at the others. 'Keep your helmets on – it'll help with identification. And the password – don't forget it.'

'Where will you be, sir?' asked Hepworth.

'There's something Sergeant Sykes and I need to have a quick look at.' He winked at Sykes. 'Then we'll be back to keep an eye on you lot. So stay put until I tell you otherwise.'

Tanner watched the men hurry off towards their posts, then turned to Sykes and said, 'Follow me.' He led him off the low ridge and down in the direction of the Knossos road.

'Where are we heading, Jack?' Sykes asked.

Ahead of them, just off the road, stood a house surrounded by a garden filled with plane trees, palms and shrubs. 'There,' said Tanner, pointing. 'It's the villa Pendlebury used to live in before the war.'

'Very nice too,' whispered Sykes. 'But what are we looking for?'

'I'll show you in a minute.'

Passing through a series of vineyards, they reached the rear of the grounds of the house. Tanner paused and listened. The place seemed quiet. Both Knossos and the villa lay in no man's land – too far south to be of use to the British and not yet discovered by the newly arrived Germans. There was no sound coming from the ridge to their right either. *Good*, thought Tanner. *The lads are still all right.*

'What a place,' whispered Sykes. 'Not a bad little basha if you ask me. But, Jack, what's here?'

'Stop jabbering, Stan, and I'll show you.'

Shadows from the protective canopy of the trees streaked across the villa, giving it a cold, deserted appearance. Insects whistled and clicked but the air felt suddenly close, every sound accentuated. Tanner led Sykes around the front of the house, past the steps that led up to its entrance and around to the side, where, tucked away, hidden by trees and bushes, there was a shed.

'Here,' said Tanner.

'It's a shed, Jack.'

'It's a lock-up of Pendlebury's. A secret arms stash. Heavily padlocked, as you can see, but I'm assuming nothing that would trouble you, Stan.'

Sykes grinned, then delved into his pack and brought out a set of short metal wires. Leaning against the door, he inserted one into the key-hole, manoeuvred it carefully and grinned as the padlock opened with a click.

'Stan, you're a genius,' said Tanner. The door creaked, the sound making him wince. Inside, he took out his torch, a small rectangular German one, carefully placed a blue perspex lens over the light and switched it on.

At the far end of the shed, a tarpaulin covered a mound. Tanner pulled it back to reveal a number of wooden boxes, perhaps a dozen in all. The top two were a little over a foot long and about eight inches wide, painted green and with '14 SLABS DEMOLITION TNT MK 1' stencilled on the side. 'Now you're talking.' Sykes grinned, moving the box onto the floor. 'Shine the torch a sec, Jack. I want to see what else we've got here.' He moved a couple more boxes, then said, 'Eureka!' He pulled out a metal tin, slightly larger than the boxes, and furiously opened it. 'Recognize these beauties?' he said, pulling out a smaller tin.

Tanner grinned. 'Pull switches, Stan.'

'Too bloody right.' He tugged out another, smaller wooden box, which was filled with reels of fuse and tins of detonators. 'Blimey,' he said, 'this is a regular bloody Aladdin's cave!'

'You know I always try to keep you happy, Stan.'

'But we can't carry this lot,' said Sykes, standing up and looking thoughtful.

'Take what we can now – enough to have some fun tonight, at any rate, and perhaps we can come back here tomorrow.'

'But who's it all for?'

'Pendlebury's Cretan *andartes*, but it *is* ours. This is British stuff. And I can't see them using it. After all, how are they going to get to it?'

Suddenly, behind them, the door swung open. Tanner and Sykes froze.

'Like this,' said a voice, in heavily accented English. 'Two thieves caught red-handed.'

'You!' hissed Tanner. 'What the bloody hell are you doing here?'

14

Alopex stood framed in the doorway, two of his *andartes* behind him. 'We have come to check on our supplies – supplies we will need when you have run away again.'

'I'm not going bloody anywhere.'

'I hope not. We still have a score to settle. Two scores to settle now. You let Pendlebury get killed.'

'He got himself killed with that hare-brained plan of his,' growled Tanner. 'As you know full bloody well. You should have persuaded him to go with you.' Tanner shone his torch in Alopex's face. 'You had no problems getting through, then? Or have you been skulking here ever since?'

Alopex laughed, then lunged forward and flung a fist into Tanner's stomach. He doubled up, gasped, and staggered backwards.

'Hey, hey, easy, mate!' said Sykes, moving between them.

'Listen, you son of a whore,' hissed Alopex, spitting at Tanner. 'We came back down from the mountains, as we have been doing every night – killing Germans. I had some business to see to in town – and I was not stopped once, not on the way in or back out again. Your men are by the Jesus Bastion, I seem to remember.'

Tanner, recovering his breath, clenched his fists.

'Easy, Jack,' said Sykes, then turned back to Alopex. 'Listen, mate, you've got a whole load of explosives here. Do you lot know how to use 'em?'

Alopex glared at him.

'Only I do,' said Sykes. 'Me and Tanner here, we've blown up a lot of Jerries since this war began and we're fully intending to blow up some more. Let us take a few bits and pieces and, trust us, we'll make good use of them.'

Alopex eyed him suspiciously. 'What will you do?'

'I haven't exactly worked it out, but we've got here fuse, explosives and pull switches, an' that means we can make some booby traps, see? There are some wells up there and old sheds and that, the kind of places Jerry's going to make a beeline for. We go up there now and arrange a few trip wires for them, and then when they're looking for shelter or a little drink to ease their thirst, they get a nasty shock instead. See?' He put two tins of pull switches into the deep inside pockets of his battle blouse.

Alopex thought for a moment. 'All right. But we'll come with you.'

'And you and Tanner will stop trying to kill each other?'

Alopex laughed. 'For tonight, yes.'

'Sir?' said Sykes, turning to Tanner.

Tanner glared at Alopex. He was about to speak, to warn him never to lay another finger on him, but then he saw Sykes shake his head. He took a deep breath, pulled out his bayonet and yanked open a box of explosives.

'You should listen to your friend more often,' said Alopex.

'Says the man with the biggest gob in Crete. Just shut up, Alopex, and let's get on with it.'

They took a box load of TNT between them, fourteen one-pound rectangular blocks, wrapped in foil and covered with light yellow paper, along with tins of both safety and instantaneous fuse. 'There are a lot of Germans maybe five hundred metres ahead,' said Alopex. 'There is an old river escarpment they are sheltering behind. But there are others closer to hand.'

As they made their way through a vineyard, the ground rose gently. Suddenly it dropped away into the valley beyond Knossos. Alopex stopped them and pointed out two buildings, silhouetted darkly against the faint glow of the sky. 'The house over there is deserted, abandoned,' he said. 'The other is a store. It has a well beside it.'

Just then they heard a wounded paratrooper cry out nearby. *'Helfen Sie mir!'* came the desperate plea. *'Helfen Sie mir!'*

'Poor bugger,' said Sykes. 'I almost feel sorry for him.'

Alopex glanced at him, then hurried forward with his two *andartes*. Sykes and Tanner followed. They soon found the German. He had cut free his parachute, but had clearly broken a leg or ankle on landing. He looked up at the men now around him, eyes wide with fear. Alopex crouched over him and pulled out a knife.

'Nein, nein!' cried the man. *'Bitte...'*

Alopex grabbed the man by his collar, yanked him up and thrust the knife into his side. The man gasped, then Alopex dropped him, and glared again at Sykes.

Tanner crouched beside the dead man, closed his staring eyes, then rifled for magazines in his pockets. 'Probably been unconscious,' whispered Tanner to Sykes. 'Imagine waking up, in pain, and it's dark, and then a sodding great Cretan comes along and shoves a knife into you. Jesus. Who'd be a paratrooper?'

A few shots rang out nearby, the enemy alerted

by the alarmed cries of their comrade.

They waited a few moments, then moved on, reaching the ruined house. Sykes worked quickly, putting a small length of instantaneous fuse into a block of TNT and attaching the other end to the fuse adaptor at the end of the switch. He then tied the block of explosive to an old hinge at the bottom of the doorway, using safety fuse as wire. Another length was tied through the eye of the pin on the pull switch, which he then ran across to the other side of the doorway, where he found an old nail to tie it to. Checking the pin would release easily and that the length of fuse was taut, he hurried round the other side of the building to the well. This time he hid the explosive behind a large stone, which he placed at the base of the wall around the well, then ran the fuse back to the house, through the grass just a few inches off the ground. Only around two pounds of pressure were needed – easily created by someone getting their foot caught in the trip wire. The pin would be pulled out from the switch, which in turn released a spring that had been holding the firing pin in place. This knocked forward a striker rod, which caused the end of the fuse to spark and, with it, the TNT to explode.

They scurried on to the old store house, and set another booby trap. Alopex was delighted. 'We could do with a man like you,' he said, clutching Sykes's shoulder. 'We shall enjoy watching these blow up.' He translated for his comrades, who chuckled in agreement.

'We need to get back to the others,' muttered Tanner, in a low whisper.

'And we need to kill a few more Germans,' said Alopex, 'then get back to the mountains.' He looked at Tanner and Sykes. 'But if you steal any more of my supplies, I'll know where to find you. I like your little friend here,' he said, 'but not that much.' He pinched Sykes's cheek and left them.

'That man,' muttered Tanner, as they scampered back in a wide arc towards the others. 'I can't bloody shake him off.'

'A useful bloke to have on our side, though. You've got to admit he's a bloody good fighter. Damn useful local knowledge, too.'

'That's as may be, Stan, but he bloody gets on my nerves. I swear that's the last time I'm going to let someone punch me in the guts and not give them a kicking in return.'

To the south, a man screamed. *Alopex*, thought Tanner. Sykes was right – he was an effective and utterly ruthless fighter. No wonder Pendlebury had sought to help men like him and Satanas. If the Germans did seize the island, they would certainly have a difficult time so long as men like them were alive. It hardly made him feel better, though. Alopex had taunted them about the British leaving the island, and it had struck a nerve. A few days before he would have thought an evacuation impossible, but he sensed the balance was shifting. An ammunition shortage already! Good God, he wished they'd used up every last round three days earlier – if they had, there would not be any Germans left on this part of the island. Yet now every day the German situation was improving while theirs was slowly but surely getting worse. If something was not

281

done about it soon, the time would come when the scales tipped against them for good. And then they would be falling back yet again, dependent on the navy to extricate them from the latest débâcle. *Jesus*, he thought, *please don't let it be so.*

The pickets had seen nothing.

'Where've you been, sir?' asked Hepworth.

'Never you mind, Hep. Now move back out of the way. Sergeant Sykes needs a bit of space.'

'Why, sir, what's going on?' He watched Sykes. 'Oh, I get it. Where d'you find them, sir?'

'All these questions, Hep. Let's just say we discovered a secret source, all right?'

They moved on to the well, calling 'yorker' in loud whispers, and then, once Sykes had set another booby trap, they carefully made their way over to the stone wall where the remainder of Hepworth's section were still keeping watch.

'See anything?' Tanner asked.

'We heard something, sir,' said Cooper. 'Jerries screaming. Was that you, sir?'

'No. Our Cretan allies,' said Tanner. He looked at his watch. 'That'll do. Come on, let's head back.'

As they gave out the password and crossed back to their positions at the edge of the town, Lieutenant Liddell was there to meet them.

'Well?' he said. 'We didn't hear anything. All quiet out there?'

'Very quiet, sir,' said Hepworth.

But at that moment one of the booby traps exploded, a shocking, jarring blast that flashed briefly and lit the horizon with a bright orange glow. Liddell flinched.

'God almighty!' he exclaimed. 'What was that?'

'A nasty shock for some Jerry, I shouldn't wonder,' said Tanner, calmly lighting a cigarette. The others laughed. 'Right, then, boys, go and get some kip.' He paused and turned to Liddell. 'It's your sergeant, sir. Very handy with explosives, he is.' He chuckled, then headed on in the direction of Company Headquarters.

Sunday, 25 May, a little after 9 a.m. Tanner sat on his rocky outcrop, peering through his German binoculars. It was another glorious early summer's day, the sky clear blue save for a few white puffs hovering over the mountains. Little seemed to be stirring ahead – and why would it? Those paratroopers would be below the ridge-line, stuck under the escarpment that Alopex had mentioned. No, he doubted they would see much movement that day. A few parachutes were still caught up in the groves, but otherwise there was little sign that there had been such a large air drop the day before.

He had heard only three explosions during the night, which left another three – those closest to their own positions – still untouched. *Ah, well,* he thought. There was always another night, and he felt little concern that any locals might disturb them in the meantime – he'd not seen a single person tending the land ahead of them since the invasion had begun.

But now he heard a faint rumble from the north, and quickly swivelled round to scan the sky. The noise was rapidly increasing and then he spotted them – more than twenty enemy aircraft approaching. The sound of aero-engines had risen to a thunderous roar as they flew almost past the town. The ack-ack had once again begun pounding, the heavy guns booming dully, black puffs of, smoke bursting out over the sky, when the lead plane flipped over and began its dive. Even before the sirens began wailing, Tanner recognized them as Stukas. One after another they were screaming directly towards the town.

Tanner hurriedly put on his tin helmet as bombs began detonating. Light ack-ack guns were pumping shells towards them but the first dozen planes completed their dives successfully. Huge rolling clouds of dust and smoke were lazily rising into the air, shrouding the town. The noise was deafening but above the whine of aircraft, the thunder of the guns and the blast of exploding bombs came the crash of falling masonry as buildings crumpled.

Having dropped their loads, the Stukas disappeared but almost immediately another wave of bombers arrived, this time Junkers 88s, more than two dozen, racing in along the coast from the west and dropping a seemingly endless number of bombs. Heraklion had completely disappeared under the pall of smoke and dust. Tanner watched mesmerized, the shock of exploding bombs shaking the ground on which he sat. Shells continued to be pumped into the air, but the gunners were now firing blind. Suddenly, a Junkers emerged, an engine alight. The men cheered as it spluttered overhead, so low the oil streaks could be seen across its underside, the black crosses clear and distinct. The great machine banked and headed north again, hidden once more by the dust and smoke.

Tanner guessed it must have crashed into the sea, but then found himself ducking as he heard the whistle of a falling bomb nearby, which exploded on some houses a hundred yards to the west. Once again, the ground seemed to tremble, and now the dust pall was rolling over their positions too. Taking his water bottle, he wetted his handkerchief and placed it over his mouth, then clambered down as another set of bombs whistled towards them. This time they were closer and Tanner flung himself onto the ground as a building just yards from Company HQ received a direct hit. With an ear-splitting crash, the building collapsed, a cascading mass of tile, stone and wood. Shards were blasted into the air and Tanner felt them raining down on him, clattering against his helmet. Men were coughing and spluttering and shouting curses. His throat felt raw despite the wet handkerchief.

And then the bombers were gone. Spectral figures stood up, emerging through the haze, coughing, staggering, numbed by the noise and weight of the attack. Tanner drank from his bottle, the already warm water as soothing as ice. Captain Peploe appeared from the direction of Company Headquarters, his face, uniform and hair covered with dust. 'The bastards,' he said, then began coughing violently.

'Is Company HQ all right, sir?' asked Tanner.

'Yes. A bit of bomb blast, but that's about it,' he replied, when he'd recovered. 'Thankfully there was no glass in the windows.' He leaned on his knees and cleared his throat. 'They certainly weren't going for the harbour that time,' he said at last. 'They were going for the whole damn town.'

Tanner offered him his water bottle. 'I pity the poor bastards in the centre. That was some bombardment.'

Peploe took a long gulp of water, then wiped the back of his hand across his mouth. 'This is not good, Jack. Not good at all.'

Captain Alex Vaughan had stayed put in his house when the siren rang out and the first bombs began to fall, but as explosions started crashing around him and buildings crumbled, he hastily closed the window shutters and took to the cellar. He prayed that the stash of armaments was safe. That morning he had paved the way for the arrival of the caique that night. The thought of it all being destroyed was doubly alarming, because of the loss to the guerrillas and because if it exploded it would tear a giant hole in the heart of the old town.

Even from his hideout in the cellar, he had heard the whistle of bombs and felt the ground shudder. Several landed uncomfortably close. He wondered whether the entire building above him might topple. Certainly plenty of dust and debris fell from the cellar's roof.

But somehow the building survived, and when at last the bombers had left, he tentatively made his way up the stairs into the main part of the house once more. Outside, Heraklion was shrouded by a dense fog of dust and smoke, so thick it was like the worst pea-souper in London. He

286

waited inside, drank some water, then a large brandy, and at last ventured out. Slowly but surely, the dust was dispersing, like a veil being slowly lifted. Vaughan gasped at the level of destruction. Rubble and debris littered almost every street. Although much of the town miraculously still stood, many buildings had been utterly destroyed and now lay crumbled in heaps as much as ten foot high. Many more had been damaged.

Damn, damn, damn. Picking his way through the ruins, he saw a woman lying sprawled in the street, her skin and clothes completely white apart from the pool of blood beneath her. He clambered over an eight-foot-high mound that blocked the road and realized it had been the barber shop where he used to go for a shave and a trim. The alley to the safe house was also partially blocked but, struggling over the loose rubble, he managed to reach the door in the wall. On opening it he saw, to his great relief, that the building above the cellar was still intact. Well, that was something.

But one thing was perfectly obvious: there was absolutely no way they would be able to shift the whole lot that night – not quickly and discreetly.

Alopex would have to wait for his stash of arms.

From the 3rd Battalion command post away to the west of the town, Oberleutnant Balthasar had also watched the bombing of Heraklion. From the first floor of the house, he and Major Schulz peered through his binoculars as the town walls slowly emerged from the haze of dust and smoke.

'Richthofen's lot did their job well,' said Schulz,

a wry smile on his face.

'It's about time we gave them a show of force,' said Balthasar, still looking through his binoculars. 'They've not been playing by the rules. They needed a lesson like this.'

He had already been feeling in better spirits before the bombardment, not least because his bout of dysentery seemed to have passed. Earlier that morning he had eaten a tin of meat spread and hard bread, some chocolate and a fruit bar, then washed it down with a mug of hot coffee and a Pervitin tablet. Two hours on, and his stomach was still at peace, no longer stabbing him with pains from bile or nauseous hunger. In fact, he felt fresh and full of energy for the first time in days.

But there was another reason for his improved humour. At just before eight that morning, they had at last made direct radio contact. For days they had heard only occasional snatches of traffic, but now at long last they had spoken directly with Athens. Ironically, there was still no link to Oberst Bräuer, only a few kilometres away, but it seemed Bräuer's headquarters was also in contact with XI Fliegerkorps HQ in Athens, so finally the separated parties could communicate with each other.

And not only had Athens warned them of General von Richthofen's plans to pulverize Heraklion, they had also relayed Bräuer's orders that all troops of the 1st Fallschirmjäger were to join together to the east of the airfield – that meant not only the 3rd Battalion but also those men who had landed the day before to the south of the town. They were to move that night, under the cover of darkness.

The prospect of leaving their river hiding place, with its stench of baking corpses, faeces and sweat, had given all the men a lift. No longer would they be isolated and rudderless. Rather, they would be massed together, no doubt in preparation for an assault on the airfield. The port, Balthasar now realized, was of secondary importance. Once the airfield was captured, troops and supplies could be flown in, rather than haphazardly dropped from the sky. The stranglehold could be tightened until the British had to flee or surrender.

It was true enough that capturing the airfield would be no easy task, but for the first time since their disastrous landing, Balthasar could see a way through. Against all the odds, they might yet win the day. And with victory would come revenge.

Balthasar lowered his binoculars and lit a cigar from his ration pack, the smoke curling around him in a thick sweet cloud that kept the insects and the cloying stench at bay. He thought of all the men he had lost since landing. Too many had been brutally butchered at the hands of the Cretans. Balthasar had seen some terrible things in his life, but deliberately hacking off the head of a man or ripping out his guts was something that belonged to a different, more bestial age. Good God, what kind of people were they? They would have to pay for what they had done. He glanced back at the still-smoking town, imagining the piles of rubble and corpses that now littered the streets.

That's just the start of it, he promised himself.

Sunday, 25 May, 8 p.m. Another sweltering day was drawing to a close – a day of back-breaking labour as platoons had been detailed in turns to help the Greek garrison and civilians start the massive task of clearing the town. There had been barely a street in the whole of Heraklion to have gone unscathed. All day, the air had been thick with the smell of dust; it rasped the back of the throat, clung to sweat-moistened skin, and the folds of clothes. The amount of stone and debris littering the myriad streets and alleyways was incredible, and with no mechanical machinery and mostly bare hands little had been achieved, despite the best efforts of soldiers and civilians alike. The priority had been to rescue any of the living still trapped.

Tanner had helped pull a middle-aged woman and her teenage daughter from underneath one collapsed house. It had been painstaking work, one block of stone at a time, with the constant fear that any movement might make the situation worse, rather than better, and with the trapped women's plaintive cries for help ringing in their ears. Eventually, however, they had pulled them clear, their hair, clothes and skin as white as if a sack of flour had been thrown over them. A few cuts and badly bruised, but otherwise, miraculously, they had been in one piece. Others had not been so lucky. Tanner saw one woman clutching her dead child, rocking and wailing with grief. He had wished then that they would be sent back to North Africa, with its wide, open desert – a place where armies could hammer away at each other with civilians well out of harm's way.

But now, back at B Company's lines, Tanner had other things on his mind. He had once more put his battle blouse over his shirt as the heat of the day was replaced by cooler night air. From the outcrop he had been watching the ground ahead once more. Still there was no sign of life and no further explosions. The enemy were keeping out of sight and it had begun to bother him that the remaining three booby traps might be left for some locals to discover.

He was about to head to Company HQ to speak with Peploe, when he saw the captain walking towards him through the olive grove to their forward positions. Tanner clambered down to meet him. 'Just the man, sir,' he said.

'Oh, yes?' Peploe looked around him. The men had dug a series of small two- and three-man trenches either side of the road and between the olives and other trees. Discarded ammunition boxes, bullet casings and pieces of kit littered the ground. 'Looks a bit of a mess, doesn't it?'

'I shouldn't worry too much, sir.'

Peploe took off his tin hat and ran a hand through his hair. 'Maybe not. Anyway, did you want me?'

'Yes, sir. I'd like to go forward and have a dekko.'

'It's certainly been pretty quiet.'

'Those Jerries aren't going to sit out there for ever, sir. After the bombardment this morning, something's got to be brewing.'

Peploe nodded. 'All right. How many men?'

'Just Sergeant Sykes, sir. I want to check those

booby traps we set.'

Five minutes later, they were on their way, Tanner glad to be doing something more interesting than watching a still landscape or shifting stone. At the goat shed they had moved up to the previous evening, they found the trip wire still in place.

'We might dismantle that and the other two, Stan,' Tanner told him, crouching beside the front of the shed.

'Might?'

'I want to see what's up ahead first. You remember that escarpment Alopex mentioned?'

'That far? Bloody 'ell, Jack, do we have to?'

'Something's up, I'm sure of it, and we need to find out what.'

They began taking a wide arc around the old house they had destroyed the previous night – Tanner did not want them to disturb any crows that might be feeding there and give themselves away. As they crouch-walked their way through a vineyard, something made Tanner stop and listen. A chink, a rustle. *Something.*

He moved on to the edge of the vineyard, which stood on a shallow terrace. Below there was another row of vines and beyond a track. And along the track enemy paratroopers were moving, rifles and packs on their backs, Schmeissers in their hands. Tanner immediately withdrew into the vines.

'Jerry,' he whispered to Sykes. 'Heading along a track about forty yards up ahead.'

'How many?'

Tanner inched forward again. He counted one

section and another. Then there was a gap but he could just see more moving in the same direction a little way to the right.

'We need to get back and fetch reinforcements,' he said, hastily pulling himself back into the cover of the vines.

'Hold on a mo', Jack,' said Sykes. He delved first into his pack and pulled out a slab of TNT, then reached into his battle blouse and took out a small, thin metal detonator and a tin of safety fuse. He cut a short length of fuse, fixed it to the detonator, then plunged the latter into the block of TNT. 'A home-made and very powerful hand grenade.' He grinned.

Tanner smiled wryly. 'What the hell? All right. You throw it and I'll give them a quick spray.'

Sykes took out a box of matches, lit the fuse, then briefly stood up and hurled it in the direction of the men walking along the track. In the dusk he had not been spotted and Tanner briefly saw the startled reactions of the enemy as the missile fell between them, then opened fire with his Schmeisser, emptying an entire magazine and seeing men jerk and fall.

'Go!' he hissed at Sykes, and they were running through the vines. Wild shooting followed them, bullets snipping wide through the vines. A moment later the TNT exploded. Tanner was jolted and the ground shook. Men were screaming, bits of stone, earth and debris pattering on the vines behind them. A minute later they had crested the shallow ridge and were now running back towards their lines.

'Jesus, what was that?' said Peploe, who was

waiting by the forward lines.

'One of Sergeant Sykes's speciality hand grenades, sir,' Tanner breathlessly told him. 'Those para boys are moving east – my guess is the whole lot of them. Listen, sir.' They paused a moment. Above the evening sounds of insects, shooting could be heard to the south, occasionally bursts of rapid fire and isolated rifle shots.

'Nothing from the west, sir. It's quiet over there.' He glanced at his watch. It was a little after half past eight and now almost dark. Only a faint glow hung on the horizon beyond the mountains. He adjusted his rifle on his shoulder purposefully, then hurried over to a half-empty ammunition box.

'You think we should be attacking, Jack?'

'Don't you, sir?' He spoke quickly. 'If they're moving east we should be attacking their flank. You know Jerry doesn't like fighting at night. I'm only guessing, but I reckon they must be trying to concentrate their forces for a move on the airfield. Even if I'm wrong, there are still lots of Jerries out there and we should be laying into them. The colonel needs to get the whole battalion moving.'

Peploe bit at his thumbnail. 'All right. I'll run and talk to Old Man Vigar. Keep 4 Platoon here, manning the positions, but get the others ready to move out.'

Peploe returned a quarter of an hour later with the news that Colonel Vigar had authorized 'patrols in force' from B and D Companies.

'He's issued a start time of twenty-one thirty,'

said Peploe. 'That's another twenty-five minutes, sir.'

'I know. But I think it's safe for us to get going. I mean, he didn't say we couldn't.' Peploe shrugged. Behind him men from 2 Platoon were already waiting in the olive grove, clearing throats, shuffling feet, adjusting belts and equipment.

'I agree, sir. We should get on with it.'

'Right, Jack,' said Peploe. 'Call the platoon commanders and sergeants together.'

Five minutes later they were all there, standing in a clearing in the olive grove by the forward positions: Liddell and Sykes from 1 Platoon, Lieutenant Timmins and Sergeant White from 2 Platoon, and Lieutenant Askew and Sergeant Butteridge from 3 Platoon. The moon was waning, but still half full, and with another dazzling sky of bright starlight, Crete was once again bathed in a milky monochrome light in which it was quite possible to distinguish features, landmarks and, in the open at any rate, moving men. To the south, rifle shots and small-arms fire continued to ring out intermittently.

'You hear that?' said Peploe. 'That's the Cretans doing their bit. With rifles and knives. We've got Brens, grenades, some captured Schmeissers. We can wreak havoc on the enemy tonight.'

He handed over to Tanner, who briefed them. They needed to clear the ridge, he told them, then move as quietly as possible further forward. As soon as anything was heard, they would fire flares and open up. 'Keep pressing forward,' he told them. 'Work in your sections around the Bren. Move forward, set up, fire, move forward, set up, fire. They'll be surprised and probably confused, so when we first let rip, we need to make it count.' They were to advance in a 'lazy L' formation: 1 Platoon would lead, representing the horizontal line of the letter; 2 and 3 Platoons would follow at a right angle, the vertical line, so as not to offer too large a target for the enemy and to protect their flank. The three leading sections would be widely spaced, so that the advance covered about a two-hundred-yard front. 'It'll get confusing out there,' he added. 'There will be lots of noise, lots of tracer, and your eyes will have to adjust from bright flashes to the night light. It'll be easy to get lost and disoriented, but white flares will show the forward line. A red flare will be the signal to halt. Tell your men to keep their heads. If they do their job and think calmly everyone will be fine.'

'Amen to that,' said Peploe. He looked at his watch. It was now just after nine. 'We move off at twenty-one ten. And in addition to the red flare, I'll blow my whistle when it's time to withdraw. Good luck, everyone.'

While Peploe moved out on the corner of the L between 1 and 2 Platoons, Tanner joined 1 Platoon by the road. They moved quickly up to the ridgeline, then crested it and pressed on, cautiously making their way through the series of vineyards in the direction of the track where Tanner and Sykes had been earlier. Suddenly a machine-gun opened up only a short distance ahead and slightly to their right, a gurgle of bullets spitting into the night and tearing through the vines. Some men cried out, and Tanner grabbed a grenade from his pack, pulled the pin and hurled it in the direction of the muzzle flash. At the same time 3 Section's Bren opened up with a steadier burst of fire.

Speed, Tanner knew, was now of the essence. 'Move forward!' he hissed and, pulling out his Very pistol, fired two flares, one after the other, which hissed through the air, crackling and shedding white magnesium light over the track and curving valley in front of them. A number of German paratroopers scurried into the vines and groves beyond, fleeing from the sudden light. All along the company's line, rifles and Brens now opened fire as muzzle flashes and MG tracer responded. The noise was incredible, ear-numbingly shrill and harsh, yet Tanner could still somehow make himself heard.

'Up and forward!' he yelled. The Brens stopped, and gasping, panting men were pressing forward through the vines, crouching as bullets scythed around them. Someone cried out on Tanner's left, but there was no time to stop. Jumping from the terrace, they crossed the track, Tanner stumbling over a fallen German. A pause in the gunfire as both sides seemed to be moving, and then a German Spandau was firing again and the night was torn apart by the din of rifles and machine-guns, spots of muzzle flashes and the cries of men. Beside him the Bren hammered out another burst, and then they were off again, Tanner now conscious that the rear of the Villa Ariadne was to his left.

'This way!' he said, and as they reached the edge of the grounds, rifle shots and MG fire opened up from the side of the road. The enemy,

Tanner realized, were trying to cross the road here and head towards the higher, more pronounced ridge overlooking Knossos, which the British had christened Apex Hill.

'Down!' he cried, as bullets tore towards them. He fired another flare, up over the road and, as it burst, he saw more enemy disappearing towards the ruins of Knossos. Beside him the Bren clattered, but then a number of bullets thumped, Lance Corporal Donnelly cried out and the Bren stopped firing.

'Charlie's been hit!' Mercer called.

'Someone take over the Bren!' shouted McAllister, but Tanner had already grabbed it, firing off another burst, then clicking out the magazine and ramming another in its place.

He knew that the Germans by the road would have to make a dash for it or surrender. Handing the Bren to McAllister, he glanced around him, then saw Lieutenant Liddell bent over the wounded Donnelly, his hands clasped to his head in despair.

Jesus, he thought. Then, moving between the men, he saw Sykes.

'Stan,' he said, his voice urgent, 'we need to keep the men here for a moment. Look for some place where we can enfilade down towards the road. I'm going to find the captain.'

Tanner scurried through the vines, shouting for the captain so as not to be mistaken. The firing had lessened again, but just as suddenly the din of battle opened up away to their left, at the far side of the road beyond the ruins. *D Company*, thought Tanner. *Good.*

He hurried on, his breathing heavy. 'Captain!' he called again.

'Here!' from just a few yards ahead.

'We should block the road, sir – try and wheel round. We can set up McAllister's section at right angles to the road on the southern edge of the Villa Ariadne and pour enfilade fire at anyone trying to cross it. The escarpment Alopex told us about runs south-west from there. If we move round behind it, we can trap whatever Jerry troops are there.'

'Yes, but we need to watch out behind us in case there are any more coming through from the west.'

'Send another section back to cover the track below the ridge.'

'Yes – good plan.'

Tanner ran back towards Sykes. The platoon was still holding a rough line extending through the vines from the corner of the Villa Ariadne grounds, but McAllister's section had moved, as had Hepworth's Bren. Ahead, one spat out a short burst, and following the sound, Tanner found Sykes and the others crouched behind a wall that marked the southern edge of the villa's grounds and which overlooked the track leading to the road. *Perfect*, he thought. And Sykes had positioned the two Brens of McAllister's and Hepworth's sections well: covered by the wall but with an interlocking line of fire down the road and across the open ground that led to the ancient palace of Knossos.

'Good work, Stan,' said Tanner. 'Make sure no one fires behind the flare line.'

'Where are you going, sir?'

'Back to the captain.'

Tanner rejoined Peploe, who fired another flare, then moved the men forward again. On his way down the shallow escarpment, Tanner saw shadowy figures flitting through the groves and fired a burst from his Schmeisser. Spandau fire erupted again, like a loud drumroll, rifles cracked and several muzzle flashes of sub-machine-gun fire shone through the trees. Someone to his right cried out, another man swore. Tanner hurled two more grenades, and as they exploded a man screamed. 'Keep moving forward!' he shouted. The firing ahead of them died – *the enemy's running* – and Peploe sent another flare into the sky, this time towards the road. McAllister's and Hepworth's Brens chattered, their bursts rattling over each other, then a short pause and one opened up again.

They reached the road soon after. Peploe fired a red flare and, as it lit up above them, shouted for his men to cease fire. Ahead, on Apex Hill beyond, fighting continued, but in their part of the valley, the shooting had stopped.

'There it is,' said Peploe, gazing towards the ruins, the columns and walls just discernible against the backdrop of the ridge beyond.

'You're getting closer, sir,' said Tanner, beside him. Beads of sweat were running down his face, his heart was pounding and his ears were ringing. The air was so still again, every sound amplified, and despite the incredible cacophony of noise just minutes before, the cicadas and crickets were still chirruping.

'I feel like Tantalus,' Peploe muttered. 'Every time I get near the place, something stops me reaching it.' He rubbed his eyes. 'We should get the wounded back, then hold a line from here up to the ridge, don't you think? There might be more still trying to work their way round.'

Both men had just turned when there was a sudden rustle nearby and a figure got up and began to run away from them through the olives.

'Who's there?' Peploe called. He held out his revolver at arm's length, fired a single shot, but the bullet and the figure were lost to the trees. 'Oh, well,' he said. 'Can't get 'em all. Good luck to him.' A minute or so later, they heard a scream from the darkness to the south.

'The Cretans don't share your forgiving nature, sir,' muttered Tanner.

B Company had done all they could. Beyond, over Apex Hill, was D Company's area of operations, so Peploe sent Lieutenant Liddell back with the wounded, and organized the rest of the men into a rough line extending from the Bren position overlooking the road back up to the ridge, watching for any further enemy approach from the west.

None came. Six hours later, Tanner sat with Peploe at the edge of a vineyard near the ridge, watching the first streaks of light appear behind Apex Hill, the long ridge that extended south and overlooked the Knossos valley.

'Sir?' said Tanner. 'I've got an idea.' He stood up and stretched. 'Come on, sir.'

Peploe followed as Tanner led them back down

301

the line, past shredded vines and trampled grass, and by the bodies of German paratroopers killed in the night. There was a stillness over the battle-field, an eerie calm. As they reached the road, they waved to Sykes and McAllister, smoking cigarettes and still manning one of the Brens. Like all the men, they looked exhausted, shirts and jackets filthy, their faces caked in dust, oil and streaks of blood.

Tanner paused and nodded in the direction of the palace. 'What could be a better way to see it, sir, than at dawn?'

Peploe smiled. 'You know what? You're right.'

They crossed the dusty road and took the track through the trees to the ruins. Painted columns, supporting great slabs of flat roof in places, rose from the ground. They stepped between half-ruined walls, across what had once been the rooms of a giant palace – Peploe was entranced – and then a large open courtyard spread before them. Leading from this was a set of wide steps, which Tanner climbed. At the top, he stopped, sat down and gazed up at Apex Hill. Birds were singing their dawn chorus, a mixture of melodious song and strange whistling calls; the air was crisp and clear, the smell of cordite, blood and sweat replaced by something purer and softer. Around the site, a blanket of firs and olives stretched up towards the ridge, and Tanner breathed in deeply, fatigue sweeping over him like a draped cloak.

He lit a cigarette as Peploe joined him at the top of the steps. An orange glimmer appeared over the crest of Apex Hill, gradually rising before their eyes and bathing first the ridge and then the whole valley in a wash of glorious, uplifting light. Tanner closed his eyes, letting the morning sun's rays warm his face.

'You were right, Jack,' said Peploe. 'This is the perfect way to see it.' He took out his hip flask, had a swig, then passed it to Tanner. They were silent for a moment, then Peploe said, 'Do you think we did enough last night?'

Tanner shrugged. 'God knows.' He drew on his cigarette, not wishing to say what he really believed – what he hardly dared admit to himself: that it had been too little too late. That, once again, they were going to lose.

15

Captain Peploe broke the news shortly after midday on Wednesday, 28 May, having just returned from Battalion Headquarters. He had called Lieutenant McDonald, Tanner and Woodman into the office at Company HQ, poured four shots of brandy, then said, 'It's all over. I'm afraid we're being evacuated tonight.' He stood, his chipped shot glass in his hand, brows knotted.

Tanner slapped the wall. 'I don't bloody believe it!' he said, his voice rising in anger. 'We've barely even bloody tried here!'

'It's not us,' said Peploe. 'It's the main force in the west, around Canea. The counter-attack at Galatas failed, they had to fall back and yesterday the C-in-C gave the order for them to withdraw to Sfakia.'

'Where the bloody hell's Sfakia?' demanded Tanner.

'On the south coast somewhere. Apparently there was little chance of the navy getting the boys out from Suda, so they're crossing country.'

'And now it's our turn,' said McDonald.

'Well, we can't very well stay here if the main force goes.'

'So what's the plan, sir?' asked Woodman.

'We tell the rest of the men at eight p.m. Secrecy is to be maintained – we don't want Jerry getting wind of it until we're safely away. A naval evacuation force will arrive tonight, at around eleven o'clock. We and the Black Watch are going to be the last to leave.'

'Jesus, what a balls-up,' muttered Tanner.

Peploe looked down at his glass. 'Yes. A lot of wasted effort. A lot of wasted lives. Christ knows what the Greeks will think of us now – I'm afraid they're being left here. We've told them there's no room for them.' There was silence in the room, except for a lone fly buzzing lazily. 'Anyway,' said Peploe, at length, and raised his glass, 'there it is. Here's to our safe return to Egypt, and as Old Man Vigar said, at least we can be proud of what we did here. The battalion – and B Company in particular – has done well. Very well.'

Fourteen hours later, Tanner and the rest of the men of the 2nd Battalion were milling around the inner harbour, awaiting their turn to be lifted. The news, when Peploe had told them earlier that evening, had been greeted with stunned silence,

304

although Tanner, who had been watching Lieutenant Liddell, had noticed the expression on the subaltern's face: eyes closed, a heavy breath – *thank God* – and then a glance up that had caught Tanner's steely gaze. Liddell had quickly looked away.

In truth, the men had had time to get used to the idea and the prospect of improved rations, fresh supplies of kit and the inevitable leave in Cairo had lifted their spirits considerably. From the harbour walls they watched the two big cruisers, *Orion* and *Dido*, set sail, followed by three of the accompanying destroyers, all now crammed with troops. Along the mole extending out from the Venetian fort, men of the Black Watch were boarding two more destroyers; next, and finally, it would be the turn of the Yorks Rangers.

So far the evacuation had gone entirely to plan. The Germans did not appear to have realized what was going on. Guns had earlier been destroyed, and stores booby-trapped; the night had been quiet, barely a shot to be heard. The biggest noise had been the singing and shouting of some of the Australians, already drunk as they lined the mole. Around 2.15 a.m., as the Black Watch's ship inched away from the outer harbour, two more destroyers sailed in to take its place.

The battalion was ordered to move down, past the fort and out onto the mole, with B, C and D Companies directed to board HMS *Karachi*, while Headquarters and A Companies were put onto HMS *Kimberley*. Once again, the men were directed onto the lower decks, except for 1 Platoon, whom Tanner volunteered to help with fire duties. It had been a self-interested decision: for once he felt in the mood for company and wanted Sykes nearby. He and Sykes watched as the brigadier and his staff boarded *Kimberley*.

'I thought he was going to be good,' said Tanner. 'The way he hid those guns before the invasion – that was a canny move. But he damn well blew it here.'

'D'you think he knows it?'

'I really have no idea at all how these blokes work.'

By 2.45 a.m. the evacuation was complete. Not a single man remained on the harbour. Tanner, standing at the stern of the ship with Sykes, leaned on the railings smoking a cigarette and looking back at the town silhouetted against the night sky. He could not stop thinking about Alopex and how he had chided them during that first meeting in the café. *Running away again. Bloody hell.*

'I know what you're thinking, sir,' said Sykes, 'but you've got to forget about it. Maybe one day, when the war's over, you can come back and give him a good kicking then.'

'He was right, though, wasn't he?' He exhaled a cloud of smoke. 'I'm absolutely bloody sick of sodding evacuations.'

'So am I, but I can't feel too sorry to be leaving. Not if I'm honest. I don't think islands are my natural habitat. I feel too cooped up, penned in. And that bloody smell.' He whistled. 'You've got to admit it was bad walking down to the harbour.' Little of the rubble had been cleared away since the bombing of the town. Those left trapped

306

among the debris had soon begun to rot in the heat. Sewers had also been broken, and the combined stench of decomposing flesh and sewage had been overpowering. Most of the men had marched through the town with handkerchiefs around their faces.

'It was a bit ripe,' agreed Tanner.

Sykes breathed in deeply. 'Sea air – that's better.'

'But I still feel bloody terrible about leaving those poor bastards. It was a half-decent place when we got here, but now...' He let the sentence trail.

'And they've got the Jerries to deal with.'

Tanner saw the ropes being cast off from the other destroyer with Headquarters and A Companies on board. Moments later, it began moving away from the mole.

'Why aren't we moving?' Sykes asked.

'God knows,' said Tanner. He looked around and saw that some of the crew seemed restless, then noticed a caique leave the inner harbour and chug past them slowly. He wondered who it was, and took out his binoculars for a better look, but it was too dark to pick out any of the features on the men's faces. He watched it leave the harbour, its masts silhouetted against the sky.

The minutes passed but still there was no sign of any movement. Peploe appeared beside them. 'We should be off soon,' he said.

'What's going on, sir?'

'It seems they were attacked as they left Alexandria. They would have had another cruiser, but it was hit and had to turn back. A couple of the destroyers also suffered near misses, including this one. There's something up with one of the engines – I'm not quite sure what – and they've decided to try and fix it.'

Tanner looked at his watch again. It was now a quarter past three. 'Cutting it a bit fine, aren't they? It'll be first light in just over an hour.'

'I said the same to the lieutenant I've just been talking to. Apparently they very nearly put us onto *Kimberley*, but they reckoned that whatever the problem was could be quickly resolved so didn't in the end. Only now, of course, it's taking longer than they thought.'

Suddenly, out at sea, away to the north-east, they heard a dull boom.

'What was that?' said Sykes. 'A mine? Or a torpedo?'

'I wouldn't like to say,' said Peploe. 'Let me try and find out.'

He returned a short while later. 'It was *Imperial*,' he said. 'The other ship damaged coming from Alexandria. Her steering gear had jammed so they had to get everyone off, then torpedoed her.'

'That's a comfort,' said Tanner. 'Bloody hell.'

As the minutes continued to pass with no apparent sign of any movement, Tanner began to feel increasingly agitated. He was not alone – as he and Sykes discovered, as they impatiently moved around the stern.

'Hope you lads have still got some ammo left,' said one of the Y Gun crew.

'I hope your aim's good, mate,' Sykes replied.

'Jesus,' said another in the gun crew. 'What a sodding dog's breakfast. The others'll be halfway back to bleedin' Alex by now, and we're still bloody well stuck in this dump.'

'Get a bloody move on!' shouted another, leaning away from the gun and looking down towards the deck.

It was well after four when they finally got going, which produced a loud, ironic cheer from the men on deck. Already, however, the first faint lightening of the horizon was discernible to the east, and by the time they were clear of the harbour, day was dawning rapidly. As they passed the island of Dia, just to the north-east of Heraklion, the tip of the sun had appeared, casting golden streaks across the sea.

No one said much; the grousing had stopped. It was a waiting game, as every man knew. If they were lucky, they still might not be picked up – it was early after all. And if they were spotted, at least there was only one of them – a single small destroyer, weaving at more than thirty knots, was a difficult target to hit.

But it was not to be. Just after five, Stukas appeared from the east, faint dots at first, quickly becoming angry wasps, and then, moments later, they were over them, diving down, sirens screaming, engines straining, and the pompom and twin cannons pumping out shells towards them. While the gunners tried to train their guns, the men on deck ducked – all except Tanner, who, with his anger rising, had unslung his rifle and begun firing as the first Stuka came out of its dive. It was too far away, he knew, but it *looked* bloody close, so he aimed and fired all the same. The first bombs fell well short, huge plumes of water erupting into the sky, and so did the second batch as *Karachi* veered dramatically. More bombs tumbled around them, the spray lashing across the deck. Suddenly a Stuka was hit, smoke and flame erupting from the engine. Screaming, it plunged into the sea. The men cheered again but then two more bombs were falling towards them.

'Christ!' said Tanner, as he realized they were going to hit. The first disappeared straight down the funnel, while the second seemed to hit the bridge. The two explosions were almost simultaneous, one a dull, muffled roar, the other a deafening crash. The ship jolted, and Tanner clutched at the railings to steady himself. A ball of angry flame and smoke engulfed the bridge and then there was a second explosion. Flame erupted out of the funnel and the ship shuddered again, more violently this time, and, with a creaking and groaning of tearing, grinding metal, the deck started to move. Men were shouting as bombs continued falling around them, Stukas diving and whirling like a swarm of bees. For a moment Tanner was too stunned to move, the noise overwhelming.

The ship lurched, and Tanner glanced around and saw Peploe, McAllister and others from 1 Platoon, all clambering onto the rails. The gun crews were hurling several rubber dinghies overboard while, further along, lifeboats were being lowered.

'Jack!' called Sykes, beside him. 'We've got to jump!'

Keeping his rifle on his back, but discarding his helmet and his Schmeisser, Tanner ducked under the railing, saw Sykes leap clear, then took a deep breath and jumped after him.

The cold sea enveloped him and he immediately felt his clothes and kit clinging to him heavily as he plunged downwards, then forced his way back to the surface. He knew he had to get away from the ship. Men were already filling the dinghies and clinging to the sides but he began to swim away, conscious of Sykes beside him.

The ship groaned again. As Tanner rolled onto his back he saw more men leaping from its side. Already his legs felt heavy, but he knew he had to keep moving – there was no time to discard his boots and kit just yet.

Sykes was gasping, arms flailing in a loose crawl, as behind men screamed and shouted. Suddenly there was a deafening tearing and grinding of metal and the ship began to turn in on itself, slowly at first, the stern and prow inching clear of the water. Tanner heard the screams of men still trapped on board, but then both ends of the ship rose high out of the sea, and seemed to hang there a moment before plunging towards the water with an agonizing screech and groan. Desperate screams from those left on board carried out across the sea, and Tanner watched as several men, arms waving helplessly, and a dinghy full of others, were sucked down with the sinking vessel.

Suddenly the ship was gone, the screaming had stopped, and all that was left were bits of flotsam and a swirling mass of white bubbles and surf.

The Stukas had flown off, their task complete. Treading water, Tanner looked around. Nearby several dinghies were filled with men and more clung to the sides. Tanner saw several of the Y

Gun crew in a dinghy no more than thirty yards away, then spotted McAllister and Mercer and, clinging to the rope around it, Captain Peploe, Hepworth, Chambers and several others from 1 Platoon. Further away, one of the lifeboats was still picking up men, who were calling out, desperate to attract attention.

Tanner swam towards Sykes, who was treading water and trying to get rid of some of his kit. 'You all right, Stan?' he asked.

'I've been better,' he muttered. He turned his head towards a second dinghy. 'We should try and grab onto that one.'

They swam towards it and found Bell and Woodman already inside, along with a few others of the ship's crew. Lieutenant McDonald and Dicky Bonner were hanging on to the outside.

'Ah, hello, you two,' said McDonald, as Tanner and Sykes reached out and grabbed the ropes around the sides of the rubber boat. 'Lovely morning for a swim.'

''Ere, sir,' said Bell, as he noticed Tanner's rifle still sticking up from his back. 'Don't you think you might be better off ditching that?'

'Not at the moment, Tinker, no,' said Tanner. 'I'm not giving up this rifle that easily. I might still need it when we get back on land.' He followed the others' gaze. Crete seemed an unnervingly long way off. 'Come on, boys,' he said. 'It's only, what, six or seven miles? We can make it, can't we?' He looked around. Men were still swimming and flailing in the water. 'Where's Mr Liddell?' He spotted him before his question could be answered, some forty yards away, clearly struggling.

312

'Bloody hell,' said Tanner. 'Stupid bugger can't even bloody well swim properly.' He sighed, then said to Bell and Woodman, 'Look after my stuff, will you?' He passed up his rifle, then his boots, and finally his belt, pack and bayonet. 'Drop any of them over the side, and I'll bloody tip you over as well.'

He immediately felt light and stronger, and swam quickly towards Liddell, reaching him just as the lieutenant's head dipped below water. Grabbing him, he put an arm around his chest and hoisted him up again. Liddell spluttered.

'Easy does it,' said Tanner, and began slowly making his way back towards the dinghy.

But just then, he heard a whir coming from the east that suddenly grew louder so that before he had realized what was happening two Messerschmitt 109s were hurtling towards them, diving out of the sun at high speed. They opened fire, lines of bullets spurting out small fountains of water. Tanner ducked, briefly letting go of Liddell, as bullets hissed through the water around him. Pushing himself up to the surface again, he grabbed Liddell once more, watched as the Messerschmitts climbed and headed on west, then heard cries. Both the dinghies near him were all right, but one of the lifeboats had been raked, several men hit, and now the vessel was sinking.

'Bastards!' said Tanner, then heard Liddell groan. Turning to look at his charge, he realized the water around them was colouring with cloudy dark blood. Liddell groaned again, and Tanner saw that blood was pulsing from his shoulder.

Damn it! Tanner cursed to himself, then grim-

313

acing, swam as quickly as he could back towards the dinghy, even though his arms and legs ached like hell with the effort of swimming and holding up Liddell.

'Here!' he said, as he reached out and grabbed one of the ropes. 'Help me get him in. He's been hit and he's losing blood. Tinker, you're going to have to duck out and make room for Mr Liddell.'

'That's all right, sir,' said Bell. 'I know my place.'

'Just be bloody grateful you're in one piece,' growled Tanner. 'Who's still got some dressings?' He managed to fish out two sodden packets from his denims, as others did the same. 'Woody, see what you can do. That hole needs filling up quickly.'

'I've been hit,' mumbled Liddell. 'Christ, I've been hit. Oh, God.' Tears ran down his face.

'You're all right, sir,' said Woodman. 'Don't you worry.'

'Where's that other dinghy?' said Tanner. 'And give Mr Liddell some water. There's a full bottle on my webbing.'

'Not far,' said Woodman.

'Then holler over to them, Woody,' said Tanner. 'We should try and stick together.'

Those outside the dinghy began kicking while those inside used their arms as paddles. They were slowly drawing towards the other dinghy, when a sailing boat was spotted coming towards them. Immediately the men started shouting and waving.

'She's coming towards us!' said Woodman.

'Good,' said Sykes, 'cos I'm getting bored of this already.'

Tanner now saw the boat: it was a caique very much like the one he had seen leaving Heraklion earlier. The two dinghies were only yards apart by the time the vessel drew towards them, and Tanner now saw that Captain Vaughan was standing at the prow alongside another British officer, ready with a rope. A wave of relief swept over him.

'Alex!' called Peploe, from the other dinghy.

'John?' called Vaughan, incredulously. 'I had no idea it was your lot. Here.' He lobbed the rope. 'Those outside the dinghies, climb aboard. The others stay where you are. We'll tow you.'

'We've got a wounded man here, sir,' called Tanner. 'He'd be better off aboard.'

'All right,' said Vaughan, then recognized Tanner. 'Good God, it's you!' he said. 'Look, bring the dinghy alongside and we'll get him out of there.'

The dinghy nudged alongside the caique. Woodman and the others in the life-craft carefully lifted Liddell, who groaned and cried out in pain. But Vaughan and one of his crew, a leathery-looking Englishman, took hold of him and hoisted him aboard.

'Get him in the cabin, Cle,' Vaughan said to his companion, 'and give him a shot of morphine.'

Tanner now clambered aboard, pulling himself up with great effort and rolling over the side onto the deck. Getting to his feet, he leaned over and helped Sykes and then Bell up too, before asking Woodman to pass up his kit.

'Damn glad to get these back,' he said, clutching his things. 'We worked hard to get those boots, Stan. I hated the thought of having to chuck them.'

315

'I lost my rifle, though,' said Sykes. 'We're going to be a bit short of firepower once we get back on land.'

Tanner patted him on the back. 'Something will crop up. We'll be all right.'

The two dinghies were roped to the back of the caique, and then they picked up a third, and finally the two surviving lifeboats. They spent a further twenty minutes sweeping the sea for any more survivors. A further six men were picked up, but many more floating corpses were left in the water.

'How many men were on the ship?' Vaughan asked Peploe and Tanner.

'Three companies, plus the crew. Over five hundred.'

'And my head count comes to eighty-two. Jesus.'

Peploe swallowed and rubbed his eyes. 'I just can't believe it,' he said. 'All those men. They were alive half an hour ago and now...' He shuddered. 'I've lost most of the company.'

'What happened?' asked Vaughan.

'The ship went down in about four minutes,' said Tanner. 'She had her back broken.'

'And the captain?'

Tanner shook his head. 'A second bomb hit the bridge.'

Vaughan scanned the sky. 'I'm sorry. But if we want to survive as well, we need to get to land quickly.' They stepped around the men crammed on the deck and moved over to the bearded, wild-looking skipper, standing beside an ageing Greek sailor at the wheel and the other British officer. 'This is Commander Mike Cumberlege,' he said,

316

'and Lieutenant Colonel Nick Hammond.'

Peploe looked at Hammond. 'Pleased to see you again, sir.'

'Again?' said Hammond.

'I attended some of your lectures at Cambridge, sir, before the war.'

Hammond smiled. 'Well, well, well. I wish we could be meeting in happier times. I'm sorry about your loss.'

'Thank you for picking us up,' said Peploe. 'I'm not sure we'd have all made it otherwise.'

'We nearly didn't,' said Vaughan. 'We've had to leave Commander Cumberlege's caique in Suda and commandeer this instead.'

'*Miaoules* is a fine vessel in many ways,' said Cumberlege, 'but the engine's on the blink, I'm afraid. Cracked cylinder head.'

'That doesn't sound good,' said Peploe.

'Might be all right,' said Cumberlege, 'if we take her steady. But we're going to head straight into Limenas. It's tucked into a headland about twenty-five miles east of Heraklion, it's – how shall I say? – discreet. I'm afraid it's way too risky to keep going along this north coast today.'

'Thank you,' said Peploe.

'But tonight we can take some of you on. I don't see why we can't try and tow the lifeboats as well.'

'I do,' said Hammond. 'It's risky enough moving a boat like this at all. As it is, we'll need to pull in for the day somewhere along the southeast coast tomorrow morning. Then we've got to get all the way across the Mediterranean with the engine under enough strain as it is. A small lone fishing vessel is not particularly conspicuous, but one towing two lifeboats most definitely is.'

Cumberlege shrugged. 'I'm prepared to give it a go. Perhaps we should put it to the men when we get to Limenas.'

'What's the alternative?' asked Peploe.

'You make your way to the mountains and hole up until things quieten down, or head straight to the south coast and try to take a boat across then. But I should warn you, the south coast is very different from the north. Lots of plunging cliffs and only a handful of places where a caique can get in.'

'Golly,' said Peploe. 'What to do for the best?'

'Was it you I saw leaving harbour earlier?' Tanner asked.

Vaughan nodded, then glanced at Hammond. A nod of consent. 'We're moving arms and explosives,' said Vaughan. 'We brought them from Suda Island at the beginning of the month and they've been stored in Heraklion ever since. I was hoping to have them moved a few days ago, but then the town was bombed and the street they were on was blocked. There wasn't any way of getting them out that night. Instead, we've been moving what we can bit by bit.'

'To Limenas?' asked Tanner.

'Yes. The Germans haven't reached there yet. We're hoping they still won't have done.'

'They'll be too busy today opening up the airfield and pushing into Heraklion,' said Hammond. 'We've got a day's grace, maybe two.'

'It's for Satanas,' said Vaughan. 'We've been moving it up to the Ida Mountains.'

'And have you got it all out now?' asked Tanner.

Vaughan shook his head. 'But it's booby-trapped.'

The sun was already warm, and the men soon began to dry, white patches of salt appearing on their uniforms. Tanner felt in his shirt pocket for his cigarettes, but the packet was still sodden. He sighed.

'Here,' said Cumberlege, passing him a crumpled packet.

'Thank you, sir,' said Tanner. He was hungry too, but he felt better for the smoke. Crete was getting nearer once more – he could see the headland Cumberlege had mentioned jutting out. It looked serenely peaceful – a beautiful island waking up to a perfect early summer's day.

The captain's cousin, Cle Cumberlege, and Lieutenant McDonald emerged from the cabin.

'How's Mr Liddell?' asked Peploe.

'Asleep,' said McDonald. 'The salt water has meant the wound is clean. The bullet also went right through him. We're pretty sure it's not hit anything vital.'

'He should live,' added Cle. 'We can take him with us tonight.'

'What about you, Alex?' asked Peploe.

'I'm staying for the moment,' he said, 'to help with the resistance. Now that Pendlebury's gone.'

'You too, sir?' Peploe asked Hammond.

Hammond shook his head. 'No, I've been ordered back to Cairo.'

The sky remained clear. Only the faintest of breezes wisped across the sea – enough to help dry

319

the men, but barely strong enough to fill the sails. That was why the caique was being powered by its engine. However, as they drew towards Limenas, it began to splutter, with thick, oily smoke puffing out.

'Bugger it!' exclaimed Cumberlege, as the men exchanged anxious glances. 'Cle,' he said to his cousin, 'go and have a look, will you?' Cle disappeared into the cabin and the skipper cursed again. 'Damn and buggeration! It's the bloody cylinder head.' He glanced at Peploe and Tanner. 'They're old, that's the trouble, and we've been pushing them too hard.'

Cle emerged some minutes later. 'She's not good. We're very low on oil.'

'Should we shut her down?'

'No, let's keep going. We should be all right, but we're going to need more oil.'

Eventually they made it, easing into the tiny harbour with its long, protective breakwater. Wearily, the men clambered out of the dinghies and lifeboats and up onto the quayside. They looked a motley bunch after their time in the water – many were without boots or any kit. Several guerrillas were waiting and eyed them with barely concealed contempt. Pushing past the men, a couple of the Cretans jumped down onto the boat and began shifting crates and boxes onto the quay, while two others loaded them onto a waiting cart.

The men, still shaken from their traumatic experience earlier, stood about helplessly, then began to sit down where they were, or drifted away to a wall across the road.

'This is no good,' said Peploe, to Tanner and

McDonald. He rubbed his brow.

They watched Cle and Mike Cumberlege talking with a Cretan, pointing to the caique, then all three jumped back on board and disappeared into the cabin. Hammond and Vaughan were helping with the boxes of supplies, but the task was quickly finished. Seeing Peploe, Hammond called, 'Let me find out what's going on.'

He emerged a short while later with Commander Cumberlege and Vaughan, and all three joined Peploe on the quayside.

'The crack is bad but it should still function. We're hoping we can get some oil and then we'll give it another go tonight,' said Hammond.

'What are the chances of reaching Egypt?' asked Peploe.

Mike Cumberlege sighed and fingered his earring. 'Well,' he said, 'the engine's losing oil. It'll splutter and cough and complain like hell, but it should keep going so long as we can keep topping it up. If we can find some spare, then we should be all right. Otherwise the engine will seize. Trouble is, we can't mend the cylinder head here. There are neither the parts nor the tools.'

'Will the number of people you take make a difference to the performance of the engine?' Peploe asked.

'If we overload the boat, it'll put a greater strain on it. We won't be carrying the supplies, but even so.' He tugged at his earring again. 'But I still think that if we can get some oil, we could tow the lifeboats tonight. If we're lucky we'll get around to the south coast. Maybe we can find another boat.'

'Realistically,' said Peploe, 'how many could

you take?'

'Twenty-five, perhaps thirty. Plus those in the lifeboats.'

'So we're a dozen too many.'

'Look, let me talk to the men,' said Hammond. He called them to gather around him. When they had done so, he briefly scanned the sky, then said, 'The caique needs oil. We're going to try and find some, and if we get it, we should be able to keep going. Commander Cumberlege will hopefully leave here at dusk. He's willing to tow the lifeboats. It may well be that we find another boat – we're going to skirt close to the shore – but we'll definitely have to moor up again tomorrow even if the boat does make it around the island to the south coast.' He cleared his throat. 'Or you may feel you have a better chance simply heading off on foot and trying to find a boat on the south coast. There's room for seventy men at a push. Have a think. I'm not going to order you to do anything.'

Peploe immediately called over McDonald, Tanner and Lieutenant Timmins. 'Well?' he said. 'What do you think?'

'I don't fancy our chances on that boat,' said McDonald. 'The skies will be full of Jerries and running adrift halfway to Alex doesn't sound like fun.'

'I must say it doesn't appeal to me much, either,' said Timmins.

'Jack?' asked Peploe.

'The more men on that boat, the less chance she's got of making it, and that's only if they scrounge enough oil. And a cracked cylinder head

322

means it'll burn the stuff like there's no tomorrow. But the colonel's right – there shouldn't be too many Jerries around inland for a day or so. That boat might pack up at any moment, but I know for certain how fast I can walk. And if I'm honest, sir, I've always been a bit of a landlubber. But we should split up. No disrespect, but I don't want lots of unarmed navy boys following me across the island. Small groups have got a better chance of moving without detection.'

Peploe nodded. 'Good point.'

'And we've got an even better chance if we stick with Captain Vaughan and the *andartes*. They know the island and we don't. Also, they've got a cartload of arms and explosives.'

'I'm with Tanner, sir,' said McDonald.

'Timmins?' said Peploe.

'Me too.'

'And I'd like to get going now, sir,' said Tanner. 'I don't want to wait a day here. What if Jerry does turn up?'

Peploe smiled ruefully. 'Let me talk to Captain Vaughan.'

Twenty-two Rangers had survived the sinking of *Karachi*. The sixteen who had kept their boots on in the sea would go with Vaughan and the Cretan guerrillas, and that included Lieutenant Liddell. Neither Captain Peploe nor Tanner would allow him to remain with the caique.

'We can't abandon him,' Peploe said, 'not when he's unable to make the choice.' But he knew that for Tanner there was more to it than that. Everyone else chose to stay with the boat.

As they climbed out of the village, Tanner paused and looked back Men were still dotted around the quayside, a long day's wait ahead of them. He glanced at the mountains away to the south and the giant Ida range looming in the distance, and wondered briefly whether they had made the right decision.

But then he thought of Alopex and the humiliation of this latest defeat. There was still a score to settle, and now, back on Crete, he had a chance to put that right.

16

A little after ten that morning, Oberleutnant Kurt Balthasar stood with the rest of the men of the 3rd Battalion on the edge of the airfield at Heraklion, watching the first Luftwaffe transports come in to land. The men all cheered and waved, raising their rifles and MP40s above their heads.

Balthasar could still barely get used to the idea. What an incredible turnaround it had been! Just a week earlier, he had been plunged into deep despair, racked with illness and facing defeat. But in seven days their fortunes had been transformed. The battle was won, and the whole of the Orion sector was theirs. He looked out at the sea, twinkling in the late May heat beyond the airfield, then watched the Tante Jus, propellers whirling, as they taxied away from the runway, orange dust swirling. As the first switched off its engines, the paratroopers hurried towards it, ready to help unload. On board there were more arms, ammunition, rations and medical supplies, while also due to arrive that day were much-needed reinforcements of men: the building blocks that would enable them to establish a new garrison in the centre of the island.

Later Major Schulz led them to Heraklion, the town in which they had fought such a bitter battle. On the way, they crossed the former British lines, littered with ammunition boxes, uneaten rations and other items of kit. The men took what they could, then continued on their way, singing as they went.

Sullen faces and rubble greeted them; and so did the stench of death. Balthasar spent much of the day with his dampened handkerchief over his face. There was much to be done, not least the disarming of the many Greek troops in the town, who had formally surrendered and were then put to work clearing the rubble, so that paths at least could be made through the tight web of roads that ran through the town. Later, they were to be corralled in the bastions until they could be shipped to the mainland, then on to the Reich.

Aircraft were still regularly flying in as Balthasar received a message to join Major Schulz at Oberst Bräuer's new headquarters in the Megaron, a large and imposing building overlooking the harbour and the Sabbionera Bastion. Already flying over the building – albeit hanging limply in the sultry late-afternoon air – was the red, white and black of the swastika.

Balthasar walked up the steps to the entrance. Guards were standing sentinel outside, and clicked impressively in salute as he went past them and into the hallway. Hauptmann von der Schulenberg was also waiting there, and rose as Balthasar entered. 'Kurt,' he said, 'our colonel has chosen well, has he not?'

Balthasar smiled. 'But of course. And even the stench is not so bad.'

A staff officer appeared and ushered them up the staircase to the first floor where, in a large balconied room, Oberst Bräuer already sat behind a large marble desk. Before it, sitting on an elegant Italianate chair, was Major Schulz.

'Gentlemen,' said Bräuer, 'let me get you a drink. Brandy?'

'Thank you, Herr Oberst,' said Balthasar. Like von der Schulenberg, he stood to attention.

Bräuer waved a hand at them, in which he held a cigarette in a holder. 'Relax, and, please, help yourselves to cigars. They're on the desk. I prefer my own cigarettes but I do so enjoy the smell of cigar smoke.'

They thanked him again and did as they were bidden. Balthasar clipped the end of his with his gravity knife and lit von der Schulenberg's, then his own. Puffs of smoke wafted into the air.

'See? A lot better than rotting corpses and open sewers, is it not?' grinned Bräuer, passing them both glass balloons of brandy. He raised his own. 'To victory, gentlemen!' The colonel was in his late forties, short but immaculate, even after nine long days of intense combat. Somehow, since reaching the Megaton, he had washed, shaved and had his uniform pressed. His hair was close-cropped and silvery, his face lined but smooth, while his eyes were pale grey and hawkish. He was something of a legendary figure within the Fallschirmjäger – a veteran of the last war, the first German to make a parachute jump, and the first and only commander of the 1st Division.

'This place, Herr Oberst,' said Balthasar, 'it is incredible. And amid all this destruction too.'

'I know. It was built only a few years ago by some wealthy citrus traders, but they did a good job. For the past few years it has been the heart of the town. Our pilots must have known we would want it, for they have very generously dropped their bombs all around but not here.' He wandered over to one of the large windows. 'And what views, too. You see our flag flying proudly over the fortress?'

'And over this building too, Herr Oberst,' said Balthasar.

'It's important to do these things straight away. To stamp a mark immediately. That is why I have set up my headquarters here, in the most important building in the town. We have to show the Cretans that we are now in charge – not their own government or king and not the British. Crete is now German.' He sipped his brandy, then turned back to them. 'It has been a hard time, these past nine days. The resistance from the local population has been surprising and shocking, but there can be no more attacks on our men. I remind you of the Ten Commandments of the Fallschirmjäger.'

'Number nine, Herr Oberst,' said Balthasar.

'Against a regular enemy, fight with chivalry, but give no quarter to guerrillas.'

Bräuer smiled. 'Yes, Oberleutnant. Exactly. We give no quarter to guerrillas. And yet they have already given us quite a headache and no doubt will continue to do so if we do not crush them immediately. Earlier today I spoke to General Student, who has already spoken to the *Reichsmarschall* about the outrages these bandits have carried out on our troops. Goring has already insisted on an immediate judicial inquiry and given us the authority to carry out reprisals.'

'This will be wonderful news for Oberleutnant Balthasar, Herr Oberst,' said Schulz 'He is particularly anxious, I know, to avenge what happened to a number of men in his company.'

Bräuer raised a quizzical eyebrow.

'There were many atrocities and mutilations, Herr Oberst, but three of my men were beheaded – with knives.'

'I feel your outrage, Oberleutnant, believe me I do. General. Student will shortly be issuing orders to every paratrooper on the island, but he is fully aware that certain members of the civilian population have been actively involved as *franctireurs*, including women and even young boys. He wants us to carry out the harshest of measures.'

'What does that imply exactly, Herr Oberst?' asked Balthasar.

'It means that we will shoot anyone known to have committed such crimes, and burn entire villages where necessary. The people need to know that if they carry out such atrocities – or, indeed, even support such actions – we will respond with the utmost severity.' He sipped his brandy. 'Personally, I dislike such actions. We are soldiers, not policemen. However, it's clear that we must show we will not stand for such behaviour. General Student,' he added, 'told me today that he wishes those units who have suffered the worst such atrocities to be the ones to undertake reprisals and punitive operations.' He sat down at his desk. 'And that means you, gentlemen.'

'We know *franc-tireurs* were operating here in Heraklion,' Schulz said to Bräuer, 'and we also know that the townspeople have strong connections with the peasant villages in the Ida Mountains.'

'We should question some of the townspeople and the Greek soldiers who fought near the Canea Gate,' said Balthasar. 'We need names. The men who were with Pendlebury.'

'Pendlebury?' said Bräuer.

'Yes, Herr Oberst,' said Balthasar. 'A British agent we captured who had been working with the Cretans. He was also implicated in the beheading of my men.'

'And where is Pendlebury now?'

'We had him shot. He deserved worse.'

Bräuer took out a gold case and fitted another cigarette into his holder. 'More reinforcements are due in tomorrow and shortly some Gebirgsjäger troops will be joining us here in Heraklion. I want you to crush these guerrillas, gentlemen. Use whatever means you see fit. You will have my support in this.'

The three men, recognizing this was the signal for them to leave, finished their drinks and, their cigars still between their fingers, saluted and turned to leave.

'Gentlemen?' said Bräuer. 'Find the leaders. Cut off the head, as you well know, and the body cannot function.'

It was late in the afternoon that they came across the wrecked plane. Since leaving Limenas, they had headed south-west, away from the coast and into the vast, wide stretch between the Dikti range in the east and the Ida Mountains to the west, a part of the island criss-crossed with valleys, narrow rivers and low ridges, most, it seemed, covered with endless olive groves, dense in places, young in others. They had passed few villages in this corner of the island, just the occasional isolated house and farmstead. They had seen few people as they tramped along the myriad dusty tracks that wove through the soft, undulating hills and valleys. Central Crete had been quiet; there had been little to suggest the calamity that had just befallen the island.

But as they had dropped down towards a wooded river valley they had smelt the familiar stench of decomposing flesh. While the Cretans had remained with the cart, Tanner and Sykes had pushed on ahead and there, across the river among the trees, they had seen the Junkers. The wings had been ripped off and lay jaggedly torn a short distance behind, but when they picked their way towards the cockpit, they saw that a row of bullets had raked the metal and windscreen. The propeller at the front had shattered and, inside, the decomposing body of the pilot

330

was still strapped into his seat, his face a deep purple where it had not already been eaten to the bone. As they neared, a thick swarm of flies rose out through the shattered perspex making both men jump.

'Argh, that's bloody disgustin'!' said Sykes, shielding his eyes.

The wreck showed no sign of having caught fire, and they went to the open door along the corrugated fuselage, Tanner poking his head through cautiously, fearing what he might find. But there were no other bodies – the crew had clearly jumped free in time. There were, though, half a dozen canisters.

He turned back to Sykes, grinning. 'It's bloody Father Christmas up there in the cockpit. Have a look at this.' He jumped up and moved down the fuselage.

'Beautiful,' said Sykes. 'Just what the doctor ordered.'

They had already begun dragging out the canisters when the rest of the men joined them, and soon they had all six clear of the wreckage and back by the track where the cart and mule now stood. One of the boxes was full of rations and medical supplies and Tanner was relieved to get his hands on some more cigarettes; his supplies were not only very low but still damp with seawater. But the others were all filled with arms. In one there were two MG34s and a number of boxes of ammunition. In two others there were rifles. The last contained a dozen MP40s and boxes of magazines.

The machine-guns were placed in the cart

beside Lieutenant Liddell, and much of the rest was divided between the men, to the annoyance of the Cretans, who remonstrated with Vaughan.

'They think their own men should have the weapons,' Vaughan explained to Peploe.

'But we need to defend ourselves too,' Peploe replied. 'Finders keepers.'

'That's what I told them,' said Vaughan. 'They can have what you don't need, but they're particularly anxious to have the Schmeissers.'

'Tell them they can have six – half of them. I don't know why they're so annoyed. It's an entirely unexpected cache.'

As the men slung rifles and sub-machine-guns over their shoulders, they began moving again, the Cretans slapping the rump of the mule and the wooden wheels squeaking.

'I have some sympathy for them, actually,' said Vaughan. 'Cairo told us to arm and prepare these men, but we've had very little help. This arms stash we've been trying to move – Pendlebury built it up over months. We could only get it in the first place by saying it was for 50 ME Commando. So then it was stored on Suda Island, and over the past few months we've been bringing it down and distributing it bit by bit.'

'And Commander Cumberlege has been helping you?'

'Yes – in those bloody useless ancient caiques. We've asked repeatedly for a couple of MTBs, but needless to say we were sent nothing of the sort.' He slapped the back of his neck as a fly buzzed around him. 'These people are still woefully under-armed. They're full of fire and determination to keep up the fight but, really, I'm not at all sure how they're going to be able to manage it.'

'I don't blame them for being angry with us, sir,' said Tanner, now walking alongside them. 'I reckon I would be too if I'd been left in the lurch by my ally.'

'Yesterday evening Satanas came to see me in Heraklion,' said Vaughan. 'Suddenly there he was, bandoliers crossed over his chest. He guessed about the evacuation – he'd seen some of the men packing up and destroying their guns, and so he came to me to ask me when it would be. It pained him to see us destroying equipment and he suggested we might leave our weapons and any ammunition we had. Well, I couldn't help him, so I took him to Brigade HQ. They were still frantically packing up when we got there, but we found the brigadier.'

'How was he?' asked Peploe.

'A bit sheepish, as you can imagine. But Satanas just put his hand on Chappel's shoulder and said, "I know you are leaving tonight. It is all right. You will come back when you can. But, please, leave us as many rifles and weapons as you can so that we might continue the fight until you return." I thought the brigadier was going to start blubbing – he was really moved, and told everyone to hand over all they had there. It was quite a stash, in fact. We got a cart and then Satanas and his men left. His magnanimity was quite astonishing.'

'It's always more effective than hurling insults,' said Peploe. Vaughan chuckled. 'If you're thinking of Alopex, remember, he's a lot younger. Satanas has lived for ever. Age has made him wise. But

333

Alopex is a wily operator. He's not called Alopex for nothing.'

'Why, sir? What does it mean?' asked Tanner.

'The Fox,' said Vaughan. 'His real name is Giorgis Kristannos.'

'The Fox.' Tanner smiled. 'Well, well.'

Not long after that they stopped for a rest, lying up in a sheltered grove by a stream. They would soon be nearing the main road that led from Heraklion, past Knossos and down towards the south of the island. Around eight miles beyond that there was another of the island's main roads, which linked the north to the south. Any of these, it was agreed, would be better crossed at night. Rations were passed around, watches posted and then the rest settled down to sleep.

Tanner found a patch of soft grass at the foot of an olive tree and, with a lit cigarette between his lips, got to work on his rifle. His oiler and small phial of gin had survived his time in the sea, and he soon had his trusted Lee Enfield cleaned, oiled and working in perfect condition. He also stripped and cleaned his MP40 and, satisfied that he was once again armed and able to defend himself properly, lay down. Cicadas were clicking and chirruping loudly, and for a minute he watched a small lizard scuttle up the bark of the tree. He never liked to think too far ahead, but he realized he had no idea at all of what now lay in store. He was still wondering whether they would ever get off the island when he fell into a deep and restful sleep.

Oberleutnant Balthasar was beginning to think he

would not even have to interrogate any of the
Greek soldiers now being held as prisoners of
war. At first light, with two dozen of his men and
a Greek officer coerced into the role of interpreter, he had led them up towards the Canea
Gate, then chosen a set of apartments that appeared to be inhabited. Forcing down the door,
they had hurried inside, gone up the staircase and
rapped hard on the first door they had come to.

A middle-aged man with greying hair, wearing
nothing more than a vest and a hastily put on
pair of trousers, had opened the door. Balthasar
and half a dozen of his men had barged in, then
pushed on through into the flat. Moments later a
screaming woman and a kicking teenage girl had
been dragged out into the hallway. *A mother and
daughter. Perfect.* The woman had tried to touch
her husband, her eyes wild and frightened, but
the soldiers had held her back. The man looked
shocked and just as terrified, but had been
desperately trying to show defiance. He shouted
at Balthasar, then glared accusingly at the Greek
interpreter.

When the interpreter began to translate, Balthasar silenced him. 'Yes, yes, I think I get the
meaning,' he said. He had learned many years
before, during his time in the SS, that the ability
to cause fear was a powerful weapon. It had been
a useful tool in Belgium and France too. He had
developed three rules in such matters. The first
was to try to gain surprise – the loud knock on
the door, the sudden shouting – which startled
people and threw them mentally off balance.
Balthasar also knew that such behaviour showed

his confidence in his strength and authority. His second rule was to instruct his men to continue to bark orders at the suspects, while he would fix them with an unwavering stare and speak slowly and clearly, as he did now.

'We are looking for men who fought against us at the Canea Gate on the evening of May the twentieth,' he said.

The interpreter repeated the words. The man gabbled, then held his hands together as if in prayer.

'He says he was not there,' said the Greek officer. 'He heard the fighting but he kept indoors, trying to protect his family.'

'Search the apartment,' said Balthasar.

His men did so, noisily, clumsily, without regard for the family's belongings. They found nothing – no guns, at any rate. That did not matter, as Balthasar was well aware.

'I want the names of anyone who fought that night, or who has fought with the British and guerrillas here.'

The man again replied that he did not know. The daughter was crying, and his eyes were darting about with horror at his defencelessness. Balthasar walked up to him and, just inches from the man's face, glared at him with unblinking eyes.

'I know you know,' he said. 'I just want names and where I can find them,' he snapped.

The man shook his head, desperation on his face.

'He insists he knows no one,' said the Greek officer.

Balthasar calmly took out his pistol, extended his arm and pointed it at the man's daughter. 'Tell him,' he said, 'that if he does not give me some names I will shoot first his daughter and then his wife.' This was his third rule: the threat of extreme violence, preferably not to the man being questioned but to a wife or child.

The interpreter did as he was told, causing more panicked glances from the man and renewed wailing from the wife. The daughter stared at him and then spat.

'Tell him to hurry,' said Balthasar. 'I am losing patience.' He moved closer to the girl, pointing his pistol to the side of her head. The man trembled and Balthasar saw a dark stain appear at his crotch.

'One,' said Balthasar, 'two...'

The man blurted out a name.

'And an address,' said Balthasar.

The man mumbled it, then collapsed on the floor, sobbing. Balthasar nodded to his men to let the women go and they rushed to the man, wailing with fear and distress.

'Well, that was easy,' said Balthasar. 'Let us go and find Herr Mandoukis.'

Mandoukis lived beyond the town walls in an old stone house with a terracotta roof in what had once been an isolated farmstead before the town had spread. He had a couple of small barns, an enclosure with a pig and some goats, a few small fruit and olive groves. Balthasar and his men found it easily enough. Nearby, in a grove a short distance to the south, stood a heavy anti-aircraft gun, its breech destroyed, and around it trenches and shell casings where two days before British gunners had been manning it.

Balthasar had the property surrounded. Already dogs were barking, tied up in the yard, and as he and six of his men entered, they growled and strained on their ropes. A moment later, a man opened the front door, a long billhook in his hand.

'Herr Mandoukis?' Balthasar asked. His men had their MP40s and rifles pointing directly at him.

The man looked at them, then turned back inside and slammed the door. 'After him,' said Balthasar.

They caught him as he tried to run out of the back of the house, then brought him back inside, to the kitchen, still quite dark in the first light of dawn. It smelt of ash and bread and sweat. Mandoukis was, Balthasar guessed, in his late thirties, with thick black hair and a three-day growth of beard. His eyes kept darting to the bedroom, so Balthasar had it searched and, in the single large wardrobe, found his wife, a good-looking girl some years younger than her husband. She struggled, scratching at the men, spitting curses.

'Search the place,' he said. 'The entire property – barns, cellar, everything.' Outside the dogs continued to bark until with a yelp they were silenced by two pistol shots. Mandoukis clenched his teeth and snarled, so Balthasar punched him hard in the stomach. He doubled up and gasped, and his wife cried out in distress.

Clutching his stomach, the Cretan stood again, his face contorted with pain.

'You were fighting against us at the Canea

338

Gate,' Balthasar said. 'You were seen. Another person has verified this.'

Mandoukis denied it.

'You were there,' Balthasar repeated, as two of his men entered, clutching an old rifle, a shotgun and two bandoliers. He glanced at the small hoard and took hold of the rifle, dabbing a finger on the barrel, which he then held up. Then he sniffed the breech. 'Recently used and cleaned.' He drove the butt into Mandoukis's stomach, and the Cretan collapsed onto the stone floor. Balthasar grabbed him by his hair and pulled him to his feet as his wife screamed.

'I know you were fighting with Pendlebury,' he said, 'but who else? Who are the leaders of the guerrillas?'

Mandoukis mumbled.

'He says he will never tell you anything,' said the Greek officer. 'You can kill him if you want, but he will never speak.'

Balthasar smiled to himself. An admission of guilt. He knew now that he would get what he wanted. 'Oh, I think he will,' he said, then nodded to the two men holding Mandoukis's wife. They pushed her forward. The woman was trembling now, her lip quivering, shoulders hunched. She was wearing only her nightdress. Balthasar grabbed the collar and yanked so that it ripped, revealing her breasts.

'*Ohi!*' shouted Mandoukis, as his wife clutched herself. *No!* Balthasar grabbed the woman by the shoulder and pushed her roughly onto the table. She was crying, sobbing convulsively, as two men held her down by her arms so that she could no longer protect herself.

'Names!' said Balthasar. 'I want the names.'

'*Ohi, ohi, ohi!*' cried Mandoukis, as Balthasar unbuckled his belt and unbuttoned his smock.

'Tell him,' Balthasar said to the interpreter, 'that if he does not talk, I will have his woman and then I will kill her.' He began to unbutton the fly on his trousers and ran a hand over the woman's body. She writhed and screamed but the men had her tightly gripped. 'She will die,' he said. 'But he can save her.' He was wondering how far he would have to go when Mandoukis gave an anguished yell and began to gabble, spurting out names as fast as his tongue would allow.

'Slower,' said Balthasar, his voice now calm, 'speak more slowly.'

'He says there were two *kapitans* fighting in Heraklion with Pendlebury. One is called Satanas, an old man who fought the Turks. He is the most powerful *kapitan* on the island. The second is called Alopex.'

Balthasar smiled. 'And where are they now?'

The floodgates were open. 'He says Satanas's base is Krousonas, in the Ida Mountains. Alopex is probably also there, but his home village is Sarhos. It lies beneath Krousonas on the lower slopes of the mountains. It is not far from here, maybe twelve kilometres.'

'What about numbers? And weapons?'

Mandoukis mumbled again, then clasped his head.

'He does not know how many men,' said the interpreter, 'but they do not have many weapons, and even less ammunition.'

340

'And this Alopex, and Satanas. These are *noms de guerre*. Their real names. I want their full names.'

'Alopex is Kristannos, Giorgis Kristannos. His family run a large olive-pressing business in Sarhos. Satanas is called Antonis Grigorakis.'

Balthasar smiled to himself, then grabbed Mandoukis, gripping his throat. 'And ask him,' he hissed, 'who cut off the heads of my men.'

As the interpreter spoke, Balthasar could feel Mandoukis break completely, his legs giving way as his whole body trembled with a mixture of fear, guilt and self-loathing.

'Alopex,' mumbled the man.

17

Around 7 a.m., Friday, 30 May. They had been walking for nine hours with barely a pause. No one had talked much; occasionally, Tanner had heard a faint murmur of a low conversation, but otherwise the men seemed content with their thoughts. He was happy to listen to the tramp of boots, the clop of the mule's hoofs and the squeak of the cart's wheels over the rough dirt tracks. Its strange rhythm was quite soothing, somehow. Then, as dawn had crept over them once more, the night sounds of the cicadas had been replaced by a different chorus as birds opened their lungs to mark another day. He had loved May as a boy – it had been his favourite month. The trees and hedgerows had been in full bloom, the mornings alive with birdsong, and the summer spread out before him, with cricket, the harvest and long light days.

They had crossed both main roads without seeing a soul, and now, a little over an hour later, had climbed down from a vine-covered ridge into a narrow valley and were walking up a track beside a stream, past clumps of bamboo and cactus on one side and chestnut and plane trees on the other. Already, dappled shadow played patterns along the track as the morning sun shone through the leaves. The air was cool and fresh, but with a faint whiff of chickens and sheep dung. Up ahead was a village where, the Cretans had told them, they would stop for some breakfast; it was the home of one of them.

'And it is also the home village of Alopex,' Vaughan told Tanner. 'He is *kapitan* here, the patriarch.'

Tanner said nothing. At the back of a house, chickens were scratching at the ground and from within he heard a child crying.

'It's a pretty place,' said Peploe. He looked up at the mountains rising away behind the houses, and Tanner followed his gaze. They towered imperiously, a hazy blue in the morning light. The Germans, he reckoned, would be hard-pushed to track down any guerrillas up there.

They turned a corner where cypress trees looked down on them and Tanner saw they had reached a meeting point of several tracks. Across the way was a *kafenio*, its doors already open. An elderly woman emerged, her arms open wide. Smiling, she hurried to one of the Cretans and embraced him. Several children suddenly appeared, shyly peering round doorways at the strange sight of so many British soldiers, then, confidence rising, stepping out into the road, pointing and sniggering. The place erupted into a hive of activity. Old men appeared, clasping the *andartes,* and then the soldiers were being ushered into the *kafenio* and urged to sit down.

The older women, Tanner noticed, were all dressed in black, with black scarves around their heads, but several younger girls had joined them and were dressed differently, in skirts and blouses, their hair loose. Some of the men had nudged each other, but Tanner found himself unable to take his eyes off the young woman now helping to feed them. She had a lean face with wide, deep brown eyes and shoulder-length hair. Certainly pretty, Tanner thought, but something more attracted him: an air of innocence, of vulnerability.

'She's lovely, isn't she?' said Sykes, sitting next to him at a table near the door.

'Very fine,' agreed Tanner. Then she came over to them and, standing beside Tanner, leaned over to put down a bowl of bread and a large pot of honey, her arm brushing Tanner's shoulder. She smiled at him. 'Eat,' she said, 'you eat.'

'*Efharisto,*' said Tanner, and she smiled again.

As Tanner tore off a hunk of bread he saw her talking with one of the other girls and looking towards him. Catching her eye, he smiled, then winked and, to his delight, saw her laugh. Soon after, she brought over some coffee.

'You like the honey?' she asked him.

'Very much,' he told her.

343

'My own bees.'

Soon after, when he had finished eating and had drunk his coffee, Tanner caught her eye again, then got up and stepped outside into the street. He paused, lit a cigarette, then walked away from the *kafenio* and down towards the small, domed church. Glancing back, he saw the girl turn into the road, heading in his direction, so he moved into a narrow lane, off which some steps led up to the door of a house. Sitting down he waited for her to pass, conscious that his heart had begun to thump.

She reached him and stopped, just as he had hoped she would. 'Hello,' she said.

'I hoped you might follow.'

She laughed, then looked away briefly.

'What's your name?' he asked.

'Alexis,' she said.

He told her his, then said, 'This is a beautiful place.'

'Yes, I think so.'

He stood up, aware of her eyes on his. An overwhelming desire to kiss her swept over him. She was standing so close to him that he could see her collarbone protruding gently beneath the soft brown skin, and the swell of her breasts beneath her shirt. She tucked a lock of hair behind her ear and looked at him, her eyes scanning his face. It was the war, he knew, that had made him so bold. He'd not even known her thirty minutes yet now he felt quite bewitched, overcome by a need to act on his impulses before it was too late.

'Tanner!' he heard Peploe call, from back down the road. 'Tanner!'

She held out a hand and took his. Her fingers felt so light, so small in his own. 'Be careful,' she said.

He nodded. 'And you.' He smiled. 'I must get back. Alexis, I hope we meet again.'

She let his hand drop. A fleeting smile and then he hurried away from her without a backward glance.

'Where d'you get to?' Peploe asked him cheerily, as he rejoined the others.

Tanner noticed one of the Cretan *andartes* glare at him. 'I just went to have a little look around the place.'

Vaughan came over. 'It looked like you made a big impression on Alexis,' he said, grinning.

Tanner shifted his feet and hastily took out a cigarette.

'Looks like the feeling was mutual,' laughed Peploe.

'She's a beautiful girl, sir,' said Tanner.

'And she also happens to be Alopex's sister,' said Vaughan. 'You might want to keep your admiration to yourself from now on, Tanner. You'll upset the *andartes* if you flirt with their women, especially the sister of their *kapitan*.'

Tanner's heart sank. 'Bloody Cretans,' he muttered. 'Can hardly breathe without offending their sodding pride and honour. It's getting on my nerves.'

'A bit rich coming from you, Jack,' said Peploe.

Tanner glared at him, and slung his rifle and Schmeisser back over his shoulder. 'Are we getting going then, sir?'

They climbed on up to Krousonas, Satanas's village, and much larger than Sarhos. It was higher up, nestling in the flanks of the mountains, the houses built around a snaking main road. Neither of the *kapitans* was there, but there were several *andartes* to meet the cart. They were surprised to see the Rangers as well, but led them on, out of the village and up a winding track that climbed higher into the mountains. As they cleared a crest, they paused. The sun was beating down on them, and the climb was hot work. Tanner stood by Sykes, drinking from his water bottle, looking back to where they had come from. Below were the low, rounded ridges and valleys they had crossed but beyond was a higher saddle, a long, low, narrow mountain that Tanner realized they must have skirted in the night. The ridge stood proud, its burnished rock faces standing sentinel over the patchwork of groves and vineyards that covered the feminine curves of the rolling valleys and hills in between.

'It's a flippin' beautiful place, isn't it?' sighed Sykes.

'And easy to hide in from the Germans. Christ, just look at all that cover.' He turned his head to the peaks rising behind them. 'And look at these.' Beyond, in the distance, lay the deep-blue sea and there, on the coast, twinkling white in the midday sun, Heraklion, only eight miles or so as the crow flew but from their current height seeming much further.

They went over to the cart, where Liddell was still lying. His shoulder was heavily bandaged but the bloodstain had not grown larger, Tanner noticed. Sweat beaded his brow and upper lip; he needed shade. As Tanner and Sykes leaned over him, his eyes flickered open. 'Where am I?' he mumbled.

'Halfway up a bleedin' mountain, sir,' said Sykes.

'A mountain?' Liddell looked confused.

'You take it easy, sir,' said Sykes. 'Get some kip now and you'll soon be better.'

Liddell closed his eyes again.

'He's a bit feverish, isn't he?' said Sykes.

'Bound to be,' said Tanner. 'But you couldn't hope for a cleaner wound. All that saltwater. He'll be all right.'

They continued, following a narrow track that led up through a ravine. The stream there was little more than a trickle, as scree-covered rock rose either side of it. The mule struggled as the ground became ever rockier. The lush slopes of the lower reaches had gone, replaced by hardy bushes and thickets. Goats bleated, their bells jangling eerily across the gorge.

'Bloody hell, sir,' said Hepworth, as he stumbled over some loose stones. 'How much further?'

'Stop mithering, Hep,' said Tanner. He was wondering the same himself, though, so he asked Vaughan.

'Just over that crest up ahead,' said Vaughan, 'there are caves and shepherds' huts. We're nearly there.'

Just then the mule stumbled too, and the Cretans rushed to the back of the cart. Tanner followed their lead. 'Come on, you lot,' he said to the others. 'Lend a hand.'

They got the cart moving again, but stayed with

it, helping to push it as its wooden wheels stuck on the rocks.

At last, they crested the mouth of the gorge, and there, up ahead, were men – men clutching rifles and raising them in salute at the sight of the latest cache to make it to the safety of their mountain hide-out. Tanner paused, wiping his arm across his damp brow. Below, at the foot of the gorge, as they had stood on the crest, half the island and more had been spread before them. Now that view had narrowed, blocked by huge peaks either side, so that all that could be seen was a tight V. No one could see them up here, Tanner realized. No German at any rate.

They had reached a kind of basin near the top of the mountains. The air was absolutely still, the only noise the jangling of goats and sheep and the cries of the Cretan guerrillas. They were led around a small spur and there, behind it, cutting into the mountain at the edge of the basin, was the cave, hidden entirely from the lowlands below and even from an aircraft above.

As they neared its mouth, Tanner saw first Satanas and then Alopex emerge. The old man leaned on a rifle and watched, while the younger came out to meet them.

'Alex,' said Alopex, embracing Vaughan. 'I *knew* I could depend on you.' He turned to Peploe and the exhausted, sweat-drenched Rangers. 'Reinforcements?'

Tanner stepped out from behind several of the men.

'You!' hissed Alopex.

As Oberst Bräuer had promised, more supplies had been flown in that day. They had arrived by sea, too, a number of laden caiques drifting into the harbour, and by road in newly landed and captured trucks. That morning, having reported to Schulz and Bräuer at the Megaron, he had watched two British trucks, laden with paratroopers, trundle through cleared streets around the harbour. It was incredible, Balthasar had reflected, how fast supplies could come once the path was cleared. In no time Crete would be a formidable garrison.

It was with some satisfaction that he had told Schulz what he'd learned earlier that morning, and then, on the major's insistence, Bräuer.

'What next, then, Oberleutnant?' Bräuer had asked.

'I thought I would lead an expedition to Alopex's village, Herr Oberst. With luck I will find some of his family there. Women and children, preferably. In my limited experience, it's only the men who think they have anything to fear from us.'

'Certainly there's no point trying to catch them in the mountains,' said Schulz.

'So flush them out, and fight them on our terms, not theirs,' said Bräuer.

'Yes, Herr Oberst. At the moment the Cretans have no experience of this. They will be surprised by our arrival in force and, I suspect, less guarded than they might be once word of such reprisals spreads. I want to use this first action to make sure we land a big fish.'

Bräuer nodded approvingly. 'Very sensible. I wish you luck, Oberleutnant Balthasar.'

'There is one other thing, Herr Oberst,' said Balthasar.

Bräuer raised an eyebrow. *Yes?*

'We seem to have some vehicles at last – I noticed a number of British trucks in the town as I made my way over here.'

Bräuer smiled. 'And you were thinking some transport would be very useful for conducting these operations?'

'Yes, Herr Oberst. The villages are some miles away and surprise is of the essence. The quicker we can get in and out again, the better.'

'He has a point, Herr Oberst,' said Schulz.

'All right, Balthasar. Let me see what I can arrange.'

Balthasar thanked him, saluted and left. He had had no intention of carrying out such an operation in the heat of the day, and in any case, there had been other matters to attend to, not least the integration of replacement troops into his company and the setting up of a camp. This he had established a couple of kilometres to the south-west of the town in a lush valley of vines, olives and citrus. Tents had been pitched in a lemon grove, the air smelling sweetly of fruit and wild grasses, not rotting corpses and effluent. There was a rocky spur to their left that jutted out into the valley on which an ideal observation post could be established, while on the far side, a track climbed out of the valley and led to the mountain village of Krousonas, the heart of the guerrillas' fiefdom. Another OP was established there.

In the early afternoon, Balthasar clambered up

350

to the OP already set up on the outcrop. The men were building a stone sangar, an MG already in position with a wide arc of fire covering the entire valley to the south and the approaches to the camp. He now had more than seventy men – men who were rested, fed and flush with victory. Here, in this undeniably beautiful valley of shimmering green, he hoped he might lure his enemy. At first glance, their canvas camp, which was now emerging between the olives, looked vulnerable yet it held well-armed and highly trained soldiers, covered by strong observation posts. If any guerrillas tried to attack, Balthasar and his men would be ready.

'Good,' he said, to his men at the OP. He drank from his water bottle then passed it to his men. All were glistening with sweat. He whisked away a fly and noticed a small black scorpion emerge from the disturbed rocks. Carefully, and deliberately, he raised his boot over it and drove down his heel.

'And that is what we will do to the Cretans, Herr Oberleutnant,' grinned one of his men.

'Precisely,' Balthasar replied.

Soon after, three trucks arrived, delivered at Oberst Bräuer's behest, two towing light 3.7cm anti-tank guns. The trucks were British, open-cab and open-back Morris Commercials, painted dusty desert yellow. Ten men could get into the back, two up front, and at a push a couple more standing and clinging to the bar behind the cab. Balthasar was delighted. They gave him speed and firepower, for they could carry more ammunition with them.

They left a little after six that evening, two under-strength platoons, fewer than forty men in all, driving off down the dirt road that wound its way gradually out of the valley and began climbing into the lower slopes of the mountains. They passed a couple of carts, forcing them off the road, and drove on, until up ahead they saw Krousonas nestling in the flanks of the mountain, a tight collection of white houses, bright against the green and grey hues of the land around. However, it was not to Krousonas that Balthasar meant to go that evening but Sarhos.

They reached a small village, Kitharida. A child scuttled across the road, women watched them sullenly, and as they passed a bar, an old man shook his fist. Balthasar ignored them and, once through the village, felt a throb of excitement. They were nearing their destination now. Sarhos, he knew, was a cul-de-sac, a dead-end village, with only paths leading out at the far end. At a fork in the road, they turned left, and half a kilometre further on the first houses came into view. The rear vehicle stopped, men quickly jumping out, while the other two pulled up at the centre of the village beside the bar and a stone's throw from the tiny white Coptic church.

Immediately his men set to work, boots and rifle butts kicking on doors. The bar was cleared, old men, children and women roughly pushed out.

'Out! Out!' shouted the men, adhering to Balthasar's first rule of acting both loudly and aggressively. Balthasar watched, his hands gripped around his MP40. There was a mixture of expressions on the villagers' faces: fear, defiance, anger; a young girl was crying, her mother trying to calm her. The men herded them down the road to the church. One middle-aged man who tried to slip away and run was chased. A short burst of sub-machine-gun fire followed, a woman screamed, and the soldiers returned.

As a show of force, the anti-tank guns were unhooked and pointed towards the church. Machine-guns were slung over shoulders, rifles and sub-machine-guns tightly gripped. The rounding-up did not take long, for Sarhos was not a big place. In no time, the village had been emptied, the population huddled in the cool, dark church. It was there that Balthasar went while his men lit their torches – long staves wrapped with cloth at one end and dipped in oil – and set fire to barns, stores, even houses.

'Kristannos,' he called out. 'Who here is called Kristannos?' Anxious faces looked at each other and feet shuffled. A low murmur arose.

'Silence!' called Balthasar, then turned to his Greek interpreter. 'Tell them anyone from the family Kristannos is to step forward. Immediately.'

The interpreter did so. A pause, then movement among the frightened throng. Balthasar saw an old, bearded man shuffle forward, then a thin, elderly woman. *The mother, perhaps?* Then two younger women pushed through, one he guessed about thirty, a small boy in her arms, the other some years younger. *A wife, son and sister*, he guessed. Surely.

It was the woman he supposed to be Alopex's sister who spoke, her face proud and defiant. And

353

pretty, Balthasar thought. Yes, definitely pretty.

'She is Alexis Kristannos,' said the interpreter. 'The women with her are her mother and sister-in-law, the boy her nephew, the man her uncle.'

'Where are the rest of them?'

'Her brother was captured in Greece with the rest of the Cretan Division,' the interpreter repeated back. 'Her father is dead.'

'What about her older brother, Giorgis?'

'He is not in the village at the moment. He is away.'

Balthasar smiled. 'Good. You,' he said sharply, pointing to Alexis, 'and you,' clicking his fingers at Alopex's wife and son, 'your names?'

'I am Alexis Kristannos,' said Alexis, 'and this is my sister-in-law, Nerita Kristannos, and her son Alexandros.'

'Come with me.' He watched them glance back, saw the mother clasp her hands together in prayer, then his men were pushing them, so that Alopex's wife stumbled and her son began to cry. A murmur from the villagers rose into cries as the church door was opened and they heard and smelt the burning.

As they emerged into the narrow road around the church, the doors were slammed and bolted. Nerita gasped, her hands to her face. The village was on fire. Alexis began shouting, hurling abuse at the Germans, and at Balthasar. She tried to claw him, but was restrained, her arms held back by one of his men.

Balthasar slapped her face, then ordered them to his truck where the women and boy were bundled into the back, the weapons of the paratroopers trained on them.

Balthasar ordered the Pak gun to be fired at the bar, three rounds that blasted holes through the wall and set the spirits on fire. More flames now erupted from a house overlooking the stream, angrily licking out through the windows. Thick, curling smoke rose into the sky, blocking out the mountains above them.

'Right,' said Balthasar, 'time to go.' The guns were hitched back on, men clambered and jumped back onto the vehicles and, turning, they sped away. From his seat in the cab, Balthasar listened to Nerita Kristannos's wails, but he was unmoved by her fear and grief. Alopex's village was burning and Balthasar had his wife, son and sister. The operation had gone perfectly to plan.

It was dusk up in the mountains. The sun had set behind Mount Ida, the largest peak in the range, and the sky above was darkening, the first stars beginning to twinkle. At last the heat had simmered down, replaced by cool evening air – air that now smelt delicious. From the mouth of the cave, the scent of roasting mutton and woodsmoke wafted sweetly over the rocky crag where Tanner and Sykes were sitting. They had found a small oak and beneath it a large smooth rock. From where they sat, they could look back down the gorge, at the interlocking spurs of jutting rock, and out to a narrow view of the valleys below and the distant ridge beyond.

'My stomach's rumbling something terrible,' said Sykes. 'D'you think they'll let us have any of it?'

Tanner scratched his chin. 'An extra sixteen mouths to feed is a lot. I won't be getting some at any rate, not if Alopex has anything to do with it.'

'You don't think it might be a good idea to make it up with him? After all, he is one of the gaffers round here. It didn't matter pissing him off before because we were in charge, but now that's changed. We need his help.'

'Stan, you're missing the point.' Tanner sighed. 'I stood up to him because he insulted us, not because we were running the show on this island.' He picked up a stick and threw it. 'I'm damned if I'm going to back down. Anyway, I reckon it's all bluster. We've both had our chances to kill each other and neither of us has taken it.'

'Maybe,' said Sykes. He sounded doubtful.

'I'll give him one thing, though.'

'What's that?'

'He's got a lovely sister. I reckon I'm quite smitten.' They laughed, and Tanner took out two cigarettes, lit them and passed one to Sykes. 'Feels very safe up here, doesn't it?'

Sykes nodded slowly as he drew on his smoke. 'I wonder how far the others have got?' They had heard that afternoon that the Italians had landed in the east of the island a few days earlier; it would make navigating safely that much more difficult.

'I suppose it depends on whether they managed to get any oil. But, Jesus, Stan, that boat didn't exactly give a man confidence, did it? All the way to Alex with a cracked cylinder head? Maybe, but you wouldn't put good money on it, would you?'

'No. We made the right decision. I hope we did,

at any rate.' He looked out at the mountain peaks rising around them. 'Feels a bloody long way from home, up here, though, doesn't it?'

Tanner drew his battle blouse around him, still stained with dried sea salt. 'I like it. Christ, where's home anyway?'

Footsteps behind them made Tanner turn. He had assumed it would be one of the men, but it was Alopex, with two of his *andartes*, one of whom had been with them all the way from Limenas. It was the same man who had scowled at Tanner earlier in the village.

Tanner eyed them, but remained sitting. 'What do you want?'

Alopex drew level with him. 'You son of a whore,' he growled. 'Is it not enough that you insult me in my town and in front of my men? But now you would shame my sister!'

Tanner still did not budge, instead looking up at Alopex with apparent indifference. 'We talked, that's all. She's a beautiful girl – a credit to your family.'

Alopex leaped at Tanner, surprising him and knocking him back so that his head cracked against the rough, knotted trunk of the tree. The shock, combined with the stab of acute pain, momentarily stunned him, and he now felt a stinging blow to his face. 'Stop!' Sykes was saying. 'Just stop!' but Alopex had landed another crunching blow. Tanner saw Sykes yank Alopex backwards so that the Cretan's next punch flailed uselessly at the air. He pushed Sykes backwards so that he toppled, but in that moment, Tanner was able to raise a leg and kick Alopex away. The

357

big Cretan staggered, but managed to remain upright on the loose rocky ground. Tanner now sprang to his feet, anger and adrenalin giving him strength. A couple of steps forward, fists raised, then a short, sharp jab that caught Alopex on the side of his chin. The Cretan staggered again, regained his footing, and charged at Tanner with such weight and force that he could only land his second punch on Alopex's back as he was rammed into the tree, an old branch stump stabbing his side, so that he gasped with pain and because the breath had been knocked from his lungs. Another punch, this time to the stomach, and Tanner doubled up. He was losing this fight, he knew. He caught a glimpse of Sykes getting to his feet, but Alopex's *andartes* were hurrying over the rocks ready to hold him back; this was not Sykes's fight – Tanner knew he had to face Alopex alone. He grimaced, stabs of pain coursing through his entire body, and a blow fell like a slab of iron on the side of his face, beside his right eye, then another caught his jaw. His vision was blurring but he knew he had to do something fast.

Bringing his arms tight around his face, he ducked and swayed, then lashed out with his leg, catching Alopex's knee, and as the Cretan tried to recover his footing, Tanner gave two quick jabs, catching his enemy on each eye. As Alopex ducked his head away from more blows, Tanner kicked his boot fiercely into the other man's groin.

It was now the Cretan's turn to gasp and double up. He stumbled backwards, nearly lost his footing again, but then recovered his balance. Tanner stayed back, unsure of the ground, his breathing heavy and laboured, blood streaming down his face and feeling his strength ebb as pain shuttled through his body.

'Why are you fighting?' he heard Sykes say.

'Keep out of this, Stan,' Tanner gasped.

'Because this dog insulted me in front of my men,' Alopex snarled, 'and now he insults my sister!'

'But you insulted me first,' Tanner retorted. He coughed, then thought he might retch.

'Stop it, please,' said Sykes. 'You two are allies. Fight Germans, not each other.'

'You are not fighting the Germans,' growled Alopex. 'You are trying to run away.'

'Stop bloody saying that!' said Tanner. He took several darting steps forward and, before Alopex could defend himself, landed three quick jabs, followed by a right hook. 'I'm not running from anyone, least of all those Nazi bastards!' The Cretan swayed, fell back a step, then reached to his side and pulled out his knife, the steel glinting in the failing light. Tanner stepped back several paces, then pulled out his seventeen-inch sword bayonet. Crouching, feeling for a position of balance on the loose rock, he waited.

Alopex shook his head. Blood was running from a wound over his eye and he dabbed at it with his sleeve. He dummy-lunged, making Tanner flinch backwards. Without taking his eye off Alopex, he squatted and picked up a small, jagged rock, deftly switched his bayonet into his left hand, and held the rock, ready to throw. He would hurl it at his head, but even if he missed, Alopex would have to duck and that would give him the chance to strike.

But from behind Alopex's shoulder, a Cretan boy was now running along the mountain track up which they had climbed earlier, calling. The *andartes* behind Alopex began talking urgently to each other and at the same time Tanner heard men approaching from the direction of the cave. He barely dared glance at the boy, but now Alopex's men were beside him, jabbering and deliberately coming between the Cretan and Tanner.

'What?' snarled Tanner. 'What's going on?' He saw Alopex lower his knife.

'We are finished here,' the *kapitan* muttered, 'for now.' He dabbed at his eye again, then put his knife away. Tanner lowered his bayonet, dropped the rock he was clasping and put his hand to his head, reaching to the tree for support. Alopex and his men pushed past, scrambled over the rocks and went back towards the cave.

'Are you all right?' Sykes said. 'I'm sorry – I couldn't help you much.'

'You got him off me to start with. Bastard might really have killed me if it weren't for that.' He breathed out heavily. 'Bloody hell. That hurt.' He sheathed his bayonet and slumped to the ground.

'I wonder what the fuss is about,' said Sykes, looking towards the cave.

'Christ knows,' said Tanner. 'But I need a beadie.' He felt for his cigarettes, took one out and lit it.

Suddenly they heard a guttural roar of pain and

anguish from the cave.

'That don't sound good,' said Sykes.

Tanner eased himself back to his feet, gasping with pain as he did so. 'No, Stan. Come on, we'd better see what's going on.'

Clambering back round the rocky spur to the cave, pain shooting through Tanner with every step, they saw Alopex clutching his head, rocking back and forth, then striding away from the others, his face turned to the sky. Alarm now struck Tanner. *Alexis*, he thought. He hoped it was not so.

'Christ, what happened to you?' said Peploe, as he and Vaughan hurried over.

'Nothing, sir. What's going on?'

'It's bad, I'm afraid,' said Vaughan. 'The Germans have torched Sarhos and taken away Alopex's wife, son and sister.'

Tanner clutched his head. 'Let me think,' he said, to himself as much as to anyone else. He drew on his cigarette, then flicked the butt away. 'Did they take anyone else or only those three?'

'Only those three. The rest they left locked in the church.'

'Then they'll be safe,' he said. 'They're trying to get Alopex out of the mountains. Let me talk to him.' He turned, but Peploe caught him by his shoulder.

'Jack, wait.' Tanner stopped and faced him. 'You and Alopex – you've just been fighting again?'

Tanner nodded. 'He came at me, sir. I've been trying to keep out of his way.'

'Jack, that's not good enough. This has to stop. Apologise to him.'

361

'Sir,' said Tanner. 'I've nothing to apologise for.'

'Tanner,' said Vaughan, 'that might be so, but this is Alopex's country – Alopex's land. You are a problem to him, because for him to back down would mean him losing face. That is more damaging to him than to you. We need him – we need these *kapitans* to help continue the fight.'

'Jack, I'm sorry. I know you have your pride, but I want you to end this now. Apologise to Alopex. That's an order.'

Tanner looked away, then wiped the blood from his face. 'An order?'

'Yes.'

Tanner swallowed, sighed and nodded. Satanas was now with Alopex, an avuncular arm around the younger *kapitan's* shoulder. 'Alopex,' said Tanner, approaching him.

Alopex turned, a look of pure hatred in his eyes.

'I–' He stopped, paused, briefly closed his eyes, then said, 'I apologize. I offended you, and I'm sorry. And I'm also very sorry to hear of your loss.' Alopex stared at him, as though not comprehending what he was hearing. Slowly Tanner held out his hand.

'Alopex,' Satanas said. 'Enough of this. Take his hand.'

Silently Alopex did so.

Tanner smiled, aware of a weight lifting from his shoulders. 'I want to say something to you,' he said. 'Your wife and son and Alexis, they'll be safe.'

'They will kill them,' murmured Alopex.

'No – no, they won't. Think about it. Why have they only taken those three?'

Alopex looked at him blankly.

'Because they're trying to lure you out of the mountains. It's you they're after – a *kapitan*, a resistance leader.'

'But how do they know of me?'

'I don't know – someone must have talked. Maybe they've rounded up people in Heraklion, tortured them. It could have been anyone, but they know. Why else would they go to your village and take your family?'

Satanas spoke to Alopex. 'I think you are right,' he then said to Tanner.

'It's a trap,' said Tanner. 'They'll be expecting you to attack in force, I'm sure. But that's not the way. Let us help you. We'll get them back for you.'

'But how?'

Tanner shrugged. 'Someone will know where they are. Do you still have people inside the town?'

'Of course.'

'Then we can find out where they are. We'll watch and wait and then we'll make a plan and rescue them. If we work together, we can do this.'

Alopex nodded. 'Yes, we must try.' He laid a hand on Tanner's shoulder. 'I accept your apology. We will work together. Our feud – it is over.'

'We will get them back.'

Alopex buried his head in his hands.

Tanner left him and walked towards the mouth of the cave, the enormity of what he had pledged now registering. He'd said it not for Alopex, but for Alexis and, he realized, because of his own-

misplaced sense of pride. Not only did they have to discover the prisoners' whereabouts, they had to defy the rapidly massing German troops now flooding into Heraklion, then get Alopex's family out and safely up into the mountains. It was, Tanner knew, with a rapidly sinking heart, a very tall order indeed.

18

Some forty miles away as the crow flew, but many more by foot, the main British evacuation was still under way. More than six thousand troops had been lifted from the tiny southern port of Sfakia on the night of 29 May. German mountain troops had dogged their retreat all the way, but as the exhausted troops of Creforce neared the coast at last, the landscape had helped them. The mountain passes had descended into a high plateau of lush meadows and groves, but from this plain ran a narrow, deep and craggy ravine, which was the only real passage to the coast and easy to defend; the Imbros Gorge had bought precious time for the mass of Creforce now waiting to be picked up on the shore beyond.

At the end of the gorge the road on which the men had been travelling finally reached a dead end. From high on a rocky headland overlooking the sea there was only one way down to Sfakia and that was by a narrow path. The signs of retreat were everywhere: trucks, cars, even a few light tanks lay abandoned, their engines deliberately wrecked. Everything too difficult or heavy to be carried down to the port lay scattered and discarded.

All the way from the bluff to the sea, men huddled in the rocks, waiting and praying that they might have a chance to leave. Major General Freyberg had made his way through the mass after he and most of his staff had finally left their cave headquarters beneath the bluff that evening, 30 May. Young men who, just ten days earlier, had looked fit, confident and brimming with youthful determination, were now haggard, dirty and unshaven, their uniforms torn and filthy. They were hungry and, above all, thirsty – damn it, who wasn't in this heat? – but there was nothing he could do for them. Before leaving, he had sent one last signal to General Wavell, urging him to do all that was possible to send more ships, but he knew that, while he would shortly be leaving the island, many of his gallant men would not. They had fought their hardest, lost friends and comrades and now faced an uncertain future as prisoners of war.

Not for the first time since the battle had begun, Freyberg wished he could have been a mere company commander once more, with the decisions of high command left to someone else. He hated leaving his men like this, cutting and running before so many others. To make matters worse, he had seen their faces in the evening dusk. Some had wished him well, but most had just stared at him, stony, silent expressions that had cut him more painfully than any sword or bullet.

Eventually they had reached the quayside, and soon after, a faint hum had been heard that had rapidly grown until, out of the sky, two Sunderland flying boats had appeared. Gracefully swooping down to the calm, gently lapping sea, they had landed a short way from the shore, waiting patiently while Freyberg and his staff clambered down into little wooden dinghies and were rowed towards them. Pulling alongside the giant grey beast, Freyberg could hear the four radial engines ticking and clicking as they cooled. There was a reassuring smell of fuel and oil, as a door opened beneath the high cockpit and he made the awkward step from the boat into the Sunderland.

And then, soon after, with the first Sunderland full of passengers, the engines began to turn and then roar, shaking the whole aircraft. Slowly at first, then gathering speed, the seaplane sped out across the water, buffeted as it skimmed over the surface, until suddenly the shaking lessened and it was climbing away. Freyberg looked out of his window and, in the last vestiges of light, saw Crete, a long, dark outline, like a sleeping giant, and a place of gentle, magnificent beauty rather than the scene of so much bitter and costly fighting.

Freyberg rubbed his eyes. He had been charged with defending Crete and yet he had failed, leading his island garrison to another bitter defeat. It was a burden he would have to live with.

As the hungry Rangers and Cretan *andartes* ate

their meal of roast mutton and bread, they were unaware that the commander of Creforce was at that very moment flying out across the sea towards Alexandria, or that the remnants of Creforce were still evacuating from Sfakia.

As it was, the mood at the cave was sombre. Several of the guerrillas were from the same village as Alopex. As for the *kapitan*, he kept apart from his men. Alopex was a solitary figure that night, and both Satanas and his men let him be. Tanner, too, was not much in the mood for talking. The cuts to his face hurt, while his head throbbed painfully. He had said nothing to Peploe about his offer to Alopex – not yet. It could wait. He needed to think. Think and rest.

He settled down near the cave's entrance. Up in the sky, stars twinkled benignly. The air was cool and still; there was no sound of cicadas in the mountains. Near the back of the cave, he heard Liddell calling out. The man had developed a fever. That worried Tanner too. He had not saved the stupid idiot just for him to go and die in some mountain cave. But Liddell was being tended by Woodman and Bonner. *He's not my concern now*, Tanner told himself. *Go to sleep.*

The other Rangers had let Tanner be in the same way that the *andartes* had recognized Alopex needed to be alone. Sykes had ensured that no one bothered the CSM; he had known Tanner long enough now to understand when his friend was not feeling sociable. Nonetheless, he also saw that the others were desperate to know what had happened between their CSM and the Cretan *kapitan*.

'So there he was,' said Sykes, in a low voice, as a number of the Rangers sat around a softly burning fire, 'with his bayonet in one hand and a sodding great rock in the other. And a few yards away there's Alopex with this gleaming dagger. Both men had already knocked ten rounds out of each other. Alopex had got blood running down his face and so had the CSM. They were quite a sight, I can tell you.'

He paused to light a cigarette, which he cupped between his finger and thumb.

'And then what?' said Hepworth.

'Well, then that nipper comes running up the track shouting about what's happened down below.'

'So they stop fighting?' said Mercer.

'Yes – that was it. But I reckon the CSM had the trump hand. He'd have flung that rock and had him. Could have been curtains for old Alopex.'

'Tanner's a hard bastard,' grinned McAllister. 'Won't back down on anything.'

'But 'e 'as, Mac. He made his peace with Alopex.'

'So we're all mates again, then, Sarge?' said Hepworth.

'For the moment. But you know what these Cretans are like. Sensitive buggers. Don't take much to get them worked up about something or other.'

They were quiet for a moment. Then Mercer said, 'D'you think we'll ever get off this place, Sarge?'

'Course we will,' said Sykes, the tip of his cigarette glowing. 'We might need a bit of help finding some kind of boat but we'll be all right. You'll see. At any rate, we're safe enough for the moment.'

'I wonder whether the others made it,' said Hepworth.

'I hope the Eyeties didn't get them,' said Mc-Allister. 'Bastard Eyeties. Always jumping on Jerry's bandwagon. Typical of them to bloody well turn up once the island's almost secure.'

'Well, I think we made the right choice, boys,' said Sykes. 'I mean, I really hope they made it but, let's face it, that old boat was knackered, wasn't it, Eyeties or no Eyeties?'

'But what now, Sarge?' said Mercer. 'Are we going to stay here or do we have to keep fighting Jerry?'

'You know what, mate?' said Sykes. 'I don't think you should worry your pretty little head about that tonight. Let's get some kip and see what tomorrow brings, hey?'

Sykes opened his eyes and saw Tanner a short distance away from the mouth of the cave, gazing out over the mountains. The air was fresh and cool, a lingering smell of woodsmoke on his clothes mixing with the sharper scent of sage and brushwood. Most of the other men were still asleep, although a couple of *andartes* were keeping watch, sitting on rocks, leaning on their rifles. Of Alopex there was no sign.

Sykes yawned, then got up and quietly stepped over the rocky ground to join Tanner, who turned as he approached. He had washed the blood from his face, but there was bruising around his right eye and on his left cheek. The cut, however, looked as though it would heal well: already, a dark mass of blood had congealed into a thick scab.

'All right, Stan?' said Tanner.

'Fine, ta. Better for a good kip, I can tell you. The old boat race don't look too bad, all things considered, Jack.'

'I've had worse.' Tanner took a gulp of water from his bottle, then passed it to Sykes. 'Could kill a mug of char, couldn't you?'

'I don't even want to think about it.' He drank. Then, passing back the water bottle, he said, 'I wonder how Mr Liddell is this morning?'

'He's not feverish any more,' said Tanner. 'I checked.'

'Then he's through the worst.'

'Should be.'

'I hope he's grateful,' said Sykes. 'You saved his life, Jack.'

'I didn't do it for him. I did it for his father. Something I owed him. In any case, I'm hardly going to sit back and let the poor bastard drown, am I?'

'Well, you did the right thing.' Sykes sniffed. 'So what's the plan?'

'Eventually to get off the island and back to Alex.'

'Eventually. But first?'

Tanner faced him. 'You don't need to come, Stan. None of you do, but we owe it to these men to help them get the women out of Heraklion. Damn it, we owe it to ourselves. Cutting and running like that – it was a disgrace, Stan, a bloody

370

disgrace. I'll go in on my own if I have to.'

Sykes took his comb from his battle-blouse pocket and ran it through his hair. 'You're not going anywhere without me. They've got a good number of explosives here.'

'And I bet not one of them knows as much about 'em as you do. And don't forget there's still the rest of that cache of Captain Pendlebury's. If they haven't already blown themselves up on it, we could make good use of that.'

'That's true. It's still going to be bleeding difficult, though.'

'I thought that too. Last night I was thinking it was nigh on impossible, but now I'm not so sure.'

'How come?'

'Well, I wonder how many troops are in the town itself. They've got pretty much the whole island to garrison after all, plus three airfields. We'll have surprise on our side and with the explosives we can create a few diversions. You've still got those time switches, have you?'

'No, but there's some in the cave here. I saw a box of them.'

'There you go, then. I'm not saying it'll be easy but I reckon it's possible. Perfectly possible.'

'And I'm sure Alopex's sister will be very grateful if we pull it off.' Sykes smirked at Tanner, who looked down sheepishly.

'I've got to admit, Stan, I can't bloody stop thinking about her. It's ridiculous – I only talked to her for about five minutes, but there was something about her, don't know what quite, but I don't like the thought of her being a prisoner of those Nazi bastards. I don't like it one little bit.'

'Just do me a favour, will you, Jack?' said Sykes. 'Don't go upsetting Alopex again.'

'Alopex? Oh, he and I are mates now. Putty in my hands.' He grinned.

'Where is he?'

'He's gone down to the village. We're going to meet him in Krousonas later.'

'And what about the captain?'

'What about him?' said Peploe's voice.

The two men turned and saw him walking towards them.

'Morning, sir,' said Sykes. 'We were just discussing a little plan of action.'

'Oh, yes?'

'Yes, sir,' said Tanner. 'You see, I was thinking that most of these Cretans here aren't exactly well trained. And, of course, no one can handle explosives like Sykes.'

'So we were thinking we should take it upon ourselves,' added Sykes, 'to get Alopex's family out of choky and carry out a bit of mischief while we're at it.'

'Oh, were you?'

'Yes, sir,' said Tanner. 'It's the least we can do after the rest of us were forced to leave them in the lurch like that.'

'If I'm honest, the same thought had crossed my mind,' said Peploe, 'but we're going to need their help too, you know.'

'Yes, but this will only work if there's a few of us,' said Tanner. 'It's a small-scale operation. You, me, Stan here. Maybe one other and perhaps a couple of *andartes*. No more. Stealth is the key.'

'I certainly doubt a few days' delay will make

any difference to our chances of getting off the island,' said Peploe, stroking his chin thoughtfully.

'It'll help them, sir,' said Tanner, 'especially if we pull this off. These Cretan lads are being good to us, but they'll be a hell of a lot more helpful if we show a bit of willing. And we'll be able to prove that, whatever the rest of the British Army might be like, we Rangers are not men to run away in a hurry'

'A matter of honour, eh, Jack?' Peploe smiled.

'If you like, sir, yes.'

Peploe thought for a moment. 'All right. This is going to need consideration but let's at least put it to Satanas and Captain Vaughan.' He paused and looked out towards the mountain peaks ahead of them. 'This is a beautiful place, isn't it? If only we weren't at war, I'd be really enjoying myself.'

'Well, sir,' said Tanner, 'I'd rather be here planning our revenge than sitting at Alex feeling fed up and guilty for running out on the place.'

Peploe laughed. 'That, Jack,' he said, 'is the difference between you and me.'

Saturday, 31 May, 6.30 a.m. Golden shafts of light now lit the mountains as Rangers and Cretans brewed up German ersatz coffee over newly made fires. Clutching an enamel mug of *milchkaffee*, Peploe spoke to Satanas and Vaughan, outlining his proposal.

'Tanner suggested as much last night,' said Satanas. 'I was sure he meant it – he is almost Cretan, he has so much pride. I was less sure you would want to risk your men on such a venture.'

373

'With the greatest respect,' said Peploe, 'we think we might be the best men for the task. We also feel we owe it to you to try.'

Satanas appeared to be genuinely touched by Peploe's offer. He smiled and clasped the captain's shoulder. 'I would not like to blame any of you for another man's folly. We know you are good, brave men.'

'And I would like to go with you,' said Vaughan. 'I know where Pendlebury's cache is and the streets and alleys of Heraklion as well as anyone.'

'First,' said Satanas, 'we must go to Krousonas. There we will meet with Alopex and hopefully learn some news from Heraklion.'

They got going soon after. Peploe left Lieutenant McDonald in charge of the Rangers, then, with Tanner and Sykes in tow, followed Satanas, two of his *andartes* and Captain Vaughan along the track down the ravine. One of Alopex's men was waiting for them on a bend in the track just above the village and led them down a long, dusty lane lined with plane trees to an ancient monastery. At its heart was the whitewashed church, twin bells raised above the roof at one end, while the monastery buildings spread around it and a narrow courtyard.

'The monastery of Agia Irini,' said Satanas. 'The abbot, Father Gregorikis, is a good man and a friend.'

As they passed through the gates, a monk appeared and led them to a room in a low terracotta-roofed building across the courtyard from the church. Inside was a long oak table with benches at either side. Alopex was there, with the abbot and another man. Alopex stood up as they entered. Tanner saw the cut around his eye and the bruising on his face, and nodded in acknowledgement; he was, he realized, glad to have the big Cretan as an ally rather than an enemy.

Introductions were made. The abbot, dressed in black, his face almost entirely covered with a thick white beard and his head with an elaborate black hat and cape, greeted them in turn, clasping their hands in both of his and muttering some words Tanner was unable to understand. The other man was Yanni Mandoukis. He looked exhausted, his eyes hollow, his lean face unshaven and dirty. Tanner watched Satanas embrace him, then sit on the bench the abbot indicated with his outstretched hand. It was cool and dim in the room, the walls plastered and whitewashed, the air slightly musty, earthy. A monk entered bearing coffee – real coffee this time, thick and sweet.

'Yanni fought alongside us in Heraklion,' said Alopex to Peploe, Tanner and Sykes. 'He has family here in Krousonas.'

'He fought well,' said Vaughan.

'The Germans have taken his wife,' said Alopex.

'But not him?' said Tanner.

'He was not there,' Alopex explained. 'They arrived two days ago, ransacked his house, looking for weapons. They took his wife too. It seems I am not the only one these bastards are trying to ensnare. They have been carrying out a number of raids on houses, taking people and questioning them. As you said, my friend,' Alopex looked at Tanner, 'someone must have talked.'

Tanner saw Mandoukis look away, at his

fingers, then at the abbot, then at some distant spot on the wall opposite.

'Do you know where your wife and the others are being held?' Peploe asked Mandoukis directly. He looked quizzically at Alopex for help.

'The Germans are using the Megaron as their headquarters,' said Alopex, 'but his wife is being held in the Sabbionera Bastion.'

'It's right next to the Megaron,' said Vaughan. 'Down by the east side of the harbour.'

'He is pretty sure my family will have been taken there too.'

'How does he know?' asked Tanner. He saw Mandoukis glance anxiously at Alopex again and then at Satanas.

'He arrived back at his house just as his wife was being taken away,' said Alopex. 'He followed them. We must get Petrina out as well.'

Mandoukis looked at Tanner, then touched his eye. He breathed in heavily, his face racked with despair.

'We need to know for certain that is where they're being held,' said Vaughan.

'Leave that to me,' said Satanas. 'I will get this information for you.'

'How?' asked Tanner.

Satanas smiled. 'You think no one will have seen two women and a child, surrounded by German troops, being driven through the town?'

'Satanas has plenty of runners,' said Vaughan, 'not least his own grandchildren.'

Satanas acknowledged Vaughan with a slight nod. 'I will have this information before the day is out.'

'And who is going to carry out the raid?' asked Vaughan. 'Not Alopex and not Mandoukis,' said Tanner.

'I am coming,' said Alopex.

'No,' said Tanner. 'Listen to me a moment. The key is going to be surprise. To achieve that, we need to get into the heart of the town without alerting a soul. So how are we going to do that?'

'By making sure no one sees us,' said Alopex.

'But how? There will be guards at every gate. No one will be able to enter the town without being stopped and checked. The alternative is to try to get through where the walls are crumbling but they'll have men there too. We won't be able to get past without killing some and then they'll be discovered and we'll be in trouble.'

'There's only one way,' said Sykes. 'We need to do some dressing up.'

'Exactly,' said Tanner. 'We need Jerry uniforms. Sir,' he said, turning to Peploe, 'you speak German, don't you?'

'So do I,' said Vaughan. 'I'm completely fluent. Tanner has a point, Alopex,' he added. 'We could pass for Germans, but neither you nor Mandoukis nor any of your *andartes* could.'

'Unless you wish to cut your hair and shave off your moustache,' said Satanas. 'No, Tanner is right. We must trust our British friends to do this for us. It is hard, Alopex, but the Germans know about us. They do not know these men are still on the island. That is an advantage we must use.'

Alopex thumped the table with his fist.

'I'm sorry, Alopex,' said Vaughan.

'No, no – you are right,' he said.

377

'Where do we get the uniforms from?' asked Peploe.

'There are still some dead ones that have not been buried,' said Alopex. 'We can have the uniforms washed.'

'But they'll be torn and covered in blood,' said Vaughan. 'I'm not sure.'

'There is another way,' said Satanas. 'There is a lot of traffic now going between Heraklion, Rethymno and Canea. Between Gazi and Arolithos there would be an opportunity for an ambush. My men can help you with that. It is only a two-hour walk away.'

'Yes, all right,' said Vaughan. 'We should go there now. Who knows how long we might have to wait?'

'Alopex can take some of his men to help,' said Satanas, 'and I will organize the gathering of intelligence.' He spoke to Mandoukis and the abbot. 'And,' he added, 'Mandoukis will stay here.'

'So, do we try and make our rescue tomorrow night?' asked Peploe.

'Yes, I think so,' said Vaughan.

'Very well,' said Satanas, clapping his hands together. 'We are all agreed. These are terrible days that we live in. Already the Germans have made it clear they intend to rule through terror. We can expect retaliation, I think, not only for what we are planning in Heraklion but for any ambush as well. They will burn houses, no doubt shoot people too. But we cannot be cowed by this. We never gave up in our struggle against the Turks and we won that battle, just as we shall win

378

this too. I truly fear what lies ahead but we cannot – we must not – accept Nazi rule. Not now, not ever. No German has the right to tell us Cretans how to live our lives. The mountains are our friends. We must use them to help us survive. I would rather die than become a slave to Germany.' He placed his hands flat on the table. 'I have said my piece. Now let us make this first stand against the enemy.'

Tanner saw silent tears run down Alopex's cheeks. He thought of the previous summer when they had returned from Dunkirk. The nation had been expecting a German invasion at any moment. There had been defiance then, a collective determination to fight on, whatever the cost. Had German troops ever reached the valley of his home, he knew he would have been compelled to kill as many of the enemy as he could, no matter what the consequences – yet home was a place he had not been in nine years and no German invasion had ever come to pass. He could only imagine the sense of bitter anger these Cretans must feel. Of course Satanas, Alopex and others would fight on.

As it happened, they did not need to go as far as Arolithos. Tilisos was a little over an hour's walk away, and as they reached the far side of the village, crossing the olive groves at either side of the road, they saw a dust cloud a mile or so off, the telltale sign of approaching traffic. Peering through his field glasses Tanner saw that it was a lone truck – it looked to him very much like a captured British fifteen-hundredweight Morris.

Through the dust he spotted a dozen paratroopers.

'We're in luck,' he said. He hurried forward through the olives to the bank next to the edge of the road and quickly scanned the ground. The truck was moving steadily up a comparatively straight stretch, but then the road curved tightly around, first, a left-hand bend and then a right. What Tanner liked about it, though, was that the road actually dropped down towards the right-hand bend: there would be some momentum behind the vehicle as it approached the turn.

Alopex, Vaughan and Peploe were beside him, crouching through the long grass between the olives. Beyond was the valley below, rolling hills covered with ever more vines and olives. Away to their left, they could see Heraklion and the azure sea beyond.

'We need to move forward a couple of hundred yards,' said Tanner, his voice quick and precise. 'As they emerge round that right-hand bend there, I'll hit the driver. With a bit of luck he'll drive on over the edge. It looks quite steep there and the olives are spaced quite well apart. The truck should roll and at the very least the men will be thrown out. It won't kill them all, but we want to shoot dead as few as possible.'

'Good plan,' said Vaughan. 'Let's move then. We need to be quick.'

They hurried forward, and about fifty yards from the bend, Alopex dashed across the road with several of his men and ducked below the line of the road in the olive grove below, while the rest stayed behind Tanner. Pulling out his Aldis scope, Tanner fixed it to his Enfield, then hastily adjusted the zero; although he knew he would be able to see the driver clearly from that distance, he wanted to be certain he made as accurate a shot as possible. He found a large rock, lay down in the grass and rested his rifle barrel on it, steadied himself and peered through the scope, waiting.

The truck was now out of sight, but he could hear it as its driver changed gear when they approached the left-hand bend. Down another gear, then foot on the throttle, engine rising, another change of gear, and then it was on the stretch down towards the second bend. Tanner pulled back the bolt on his rifle and felt his finger lightly caress the trigger. Now the engine was changing tone again as brakes were applied and it approached the second bend. Tanner breathed in, then held his breath. *Come on, come on,* he thought. And suddenly there it was, the front of the truck appearing around the bend, filling his scope. Tanner took a second to focus on the driver, aimed for the centre of the man's cloth-capped forehead and squeezed the trigger.

The butt lurched into his shoulder, the crack of the rifle rang out sharply, and the driver's head snapped backwards. The startled passenger reached for the steering wheel, but Tanner had already pulled back the bolt again and fired. The second man fell backwards just as the front of the truck tipped over the edge of the road. For a moment it rolled and bounced forward, men jumping free from the back, but then hit a tree with a glancing blow, toppled over and began to roll down the steep slopes until it was lost to sight.

'Quick!' said Vaughan, and now they were all jumping down onto the road and scampering across. With his rifle hastily slung across his back and his Schmeisser ready, Tanner reached the lip of the road as, with a crash, the truck at last came to a halt a hundred yards below, mangled and bent between two olives, while in front of him Alopex and his men were using knives and rifle butts to kill those who had jumped.

Tanner ran down through the trees. Several men, he saw, were lying spreadeagled around the smashed truck, but at least two were moving. He ran on and was conscious of Alopex beside him, bloodstained knife in his hand, flitting between the trees.

A paratrooper saw them and tried to manoeuvre his rifle but Alopex reached him before he could fire, knocked the weapon clear and swung his fist hard into the side of the man's head. Tanner pounced on the second man, clenched his arm around the German's neck so that he gripped the back of his head, then with his other hand gave a sudden, firm jerk that broke the man's spinal cord, killing him instantly.

'A fine shot, Jack,' said Alopex, using Tanner's Christian name for the first time. 'Your plan worked perfectly.'

'Are there any others?' said Tanner. There were loose pieces of paper scattered around the truck, which hissed and ticked as its now broken engine cooled. He grabbed a sheet.

'Here,' he said, passing it to Alopex. 'It's all

382

Greek to me.'

Alopex took it. 'A warning from General Student, whoever he may be,' he said. 'Threats – the Germans will shoot us, burn villages, execute male populations as a reprisal against any sabotage or atrocities by us Cretans.' He screwed it up. 'They must have been on their way to put these up around the villages. They were wasting their time.'

'You'd take no notice?'

'No – hardly anyone can read.' Alopex laughed. 'Stupid Nazi Sons of whores.'

Tanner grinned, picked up another of the notices and tucked it into his pocket. Further back up the hill he saw a guerrilla raise his rifle in salute. 'We should hurry this up,' he said to Alopex. 'We need to get these men stripped and bundle some of them back in the truck. If we set fire to it, it's just possible the Germans will think it was an accident – after all, they're mostly young troops driving an unfamiliar vehicle on unfamiliar roads. We can leave a couple of the men on the slopes here, but they need to be dressed still and to look as though they were killed as the truck fell.'

'Good idea. I will tell the others,' said Alopex.

Tanner began to strip the two men they had just killed: boots, trousers, jump smocks, which, he noticed, both men had rolled up to the elbow, shirts, belts, webbing, field caps and helmets, which were quite different from the normal German coal-scuttle design. He felt in the pockets and found some cigarettes, but also letters and a few photographs. Tanner looked at them: a family shot, a mother, father and younger sister. Tanner sighed, and wiped his brow. 'Bloody hell,' he muttered. Both men had been young – early twenties, he guessed. Maybe even younger. *Just kids*. Having made a pile of their kit, he moved the bodies beside the truck. Alopex was returning with Vaughan and several of the *andartes*, each carrying a stripped and dead German.

'Here,' said Tanner. 'Put them in the back.'

'We'd better not take their weapons,' said Vaughan.

Alopex looked disappointed and threw a Schmeisser into the back of the truck. 'No, you are right – but it is hard to throw away guns.'

Seeing an oily rag in the open store box between the off-side wheels Tanner took it, hurried around to the other side, drew out his sword bayonet and punctured the fuel tank then held the rag under it until it was soaked in the fluid.

When the bodies had been dumped in the back and the men had moved out of the way, Tanner wrapped the rag around a stick, lit it and threw it at the truck. The petrol seeping onto the grass immediately flared up and, moments later, the rest of the petrol tank exploded. In no time, the entire truck was engulfed in livid flames, thick smoke billowing into the sky from the rubber tyres, the wooden flooring and sides. The bonnet burst open as fire from the ignited oil in the engine caused the metal to twist.

'Come on,' said Peploe, 'we need to get out of here quickly.' Alopex cuffed one of his men, who was still watching the spectacle, but then all of them were scampering back up the slope, through the trees, German boots around their necks and uniforms bundled under their arms. Crossing the road, they clambered back up the other side and, using the olives as cover, hurried back towards Silhos.

Only when they were halfway back to Krousonas and well clear of the burning truck did they slacken their pace and begin to relax their guard. As the village came within easy sight, its collection of largely white buildings nestling beneath the mountains, they paused to look back in the direction from which they had come. They could still see a faint wisp of dark smoke.

'I don't think it'll take the Germans long to come out and investigate,' said Vaughan.

'Hopefully they'll think it really was an accident,' said Peploe.

'Here, sir,' said Tanner, passing to Vaughan the notice he had picked up. 'Looks like they were on a trip to post these up round about.'

Vaughan took it. 'The bastards,' he muttered. 'There's going to be a reign of terror. This isn't a modern war, it's worse than the Middle Ages.'

They walked on, following Alopex and his men.

'I've been meaning to ask, sir,' said Tanner, at length. 'That bloke Mandoukis.'

'What of him?'

'Do you believe him?'

Vaughan sighed. 'Why do you think Satanas insisted he remain in the monastery? Honestly? I don't know. He fought bloody well in Heraklion. He has family up here in the mountains, and has known these men all his life.'

'But his wife is being held by the Germans,'

said Peploe, 'so they could have something on him.'

'Maybe,' said Vaughan. 'I hope not. But we need to be careful. If we can get his wife out as well, then I'd say we have less reason to worry. If he has betrayed them, though...' He did not finish the sentence.

'I can imagine,' said Peploe.

They returned to the cave, climbing back up through the ravine in the scorching afternoon sun, their backs slick with sweat. Later, at dusk, Satanas arrived with one of his teenage grandsons, a number of armed men and several other new faces, not least Jack Hanford, an agent who had been working with Pendlebury, and another of the *kapitans*, Manoli Bandouvas. The latter was a large, moutachioed, broad-faced man of perhaps forty, Tanner guessed, booted and armed with no fewer than three bandoliers around his waist.

The new arrivals had brought with them important news.

'Mandoukis was wrong,' said Satanas. He sat on a rock before the fire, Bandouvas on one side of him, Alopex on the other. Hanford, Vaughan and Peploe sat opposite. There was, Tanner realized as he stood behind Peploe, a distinct pecking order: Satanas at the top, then Bandouvas and then Alopex. All three men, however, showed obvious regard and respect for Vaughan and Hanford. Behind them all were the *andartes* and the Rangers, some standing and listening, others sitting around the cave's edge. Bottles of raki were passed around, while on another fire, meat was

386

cooking. Tanner watched the flickering flames cast shadows and an orange glow across the old man's face.

'They are not being held in the Sabbionera Bastion,' he said. 'They are in the fortress.'

'Damn it!' said Vaughan.

Peploe rubbed his chin. 'That's not going to be easy.'

'No,' said Satanas, 'although if you can get in it should be easy enough to find them. The fortress is not as big as it looks.'

'And we know this for certain?' said Peploe.

'Yes. They were seen being taken there. A number of witnesses have confirmed this.'

'I suppose it is the obvious place,' sighed Vaughan. 'What about the stash?'

'So far, it seems no one has found it.'

'Well, that's something.'

'And there's a fair amount of explosives up here already, Alex,' added Peploe. 'Sergeant Sykes has enough switches and fuse to wreak considerable havoc.'

'Do we have any idea how many men there are actually in the town?' asked Tanner.

Satanas smiled. 'Not so many. A number have moved to Rethymno, but most are out by the airfield and outside the town walls. There are perhaps a hundred at the Megaron and around the Sabbionera Bastion. There is also an encampment of paratroopers in the valley south of Gazi and at Knossos. There are guards at all the gates and troops wandering freely through the town.'

'What we need is a big diversion,' said Tanner. 'Several different explosions going off in different parts of the town. At the bastions, preferably, then none of the townspeople will get hurt.'

'That should be possible,' said Sykes. 'We've got a whole crate of time pencils back here.'

'So we get into the town, set the explosions, lie low and then, when they start going off, make for the fortress?' said Peploe.

'In a nutshell, sir, yes,' said Tanner.

Vaughan nodded. 'I can't think of a better plan.'

'Pendlebury would approve,' said Hanford. 'Just the kind of madcap scheme he would have come up with.' He smiled, then said to Peploe, 'And assuming you're successful and make it safely back here, we need to get you and the rest of your men, John, off the island.'

'Yes. Do you have any ideas?'

'I do, as it happens. I don't know how much Captain Vaughan has told you, but Major Bruce-Mitford and I had been working with Pendlebury for some time over here, and will continue to work here on the island. Bandouvas and I have just come from the Amari Valley where, with Bruce-Mitford, we've set up something of a base in a village called Yerakari. Bruce-Mitford's still there and we've been in touch with Cairo.'

'You've got a wireless set?' said Peploe.

'One of the very few the British Army ever had on the island.' He smiled ruefully.

'It's one of the disgraces of the war,' said Vaughan. 'Why the hell the powers that be didn't twig this earlier, God only knows.'

'It was the same in France,' said Peploe. 'No one had a clue what was going on half the time and all the while it seemed like every other Jerry

388

had a set.'

'Anyway,' said Hanford, 'fortunately we do have a set and we're in touch with Cairo. They're sending a submarine. It's coming in a week with a Commander Pool on board, a naval man who apparently knows Crete intimately from before the war. He's suggested Preveli.'

'A good choice,' said Satanas. 'It is a monastery on the headland overlooking the sea, but there are paths leading down to the shore. Father Langouvardos will help. I know him and he is not only a very holy man but also a true Cretan patriot.'

'In a week?' said Peploe. 'Did they say when exactly?'

'Not yet. Major Bruce-Mitford is going to make contact with Father Langouvardos and then we'll await confirmation from Cairo. But if we can, we'll try to get you out on the sub when it comes.'

'Thank you,' said Peploe. 'But, first, some of us have a mission to carry out.' He looked at the Cretan *kapitans* opposite him. 'Tomorrow night, then?'

'Yes, tomorrow,' said Satanas.

Tomorrow, thought Tanner. He knew it was a mission fraught with danger, that there was every chance something would go terribly wrong and that they might all get themselves killed. And yet it would give them a chance to fight back, to show those bastards that not all British troops on Crete had been ready to roll over. And he also wanted to get Alexis out of there; he wanted that badly. He was taking it far too personally, he knew, but unless they attempted this mission, his conscience would never rest. Honour demanded it.

19

Sunday, 1 June, a little after 6 p.m. Oberleutnant Balthasar walked around the blackened remains of the British truck. The paint had gone entirely, leaving patches of bare steel; so too had the tyres and the timber. Of the driver and his companion two charred corpses could just about be recognized while several bodies were discernible among the ash and debris in the back. On the grass nearby two more badly burned bodies lay where they had died – their blackened forms more obviously once human. Three others had been found the day before among the olives.

Balthasar had not seen them. Indeed, he had been in Heraklion at the time at a meeting with Major Schulz, and so in his absence Leutnant Eicher had sent Mittler's *gruppe* to investigate as soon as they saw the smoke pitching into the sky. One of the men had claimed he had heard shots, but Mittler had returned convinced that the loss of the men and the truck had been an accident and nothing more. The men had still had their weapons, and although there were signs of trampled grass, he had concluded that had been caused by the truck as it had fallen down the slope. Hitting two trees had caused the petrol to explode, killing most of the men before they'd had a chance to jump clear.

The three men from the olive groves had been

brought back and buried and were already under the ground by the time Balthasar had returned and been given the news. He wished he had had a chance to examine the bodies, but although he had accepted Mittler's version of events initially, there had been something about it that did not seem quite right to him – something he had not been able to put his finger on until that afternoon. Then it had dawned on him: any Cretan for miles around would have seen the smoke – would have probably heard the crash and any explosion. Surely someone would have come along and picked the men clean of weapons – Balthasar was not so naïve as to believe the burning of Sarhos had brought about the end of all Cretan resistance. No, what was strange was that the three men who had been found had still had their weapons with them.

Balthasar had mulled this over that afternoon and then had decided to go and look for himself.

'Perhaps the brakes failed,' said Unteroffizier Mittler, as they had stood on the road where the truck had come off.

'Perhaps,' Balthasar had replied, his voice terse. And now he was looking over the wreck itself. He peered closely at the bodies on the grass beside the truck. Both men were face down, so he turned the first over. Patches of skin on his chest had been roasted dark, but not black.

'Here,' said Balthasar. 'What do you make of that?'

Mittler looked. 'The flames have not burned him so badly where he has been lying in the grass.'

'They have hardly burned him at all in places,

391

Mittler. That tells us something, does it not?'
Mittler looked blank. 'It tells us; Mittler,' said
Balthasar, exasperation creeping into his voice,
'that there should be bits of uniform still clinging
to his front. But there is nothing, is there? No
scraps of cotton, no belt buckle. No helmet for
that matter. Where is it?'

'You think they have been stripped?'

'Yes, Mittler, that is exactly what I think.' He
now peered into the remains of the truck. 'Here,'
he said, examining the driver. 'A belt buckle.' He
then looked into the mess that had once been the
back of the Morris. 'But nothing among this lot.
Even if they were wearing their field caps they
would have had their helmets with them.'

'They did, Herr Oberleutnant,' said Mittler. 'I
saw them leave.'

'And yet they are not here any more. Something should have remained of them.' He
whisked away several flies now hovering around.
It had been another hot day, and even now, as
evening was drawing in, the heat sat heavily in
the air. 'Get a party up here to collect and bury
the remains of these men, Mittler. And try to be
a bit more observant in future.'

'Yes, Herr Oberleutnant. But why would the
Cretans want our uniforms?'

'If they had taken only boots, Mittler, I would
have said it was because they were after decent
footwear. But they have taken everything, yet
wanted us to believe this was just an accident and
nothing more. If you can't work it out for yourself, then I'm certainly not going to tell you.'

They headed back, Mittler driving, Balthasar

deep in thought. Having reached the camp he ordered Mittler to drive on, to Heraklion and to the Megaron. To his intense frustration, neither Schulz nor Bräuer was there – Schulz was visiting the 1st Battalion at the Jesus Bastion and Bräuer was at the airfield although due back any moment. Balthasar looked at his watch, uncertain whether to head straight to the bastion or to wait for Bräuer. It was now half past seven, the light beginning to fade.

'When exactly are you expecting Oberst Bräuer?' he asked the clerk in the office adjoining Bräuer's.

'Half an hour ago, Herr Oberleutnant.'

Balthasar looked at his watch again, then left and began to pace the corridor on the first floor outside Bräuer's office. He would stay where he was, praying he was being both overly cautious and that the colonel would return soon.

It was just after eight when Bräuer appeared, his voice ringing out before Balthasar saw him as he climbed the staircase.

'Oberleutnant Balthasar.' He smiled. 'Have you been waiting for me?'

'Yes, Herr Oberst,' said Balthasar, saluting.

'Come in, come in,' said Bräuer, leading the way into his office. He paused by his desk to fit a cigarette into his holder then lit it with a gold lighter. 'How can I help?'

Balthasar told him about the truck and what he had discovered. 'The uniforms could have been taken for a number of reasons, but one cannot rule out the possibility that they were intended as a disguise. It seems a coincidence that the day after I capture a leading bandit's family, a number of my men are killed and stripped not five kilometres away.'

'Yes, I agree with you, Balthasar. Although even after a shave – which, let us face it, most Cretans seem incapable of doing – I think they would still stand out.'

'Yes, but it would be easy for the unsuspecting sentry not to notice any imposters passing at dusk or even at night.'

Bräuer exhaled a large cloud of smoke. 'Yes, yes – you're quite right, Oberleutnant. I still doubt that a handful of Cretans in disguise could cause too much mischief, but the men must be warned. I'll send out word immediately. Thank you, Balthasar. You were right to tell me.'

'And perhaps, Herr Oberst, if you will forgive me saying so, it might be prudent to put extra guards around the fortress.'

'Yes, Balthasar, I'll do exactly as you suggest, and without delay.'

Around a quarter to nine six men walked towards the Kenouria Gate beside the Jesus Bastion, approaching from the east as though they had come from the direction of the airfield. They had not, as it happened. Rather they had woven their way down from the mountains, carefully crossing the road beyond the crest of the low ridge that led from the town towards Knossos, then working their way first through the groves and then the houses and back alleys of the sprawling town beyond the great walls.

Six of them: Vaughan, with the gull-wing insignia of an *Unteroffizier* on his left sleeve, Peploe

394

beside him with a single V-shaped chevron. Behind them came Tanner and Sykes, then Chambers and McAllister. They all looked battle-hardened: tanned, faces smeared with sweat and oil; Tanner with his bruising and cut eye. They all had Schmeissers slung from their shoulders, except McAllister, who carried an MG34 across his shoulders, despite its sling. From Tanner's shoulders hung another strap from which he carried two aluminium ammunition boxes full of MG belts. Peploe, Tanner and Sykes also wore long cloth bandoliers draped around their shoulders, five pouches each side, which they had gleefully discovered were just the right size for a half-pound packet of TNT. German paratroopers, they had found out, did not carry the kind of packs an ordinary infantryman wore as a matter of course. Instead they used the plentiful pockets in their cotton jump smocks. These now bulged with more rounds, stick grenades and explosives. And while Peploe and Vaughan wore Luftwaffe blue wool side caps, the rest had on the distinctive paratrooper helmets, in Tanner's case low over his eyes.

'Now just act naturally, boys,' said Vaughan, in a low voice. In the dim dusk light they saw guards moving towards them either side of the gate. Tanner's heart was thumping heavily. They had managed it this far, but he knew that getting through the town gates was going to be one of the potential stumbling blocks of the entire operation. But then again, when he thought about it, there were many...

A guard pointing a Schmeisser came towards

them and ordered them to halt. Tanner listened as Vaughan said something in German to Peploe, who laughed. It sounded convincing enough to him, but now a lance corporal was ambling over to them, the same single chevron on his sleeve as Peploe wore.

'*Seid ihr vom Flugplatz gekommen?*' he asked.

'*Ja,*' said Vaughan. Tanner watched him wipe the side of his face. '*Es ist immer noch heiß, nicht wahr?*'

What the hell are they talking about? Tanner wondered. The NCO seemed friendly enough. *Thank God for Vaughan.*

'*Ja, ja. Sind Sie für die Verstärkung der Festung?*'

'*Ja. Was ist los?*'

The German grinned. '*Wir suchen einige Kreter als Fallschirmjäger verkleidet. Ihre Soldbuch?*'

Vaughan and Peploe handed over their pay-books, found inside the uniforms of the dead men. The German looked at them briefly with a torch, then said, '*Gut,*' and waved them on. No other paper required, no careful scan of the face. Tanner felt himself relax. They walked on, the guards talking casually as they passed, and then they were under the gate, the rubber soles of their boots drumming softly on the dirt road as they walked straight on down Evans Street – it had been named after the British archaeologist – as though going towards the port. Only when they were out of sight of the men at the gate did Vaughan lead them off the main road and down a narrow back-street.

'They know something's up,' said Peploe, his voice quiet and urgent.

Vaughan nodded and turned to the others. 'That guard asked me whether we were reinforcements for the fortress. I said yes and asked him what was going on. Apparently they're looking out for some Cretans dressed up as paratroopers.'

'Could be worse, sir,' said Tanner.

'I don't like the sound of the reinforcement bit,' said McAllister.

'It'll be all right,' said Tanner. 'We're in, aren't we?'

They had agreed they would lay a series of charges at each of the four bastions from the Martinengo Bastion in the south, all along the west side of the walls to the Ayios Andreas Bastion by the sea's edge, but avoiding the Canea Gate, which, as a major entrance to the town, was likely to be more heavily guarded. First, however, Sykes had to prepare the charges, so Vaughan led them down through a web of narrow streets until they found a small courtyard beside a destroyed house. With Peploe shining his blue-filtered German torch, Sykes got to work, deftly pulling out a time pencil, fixing a small length of instantaneous fuse into the fuse adaptor and then wrapping it around two half-pound blocks of TNT. A cat suddenly mewed above them; none of the men had heard it approach and they flinched.

'Bloody cat!' hissed Vaughan. 'Too damned many of them in this town.'

'That's one done,' said Sykes. The time pencils were colour coded by the metal strip that acted as a safety pin and protruded from one end of the switch. What they had really wanted was an hour's delay but the choice was either red, which was half an hour, or white, which was ninety minutes. They had chosen white.

'Ssh!' hissed Chambers, from the doorway. Footsteps. The men froze, but then the person passed and they relaxed once more. Tanner moved over beside Chambers and listened. The night was still with barely a breath of wind. The stench of rotting corpses had gone, but the air remained heavy with the smell of sewage; a body might rot away but the living still produced effluent. Broken sewers could not be repaired overnight.

In less than ten minutes they were ready, six bundles of explosives prepared with their timers set to begin the moment Sykes broke the acid phial in each of the switches. From that moment the acid would begin to corrode the wire that held the striker away from the fuse adaptor. They had discussed whether they should be set to detonate simultaneously but had decided that staggering the explosions would be more effective. With luck, as soon as troops were drawn to one explosion, another would go off. Sykes now handed out the charges, which they each put carefully into the front pockets of their jump smocks.

'Just make sure you don't break the fuse or knock the switch out of place,' said Sykes. 'Obvious, I know, but it don't take much for this stuff to go whoosh.'

Vaughan nodded and took a deep breath. 'All set?' he asked.

'Yes, sir,' said Sykes.

'Right – let's go.'

He led them back up to Plastira. It was now completely dark, with only a sliver of moon and the stars providing any light. Having paused to check there were no troops about, they moved onto the main road that ran beneath the walls. Opposite the entrance to Martinengo Bastion, they crossed to the wall, where they were hidden by dark shadow. A set of steps led up to the walls and Sykes now took out the first of his bombs, broke the phial, placed it on the ground and covered it with a piece of loose paper lying discarded on the street.

They moved on. Two officers walked past, not paratroopers but ordinary army. Vaughan and Peploe saluted, and as the Germans passed them Tanner saw the white Edelweiss symbol on their sleeve. Mountain troops. *So they're here now too.*

Another package was dropped by the Bethlehem Bastion and then they were by the break in the wall where there had been so much fighting ten days earlier. This was the stretch of the walls they had briefly manned afterwards and they saw that German troops now occupied the building opposite that had earlier been a Greek company headquarters. There were men inside – they could hear them talking and laughing. Tanner felt his heart quicken again.

'Here,' whispered Vaughan, and now Tanner carefully placed a package on a ledge by a shuttered window. Then Vaughan took them off Plastira and halted them by the alleyway that led to the rear of the building. 'What do you think?' he said. 'Worth risking?'

'Hold on a moment, sir,' said Sykes. He crept

soundlessly along the alley. Watching from the end, Tanner could barely see him. Suddenly voices rang out – someone was leaving the back of the building – and jarringly loud in the still night air. Quickly they moved back, away from the mouth of the alley. But Tanner stood right on the corner, protected by the shadows. The German paused, lit a cigarette, then walked towards them. *Damn it*, thought Tanner, but somehow the man walked straight past where Sykes must have been. *Of course*, thought Tanner, *he's not expecting trouble.* He now felt in his trouser pocket and closed his fingers around his small knife, silently pulled it out and opened the blade. The German was almost upon them, only the faint shape of his side cap showing in the light of the stars and the red glow of his cigarette. Tanner let him draw level before quickly moving forward, bringing his arm tightly around the man's neck and in the same moment plunging the knife into the German's side. The man was dead – his body shutting down the moment the blade had skewered his kidney – but Tanner held him upright and dragged him clear of the alleyway.

Moments later, Sykes was back beside them.

'Blimey,' he whispered, 'that was a bit bloody close.'

'You dropped the TNT all right?' asked Peploe.

Sykes nodded. 'What are you going to do with him?'

Tanner hoisted the dead man over his shoulder and, seeing a bombed house a short distance across the street, hurried over and dumped the body among the debris.

They moved on, making the most of the rubble still piled high along Kalokerinou and Dedidaki to cross those two main streets without being seen, and dropped the last of the packages near the Ayios Andreas Bastion by the sea. Barely a soul moved – a few guards on the walls, but that was all. A curfew had clearly been imposed on the town and, with the blackout as well, the six men were able to slip through the streets of Heraklion with ease.

The rubble had still not been cleared from the narrow lane that led to Pendlebury's arms store. Clambering over it, they reached the wooden door in the wall, passed through into the courtyard, and took the steps, Vaughan leading the way. In the first chamber of the cellar, Vaughan took out his torch and quickly dismantled the trip wire he had set a few days earlier, then led the others down into the lower depths of the cellar. A stack of boxes of various sizes stood in the far corner of one room.

'What have you got here, sir?' asked Sykes.

'I can't quite remember, to be honest,' said Vaughan, 'but there are some grenades and more explosives. No more weapons – they've all gone.'

'It's the explosives we want, sir.' There were three wooden boxes of Nobel's Explosive No. 808, which Sykes immediately opened. 'This stuff is beautiful,' he said, grinning. He took out a cardboard carton. 'It's the way they're packed, you see. There's five pounds' worth of four-ounce cartridges in each of these packets. Now, twenty pounds of gelignite makes a very nice bang. A very nice bang indeed.'

'Excellent, Sergeant,' said Vaughan. 'Well, let's take what we can, then get rid of the rest. It's a shame to blow this place up after hundreds of years, but such is life.'

'Can't let Jerry get his hands on it, sir,' said Tanner. 'And the buildings nearby are either destroyed or empty. We won't be killing anyone.'

'Set to blow with another time pencil?' Sykes asked.

'Yes,' said Vaughan.

'What length of time, sir?'

They looked at their watches. 'The first bomb is due to go at twenty-two fifty hours,' said Vaughan.

'It's nearly ten now, sir,' said Tanner.

'Another white?' suggested Sykes. 'It'll blow just as they think everything's calmed down.'

Vaughan nodded. 'All right.' He glanced around the room, and at the ancient vaulted brick ceiling.

'I know,' said Peploe, 'but Sykes is right. You didn't struggle with this stuff all the way from Suda for the benefit of the Germans.'

'I was thinking about Pendlebury,' said Vaughan. 'He would have loved being part of an operation like this. In some ways he did regard it all as something of a game, yet he passionately believed in the cause too. He really, truly loved Crete.' He hitched his Schmeisser over his shoulder. 'Anyway, no time for sentimentality. We should get going. There's a partly bombed-out house overlooking the harbour. I thought we might hole up in it for a while. We can do a visual recce from there.'

Having stuffed their pockets with packets of gelignite and grenades, and with Sykes having set another time-delay switch, they climbed back up

402

and out into the courtyard, then scrambled over the rubble once more. As they worked their way the short distance down towards the harbour the sound of traffic – engines and squeaking tracks – suddenly filled the night air. Pressing themselves into the shadows of a side-street, they watched a small column of three trucks and two British Bren carriers head down the Street of the August Martyrs, the main road that led from the centre of the town down the hill to the harbour.

'Damn it,' whispered Vaughan.

'On the other hand, sir,' said Tanner, 'it means there's some transport about.'

They moved on, picking their way down a back alley until they reached the rear of the bombed house. Part of the roof had collapsed, but the back of the building was still intact, so they climbed over a pile of rubble to the rear doorway and stepped inside. The building was little more than a shell. Several rats scurried past, and grit and stone crunched underfoot, but having climbed the stairs they entered a dark room on the first floor and, feeling their way, reached one of the windows, stepping over broken glass. Tanner tensed at the sound – it seemed so loud suddenly in the confines of the empty house – but from the window they had a clear view of the harbour, the arsenals and the Megaron building, sticking up over the domed roofs of the arsenals.

The motorized column they had seen a few minutes earlier had now come to a halt by the harbour's edge. The two Bren carriers and one of the trucks were in front of the row of Venetian houses along the southern edge of the harbour, while the two other trucks had parked at the mouth of the harbour wall. Men were milling about the vehicles, then the Brens started up again and drove off in the direction of the Megaton and the Sabbionera Bastion.

'What are they up to?' whispered Vaughan.

'I like the look of that Snipe,' said Tanner, pointing towards the Humber. It was an eight-hundredweight truck, with room for three up front and half a dozen in the back. More importantly, however, it had a six-cylinder engine and four-speed gearbox that gave considerably greater speed than either the carriers or Morris Commercials the Germans had taken from the British.

Tanner looked at his watch, angling it so that the light of the stars shone on the face. It was nearly half past ten. Another engine started up and this time it was the Snipe. Thin blackout lights shone from its headlamps and it now drove on down the harbour wall, stopping thirty yards short of the fortress in front of some tracked derricks that overlooked the water. Men clambered out of the back and appeared to go into the fortress.

'Ideal,' said Peploe, in a low voice. 'Look, I've got an idea.'

'Yes?' said Vaughan.

'We move back down to the street and get as close to the mouth of the harbour wall as we can. As soon as the first bomb goes off, there's going to be confusion, isn't there?'

'I should think so,' said Vaughan.

'They'll probably load up into that truck. If they do, we could walk straight past them and

404

down the harbour wall. Tanner's right: we need that Snipe. If anyone tries to move it out we stop them.'

'How, sir?' asked McAllister.

'Preferably verbally. Captain Vaughan can just tell them to wait. I can do the same – we can give them spiel about being ordered to stay put.'

'It's a good idea, sir,' said Tanner. 'They'll be surprised, and hopefully not thinking quite right.'

'And assuming we get the truck?' said Vaughan.

'Then we get Mac in the back with the MG,' said Tanner, 'and you, sir, sit in the front. The rest of us then go into the fortress.'

'Yes,' said Peploe, 'and if anyone comes down the harbour wall causing trouble, McAllister can open up.'

'All right,' said Vaughan. 'Are you sure, Peploe?'

'As I can be, yes. The whole operation now seems absolutely lunatic, if I'm honest, but I can't think of a better plan.'

They began moving back downstairs but heard voices and the sound of footsteps coming towards the building. They froze. The building had been a shop before it was bombed and the large window at the front had been blasted in, while the door had also gone. They could see three soldiers walking towards the building's edge, their forms quite distinct. It was as though the men were looking directly at them. They paused, lit cigarettes, then stood there, chatting. Tanner cursed to himself. They were stuck, unable to move or make a sound. Several minutes passed but still the Germans remained where they stood. Tanner could feel his feet going numb and his back had begun to itch – lice, maybe – but he dared not move. *Come on, come on,* he thought. *Move away.* He wondered what the time was. It couldn't be long now. The men were laughing, then one flicked his cigarette through the gap where the shop window had been. From the staircase Tanner could see it lying on the ground, its end still glowing a faint orange.

The first bomb exploded.

Tanner flinched. A moment's pause, then urgent, anxious voices and someone was shouting to the men from across the road.

'Quick!' hissed Vaughan, and led them out of the back of the building. An engine started up – *the Morris* – and Tanner heard more shouts and yells and the sound of the truck reversing. Scrambling over the rubble, they reached the road by the harbour as the truck moved out. Pressing himself into the shadows, Tanner saw Sykes deftly step out, crouching, as the truck went past, then duck back into the shadow again.

'Come on!' said Vaughan, and they now ran down the harbour wall. Two Germans were standing by the Snipe.

'*Warum steht ihr da?*' barked Vaughan.

'*Uns wurde gesagt, hier zu warten,*' sputtered one of the men.

'You take the right, I'll take the left,' whispered Vaughan to Tanner. Reaching the car, Tanner glanced at Vaughan, saw him draw level with the first man. He heard a muffled cry and in the same moment rammed his forearm into the other man's throat, quick and hard, before the German had time to realize what was happening, then plunged his knife into the man's side. The soldier gasped and crumpled to the ground.

'Mac, get in the back!' said Peploe. As McAllister clambered in, Tanner handed over the twin ammunition boxes, his heart pounding. Just then the second bomb exploded, and now the four of them were running to the entrance of the fortress. Across the harbour, the two carriers they had seen earlier were speeding back along the road. *Good*, thought Tanner. *So far so good.* As they reached the entrance they heard orders being barked and men hurrying towards them from within.

'Try to hit them as they come out,' said Vaughan. 'Don't shoot unless you have to.' Tanner and Sykes stood to one side, Chambers and Vaughan to the other. Suddenly the door opened and eight men hurried out, oblivious of the four waiting either side of the entranceway. Tanner sprinted forward and charged at them, pouncing on the last two, tumbling them and knocking over the others like dominoes. He plunged his knife in quick succession into the sides of two men as Vaughan, Sykes and Chambers jumped on the rest. It was over in seconds – a few startled shouts from the Germans but not a shot had been fired. Tanner pushed himself up as Vaughan dragged a man clear and rammed him against the fortress's walls.

'*Wo sind die Gefangenen?*' growled Vaughan. *Where are the prisoners?*

'*Töte mich nicht,*' said the terrified man.

Vaughan yanked him around and shoved him back through the entranceway. 'Come on,' he said. 'Let's go and find them.'

Inside, the fortress was dimly lit. They hurried through into a high arched and narrow hallway, off which were a number of heavy curve-topped wooden doors.

'*Wo sind Sie?*' demanded Vaughan.

'*Auf der nächsten Etage,*' said the German.

'They're on the next floor,' said Vaughan. He shoved the German forward. '*Schnell!*' he said. '*Schnell! Schnell!*' Voices could be heard from further along the hallway and now, more urgently, from above. Dimly, from across the town, they heard another explosion and Tanner felt the pulse of the blast through the stone floor.

'I think we're going to have to open fire soon, sir,' he said.

The German led them through a door, then up a stone staircase. Tanner now pushed ahead past their captive and, at the top of the stairs, turned into another long corridor, this one with a lower arched ceiling. A row of doors ran along the passageway and outside one he saw several soldiers, all mountain troopers. An officer saw him and started shouting and pointing.

'Haven't a clue what you're on about, mate,' said Tanner, and opened fire. The noise was deafening, as the men jerked and flailed and collapsed on the floor. The others were now beside him.

'My guess is they're in there,' said Tanner, pointing to the heap of dead Germans and moving to the mouth of an arch from which a ramp rose upwards, perhaps to the battlements above. He saw booted feet and fired again. Several men collapsed and he fired a second burst. Three men rolled down the stone ramp, but Tanner now saw two thick, heavy wooden doors that could close off the ramp and moved to shut them. He had closed one half when a stick grenade landed at his feet. He grabbed it and hurled it back, the charge exploding before it landed a second time. He rammed shut the other half of the door and drew across the bolt as another grenade exploded. He felt the blast but the door stood firm – eventually it would give way. They had to hurry.

Glancing back he saw their captive sprawled on the floor and Vaughan ushering two women and a child out over the dead by the door, then saw that one was Alexis. Relief swept over him, and he grinned at her. She smiled back fleetingly.

'Where the hell is Mandoukis's wife?' he called, suddenly remembering.

'I do not know,' said Alexis.

'Come on, quickly,' said Vaughan. 'We'll have to forget about her.'

Then Nerita slipped in some blood, and cried out in horror. More grenades were exploding against the door, and Chambers, keeping cover at the top of the stairs, opened fire. Alopex's son put his hands over his ears. Tanner helped usher them forward and saw Sykes fiddling with a length of fuse, which the moment they had all passed he tied around the hinge of a door, then across the passageway to the hinge of another door on the other side.

Tanner was now at the top of the stairs beside Chambers. Taking out two grenades, he pulled the pins, counted to three, then threw them and, as they exploded, hurried down the steps and opened fire. Two men, one dead, the other badly wounded, lay at the foot of the stairs, but there were more enemy further along the main passageway to the right. Tanner knew he could not step clear of the stone staircase without being hit.

'What's holding you, Tanner?' shouted Vaughan.

'Won't be a moment, sir,' said Tanner, pulling out a packet of Nobel's and ripping open the cardboard to take out one four-ounce stick. Then he took another two grenades, pulled out the pins, counted and threw them. Bullets spat out, one nicking his arm, but as the grenades exploded and filled the passageway with smoke and dust and, he hoped, stunned the men, he threw the stick of Nobel's and opened fire. The stick exploded, men cried out, and Tanner yelled at the others to hurry down. At the same moment Sykes's trip wire detonated with another deafening explosion. Smoke, dust and cordite filled the air.

'Hurry! Hurry!' rasped Tanner, ushering them forward.

'Follow me!' called Vaughan, and ran to the entrance. He stopped them all briefly and spoke to the two women and the boy in Greek. The three nodded, their eyes wide and frightened.

'We need to watch out for the men on the battlements,' said Tanner.

'We need to run,' said Vaughan. 'Don't forget it's dark.' He looked at them all. 'Ready? Let's go.'

Vaughan and Chambers went first, then the women and the boy, and then Tanner. Sub-machine-gun and rifle fire cracked out from above and Tanner felt himself crouching, instinctively trying to make himself smaller. Bullets pinged and fizzed, ricocheting off the stone. He heard Vaughan gasp, but then, in the same moment, return machine-gun fire was peppering the battlements. *Well done, Mac,* thought Tanner, ducking behind the harbour crane.

As he reached the Snipe, he saw that McAllister was not in the back but on the ground to the side, using the base of the cranes as cover. Peploe had also reversed the truck tight behind the derricks so that it lay out of the line of fire from the fortress. Bullets zinged uselessly into the metal behind them as, with the engine running, Chambers helped the women into the back.

Tanner now joined him, hoisting the boy up beside his mother. 'Where's Captain Vaughan?' he asked.

'In the front,' Chambers told him. 'He's been hit.'

'And where the hell's Sykes?'

'Here, sir,' gasped Sykes, from behind.

'Good – now get in quick. Mac – time to go.'

Moments later they were all in, the boy and the women crouched in the middle, Tanner and Chambers at either side, with Sykes next to McAllister and the machine-gun.

'Go, sir!' called Tanner, and now they sped along the harbour walls, bullets continuing to ring out behind them. They raced to the end of the harbour wall, as another machine-gun opened up from the direction of the arsenal. Tanner could feel Nerita trembling with fear, but the lines of tracer from the enemy machine-gun were both wide and too high and now Peploe had turned up the Street of the August Martyrs and out of the line of fire. Suddenly another explosion rocked the town to the west as they continued to speed along.

And now they were back on Evans Street, seemingly deserted.

'Nearly there,' said Tanner.

'Here,' said Sykes, passing Tanner a twenty-ounce packet of Nobel's. In his own hand he held two blocks of TNT. 'Reckon you can hit these, Mac?'

'I'll give it a go, Sarge.'

'Punter, jump up with me,' Tanner said to Chambers, and pulled himself up so that he was clutching the rail around the cab. They were now nearing the Kenouria Gate and up ahead, in the faint night light, he saw guards stepping out into the road. They would not be stopping this time, and at thirty yards he opened fire,

Chambers following a split second later, the men collapsing by the side of the road. As they reached the gate, Sykes threw out a block of TNT, and McAllister's MG spat bullets, livid darts of tracer soon finding their mark, the packet detonating with a bright eruption of flame and a million stone shards. Tanner opened fire again, blindly into the dark on either side of the road, as they sped on through the archway. Then Sykes lobbed another block, which, seconds later, McAllister hit, and then finally the packet of Nobel's. From the bastions rifle shots cracked out, but already, as the packet of gelignite exploded behind them, they were away, speeding

412

clear of the town and up the low ridge to safety.

'We've done it!' laughed Sykes. 'We've bleedin'
well gone and bloody well done it.'

20

But they had not made it. Not yet, at any rate –
Tanner knew he would not relax until they were
safely at the monastery above Krousonas. As they
crested the ridge they now knew so well, Peploe
turned off the main Knossos road, taking a rough
track that led them through the vineyards to the
west of the ruined palace where they had fought
just days before. *Was it really so recent?* Tanner
thought, as they bumped slowly along the rocky
track. It seemed longer than that – a lot longer. *A
lifetime ago.*

Peploe was taking them south-west, towards
the mountains, which even in the darkness of
midnight loomed heavily ahead. The countryside
was alive once more with the sound of the night:
cicadas with their strange chirruping noises. It
was still warm: the heat was no longer completely
dying each day, but lingering throughout the
hours of darkness. No one spoke now, as though
to do so would be to tempt the good fortune they
had enjoyed so far. And then, from Heraklion,
came one last explosion, bigger than any before
it, which, even several miles away, was so loud
and distinct that the women and the boy started.

'It's all right,' said Tanner, softly. 'Just one last

413

little message to Jerry.'

Alexis repeated the words to the boy, then touched Tanner's hand. 'Thank you,' she said.

Soon after they reached a stream, and there they left the Snipe, having first filled the engine with loose soil, and made a sling for Vaughan, who had been shot in the arm. It was not far – a three-hour walk at most – but as they moved through the groves and vineyards and climbed into the foothills of the Ida Mountains, Tanner felt overcome with fatigue. The adrenalin had worn off, and the sudden peacefulness, with the night-time beauty of the countryside, bathed as it was in an ethereal glow, contrasted too starkly with the din and violence of the action. He sensed the others felt the same.

When they finally reached the monastery and Alopex was reunited with his wife, son and sister, he wept quite openly, overcome to see them alive. For Mandoukis, however, their arrival prompted an outpouring of despair. Clutching his head and tearing at his hair he was inconsolable.

'I told him we looked for her,' Vaughan explained to the others, 'but she wasn't there. He said she was in the Sabbionera Bastion, as he'd told us.'

'But that's not what Satanas said,' Peploe reminded him.

'Poor bugger,' said McAllister.

'He'll need watching,' muttered Tanner.

In the monastery's refectory, they were fed, given wine and coffee, then set off on the final stage of their journey, back up to the cave in the mountains.

Tanner slept. He'd dressed the gash on his fore-arm, changed back into his old uniform of denims, shirt and battle blouse, then with his German trousers and shirt as a pillow and the jump smock as a rug, he had settled down in a soft hollow in the ground he'd discovered a little way from the cave. Almost the moment he closed his eyes, he succumbed to deep, dreamless sleep. When he awoke, Alexis was standing over him with an enamel mug of coffee.

'Here,' she said.

Tanner rubbed his eyes, thanked her and looked at his watch. It was after nine; he hadn't slept that long in ages.

'Thank you,' he said, but now sitting up he saw bruises on her cheeks. 'Are you hurt anywhere else?'

'It is nothing.'

'The bastards,' he muttered.

'But it is not as bad as the ones my brother gave you.'

Tanner smiled. 'Nor the ones I gave him.'

'He will not fight you again,' she said, returning his smile. 'I owe you my life, Jack. They would have shot us all.'

'Not just me, Alexis.'

'But it was your idea. Giorgis told me. You risked everything.'

'I couldn't bear the thought of them taking you,' he said.

She sat down beside him and clasped his hand. 'I do not know you at all,' she said, 'but still I feel as though I do.' She lightly kissed his cheek, then stood up. 'Thank you, Jack. Thank you for what you did.'

Tanner smiled. She left him, and Tanner remained where he was, thinking. Woodsmoke wafted towards him, sweet and soothing – unlike cordite or the dust of explosives. His throat was dry after the night's fighting, and having drunk the coffee, he reached for his water bottle. He was about to begin cleaning his weapons when Sykes and McAllister joined him.

'Morning, sir,' said McAllister. 'That was quite a bloody night.'

'It certainly was,' said Tanner. 'You did well, lads.'

'I still can't quite believe we got out alive,' said McAllister. He was a small lad, still not quite twenty, but stockier now than when Tanner had first known him – many of the boys were better fed in the army than they had been back home in the working-class areas of Leeds and Bradford, the recruiting heartland for the Yorks Rangers. McAllister had been in the Territorial Battalion along with Hepworth, Chambers and Bell when Tanner had first known them. They were not Territorials now, though. Tanner reckoned they were as good as any regular soldiers he had ever known.

'As I always tell you, Mac,' said Tanner, 'surprise is one hell of an advantage. We knew exactly when we were going in and pretty much what we were going to do.'

'Glad you did,' said Sykes. 'I thought we were making it up as we went along.'

'Improvising, Stan, we were improvising.'

Tanner chuckled. 'But we knew we were going to set off some pretty big bangs. Now Jerry hadn't really got a clue what we were up to. Someone had got a scent of something, but they were looking for Cretans and they certainly weren't expecting loads of bloody great explosions. It's amazing what you can get away with if you're prepared to brazen it out. By the way, Stan, what were you doing with that truck as it passed? I saw you crouch down beside it.'

Sykes grinned. 'I was quite pleased about that one,' he said. 'I saw the store box hatch was open so I put in a block of TNT with a black time pencil on. It was barely moving so it was quite easy. Ten minutes after I done it – boom!'

'You sly old bugger,' said Tanner, taking out a cigarette. 'How's Captain Vaughan this morning?'

'He should be all right,' said Sykes. 'The bullet broke his arm, though.'

'Have they got it out?'

Sykes nodded. 'He's been stitched up and dressed, thanks to that Jerry first-aid kit. Mr Liddell's still not so good, though.'

Tanner looked at him. *Oh, yes?*

'His fever's gone but he's still pretty ill. Seems to be asleep most of the time.'

'Should pull through now, though,' said Tanner. 'Bastard better had.' He took out his oiler, phial of gin, rag and pull-through.

'I'll tell you one thing, though, sir,' said Mc-Allister. 'That Alopex. He's not as tough as he likes to make out, sir, is he? A grown man like that and he was blubbing like a baby.'

'It's these Mediterranean types,' said Sykes. 'They're an emotional bunch.'

'I'd rather have him blubbing than knocking ten rounds out of me,' muttered Tanner, and felt the scab above his eye. 'He's got a hell of a fist on him.'

'Talk of the devil,' said Sykes. 'Here he is now.'

Alopex climbed up towards them, black beret on his head, bandolier around his waist, wearing his supple black leather boots and pantaloons. 'I need to speak to you alone, Tanner,' he said.

Tanner clicked his tongue, and stood up. 'Give us a moment, will you, lads?'

When they had gone, Alopex embraced him. 'What you did – I cannot thank you enough. How could we have ever been enemies? I misjudged you.'

'Forget it,' said Tanner.

Alopex now drew out his knife, and Tanner took a step backwards, alarm on his face. But Alopex laughed, held out his palm and drew a small cut across it. He then took Tanner's hand and did the same. Tanner flinched, but Alopex took both their hands and clasped them together. 'Once enemies,' said Alopex, his face solemn, 'but now blood brothers. This,' he said, releasing his grip and holding up his hand, 'is the blood of honour.'

Tanner nodded. 'And your wife and son – they were not harmed?'

'My son, no. But those sons of whores struck Nerita and Alexis. What kind of a coward does that?'

Tanner said nothing.

'His name is Balthasar,' said Alopex. 'Oberleut-nant Balthasar.'

'The women told you this?'

Alopex nodded. 'They heard his men say it. Balthasar and his men are camped in the valley to the south of Gazi.'

'Don't go after him there,' said Tanner. 'It's like I said. He captured your family to lure you out. I'm sure of it. But you've got them back now, so don't ruin it by falling into the trap. He'll be expecting you.'

Alopex wiped his moustache, then put his hands on his hips. 'At night, though, maybe we could go down.'

Tanner shook his head. 'You might kill some of his men, but you won't get him. Be patient, Alopex.'

The Cretan smiled and clapped him on the back. 'Yes,' he said, 'you are right. And we must try to get you off the island. Hanford has gone to Yerakari. He'll be back here tomorrow, hopefully with news. Much as we could do with you and your men, you are not Cretans. This is our battle now.' He turned to leave, but Tanner called him back.

'I'm sorry about Mandoukis's wife.'

Alopex took off his beret and rubbed his brow. 'I am sorry too,' he said. 'I feel his pain.'

'Don't take this the wrong way,' said Tanner, 'but you will watch him carefully, won't you?'

Alopex sighed and sat down beside him. 'I have known Mandoukis all my life. His younger brother is one of my oldest friends – he was with the Cretan Division as well. Both our brothers are now prisoners of the Germans. I still do not understand why they were abandoned – but there it is. I understand what you are saying, Jack, and if I were you and did not know him, I would wonder the same. But I cannot believe he would betray us. I simply cannot. You should have seen him fight at Heraklion.'

'Then I'm sure I'm wrong about him,' said Tanner. 'But keep your eye on him, eh?'

'Of course,' said Alopex, standing up and leaving Tanner to clean his weapons. Tanner watched him go, then began stripping his Enfield and rubbing it down with oil. Blood dripped from his cut hand into the breech and he cursed. Alopex had paid him a great compliment, but he wished the Cretan had not made such a dramatic gesture. With the gash over his eye, the nick on his arm and the bruising to his face and back, he felt quite knocked about as it was without the need to lose any more blood.

Tanner had kept his own close watch on Mandoukis. The man had seemed quite broken, keeping away from the others, and barely speaking a word. In the evening he had hardly touched any food, instead retreating to a corner of the cave where he had remained. Later, Tanner had glanced at him before heading off to his hollow in the ground. Mandoukis had not moved all evening.

Tanner had lain awake for a long time, thinking. At some point, however, he had drifted off to sleep, but now, as someone shook his shoulder, he was suddenly awake.

'Tanner!'

It was Alopex.

'What?' whispered Tanner. 'What the hell is it?' He was sitting up now, feeling for his rifle.

'Mandoukis,' said Alopex. 'He is leaving.'

'We should follow him.'

'I agree. I have two of my men ready. Quick, we must go now before we lose him.'

Grabbing his rifle, Tanner quietly followed Alopex to the track that led back down through the ravine where his two men were waiting. The three Cretans spoke in whispers, then Alopex said, 'He's a hundred metres or so ahead. We must hurry.'

They moved as quietly as they could but the night air was still and it seemed to Tanner as though every step would alert Mandoukis to their presence. It was dark, but the great canopy of stars and a quarter-moon gave a faint, creamy glow. It was enough for them to see where they were going – and to reveal Mandoukis as the track led him around a spur and silhouetted him against the sky.

'I warned the sentries,' Alopex whispered to Tanner. 'They pretended to be asleep. I think it is better to follow him.'

'I'm sorry, Alopex,' said Tanner. 'I had hoped I was wrong.'

'Maybe we still are. This way we will know.'

A couple of times Mandoukis paused, seeming to listen, then continued. He emerged from the end of the ravine, but instead of walking down past the monastery and into Krousonas, he cut across country, through the olive groves above the village. Now that their eyes had become more accustomed to the night light Tanner, Alopex and the *andartes* followed him easily.

Having skirted Krousonas, Mandoukis rejoined the track, but instead of following the path to the mountain villages of Korfes and Tilisos, he took the road that led to the valley below.

The German camp, thought Tanner. Briefly they lost sight of him as the road curved, but then they saw him again, and then at last, a few hundred yards further on as they neared the base of the valley, they saw, glowing dimly, the pale cream canvas of the German tents nestling between the olives.

'Mandoukis,' whispered Alopex, 'I can hardly bear to believe it.'

'We need to be careful,' said Tanner. He un-slung his rifle, gripping it in his hand.

Moments later they heard a sharp German voice cry, *'Halt!'* ahead. Pressing themselves into the side of the road, they heard Mandoukis call in response. More German voices and then one man was moving towards the Cretan. Tanner could just make out that Mandoukis had his arms in the air.

'We've got to kill him,' whispered Tanner, bringing his rifle to his shoulder.

'No,' said Alopex, pushing the barrel away. 'Let me.'

'Be quick then,' said Tanner. It was hard to see them. Dark shapes – that was all. He glanced at Alopex. *Don't miss*, he thought. Up ahead the figures seemed to be moving, but then Alopex fired, the single shot cracking out sharply, the

422

report echoing around the narrow valley. Had he hit the man? Tanner couldn't be sure, but voices were shouting in alarm and then he heard Mandoukis jabbering. *Professing his innocence*, thought Tanner, bringing his rifle to his shoulder. He fired, wildly, blindly, but already a machine-gun had opened up, a rapid *brurp* that sent lethal darts of tracer pulsing towards them.

Alopex hissed an order to his men but not before one cried out and collapsed on the road. Tanner felt bullets hissing past him, smacking into the dirt road, as he scrambled up the bank and among the olives above them. He glanced around and saw the heavy shape of Alopex dive into the cover of the tree-lined hillside. 'Keep moving!' whispered Tanner, as a flare whooshed into the sky above them. It burst and crackled, bright magnesium lighting the ground around them.

'The sons of whores!' hissed Alopex, a few yards away, as they pushed through the dense olives. More machine-gun fire rang out, bullets thudding into the tree trunks. Tanner's chest was tightening as he fought his way through, ducking under branches, gasping for air, legs throbbing as he climbed up the slopes through the thick grass. Another flare burst above them but, glancing back, he saw they were now out of any direct line of fire. Away to his left he glimpsed Alopex and one of his *andartes*.

'Are you all right?' he called.

'Yes,' came the reply, but then he heard the faint thwack of a mortar followed by its hollow whine and flung himself to the ground. A second later the shell exploded thirty yards ahead. He was on his feet again now, climbing to his right, away from where the mortar had landed. The hollow whine rang out again and he flung himself face down once more, his hands over his bare head. This time the explosion was closer, so that earth and grit showered down on him. As the rain of debris stopped, he glanced around. The light of the flare was dimming but he saw that Alopex and his *andarte* were still with him. He got to his feet and, a short distance above, spotted a small rocky outcrop. He pointed to it, saw Alopex nod, then scrambled towards it as yet another mortar whistled down, crashing into a tree, which split, sending not only soil into the sky but also woodchips. Diving behind the safety of the rock, Tanner clutched his head. Moments later, Alopex and his *andarte* were beside him.

'You were correct,' said Alopex, as he gasped for breath. 'They were ready for us.'

'Are you all right?' asked Tanner, as another mortar whined into the sky.

'A piece of wood in my arse, that's all. But I had to leave Andreas.'

The mortar exploded twenty yards below them, but although they pressed themselves against the rock, they were safe from any flying shrapnel. As the clatter died down, Tanner listened. He could no longer hear any voices. The second flare had faded, so they were in darkness once more, their eyes struggling to adjust.

'Wait a moment longer,' whispered Tanner. He was expecting to hear another whoosh of a flare, but there was nothing. 'Let's move,' he said, after

424

several minutes had passed. Carefully, quietly, they began climbing through the grove once more, their legs swishing through the long grass. Cicadas chirruped around them and Tanner paused to wipe the sweat from his eyes, his breathing still heavy. A short while later they reached the higher road that joined the mountain villages, and turned towards Krousonas, the village glowing dimly as it nestled in the cradle of the mountains.

Tanner paused to drink from his water bottle, then cupped his hand and splashed his face, his heart still hammering. Damn it, but that had been close.

'How could he have betrayed us?' snarled Alopex. 'How could he?'

'They still have his wife,' muttered Tanner. Not for the first time, he regretted their failure to find her the previous night. He wanted to lash out at Alopex, to yell at him for being so stupid. *Damn it!* Tanner knew he should never have allowed Alopex to take that shot – he should have killed the man himself while he had had the chance. *No* – they should never have allowed Mandoukis to reach the Germans in the first place. What had they been thinking? He should have been made to prove his innocence, not allowed to betray his guilt, and locked up out of harm's way. *We've been idiots*, thought Tanner. And Mandoukis was still a dead man. Even if they did not shoot him there and then – even if he survived a long incarceration – his people would not forgive him for what he had done. Tanner doubted Mandoukis would be saving his wife either. *The damn bloody fool.* Damn it, shooting Mandoukis would almost have

425

been a mercy killing. But instead of lying dead on the road, Mandoukis was now spilling all he knew to the enemy.

Tanner sighed wearily and slung his rifle across his shoulder. How much Mandoukis could reveal, only time would tell.

21

Oberleutnant Balthasar had woken at the sound of the shooting, swiftly got out of his camp bed and dressed, praying this had been the attack by Alopex and his men that he had hoped for. He was therefore not best pleased to learn that only one Cretan bandit had been killed and that whoever had opened fire appeared to have melted back into the night. On the other hand, at least his men had not shot Mandoukis. That was something.

The Cretan was brought before him in the company command-post tent. In the yellow half-light provided by a lone paraffin lamp, Balthasar was struck by how much the man had changed in just a few days: the growth around his face had become a rough beard, his hair and face were filthy, his cheeks gaunt and his eyes wide with fear but showing extreme fatigue. He smelt too – of piss and grime. Really, Balthasar thought, it was hard not to think of these people as inferior beings – they were little more than filthy, vicious, uncivilized animals. Balthasar could hardly bear to look at him.

The Cretan began to speak wildly. Balthasar raised his hands to silence him, turned to his interpreter and said, 'Tell this man to be quiet. What is he saying?'

'He wants to know that his wife is still alive, or he will not tell you anything.'

'I hardly think he's in any position to bargain,' said Balthasar, then turned back to Mandoukis. 'Let me get this straight. You joined your bandit friends and discovered they were planning an attack to free the women and child we imprisoned, so you thought you would wait and see what happened before coming back to me? It did not occur to you that, had you warned me, I might have set your wife free?'

'He says he knew nothing about the plan. He was not with all the guerrillas at that time.'

'Hmm. I find that hard to believe. What can he tell me now?'

'He wants to know that his wife is safe.'

'Yes. He will have to take my word for it, though, just as he expects me to take his.'

Relief appeared to sweep over the Cretan. As it happened, his wife was still alive, although she would soon be leaving Crete. There was no point in keeping prisoners on the island. Not only were they an unnecessary strain on resources, they were of use in labour camps in the Reich.

'He says the attacks on Heraklion were not carried out by Cretans but by six British soldiers still on the island.'

Balthasar was certainly interested in this. It explained how they had managed to get into the town undetected. *Wearing the uniforms of my men*, he thought. 'Tell him to describe them,' he said.

'Five of them were from a unit called Yorks Rangers. There are sixteen of them – they had sailed from Heraklion but their ship was sunk and they managed to get back to land and make their way up to the mountains.'

'What did they look like?'

Mandoukis described them, gesticulating to emphasize size and features.

'There was an officer, a captain called Peploe. Light ginger hair, round face, medium height. There was another man – a man all the others look up to. His name is Tanner. He has medals for bravery. He is tall, with dark hair and pale eyes.'

'I know this man,' said Balthasar. 'It must be the same one. I'm sure of it.' *Well, well, well.* 'And the others?'

'There was a sergeant called Sykes. Small – an explosives expert. And two others but he does not know their names. The explosives came from one of Pendlebury's arms dumps. He had been bringing them to Heraklion before the invasion. They were moving them out again before the British evacuated. Most of it is in a cave in the mountains, but they blew up what was left in the town.'

Balthasar nodded. 'That explains a great deal. And what about the sixth man?'

'Captain Alex Vaughan. He worked with Pendlebury in Heraklion. Mandoukis knows this man. He is a soldier but with a unit called Middle East Commando.'

'So how much in the way of supplies do they

still have?'

'He thinks a fair amount. They do not have much ammunition but plenty of explosives.'

'And where are they being held?'

Mandoukis described the cave and how to get there. 'It's not far. An hour's walk from Krousonas. He does not think there are any immediate plans for them to leave this base. There are other *kapitans* – Manoli Bandouvas is one – but he does not know where they are based at present.'

Mandoukis was speaking again, jabbering rapidly.

'For God's sake,' said Balthasar. 'What is he saying now?'

'The British soldiers are due to leave soon,' the interpreter told him. 'He says a British U-boat is coming.'

'Where?'

'It has not been decided exactly, but they are planning to use the monastery at Preveli. It is quite isolated down there, but there is a beach below the cliffs.'

'And where is this place?'

'On the south coast. A few kilometres east of Plakias and southwest of Spili.'

'Spili? A command post is being set up there already. And when is this submarine due to come?'

'He's not certain. They were awaiting confirmation but hoping it would be soon, either Saturday or Sunday. The Tommies will travel to the monastery overnight, remain there for a day and leave the following night. That is the plan.'

'That's four days' time.' Balthasar clapped his

hands together. 'Good. This is all most useful.' He stepped outside the tent. Dawn was spreading across the valley, the air alive with birdsong. He stretched. It was not only Alopex and his guerrillas who had been a thorn in his side, it was those damned Yorks Rangers too. But a plan was now formulating in his mind. A plan that would kill two birds with one stone. He smiled to himself. He would have his revenge yet.

At the cave, the mood had been tense that day, Tuesday, 3 June. No one was quite sure how much Mandoukis knew or, indeed, what he might have told the enemy. Among the Cretans there was widespread disappointment, anger and even incredulity that one of their people could betray them all.

'You know how proud they are,' Vaughan told Tanner. The captain was up and about, his arm in a sling. 'They're very nationalistic, fiercely independent. Cretans first, Greeks second, and slaves to no one. But now they're waking up to the reality of the situation. Crete is occupied by the Germans. Old feuds will be reopened, men will be betrayed. Long-valued friendships will be tested and trust replaced by suspicion.'

'It seemed so obvious to me,' said Tanner, as they sat beneath one of the mountain oaks, the leaves offering them dappled shade. 'Mandoukis, I mean. Even if there was only the faintest of suspicions, he should have been locked up somewhere.'

'They didn't want to believe it, though. It's different for you. Until the other day you had never met Mandoukis. You could see the implications of his wife's imprisonment and his freedom with an entirely pragmatic eye. You might have reacted the same way if this was England and one of your oldest friends was in Mandoukis's position.'

'Maybe you're right, sir,' Tanner conceded.

'It's taken a bit of the gloss off our venture the night before, though, hasn't it?'

'Yes.' He picked up a small stone and threw it away. 'These people are brave, but they're not trained. Alopex and Satanas are good leaders, I'll give you that, and men like Alopex are prepared to fight hard and dirty, but there will always be a limit to how much irregular troops can achieve. There's a bit of ammunition now but it won't last. How are these people to keep going? They can't live in the mountains for ever.'

Vaughan smiled. 'You sound just like Pendlebury. He had exactly the same concern. It's what he kept trying to get across to our masters in Cairo and London.'

'And these mountains,' said Tanner. 'It's all right now. It's summer and warm, and it's only been a few days. But it'll be a different kettle of fish when winter comes.'

'There'll be snow. I worry how they'll survive. These men are loyal enough towards the *kapitans* now, but will they be by January?'

'I've half a mind to try and stay here, you know. I like this place. I could help them.'

'And there's Alexis Kristannos too.'

'Well, yes, there is.'

'You'd find it very frustrating, Jack. And you

431

really do need to speak the lingo, and have the patience of a saint. It would be one disappointment after another – supplies not arriving, headstrong Cretan guerrillas doing the opposite of what you tell them, shortages of everything. You're a fine soldier, but the liaison officers here need different skills. Military prowess is almost the least of it.'

'I'm sure you're right, sir. And the ammunition will soon run out. Without it, we'd not be helping at all. We'd just be extra mouths to feed.'

'We already are. We've done our bit – and you have especially, Jack – but most of your men have done nothing since they arrived. Cleaned weapons, slept, eaten the guerrillas' food – and that's been about it. Ten men who have done nothing but eat their food. That's why we need to get off the island as quickly as possible. The best help we can be is to keep fighting the Germans – and at the moment, that means in North Africa. I also think they hope that if they help to return lots of our stranded soldiers, we'll give them more arms and supplies.'

'They need to keep us sweet, eh?'

'I think they assume so.'

Tanner wiped his brow; even in the shade and high in the mountains, it was warm. 'And when it's all over,' he said, 'I wonder how many of them will still be alive. How many villages will have been razed.' He shook his head. 'It's going to be tough for them, isn't it?'

'Yes.'

'And all because our commanders keep making such bloody stupid mistakes.' He flung a stick

432

onto the ground. 'When are we going to get someone who's got a bit of fire, sir? That's what I'd like to know.'

Soon after, Alexis found him. 'Come with me,' she said. 'I want to show you something.'

Tanner followed as she led him up the spur above the cave. Climbing a goat track through the thick vetch, they had soon left the secluded encampment behind.

'We are nearly there,' she said, taking his hand in hers. Tanner's heart quickened, not from the exertion of the climb but from the touch of her skin on his. At last, they crested a ridge and suddenly the mountain range was spread before them all the way to the coast. And there was Heraklion, not the bomb-damaged mass of rubble, but a patch of white, dazzlingly bright against the deep blue of the Aegean. The folds and ridges of the valleys below spread away from them, while beyond, hazy in the distance, was the next great chain of mountains.

'It's incredible,' he said. 'Yours is a truly beautiful island, Alexis.'

'I can still believe it is a peaceful place when I'm up here,' she said. She turned him around so that they were looking at the highest peak of the entire chain. 'And that is Mount Ida. The birthplace of Zeus.'

Tanner followed her gaze, then clasped her shoulders, bent down and kissed her. 'I've been wanting to do that since the moment I first saw you,' he said.

'I wanted you to.' She laughed, then placed her

arms around his neck and pressed herself into him.

'What will you do?' he asked.

'We have cousins in Fourfouras,' she said, 'on the other side of these mountains. It's in the Amari Valley. When you leave, we will come with you.'

'Will you be any safer there than you were in Sarhos?'

She smiled. 'Oh, yes. When you see the Amari Valley you will understand why. It is surrounded by mountains. The valley is not really a valley at all, but a bowl. A secret bowl.'

'And what will you do?'

'I want to help, Jack. I have told my brother I want to be a runner for him. I know these mountains as well as anyone.'

'And what did he say?'

'I think he will say yes.' She raised her mouth to his.

'And what will he say about this?'

'Nothing. Now you two are friends. Anyway, I do not care what he says.' She put her hand to his cheek. 'When I was in that prison, I thought at first that they would shoot us all. Then they told us we would be sent away, taken from Crete to a prison camp in Germany. But I would not have let them. I would have killed myself before they took me away from here. I thought my life was over, but here I am. It made me think I must make the most of what life I am given. Soon you will be gone. I would rather have a few days with you, Jack, than none at all.'

'I'm glad,' he said. 'And you're right. We

434

mustn't die full of regrets.'

He held her face in his hands, then pushed his fingers through her hair. She looked so determined, but vulnerable, the bruising on her cheek still quite marked. He kissed her again.

'We should go back to the cave,' she said, and taking his hand, led him back down the stony track.

The sun was setting behind the mountains when Jack Hanford arrived at the cave, bringing with him confirmation that the British submarine, HMS *Thrasher*, would arrive on the following Sunday, 9 June, a short distance from the beach at Preveli, as had been initially suggested. He also reported that contact had been made with a party of Australians from Rethymno, who were making their way south into the Amari Valley. Commander Pool was going to arrive in the submarine and hoped to talk with the abbot of Preveli, Father Agathangelos Langouvardos, about using the monastery as a mustering point.

'Father Agathangelos will agree to this,' Satanas told him, as they once more sat around the fire at the mouth of the cave. This place, perched on a rocky lip to the side of a spur at the head of the ravine, had become the focus of the guerrillas' command post. And as ever, a strict protocol was observed: guerrillas on one side, British on the other, officers and *kapitans* sitting on rocks nearest the gently burning flames, their men standing behind.

'I have known him a long time,' Satanas continued. 'He will do as Commander Pool asks.'

'He's already agreed to take these men in and any Australians who can reach Yerakari in time,' said Hanford. 'I saw him last week.'

Satanas stroked his white goatee beard. 'You should move tomorrow. You will be safe to move by day up here. Alopex will accompany you with some of his *andartes*.'

'We will stay in Fourfouras tomorrow, then go on to Yerakari,' said Hanford. 'We'll move out again on Saturday evening, cross the main road at night and reach Preveli early on Sunday morning. We'll be safe to wait there until *Thrasher* arrives.'

'And what about you, sir?' Tanner asked Satanas. 'Will you stay here?'

Satanas looked at him, his eyes bright. 'You don't think we should?'

'No – no, I don't, sir. Mandoukis will surely have told them about this place. Jerry may still not want to attempt any attack this far into the mountains, but I don't think it's worth taking a chance.'

'I think you're right,' said Satanas. 'We will be fighting the Germans for some time yet. We must learn to be patient.'

'I agree,' said Alopex. 'God knows I want to kill those sons of whores and especially this Lieutenant Balthasar, but we need the Germans to dance to our tune, not the other way around. We should get the supplies here away to safety – to the Idean cave. No German will go there.'

'Then we are agreed,' said Satanas. 'Tomorrow morning, we will all go.'

The mood among the men, both Cretan and

British, seemed to improve with the announcement of these decisions. Wine and raki were produced and they remained sitting around the fire, drinking and talking, until long after dark. Yet despite the wine and raki, when Tanner returned to his small hollow in the rocks, he lay awake for a long time, unable to sleep, his mind a jumble of conflicting emotions. It pained him to think that all too soon he would be bidding farewell to Alexis, probably for ever. Something about her had got under his skin; his head had been quite turned. And yet he wanted to get back to Egypt too, to be part of a battalion and army once more. Damn it, he also wanted some leave: the thought of the bars and restaurants of Cairo made his stomach rumble with yearning. More than that, he knew he could not stay – Vaughan had been right. Yet to walk away from this place and the woman who had entranced him made his heart ache.

Eventually, he had fallen asleep. He must have done, because when he opened his eyes it was no longer dark and the mountains were emerging into the first light of early dawn. But what had woken him was not the sound of men stirring, but of rifle fire, which could mean only one thing.

The enemy had come up the mountain after all.

22

Only a few days earlier, Oberleutnant Balthasar had decided he would never venture into the mountains in an effort to track down the Cretan guerrillas. He had always believed it was important to play to one's strengths, but more than that, he had counted on being able to draw the enemy down into the valleys. He had no doubt the ploy would have worked had those Tommies not infiltrated Heraklion and freed Alopex's family from the fortress. He had been furious about that, especially since he had warned Bräuer, but it had been a brilliantly carried-out raid. Only twenty-eight men had been killed and half a dozen wounded – a small casualty bill, all things considered. Neither had there been that much damage. A company headquarters had been destroyed, but most of the charges had been laid against the walls; their immense thickness had absorbed most of the blasts. No, what those Tommies had done was to outwit them, through the use of surprise and clever diversions. In many ways, he had already believed himself to be part of a game of cat and mouse, but the escape of the prisoners – his bargaining chips – had only reinforced this opinion. Now he had to outfox them in turn.

The information from Mandoukis had been a stroke of luck. He had assumed he would not be seeing the Cretan again, but then he had turned up suddenly, out of the blue. Of course, he might have been lying, which was why he had taken him into Heraklion to the Sabbionera Bastion. There he had allowed the couple a brief reunion. It had been quite touching, really, but then he had pointed a pistol at the wife and threatened to kill her if one word of what Mandoukis had said proved to be untrue. The tears, the trembling, the imploring that had followed! Balthasar had been convinced by that, and for a brief moment he had thought of sparing both of them. That could not happen, however. It was likely they would have been murdered by their own kind – but it was a risk he could not take. In any case, Mandoukis had been involved in atrocities against his men and the punishment for that was death. So Mandoukis's wife remained a prisoner awaiting passage to the Reich, and Mandoukis, his useful-ness over, was taken into the courtyard and shot.

But it was not only the Cretan's information that had persuaded him to try a dawn assault on the guerrillas' mountain lair. The build-up of German forces on the island had been running smoothly since the British evacuation. Three airfields and three ports had been put to good use. More arms, guns, ammunition and motor transport had arrived over the past few days. There were more troops on the island now too, not only Fallschirm-jäger, but also a whole division of Gebirgsjäger – mountain troops. Mountain troops for mountain operations.

Balthasar had gone straight from the Sabbionera Bastion to Major Schulz's office in the Megaron,

439

and outlined his plan. For the time being, he proposed, he would stop his own reprisal operations against the villages. Instead, he wanted to make a joint-force dawn assault on the mountain. With luck, he would be able to surprise the guerrillas and, at the very least, destroy their base. Then he proposed to lead his company to Spili, in the south, to lie in wait for the Tommies, prevent their evacuation attempt and put paid to any future escape line from that part of the south coast.

It had needed the authority of Oberst Bräuer, but Balthasar had been given all that he had asked for: two platoons of mountain troops and, for transportation to the south, trucks from the divisional services. Furthermore, his own company was now some two hundred men strong. That meant it was approaching full strength again; more importantly, they were fully armed.

Now, at a little before half past four on the morning of Wednesday, 4 June, Balthasar was leading his men up the track that wound its way around the spurs that fed into the ravine. Below, in the gorge, and picking their way over the rocky slopes opposite, were the Gebirgsjäger troops. The air was fresh and clear, the dawn light creeping slowly over the mountains from the east behind them. Up ahead, Balthasar could see the mouth of the gorge. Soon they would be there.

Darting figures on the track ahead caught his eye. Two guerrillas were running back up, and Balthasar smiled to himself at the ill-discipline of these sentries. A man paused, knelt and fired, but Balthasar signalled for his men to hold their own

440

fire, then glanced across the ravine and saw that the mountain troops had almost reached the head of the gorge and were now picking their way past a small mountain shepherd's house. Sheep, bleating anxiously, the bells around their necks ringing, scuttled clear of the men.

Balthasar now urged them forward, and ran up the last part of the winding track. The lip of the ravine was only a few hundred metres away. Mandoukis had told him the cave was to the right, behind the spur that led to the mouth of the gorge. And that was now not very far away at all.

The instant Tanner was awake, he had grabbed his rifle and pack and hurried to the little oak perched on the spur from which he could see down the mountain, aware that behind him both *andartes* and Rangers were hurriedly emerging from the cave, weapons in hands. Enemy troops were swarming up the mountain track and in the ravine there were paratroopers and, he saw, mountain troops too. Quickly fitting his scope, he picked out first a paratrooper and fired, then moved his aim to the mountain troops threatening to come around the spur right on top of them. Hitting two in quick succession, he was spotted: a bullet zinged from the rock only a foot away, and he leaped back, out of the line of fire.

McAllister was emerging with the MG34, Peploe urging him to hurry and take up a position at the head of the gorge.

'We need sharpshooters and the MG,' said Tanner, running over to the captain. 'There are mountain troops swarming up the other side of the ravine. We just need to hold them up for a bit.'

'You get up there and keep shooting, Tanner,' said Peploe. 'Satanas and Alopex are loading the cart.'

'We haven't got long, sir.'

'I know, Tanner, I know.'

Tanner ran forward, met Sykes, and together they headed over to the mouth of the ravine. McAllister was already lying down between two rocks, the barrel of the Spandau poking between the two, hastily feeding in a belt of ammunition.

'Come on, iggery, you two!' Tanner shouted at Mercer and Hill, who were hurrying along with boxes of ammunition. As he found a rock from which to fire, he heard McAllister pull back the bolt on the MG, then open up. Several men cried out and collapsed on the track, as Tanner brought his own rifle into his shoulder and picked out another mountain trooper.

'Short bursts, Mac!' Tanner shouted out. He was worried not only about overheating the barrel but also about ammunition. 'Keep your firing to an absolute minimum.' Bullets were zipping around them, pinging off the rock, but the combination of rifle and MG fire was checking the advance of the paratroopers. Those on the track were hidden in the lee of a spur, while those picking their way across the rocks above had now taken cover. Tanner spotted one soldier emerge to take a shot, and was able quickly to take a bead and fire, the bullet hurling the German backwards. More mountain troops were pressing forward on their left, however, using the broken lie of the land to scurry between rocks.

'Stan, we need to move our arses,' he said, then called to Hepworth, Bonner and Cooper to follow him. Quickly pulling out of the line of fire, he led them around the spur, then clambered up the slope. Tanner was just making for a large rock when a German appeared not ten yards from him. He fired his rifle from the hip and the German fell backwards. Racing to the rock, Tanner now saw more only yards ahead. Rifle bullets clattered against the rock as Tanner felt in his pack for a grenade, pulled the pin and hurled it in front of him. As it exploded he stood up and, with his Schmeisser, fired a long burst, saw men either fall or duck back for cover, then sank down out of sight.

His position was better than he had first imagined. From where they were they could see down onto the mountain track, and although the mass of paratroopers was still out of sight, pinned down behind a bend in the path, he could now see several men crouching in the rocks above and below. Carefully taking aim he fired, hitting one, then two, and a third man before more bullets were hissing past.

He looked back down towards the cave, and wondered how the loading of the cart was going. He hoped that the women and the little boy, Alexandros, had been sent on and were hurrying to safety. Below, men were scrambling over the rocks, their studded mountain boots crunching on the stone. How long did they have? He jolted as a loud explosion shook the mountainside just a short distance below.

'Bloody hell!' he muttered, then turned to see Sykes lighting a stick of explosive. He winked at Tanner, let the fuse burn, then hurled it from behind his rock down the slope. Moments later there was another loud boom, the report echoing through the ravine, and Tanner heard men scream. Sykes lit another, Tanner watched the fuse burn, and then, when he thought his friend was about to blow himself to smithereens, saw him throw it. This time the deafening explosion was followed by a rumble of rocks, cries of alarm, then more screams.

But in return the enemy was now firing mortars. Tanner heard the hollow whine and then the explosion below, near the mouth of the ravine. Another burst of MG fire, and a few more rifle cracks, then another whine and this time the mortar shell landed thirty yards below them to the left. Grit and debris clattered against the rocks. *We're running out of time here*, thought Tanner. He moved back, clear of the ridgeline, and saw the laden cart moving, Alopex and the *andartes* urging on the mule. Boxes were piled high, Lieutenant Liddell sitting upright near the back. *Come on, come on*, thought Tanner. He ran back to the others as two more mortars crashed nearby, then a bullet flew past his head and he looked across the valley to see another paratrooper taking aim. Swiftly training his scope on the man, Tanner fired again, saw him fall, then felt in his pocket for another two clips.

'Stan!' he called. 'Have you got any sticks left?'

'Yes, and a few grenades. So have Coop and Bonny.'

'Good. Chuck the grenades and pull back. Head round the spur and up and follow me.'

They hurled their grenades in turn, heard them explode, then scampered back. Down below, he saw McAllister, Peploe and the others packing up and running. Another mortar shell burst and they fell flat on the ground. 'Come on, up you get,' muttered Tanner. Then, to his relief, they did so and began to run again, although one – Hill, maybe? – seemed to be limping. From their cover around the bend in the track, he saw the para-troopers inch forward once more – an MG team nipped ahead, crouching, while several riflemen moved on, finding cover in the rocks below the track. Tanner quickly drew his rifle to his shoulder, aiming for the machine-gunner, fired, saw him fall, then fired again. Behind him, Sykes and the other two had followed his lead, a fusil-lade of rifle fire cracking out. The enemy soon replied with a volley of bullets.

'The bastard!' called Sykes.

'You all right?' shouted Tanner.

'No!' said Sykes. 'Some Jerry's just nicked my bloody ear!'

Tanner aimed again, searching his scope for an officer, then spotted him, urging his men forward, Schmeisser in hand. 'Well, I'm damned,' he said to himself, recognizing him. Carefully, he homed his scope on the man's chest. This time, he was not in the mood for mercy. Breathing out, he squeezed the trigger – but at that precise moment another paratrooper entered his sights, the bullet hitting the man neatly in the head instead, and spraying the officer behind with blood and brain.

'Damn it!' said Tanner, then saw the officer glance in his direction. Tanner pulled back the bolt again but now bullets peppered the rock around him and he dived for cover, then ran clear.

'Come on!' he shouted to Sykes and the others. 'We're going over the top here.' Following the goat track Alexis had shown him the day before, they were soon out of the line of fire from the ravine below, but pausing briefly to glance back, Tanner saw the enemy had now almost reached the lip. In no time, they would be at the cave.

'Keep going!' he urged his men. Sykes was clutching his ear, still cursing, but as they reached the summit, they could see the lie of the mountains stretching away from them. A track climbed around the spur behind them and now the cart was cresting the ridge beyond. The track tucked around another spur and passed through another even narrower ravine. If they made it through there, Tanner realized, they would be safe, because no German, not even mountain troops, would be able to climb the steep slopes on either side.

Balthasar wiped the blood and gore from his face, and wondered why he seemed to be so lucky. It had been the Tommy Mandoukis had called Tanner, he was sure; he had seen him. A split second earlier and that British bullet would have hit him square in the chest, not the head of Obergefreiter Möhne. After a fusillade of bullets had been directed at the Tommy, he had seen him dive backwards and wondered whether he had been hit.

His men were now pressing forward, cautiously inching their way along the track and through the rocks below. Gebirgsjäger troops were clambering up over the mouth of the ravine, having recovered from the landslide some minutes earlier. Mandoukis had mentioned a Tommy who was an explosives expert. *Sykes.* He wondered whether it had been the same man who had caused the rockfall.

There was now no return fire from the enemy, and Balthasar could see his men pressing forward with mounting confidence. Still wiping the blood from his face and uniform, he hurried on, up the track, pushing past his men and rushing around the spur that hid the cave. There were a few bodies lying over the rocky ground – several Cretans and two Tommies. And there it was, a fire still smoking gently, an upset billy-can of coffee, empty boxes and clutter lying about. Balthasar ran on, reached the mouth of the cave and cautiously walked inside. It was cool in there, a strong smell of woodsmoke, mustiness and stale urine heavy on the air. Taking out his torch, he shone it around. Any boxes of ammunition and supplies seemed to have gone, but then he noticed one more, tucked away at the far end, obviously missed as the guerrillas had packed.

Grabbing it, he carried it outside, saw 'Demolition TNT' stencilled onto the side, then prised it open with his knife. Inside he found a number of slabs of explosive. He picked one up, thinking.

'Herr Oberleutnant,' said Leutnant Hilse, the Gebirgsjäger platoon commander, 'should we pursue the enemy from here?'

447

Balthasar nodded. 'Follow them as far as you can, but if you receive heavy return fire pull back. We will have achieved enough here.' He stood up and called over Unteroffizier Rohde.

'Here,' he said, passing him the block of TNT. 'Get the pioneers up here. They can use this to prepare charges on this cave. We are going to make sure these bandits cannot use it again.'

Rohde saluted and hurried off, and Balthasar began to climb the spur above the cave. It took him a short while to find the spot but, to his great disappointment, there was no sign of the Tommy, only sharp strikes against the rock where bullets had hit and a number of empty rifle bullet cases. He looked around further then, noticed blood on a rock, and a line of drips spreading up the slope. He paused, wiping his brow. Away to the east, the sun was rising, the great orange orb almost visibly moving up over the mountains in the distance. Balthasar felt a mixture of emotions: annoyance that so many of the Tommies and guerrillas had got away, but satisfaction that a mountain hideout had been overrun and was about to be destroyed. Guerrillas could not stay in the mountains for ever. *Patience*, he told himself. He would get Alopex yet.

He turned and began to climb back down the slope. This part of the operation was over. Now it was time to head south.

Catching up with Peploe, McAllister and the other Rangers, Tanner was pleased to see Hill was still with them.

'I thought you'd been hit,' he said.

'No, sir,' said Hill, 'just turned my ankle on a stone. Bloody hurt, but it's worn off now.'

'Glad to hear it,' said Tanner.

They ran on, pausing repeatedly to check if they were being followed. Up ahead was the narrow ravine Tanner had seen earlier, the track winding up towards it. Now, though, as he turned, he saw a number of mountain troops clear the crest of the ridge a few hundred yards back. He stopped, knelt and, using his scope, picked out a man and fired. His victim jerked backwards, clutching his shoulder, while the others made for cover.

'Run!' shouted Tanner.

Sykes was now kneeling and fired, and then a lone shot whipped past them. Tanner glanced back but the enemy were hidden from view. He ran on, his chest tight, his breathing heavy, and now the track was curving to the left. Tanner looked back again and saw they were clear of the enemy line of fire.

Thank God, he thought.

They caught up with the cart a short while later and soon after that reached the end of the ravine and emerged onto a high mountain plain, following an ancient shepherds' track that wound its way towards Mount Ida.

Sykes had lost part of the top of his ear. 'That's my good looks gone for ever,' he grumbled. 'What girl's going to look at me now?'

'What girls were looking at you anyway, Sarge?' said Hepworth.

Sykes cuffed him. 'Don't be so bloody insolent, Lance Corporal. I'll have you know I've had my fair share of women, which is more than can be said for you.'

'You should be bloody grateful, Sarge,' said McAllister. 'Another half-inch, and you'd have been a croaker.'

'Mac's right,' said Peploe. 'Anyway, I think it'll give you a touch of distinction.'

Tanner smiled, listening to the banter. They had lost five men in all. They had been lucky; it could have been so much worse. Once again, the men had kept their heads and used what limited resources they had to good effect – Mac on the MG, Sykes lobbing sticks of dynamite. It had bought them precious minutes – minutes in which the rest had been able to get away.

They reached the Idean cave just before midday, having followed a path through a narrow gorge. The peak of Mount Ida towered above them, but there, at the base of a vast rockface, was a dark, rectangular gash. Inside it was gloomy and dank, stalactites further within dripping audibly. It would hardly be comfortable, but as a hideout Tanner could not fault it.

It was here that they bade farewell to Satanas. He embraced Peploe and Vaughan, then shook hands with the men in turn. 'We have much to thank you for,' he said, 'not least your help this morning. Without it, I fear none of us would be standing here now. Good luck – and come back when all this is over. You will always be welcome on this island.'

It was a harder onward journey, the mountain tracks rockier, narrower and, in places, considerably more precipitous. There had been no question of taking the cart. Lieutenant Liddell had been carried in shifts on a makeshift stretcher, but Vaughan had had to walk, which he did without complaint. By late afternoon, however, they were at last dropping down into the Amari Valley.

Tanner was stunned by what he saw. Mountains seemed to ring the entire valley, which lay before them in a wide bowl, a sylvan carpet of olives, ilex and plane trees, lush and fecund. On the flanks of the mountains, overlooking the valley, were numerous small villages, each a collection of mostly white houses, terracotta roofs and small, domed churches.

'What a vision!' said Peploe, as he and Tanner walked beside Alexis. 'It's like some forgotten Eden.'

'You see, Jack?' said Alexis. 'I told you it was well hidden.'

'And you were right. It's beautiful, Alexis. And so – so *green*.'

Alexis laughed. 'Yes, it is. Always, even in the middle of summer.'

Peploe was shaking his head in wonderment. 'There's a lot more to this island than meets the eye – honestly, I had no idea such a place existed.'

Their path now passed through groves and beneath long lines of eucalyptus and plane trees, and suddenly the air was alive with crickets chirruping, bees buzzing and birds singing from the foliage above.

Soon after, with the sun beginning to set behind the mountains and the valley bathed in a rich, golden light, they reached Fourfouras. Alopex led them to his uncle's house, a large, imposing property on the edge of the village, three storeys high and with a cluster of outbuildings surrounding it. Beneath, running away from the house into the heart of the valley, there was a long, wide olive grove, bigger than any Tanner had seen before. Olives, it seemed, were a family business.

The men were fed, given wine, then taken to a stone barn. It was dusty but dry and they were all tired; it had been a long day, and they had barely rested so sleep came easily. In any case fighting, no matter how quickly it was over, was tiring in itself. Yet, despite his exhaustion, Tanner woke before midnight. A number of the men were snoring – too much wine, Tanner guessed – and he found it hard to get back to sleep again. He was hot, too, so he got up and went outside into the courtyard between the house and the barns, sat on the edge of the stone well in the centre and lit a cigarette. There was a faint light from inside the house and he heard laughter – the Cretan men were drinking late. Tanner didn't blame them. Alopex, he knew, was relieved to have got his family here, to this extraordinary haven. No wonder the fellow was letting off a bit of steam.

A door opened at the side of the house and he looked up. In the light from the doorway, he saw Alexis and his heart lurched. She came over to him, then held out her hand, beckoning him. Tanner followed as she led him out of the yard and down a cart track that ran to the edge of the giant grove. Away from the track there was a grassy bank and she sat down, beckoning him to join her. He did so and looked up at the vast canopy of stars.

Above them, an almost half-moon shone, which, with the stars, cast a glow over the valley.

Alexis leaned over and kissed him. 'At last,' she said, 'we are alone.'

'I was waiting for you,' he lied.

'I hoped you would be.' She sighed happily. 'It is still so warm.'

He touched her cheek, and she smiled. 'We have so little time...'

'A few days, that's all.'

'Then stay with me now. For a few hours I want to believe that we are the only two people in this valley. I want to believe that and to remember this night for always.'

Later, much later, with Alexis's head resting on his chest and her arm across him, he thought again about what she had said. Truly, in these precious hours, it had seemed as though they really were alone in the world and that the war was no more. And he knew then that, no matter how long he lived, whether it be for a few days or until he was an old man, he would not forget this night either.

Around nine the following morning, a German reconnaissance aircraft flew over the Ida Mountains, then dropped height as it continued over the Amari Valley. Slowly, the Storch banked, circled, then continued on its way to the west, then down towards the sea.

Oberleutnant Balthasar was sitting beside the pilot. The previous evening he had requested an aerial recce and had been granted one. It had not been hard to justify, and his request had been perfectly reasonable: he wanted to get an appreciation of this central part of the island and a glimpse of its hidden tracks and valleys that would be quite impossible from the ground, and although the Luftwaffe had already begun to produce aerial reconnaissance photographs, he knew there was no substitute for seeing it for himself, in its full dimensions and colour.

Already, the flight had proved more than worthwhile. With his map spread out over his knees, he had been able to look down and mark up numerous tracks and villages. He had circled the Amari Valley on the off chance that he might spot the Tommies; with binoculars and with the Storch's slow speed it might have been possible, but he had seen nothing that caught his eye – just a lush valley, dotted with small villages.

It was the southern coast that had been his main objective, however, and it was towards it that he now asked the pilot to fly. Both the tiny coastal village of Plakias and the monastery of Preveli were marked on his map, but this told him very little. He wanted to see it for himself – the tracks, the coves, the beaches, the course of the rivers. What surprised him, as they cleared the mountains and flew over the narrow ten-kilometre strip of land to the coast, was just how different it was from the rest of the island. It was altogether wilder, more remote, with fewer villages, and while there were still olive groves, they were small and sparse. And it was mountainous too. Gone were the high peaks of the Ida range, but these lesser mountains were craggy and inhospitable. They flew over a narrow wind-

454

ing gorge, then south to the coast. As they cleared a high, rocky hill dotted with sheep, Balthasar suddenly saw the monastery of Preveli, perched back from the cliffs above the sea. It was, he realized, entirely hidden from the north, tucked away and isolated, the hill behind, the sea in front. They flew over the coast and he noticed a beach at the foot of the cliffs below the monastery, then, a little way further along, a gap in the cliffs where a river flowed out into the sea.

'Turn back up there,' said Balthasar. 'I want to follow that river.'

The pilot did as he was asked.

'Lower,' said Balthasar. A lone track ran above the river, winding through the hills from the monastery. They followed both the track and the river until one crossed the other by means of a small stone bridge.

'Now follow that track,' said Balthasar. The pilot banked again, keeping above the course of the track, which wound through the hills and mountains until it reached the dirt road that ran from Rethymno, through Spili and on along the south coast.

'Thank you,' said Balthasar, satisfied. 'Now we can return to Heraklion.'

The flight had cleared up a great deal. Before, several conundrums had been troubling him, but now his plan was clear in his mind. Later that afternoon, he would lead two platoons to Spili, which would leave him just enough time to make his preparations. Then, when the Tommies tried to make their bid for freedom, he and his men would be ready to strike.

23

Saturday, 7 June, around 9 p.m. Their final journey to the coast had just begun. There were nineteen of them in all: fourteen Rangers and Captain Vaughan, and four Cretans, including Alopex, walking up the winding road through the village that snaked like a giant S up the steep mountainside on which Yerakari had been built.

Some of the men chatted easily among themselves, relieved to be on the move again. Laughter, garbled words – it was the banter of men who were both excited about and daunted by what lay ahead. Tanner did not join in: he was in no mood to talk. In the rapidly fading light, he looked hard at the village as they walked, determined to remember as much of it as possible: the limes and plane trees that lined the road with the bases of their trunks whitewashed, the flat-roofed houses, and the white church with its thin, high tower. And the orchards: figs, apples, oranges and lemons – the village was a haven of fruit, growing on the terraces and behind the houses at either side of the road. Shed blossom still lay beneath the apples, a white carpet on the grass.

His heart was heavy. That morning he had bade farewell to Alexis and now he was leaving this enchanted valley too. Only twelve hours earlier he had been as close to her as two people could be but now she was gone, out of his life for ever, as this valley soon would be too. It was the finality that he found so difficult: he was as sure as if she had died that he would never see her again. And then it struck him that what he was feeling was a kind of grief. *Snap out of it*, he told himself. He had lost good friends before and had dealt with it by simply putting them out of his mind and getting on with the job. The trouble was, there was little distraction just now – only walking, up and over the mountains. For the next few hours, at any rate, their journey was likely to be uneventful.

He tried to think of other things. The growing shortage of ammunition was a concern. Thanks to Sykes's raid on a box in the cave, he had around forty rifle rounds left. He had chided his friend for taking precious supplies from the Cretans but had been glad of them all the same. On top of the rifle rounds, he also had six magazines for his MP40, four grenades and, in the loose cotton German bandolier he had kept and which hung around his neck, a number of slabs of TNT. He was conscious, though, that he and Sykes were considerably better armed than the others. With a bit of luck, they would need none of it, yet concern at what Mandoukis might have told the enemy nagged at the back of his mind. They had all agreed that he must have known about the planned evacuation from Preveli; there had been no precise details at that time, but it might have been more than enough for the Germans to scupper the plan. Not for the first time, Tanner cursed Alopex and the other Cretans for their mishandling of Mandoukis.

Only time would tell whether they would soon be paying the price.

On the other hand, all of them were now fit enough for the trek to the coast. Vaughan's strength had been building, but it was Liddell who had really benefited from their three days in the Amari Valley. Food, sleep, a degree of comfort and careful nursing had helped him through the worst, so that the previous day he had got up and begun moving about. Another long night of sleep and now he was, he declared, fit enough to walk – and so far, by the look of it, he was managing well.

He had found Tanner earlier that afternoon, dozing in the orchard behind the barn that had been their base since reaching Yerakari. Tanner had looked up at his approach, his heart sinking; since he had rescued Liddell, he had largely avoided him, letting others carry out nursing duties. What Liddell had done in those first days of the invasion still rankled but, more than that, he did not want any more conflict with the man. He had too much else to think about without worrying about Mr Liddell.

'How are you feeling, sir?' Tanner had asked. He should have stood up with an officer before him, but he stayed where he was, leaning against his apple tree.

'A lot better, thanks,' said Liddell. The sub-altern had then produced a packet of cigarettes and offered one to Tanner. 'Here,' he said.

'Thank you, sir.'

Liddell lit Tanner's, then his own. After a brief pause, he said, 'I want to thank you, Tanner. You

458

saved my life. I wouldn't be here now if it wasn't for you.'

'It's all right, sir. Anyone would have done the same.'

'Well, I'm not sure about that, actually. But I'm most grateful.' He sighed heavily. 'You know, Tanner – Jack – I've been doing a lot of thinking these past few days. I'm afraid I behaved badly. Like a bloody prig. I'm not really cut out for soldiering, you see.'

'You could have stayed on the farm, sir. We need people to feed us, as much as we need officers to lead us.'

Liddell looked away. 'Yes, I know. I wish I had, really. But you see – well, it's complicated, but when my father died, my sister came home.'

'Miss Stella, sir?'

'Yes. My older brother was killed – in France.'

'I'm sorry to hear that.'

'Yes, it was bloody awful. Anyway, Stella came back and she started helping on the farm too, and I could see that she was making a bloody good job of it. The farm didn't need me with her around.'

'You thought you'd be more use in the army.'

'Yes. I was being bloody-minded too, I suppose. So I did my training and got sent out here and then you of all people showed up. I want to be frank with you, Jack. I was always rather envious of you as a boy. You were so good at the things my father loved – so much better than me. And then I discovered you'd already proved yourself to be a far better soldier than I could ever hope to be. It made me angry and I suppose I also felt I needed to show my authority. To make you understand that I was an officer who demanded your respect. Of course, respect is earned, not given. I see that now.'

'I respect you, sir, for your honesty.'

Liddell smiled. 'I'm sorry, Jack. I made some bad mistakes. And I was wrong to bring up your past like that. You were right. I don't really know what happened. I wasn't at home then and it's none of my business. Your father was a fine man and I'm sorry about what happened to him. What happened to you – well, that's your affair. I promise you won't hear me mention it again.'

'What happened after my father died was a dark time for me – a very dark time. I try not to think about it and I certainly never talk about it. It's best forgotten.' He sighed. 'But your father was a fine man, too, and someone I had the utmost respect for. I certainly wouldn't be here now if it wasn't for him.'

'I miss him very much,' he said, 'but the point is, Jack, if it's not too much to ask, perhaps you could give me a clean slate. Can we put all that behind us now?' He held out his hand.

Tanner stood up and took it. 'Of course. We Wiltshiremen should stick together, sir.'

Liddell laughed. 'Yes. We're certainly a minority breed here.'

Tanner had been glad of that conversation. It took a lot for a man to admit his mistakes and to apologize, as he well knew. And it was a weight off his mind to know that he no longer needed to pussyfoot around the man. Having enemies within the battalion caused problems; Liddell's

460

olive branch was one Tanner had been pleased to take.

Their small column left the village behind, taking a track that led them up and over the mountains to the valley below. It was after one in the morning and inky dark when they reached the main Rethymno road at an isolated stretch a couple of miles to the south of Spili. Not far off a dog barked, but there was no sign of any traffic and they crossed the road easily and continued, following a track that wound through the mountains. By first light, they were entering a narrow pass, and by the time the sun had risen, they were out into a secluded valley. The lushness of the Amari Valley had gone: this was a quite different corner of the island. Not a house could be seen, while either side of the valley grey mountains and hills loomed over them.

They dropped down towards the river, the track leading them to an isolated and ancient stone bridge. It rose in a high arch over the river and at its halfway point, Alopex stopped and pointed. 'Look,' he said, 'the sea.'

Tanner looked and there, a couple of miles away through the narrow V of the valley, he saw it too, deep and blue and enticing.

'Nearly there,' grinned Alopex. 'Freedom within your grasp.'

'You know, I can almost believe it,' said Peploe. 'Look at this place – there's not a soul to be seen.'

'Just sheep,' said Alopex, and then, spotting a circling hawk, 'and a few buzzards. Your man has chosen this place well.'

Tanner wished they would be quiet. He hated

461

hearing such talk. Yes, it was quiet all right – but that meant nothing. The sun was up, they still had a little way to go, and the best part of the day to survive. In any case, he could not shake from his mind his anxiety about Mandoukis. Much could still go wrong.

It was around half past eight that the message came through. Balthasar had been awake since before first light. It was the third night his men had been on alert and although logic told him that the evacuation had been unlikely to take place on Friday and as likely on the Sunday as the Saturday, two whole nights with no news had made him wonder whether he had been entirely misinformed. As first light blossomed into sunrise and then into day, Balthasar had become increasingly impatient, pacing about his command post in Spili, hovering over his radio operator, and smoking one cigarette after another.

But then the magic words.

'Receiving you, Asgard, this is Baldur. Yes. Yes.' Gefreiter Schieber turned and grinned at Balthasar. 'Yes, understood, Asgard. Over.'

'He's spotted them?' said Balthasar.

'Yes, Herr Oberleutnant. Nineteen men – fifteen Tommies and four Cretans. They're nearing the monastery now. There is still no sign of any enemy U-boat.'

Balthasar gave immediate orders for his men to be ready to move out in fifteen minutes. So he had been right, after all! All that planning, all that waiting – it had come to something, just as he had hoped.

It was a plan that had evolved in his mind as he had flown over the coast a few days earlier. He had no intention of chasing the Tommies around the mountains. Rather, he wanted to trap them escaping, and Preveli, lying at the end of a dead-end track and narrow strip between the hills and the sea, was as perfect a place as any. Furthermore, he wanted to ensure that Preveli would not be used as an evacuation base in the future. There were, he realized, only two real ways of reaching the monastery. One arced round to the west of Spili through a narrow gorge, the other looped to the east, along a pass that was almost as narrow through the mountains. The two roads met in the valley that led to the sea a short way to the east of the monastery, becoming one at the only bridge across the river. From there, just that lone track led to the monastery. It was possible that the Tommies might try an entirely cross-country route, avoiding any established track, but that seemed to make little sense, and in any case, if they were planning to leave from Preveli they would have to travel along the narrow stretch of land between the sea and the long ridge of mountain behind.

Therefore all he had to do was have a radio operator watch from the mountain above and wait for the Tommies to appear. Again, logic told him that they would move down to the coast overnight, hole up at Preveli during the day, then leave the following night and, indeed, that was precisely what Mandoukis had indicated. Certainly, he reckoned the British were unlikely to risk leaving by day if they did not need to. Armed with a radio set, Balthasar had sent Gefreiter Tellmann and a *Gruppe* of his men to Preveli on Thursday evening, the first night of their arrival in the south. They had been guided to the valley by a local man who had been bribed heavily. Leaving Tellmann and two others in the valley, the squad had returned to Spili with their guide, who had since then been locked up; Balthasar certainly had no intention of letting some Cretan loudmouth spill the beans on his plan. He had told Tellmann to climb the hill above the monastery to find a place to hide among the rocks, and to remain there, watching.

He now split his force into two. One platoon would approach through the route that ran from the west of Spili, the other from the east. They would rendezvous at the bridge and proceed towards the monastery together.

Balthasar glanced at his watch. It was approaching nine o'clock. The divisional transport had returned to Heraklion, but even travelling by foot they would be at the coast by mid-afternoon. That would give them plenty of time in which to reach the monastery, round up the Tommies and wait for the British U-boat.

It was a shepherd who spotted the men up on the mountain. He had been checking his flock that morning and had heard them speaking in an unfamiliar language, and so had lain low, then crept forward until he could see them. They were in a little hollow beside a large rock and surrounded by vetch. They had guns, but also a box, he said, with a long thin bit of metal sticking up.

'Did the Germans see him?' Peploe asked Alopex. They were in a low, flat-roofed building on one of the terraces below the monks' accommodation. It was where Father Langouvardos had taken them on their arrival, and where they had since been brought some food and coffee. And where, now, an hour later, this young shepherd had been brought to tell them his news.

'No,' said Alopex. 'He is certain they did not see him. At least, they did not once look round and no one came after him.'

None of them needed any guesses as to what the boy had seen.

'Damn Mandoukis!' said Tanner, kicking angrily at the ground. 'So now Jerry's spotted us and soon loads more Jerries will descend on us.'

'All right, Jack,' said Peploe. 'Let's just try and think calmly here. I doubt they'll send a whole battalion to deal with us.'

Tanner now turned to Alopex. 'Ask this boy if he'll take us back up there. You and I could go, Alopex. If the boy could get close to them without them noticing, there's no reason why we can't. If we can get one of the men alive, we can at least find out what we're up against.'

Alopex nodded and relayed the message. 'Yes, he says he can do that. It will only take a half-hour, maybe a little more.'

'All right, Jack,' said Peploe, 'but let me come too. I can speak German, remember.'

They left immediately, following Father Langouvardos as he led them through the collection of buildings and courtyards so that they could not be observed from the hill behind. Beyond the western end of the monastery, the ridge of the hill ran down towards the sea and it was around this spur that the shepherd now led them. They followed him closely, climbing once more, but on the reverse slopes, walking along narrow sheep trails through the vetch until they were approaching the ridge of the hill above the monastery, but from the other side.

The shepherd boy crouched, turned to them and put a finger to his lips. Slowly, quietly, they crept forward. Tanner strained his ears – there was a breeze blowing in from the sea – and then, as the boy had said, they heard voices. They paused to listen.

'Sir, you stay here with the boy,' whispered Tanner. 'Let me and Alopex deal with them.'

Peploe nodded.

'We'll keep the radio operator alive and shoot the other two,' Tanner now whispered to Alopex. 'But we should get as close as possible before we shoot – we need that radio man alive.'

'The wind should help us.'

'I agree – that's in our favour, at least. Ready?'

Alopex nodded and they began to edge forward. As they crested the ridge they saw the three men not twenty yards ahead, their heads sticking up above the hollow. They were facing towards the sea, two with binoculars to their eyes. Tanner moved closer, one step at a time, until he was just fifteen yards away, and conscious of Alopex on his right. One of the Germans lowered his binoculars, turned and saw the two men. For a split second he looked at Tanner and Alopex with wide-eyed surprise and horror, but in that moment Tanner had raised his rifle tightly into his shoulder and shot the man clean through the forehead. At almost precisely the same moment, Alopex had hit the second through the back, so that he slumped silently forward. The third man, the radio operator, his headphones still around his head, had barely a chance to register what was happening before Tanner was charging down on him, leaping into the hollow and grabbing him. The German struggled at first, but Tanner brought one arm around his neck and yanked one of the man's arms back with his other hand, then shoved him to the ground at the edge of the hollow. While Tanner held him down, Alopex tied the German's hands behind his back with his scarf, then yanked him to his feet.

'Sir,' Tanner called, and a moment later Peploe and the shepherd appeared.

'We can start walking straight back down,' said Alopex.

Taking the radio set and the weapons, they pushed the German forward as Peploe questioned him.

'He's being stubborn,' said Peploe. 'Won't say a word.'

Alopex now pulled out his knife, grabbed the prisoner and ran the tip of the blade across the German's neck. 'Tell him,' he said, 'that if he starts speaking now we will not harm him. Otherwise I will cut off first his ears and then his fingers, one by one, until he talks.'

'That's not how I prefer to do things,' said Peploe, 'but in the circumstances...'

Alopex continued to hold the man, his eyes

boring into him, the tip of the knife just breaking the skin. Tanner watched as a large stain spread around the German's crotch and down his trouser leg. 'I think that's done the trick.' He grinned.

The German started to talk, his eyes darting from Peploe back to Alopex.

'All right,' said Peploe to Alopex, 'you can let go of him now.'

The German continued to speak, eyeing Alopex with a look of fear.

'It's Balthasar,' said Peploe, as they continued down the hill towards the monastery. 'He's got two platoons with him – around sixty men, this fellow reckons. They'll have machine-guns and rifles but nothing heavier. And they're coming on foot.'

'When did he warn Balthasar of our arrival?' Tanner asked.

'He says at about half past eight.'

Tanner looked at his watch. It was now nearly eleven o'clock, the hot sun high in the sky above them. 'We've not got long. A few hours, maybe.'

'What do you think?' Peploe asked.

'Could be worse, sir. It could be a lot worse.'

'But hardly ideal.'

'No – it's certainly not that.'

Peploe slapped at an insect. 'Damn it, Jack, why do I have the feeling this is all rather personal with this bloody Balthasar fellow?'

'Because, sir,' said Tanner, 'I think it probably is.'

Balthasar's force was spotted a little after half past three that afternoon, emerging around the bend in the road above the mouth of the valley and heading along the track that led towards the monastery. Tanner could see them marching in two long columns, and through his binoculars spotted Balthasar near the front of the lead platoon. The temptation to raise his rifle now and shoot the man dead was considerable, but to do so would have been to ruin their chances of escape.

'Here,' he said to Alopex, passing him the binoculars. 'You want to see what he looks like? That's Balthasar, up at the front.'

Alopex took them. 'So that's the son of a whore. At least I now know who it is I am going to kill.'

With Vaughan and the other officers, Tanner and Peploe had worked out a plan of sorts. As Tanner had pointed out, they not only needed to kill as many Germans as possible, they also had to play for time. None of them was quite sure when the submarine might arrive. Hanford had said some time in the afternoon, which meant it might appear at any moment but, equally, it might be late. Clearly, however, it was best to have the men as close to the sea and ready to leave as possible.

Furthermore, the ground below the monastery favoured defence. It was a good five hundred yards to the sea, but the high point on which the monastery was perched fell away only gradually through rocky, broken, uneven ground. There were trees, too, cypresses as well as olives, and thick gorse bushes. Tanner was perched now on a jutting mound of rock. It gave him a clear view up to the track and monastery, but behind him he could also see almost down to the beach, although the narrow strip of shingle was hidden by one last shallow cliff. That, too, would help.

A track from the monastery led down to the beach, winding through the folds and between rocky outcrops. Sykes had laid two trip wires along it, one near the monastery, and the other a little further down. There was no guarantee the enemy would use the track but Sykes for one had felt it worth laying some charges in case. Elsewhere, at intervals all the way down to the beach, they had placed slabs of explosive, which, as enemy troops neared, would be fired at by Tanner, the bullet causing the highly volatile charge to blow. It was a trick they had first used to good effect in Norway; Sykes had called them 'Jelly Surprises', although, as Tanner had pointed out, in this case it was not gelignite but TNT.

'Don't matter, sir,' Sykes had said. 'The effect's the same, so they're still Jelly Surprises as far as I'm concerned.'

'As you like, Stan,' Tanner told him. 'Just so long as they kill lots of Jerries – that's all that matters.'

While Liddell and Vaughan had been sent down to the beach to keep watch for the submarine, the rest of the men had been positioned over a comparatively wide area covering the approach to the beach. Their instructions were to hold fire until the last moment, and to make the most of what limited rounds they had left; some had barely more than the ten in the breeches of their rifles.

And there was one further reason for taking up

470

positions down towards the coast. They had reckoned that the enemy would head first for the monastery. Approaching the place, then searching every part of every building, would take Balthasar's men time. Precious time.

Beside Tanner, Alopex chuckled. 'You were right, my friend. Look.'

'Good,' said Tanner, as he watched the columns now deploy into a more open formation. Men were scampering forward, off the road, moving to encircle the entire monastery. 'Jerry can take as long as he likes.'

Minutes passed. From the monastery they heard shouts, orders being barked.

Alopex chuckled again. 'They'll be furious.'

Tanner and Peploe had urged Alopex and his men to leave, to get away while they had the chance, but the Cretan *kapitan* had refused. 'I might never have a better chance to kill that son of a whore,' he had said. 'I am not going anywhere until this is over, and neither are my men.'

Both Tanner and Peploe had not argued further – after all, they could use four extra rifles – but it worried Tanner that the Cretans might not be able to get away.

'Don't worry,' said Alopex. 'We can always lie low until nightfall. In any case, we might have killed them all by then.'

Perhaps, but a more likely scenario was that it would be they who were dead, rather than the Germans. Tanner lit a cigarette and saw his hands were shaking. He wanted the enemy to take as long as possible, but he also wished the fighting would begin. He would be fine then, adrenalin dispelling any nerves. He looked at his watch – it was now after four o'clock – then glanced back at the sea, deep and blue and peaceful. Where was that submarine? 'Come on, you bugger,' he muttered to himself.

They continued to watch the Germans search the monastery. It seemed as though one platoon had been sent to encircle the walls while the other was there to carry out the search. Occasional shouts, but otherwise nothing. More minutes passed, but eventually they heard orders being called and saw the troops around the outside of the monastery begin picking their way down through the animal pastures, then the fruit and vegetable garden below. Soon after, the men searching the monastery emerged, assembling outside the main entrance.

'Go on,' said Tanner. 'You just walk right on down that track.'

'What would you do?' Alopex asked him. 'If you were Balthasar?'

'I'm not sure. I think I'd use the track to take me away from the monastery because it's so obviously easier than jumping down off those terraces. But then I'd move into open formation.'

'Looks like our man thinks the same as you,' said Alopex.

They watched now as Balthasar ordered his men forward down the steep track that led from the entrance towards the coast. The lieutenant followed, walking slowly, binoculars to his eyes.

'Come on, come on,' said Tanner. He had stood over Sykes as he had set the trip and knew exactly where it was – tied between a young cypress and a fence post beneath the monastery terrace. The lead section was now just yards away.

'They're going to hit it,' grinned Alopex.

Tanner held his breath. *Just a couple more steps.*

A flash of flame and a deafening boom, and the leading men were blown to pieces, others thrown high into the air along with a fountain of stone, smoke and grit. The report resounded off the mountains, and even on their rock Tanner and Alopex felt the ground tremble. Immediately the enemy hit the ground, diving for cover. A couple of Rangers rifle shots rang out but that was all. *Good*, thought Tanner, *they've listened.* The men were using their heads.

But as the dust began to settle he saw the men behind the explosion start to get up and try to take cover. With his scope ready on his rifle, Tanner peered through the lens, spotting a crouching figure clutching a machine-gun. He fired and saw the man drop, then aimed again at another darting figure, but this time missed. He cursed – they could not afford to waste a single bullet. And where the hell was Balthasar? Vanished.

'That must be ten less to worry about at least,' said Alopex. 'Only fifty to go.'

'Just keep watching,' said Tanner. He wished they still had the machine-gun, but they had left that with Hanford at Yerakari. Men were darting between the rocks, the vetch and gorse. It was hard to get a bead, but Tanner now saw several men scampering near to the first block of TNT. It was perhaps still a hundred yards away, but through his scope he could see it well enough. Focusing on it, he saw a blurred figure move

473

behind it and squeezed the trigger. Another ball of flame erupted into the sky and as the blast subsided they heard a man screaming.

'Shall we say forty-seven now?' said Alopex.

The enemy seemed to take to the ground after that. Shots rang out, bullets zipping and whining off the rock, but the advance for the moment seemed to have been stopped dead. Strain as he might, Tanner could not see any movement at all.

'They've gone to ground,' he said. Then, leaving Alopex, he clambered across the rock to speak to Peploe.

But the captain was not there. Desperately Tanner looked around, spotted Sykes and saw his friend point to the sea: the long, narrow, grey shape of a submarine lay a short distance from the shore.

Thank God, he thought, then realized with a sinking heart that any German machine-gun could make mincemeat of them as they swam and rowed out to the waiting vessel. He looked around and saw Peploe again, running between the rocks and gorse. A shot rang out and Peploe ducked, then scurried on until he was clambering up the rock once more.

'Can you believe it?' he said breathlessly. 'The sub's actually here.'

'But the men can't go out to it yet, sir. They'll be massacred.'

Peploe's face fell. 'How much longer do you think we can keep this lot at bay?'

Tanner scratched his forehead. 'It's their machine-guns that are the problem. We need to pin those down.' He thought a moment, then said,

'Sir, I've had an idea. Send Sykes over here – he's got more ammo than anyone else – then pull the rest of the men back. When you're nearing the cliff over the beach, fire off a couple of shots. That way, Jerry will think we've all pulled back. Then, when they start moving forward again, Stan and I will set off the rest of the Jelly Surprises, spray the bastards with MP fire and grenades, then make a dash for it. We've a cracking little redoubt here – we can see any Jerry that moves forward or either side of us.'

Peploe thought a moment, rubbing his chin. 'Seems awfully risky for you two. I'm not sure, Jack.'

'Have you got a better idea, sir?'

'Well, no, I can't say I have.'

'Sir, this way we might just get rid of nearly the whole bloody lot of 'em. One thing's for sure, though: we won't be able to get away while those MGs are still operating and I doubt we'll be able to hold them until nightfall either. This just might give us a chance.'

Peploe sighed. 'All right. You're a brave man, Jack. I'm not sure Sykes will thank you for this.'

'His fault for nabbing all that ammo.'

Reluctantly, Alopex now agreed to fall back with his men and the others, swapping places with Sykes, who had deftly darted between the rocks to join Tanner. 'I'll wait for you at the cliff,' Alopex told Tanner. 'Good luck, my friend.'

Tanner watched him go, then turned to look for any movement up ahead. An occasional shot rang out, a glimpse of the enemy among the rock and gorse, but that was it. A lull had settled on the fighting, but further down towards the sea, he saw figures moving, and then, as several Germans opened fire, a single crack of a rifle responded. *Just the one – that'll do*, thought Tanner. *Good lads.*

A short distance ahead he saw movement and then a machine-gun opened fire. So the enemy was moving forward, just as he'd hoped. Peering through a crevice in the rock Tanner could see the Spandau, and two men crouched amid the gorse only fifteen yards or so from another block of TNT. That was close enough, he reckoned.

'They're starting to move up!' whispered Sykes.

'And I've got an MG team in my sights. Get everything ready, Stan – grenades out, the lot.'

Tanner pulled out his four grenades from his pack, and although his heart was hammering, his hands were no longer shaking. Really, he felt quite calm. Aiming through the crevice, he sighted the block of TNT, then said to Sykes, 'I'm about to fire, Stan, all right?'

'Go ahead,' came the reply. 'I'm ready.'

Quickly checking that the MG team was still in the same place, Tanner focused on the explosives and fired. A deafening boom – more flame and debris erupted into the air, then bits of rock and earth were pattering back around them, but Tanner had pulled the pins from two grenades and had hurled them towards the rustle and movement ahead of him. Bullets smacked into the rock in reply, but then a further explosion erupted from his left, followed by another grenade blast. *Good lad, Stan,* thought Tanner. His ears were ringing shrilly, the stench of cordite and smoke was thick in the air, but he now brought his Schmeisser into his shoulder and, moving around the rock, sprayed an entire magazine in a wide arc in front and to the right of him. More men cried out as Tanner brought his rifle back to his shoulder, watching for any movement to the right of their position. A figure was running a hundred yards away, but Tanner quickly drew a bead, picked out the man through his scope, fired and saw the paratrooper drop. Bullets continued to zip and whiz off the rock to the front of them, but although a splinter of stone pinged off his helmet, Tanner was unscathed.

'How are you doing, Stan?' he asked.

'All right. I got a machine-gun.'

'So did I.' He glanced back briefly and saw what looked like a canoe moving towards the waiting submarine. 'Go on,' muttered Tanner, then further movement away to his right caught his eye. Two Germans were hurrying forward. He aimed and fired in quick succession and saw one knocked over for sure. He glanced back at the canoe and saw it had now nearly reached the submarine. How far was it to that sub? he wondered. Six hundred yards? Seven hundred? A machine-gun could hit it, he knew, but still none was firing. Perhaps they really had got them all. Now his spirits began to rise. He took out the empty magazine from his Schmeisser, replaced it, then called to Sykes, 'If those lads get to the sub, we make a run for it. What do you say?'

'They just have, sir – have a dekko.'

Tanner looked back as two men were helped out of the canoe and onto the back of the sub. *Liddell and Vaughan?*

'Hold on,' said Tanner. He looked out, using his scope. There were three more blocks of TNT to explode, one further away to the right, one away to the left and another not far from Sykes. Spotting the first through his scope, he aimed, fired, and immediately the block exploded with another deafening blast of flame, rock and smoke. He shuffled around to Sykes. 'Stan, cover the right flank, will you, while I get these Jellies?'

He had carefully memorized their location earlier and soon spotted them. The furthest was more than a hundred yards away and only just in his line of fire. A single shot and the block exploded. It was the shards of rock, many of them razor sharp, that were so lethal, he realized, the blast sending them in a wide radius. He heard more men cry out, but was already drawing a bead on the last block, no more than thirty yards to his left and slightly forward. *Good*, he thought, as he saw movement in the thicket nearby. Again, his aim was true and this time he saw a paratrooper flung into the air by the blast. The slopes were thick with smoke and he grabbed Sykes.

'Right, iggery, then, Stan,' he said. He took another grenade, pulled the pin and hurled it, then clambered from his perch, and slid down a steep rockface.

Sykes was already there, crouching at the base of the outcrop. 'Ready?' he said.

'After you.' Tanner grinned. Crouching, they scurried between the rocks and gorse, using the broken ground to mask their withdrawal, so that it was not until they had made more than a hundred yards of ground that a single bullet whistled near them. Tanner hurried on, following Sykes and sliding down over the lip of the Cliff.

Peploe was there, with Alopex and his *andartes*.

'I'm pleased to see you two,' he said. 'That sounded like a pasting you gave them.'

'I think we've nailed those MGs,' Tanner said. 'Liddell and Vaughan are aboard.'

'Good. I thought it was them. What about Commander Pool?'

Peploe smiled. 'He's coming back with us to Alex. Feels his mission has been compromised. He says he'll try again in a few weeks.'

'I suppose it has. Can't say I blame him.'

'How many do you think are left – up there, I mean?' Peploe nodded in the direction of the rocky slopes above.

'God knows, but not that many, I'd have thought. We've certainly pinned them down. I think those that are still up there are lying low. I suppose it must be unnerving to think a big block of TNT might go off in your face at any moment. A bit like walking through a minefield – no one wants to do it if they don't have to.'

'Have you seen that bastard Balthasar?' said Alopex.

'No – not since the trip wire blew. Maybe he was killed then. Maybe that's why they're not exactly hurrying forward.'

'In any case, let's get the rest of these men on board,' said Peploe. He waved down to Lieutenant McDonald on the beach below and indicated to him to get the men to start swimming. Tanner watched as Hepworth, Bonner, Hill and Lieutenant Timmins stripped off their webbing, packs and helmets, then saw Hepworth wade into the sea and begin to swim.

An occasional bullet fizzed near, but otherwise it was now quiet. One by one, the men clambered down onto the beach, stripped off their equipment and headed into the water, until, apart from Alopex and his men, only Tanner, Sykes and Peploe remained.

'Go on, Jack,' said Peploe, 'your turn.'

'No, sir, it's all right,' said Tanner. 'You go.'

'Very well.' He turned to Alopex. 'Thank you,' he said. 'Thank you for everything. And good luck.'

'Long live Crete.' Alopex grinned. They watched Peploe slide down the cliff, then dash across the beach to the water's edge.

'And now it's your turn,' said Alopex, to Tanner and Sykes. He shifted his position and then raised himself slightly above the lip. 'It still seems quiet enough,' he said. 'I told you, get them all and you'll get away. I think maybe you have killed more than you think.' He turned – but in that moment his expression changed. 'Balthasar,' he muttered, and a split second later a single rifle shot cracked out, blood spat from his neck and he slumped beside them on the edge of the cliff. Blood was gushing from his neck, thick and dark, and running from his mouth.

'Christ, no!' muttered Tanner. Another shot cracked out and this time the shot was aimed at Peploe now swimming out to sea. Tanner saw him dive then emerge again. 'Damn! Damn!' The *andartes* were now crowding around him and he pushed them away. 'Stan!' he hissed. 'Have you

480

got any grenades left?'

'No, but I've got a stick of Polar.'

Grimacing and cursing, he looked back down at Alopex.

'Get him,' Alopex gurgled. 'Promise me.'

His teeth clenched, Tanner said, 'Yes. I promise you I'll get that bastard.' He gripped Alopex's shoulders, then saw the Cretan's eyes flicker and his head loll limply to one side.

'No! No! No!' said Tanner, then turned to Sykes. 'You got that stick, Stan?' he said, pulling his last grenade from his pack.

'Right here.'

'Then light it and when it's almost ready to blow, hurl it as hard as you can in the direction of those shots.'

Moving forward under the brow of the cliff, Tanner inched forward, then glanced back at Sykes, who hurled his stick of dynamite. At the same time, Tanner had pulled the pin on the grenade and threw that too. One explosion then another, and now Tanner was up, cresting the lip of the cliff and running forward, blindly firing his Schmeisser, emptying the magazine through the haze of smoke and dust. He heard several men cry out and then, leaping through the smoke, glimpsed the man he was after, shaking his head and staggering. Seeing Tanner, Balthasar reached down to grab his rifle but he was not quick enough and Tanner charged into him, flinging him to the ground. He punched his face once, then again, and then closed his hands around the German's neck.

Balthasar gasped, flailing for his rifle, but then

481

his fingertips closed around the breech and now he had it firmly in his hand. He swung it round onto Tanner's back, knocking him sideways, but Tanner did not loosen his grip, so that as he fell he pulled Balthasar with him, over the edge of the cliff, the two men tumbling towards the beach. Both men gasped as they rolled to a halt on the shingle, Balthasar now free of Tanner's grip.

It was Balthasar who was on his feet first. 'You,' he said in English. He could not believe his plan had gone so wrong, that so many of his men were either dead or wounded. Even his attempt to outflank them had failed. He had killed the Cretan *kapitan,* but most of the Tommies had got away, and now Tanner had killed even the half-dozen men he had had with him. Well, no more. As Tanner got to his feet, Balthasar pulled out his pistol.

'You,' he said again, as he pointed the Sauer at Tanner, 'you should have killed me when you had the chance.'

'Yes,' said Tanner, 'I reckon I should.'

A rifle crack rang out behind them, further along the beach, and Balthasar instinctively ducked. In that same moment Tanner swung his arm, knocking the German's hand clear so that the shot fired harmlessly into the shingle. At the same moment, he drove his boot into Balthasar's crotch, then swung with his left fist. Balthasar cried out in pain, his pistol fell from his hand and Tanner drew out his German knife and thrust it hard into the man's chest.

'But I'll not make that mistake again,' he said. Balthasar staggered back a few steps, a look of astonishment on his face. He glanced up at Tanner, blood already running from the side of his mouth, took another step, then fell.

Tanner walked over, pulled the knife from Balthasar's chest, wiped it against his trouser leg, then stumbled towards Sykes, who was waiting for him at the shore's edge.

'Cheers, Stan,' said Tanner. 'Reckon you saved me there.'

'Couldn't have him shoot you, sir.' Sykes grinned.

'You might have hit him, though.'

'I didn't want to deny you the pleasure.'

Tanner looked back towards the cliff and saw the three *andartes* carefully bringing Alopex's body down to the beach. He raised his hand to them, saw them wave their rifles in return, then turned and stepped into the water.

'Leaving your boots on, are you?' said Sykes.

'Yes, Stan, I bloody well am. And I'm keeping my rifle on my back as well.'

Not a single shot rang out as they swam to the waiting submarine. When they reached the hull, waiting crew heaved them aboard, and then, dripping, their clothes clinging to their bodies, they climbed the conning tower. Sykes entered the hatch first, and Tanner followed, but as he was about to duck down, he paused and looked back towards the shore and the mountains beyond. He was leaving the island that had entranced him with not a few regrets, and yet his conscience, at least, was clear.

HISTORICAL NOTE

Tanner had good reason to feel let down by the British commanders on Crete, a failure one year on from Dunkirk that should have never happened. The German Fallschirmjäger units dropped on Crete on 20 May 1941 were absolutely slaughtered, most units suffering between 50 and 70 per cent casualties and some even higher than that. There is no way a defending force of superior numbers, armed with rifles and machine-guns with an effective range of four hundred yards or more, should have lost ground to an attacking force, hideously mauled in its first moments, armed principally with sub-machine-guns with an effective range of twenty–forty yards. For that to happen, some monumentally bad judgements and decisions had to have been made.

A lot of the blame lies with Major General Freyberg. Although he did not know it, Freyberg was being fed Ultra, the decrypts from the German Enigma machines, but he became so concerned by his instructions to preserve the secrecy of what he knew that he was unable to act upon them. Even worse, he developed a strange obsession that the main threat would come from a seaborne invasion. A cool head and some logical thinking would have shown the unlikelihood of this, not least because the Germans had almost no surface fleet, and no ships within the Mediterranean. Furthermore, he misread the decrypts, clinging to any mention of a seaborne invasion and overlooking the greater threat – namely an attack on Maleme airfield. Thus he failed to move troops to reinforce that vital airfield when he had the chance. The extraordinary conversation he had with Monty Woodhouse on the morning of the invasion occurred in much the same way as depicted in the book. Such sangfroid was not the sign of a commander with a full grasp of the situation.

Freyberg was, by all accounts, a thoroughly decent fellow, but he was no great intellect and had been promoted well above his capabilities. His reputation for bravery and his status as New Zealand's most famous soldier had seen to that. But this also made him very difficult to sack – Britain depended on New Zealand's not inconsiderable contribution and could not afford to threaten her cooperation by getting rid of someone as well known and decorated as Freyberg. Sadly, the Crete fiasco would not be the last time Freyberg messed things up. Three years on, after an undistinguished period of command in North Africa, he oversaw one of the worst-planned battles of the entire war – the Second Battle of Cassino.

At Heraklion, Brigadier Chappel, despite clever deployment of his forces, was overly cautious. Perhaps he was undone by the formidable, all-conquering reputation German – and especially Fallschirmjäger – troops had acquired by this stage. British confidence was low, but again, cool logic should have told Chappel and his commanders that a quick, decisive counter-attack could and should have seen off the German invasion efforts in that part of the island in one neat blow. Tanner's exasperation was understandable.

The British forces on Crete also suffered from the appalling shortage of wireless radio sets. The perils of any over-dependence on easily broken land lines had been demonstrated all too clearly in France the previous year, but this was a lesson, it seems, that had not been learned. It is true that an army lacking radios cannot become equipped and trained with them overnight, but the battle for Crete was a whole year on, and the provision of ample radio sets should have been a priority, as Pendlebury had correctly recognized.

Most of the events depicted occurred pretty much as is written here, although it is often hard to piece together the precise details. On the British side, battalion war diaries were often written up some days after the events, or even only once evacuated, and personal testimonies are frequently contradictory. German records are even less reliable. Paratroopers carried little with them into battle – typewriters, paper and pencils were not a top priority – and again, events were often recorded some days, or even weeks afterwards, and in the case of personal accounts, sometimes years later. It was, for example, very hard to piece together the nature of the III Battalion, 1st Fallschirmjäger Regiment's attack on Heraklion following their landing. Major Schulz's men (he was very much a real person) did land west of the town and did attack Heraklion but were eventually forced back. However, no single account that I have read agrees with another as to when this took place. Some suggest it was that first night, others after the bombing attack the next morning. Several accounts claim the fighting continued well into the following day and that the town mayor had already surrendered when a British, Greek and civilian counter-attack forced them back again.

I have opted for what I think is most likely. An attack would probably have been launched at dusk or first light, when the light was changing quickest, making it hard for the defender to adjust and pick out figures and shadows, but allowing enough light for the attacker to see what he was doing. Since Schulz would probably have known the Luftwaffe would be over in the morning, but with no way of contacting them himself, it seems likely that he would have opted for a dusk attack so as not to get caught out by his own side's bombs.

It also seems to me very unlikely that it would have been a long battle. Schulz's men would have been mostly armed with MP38 and MP40 sub-machine-guns, and would have had, on average, six or so magazines per person. These contained thirty-two rounds each, which would be fired in three and a half seconds. In other words, six magazines gave his men little more than twenty seconds' worth of fire. This being so, there is absolutely no way Schulz's men could have attacked at dusk and still have been fighting the following afternoon. Their ammunition would have run low long before that.

What is agreed upon, however, is that a final charge was made by a combined force of Greek soldiers, Cretan guerrillas and civilians against Schulz's men as they fell back against the Canea Gate. This was also led by John Pendlebury, British vice consul, SOE agent and former curator of Knossos. He was an extraordinary man, who did carry a swordstick, had a glass eye, and broke out of Heraklion through the Canea Gate, a brave but foolhardy plan to put it mildly. He had also established an arms dump in Heraklion, which he had laboriously shipped from Suda Island.

Pendlebury was executed some time soon after his break-out from the town. How his last hours were spent has also been the subject of highly contradictory reports, but it seems he was wounded in a firefight and a day or two later shot. I have tried to make my fictional character as much like the real figure as possible. However, I have no idea what his last thoughts were, or even if he was conscious at the time. This is fiction based around real events; but it is fiction, all the same.

Today, Heraklion sprawls a long way beyond the town walls, but back then Knossos was some miles to the south. The Villa Ariadne was reputedly a British field hospital during the invasion and battle for Crete, but since this was well beyond Allied lines and, as described in the book, Germans were landing nearby, it seems rather improbable. Perhaps it was a field hospital before the invasion, but any doctors working there after 20 May would soon have found themselves overrun.

Heraklion itself has been massively spruced up since 1941. Even before the heavy air attack on 25 May, much of the town had become run-down. The walls had taken a battering over the centuries, and once the Turks had finally departed in 1898, they had been left, often plundered to build further houses. Certainly they were not as pristine as they are today. One of the few new buildings in Heraklion was the Megaron, however, built in the 1930s and dominating the harbour next to the old arsenals. Today it is Heraklion's smartest hotel.

Colonel Bruno Bräuer, like Major Schulz, was a real person. He later went on to be promoted to major general and to command the German garrison on Crete. He was actually known to be more lenient than some German commanders on the island and generally disliked violent reprisal actions. It didn't stop him being tried for war crimes, however. Found guilty, he was sentenced to death and executed by firing squad.

Mike Cumberlege was also a real character, as was his cousin, Cle. The former and the faulty caique made it back to North Africa, although they were shot at en route and Cle was killed. Mike Cumberlege died later in the war. Satanas was also a real character, as was Manoli Bandouvas, and both were legendary *kapitans* of the Cretan resistance. Satanas's magnanimity towards the British, especially, was extraordinary, and his appearance at Brigade Headquarters on the night of the British evacuation took place much as depicted. For Cretan guerrillas, life as resisters was incredibly tough, as it was for all partisans in Nazi-occupied Europe. Underarmed, underfed, with few if any home comforts and with the threat of torture and death if caught, they were, to a man, incredibly brave. Britain continued to send agents to Crete, but theirs was a long, hard, three-year struggle. Anyone wanting to understand what life was like as a Cretan *andarte* should read *The Cretan Runner* by George Psychoundakis. It's harrowing, compelling stuff.

British troops stranded on Crete continued to escape from the island for many months to come, not least via the monastery at Preveli and the escape line established by Commander Pool and the submarine HMS *Thrasher*. In fact, Pool did not reach Crete until the end of July 1941, some six weeks after his first appearance in this book.

Visiting Crete today, however, it is easy to see why Tanner became so bewitched by the island. It is a stunningly beautiful place, more green and lush than many of the other Greek islands, and with an atmosphere of incredible hospitality suffused by its long and ancient history.

Yet, as Tanner understood, there was a lot of the war still to be fought, not least in North Africa, where the British Eighth Army was already slugging it out against the combined Italian and German forces under General Rommel. Tanner and Sykes made it safely back to Alex, but all too soon they would find themselves in the thick of the action once more, this time across the vast sands of the Western Desert…

I have used contemporary spellings for place names, and hope this small glossary might be useful:

CP command post
DCT Director Control Tower
Goojars thieves
Iggery get a move on
M/T motor transport
MTB motor torpedo boat
OP observation posts
ORs other ranks
Schmeisser British name for the German
          MP38 and MP40 sub-machine-guns
Spandau British name for a German machine-gun

I owe thanks to the following: Oliver Barnham, Dr Peter Caddick-Adams, David Cross, Rob Gallimore, Jans and Martin Holland, Tom Holland, Fred Jewett, Steve Mulcahey, Hazel Orme, Bill Scott-Kerr, Mads Toy and everyone at Bantam, Giles Vigar, Patrick Walsh and all at Conville & Walsh, and Rachel, Ned and Daisy.

The publishers hope that this book has given you enjoyable reading. Large Print Books are especially designed to be as easy to see and hold as possible. If you wish a complete list of our books please ask at your local library or write directly to:

Magna Large Print Books
Magna House, Long Preston,
Skipton, North Yorkshire.
BD23 4ND

This Large Print Book for the partially sighted, who cannot read normal print, is published under the auspices of

THE ULVERSCROFT FOUNDATION